Sarah M. M. Turner has always loved writing and weaving fantastic stories filled with heroic characters and evil villains. As the third eldest of seven children, she took pleasure in reading bedtime stories to her young siblings – including numerous fanfictions she wrote herself. When not writing, she enjoys rereading a selection of stories by her favourite authors, singing opera and musical theatre, and dressing up in costume for a concert or Shakespeare Party.

Sarah loves to hear from her readers. You may contact her in one of the following ways:

sarahmmturner.com

facebook.com / SarahMMTurner

instagram.com / sarah.m.m.turner

Want to be among the first to know the release date for the next book? Please join her Reader's List here:

sarahmmturner.com / contact-me

Titles available in the Rhiannon McBride Trilogy
(in reading order):

Rhiannon McBride and the Dragon's Cup
Rhiannon McBride and the Dragon's Eye

Rhiannon McBride and the Dragon's Eye

~A Fantasy Novel~

Sarah M. M. Turner

Published by Sarah M.M. Turner
sarahmmturner.com

First published 2025

 A catalogue record for this
book is available from the
National Library of Australia

ISBN 978 0 6456125 5 4 (pbk–YA)
ISBN 978 0 6456125 6 1 (ebk–YA)

Cover design by Joolz & Jarling—Julie Nicholls & Uwe Jarling
Map design by Sarah M.M. Turner and computerised by Peter Turner
Typeset by Helen Christie, Blue Wren Books

To my new nephew,
Maximilian.
Thank you for bringing more light
and joy into my life.

CONTENTS

	Map of the Kingdom of Álnair	ix
	Author's Note	xi
	Prologue	1
1.	The Dryad's Warning	3
2.	A Grand Party	19
3.	Of Troubling Reports and Strange Birthday Wishes	37
4.	More Than Friendship?	53
5.	A Lurking Threat	68
6.	Confessions and Laboratories	70
7.	The Hall of Archives	100
8.	Stunts and Stratagems	121
9.	Villainous Deeds	147
10.	Fumes of Confusion	149
11.	Treachery Unmasked	170
12.	A Disastrous Outing	201
13.	Far From Home	211
14.	Concerned Minds and Anxious Hearts	235
15.	Dark Delight	249
16.	A Surprising Encounter	250
17.	Fists and Fangs	272

18. A Shot in the Dark   283
19. Grim Revelations   292
20. Sir Raeden the Counsellor   311
21. A Pledge of Hearts   318
22. A Trove of Secrets   333
23. Cruel Motivation   362
24. Shadows in the Water   364
25. Malevolent Conspiracy   380
26. A Grievous Betrayal   382
27. Of Salt and Arachnescopes   397
28. Web of Traitors   403
29. Strength in Adversity   405

KINGDOM OF ÁLNAIR

SEA OF DORLAND
Deadwater Cove
Merosorc (Place of Exile)
Titus River
Enchanted Barrier
Ruined City of Glenwing
OLD ROAD OF VAROS
Forbidden Mountains
Pine Woods
SEA OF NILOR
White Rock Bay
Caves of The Fallen
Farmland
To the ISLE OF FIRE
Wastelands
Thaos Wood
Coral Bay
Mt Perdus
Farmland
Town of Tolgor
The Fell of Fiachra's Woe
Lake Tamesis
City of Lothian
Farmland
City of Ardara
GRAYNOR ROAD
Langwell Hills
Valley of Dreams
Gulf of Amdon
Finbar Forest
Village of Wynoras
Shadow Pass
Idon River
Pool of Rememberance
Norgan Bight
Wildlands
Mt Solus
Del Enger Mountains
Underground city of the Rolvian Clan
Black Forest
Larnen Sea
Town of Belnight
ROAD
ROAD TO SHADOW PASS
Wildlands
Aidan Dessert
SOLVANUIN OCEAN
Farmland
Ryegoth Academy
Realta Lake
MAIN ROAD
Town of Salrock
Shaimar Forest
Deora River
The High Wolds
Radamus Point
City of Cendillis
Cendillis Harbour
ROAD
Heart of the Black Forest
Farmland
ROAD TO ARDARA
Haldoron Bridge
Town of Kelmore
Valieoth Castle
Deer Park
Lagoon
Luwyneth Cove
Kinpar Rocks
Wildlands
Idon River
ISLE OF CULHOS
Aureus Bay
Town of Melson
Boffin Bay
City of Graynor
DAIRION OCEAN
MALPARS
N NW NE W E SW SE S
To the uninhabitable REALM OF KHOSHEK

Author's Note

There are several names used in this book which are taken from various cultures in our world, along with many names and words from the ancient tongue of the dragons (Drakaron). The writer has done her best to provide to the reader a pronunciation guide for these words. However, she cannot guarantee they are 100% accurate. The reader should remember there may exist different versions of the spelling and pronunciation for the names from our world, and that Drakaron is a very old language, which is no longer spoken here.

Names

Aleda	*A-lee-da*	Fendrel / Sados	*Fen-drel / Sar-dos*
Apollinaris	*A-pol-ee-nair-is*	Fíachra	*Fee-ach-ra*
Orlone	*Or-lawn*	Fjenador	*Fee-en-a-dore*
Arastar	*Ara-star*	Funabe	*Foon-ah-be*
Asaph	*A-saff*	Izana	*ee-zah-na*
Baegolz	*Bay-golz*	Janarius	*Ja-na-re-us*
Cináed	*Kin-ahd*	K'el	*Kay-EL*
Dairíon	*Die-re-on*	Kelandrus	*Kel-un-drus*
Daiki	*Die-key*	Lamorak	*Lam-oh-rack*
Eirehon	*Eye-er-ah-hon*	Leronus	*Lur-ro-nus*
Elaros	*El-ah-ros*	Lystro	*Lie-stro*
Elvanor	*EL-va-nor*	Maiwen	*My-win*
Endrille	*En-'dril*	Mórell	*More-el*

Mórfran	*More-fran*	Phalóran	*Far-lor-an*
Níping	*Nee-ping*	R'lon	*R-lon*
Nuallán	*Noo-al-ayne*	Raeden	*Ray-den*
O'Faenart	*O-'Fay-Nart*	Ryegoth	*Rye-Goth*
Oraun	*Oh-rawn*	Valieoth	*VAL-e-oth*
Orthoríon	*Or-thor-re-on*	Valnas	*VAL-nas*
Polansi	*Poe-lan-see*		

Herbs/Plants   Dragon Breeds

Mëlu	*May-lou*	Erímos	*air-ih-mos*
Myaelan	*My-ay-lan*	Gora	*Gore-ah*
Narapet	*Nar-ah-pet*	Parvus	*Par-vus*
Somlyne	*Som-lin*	Ríyun	*Ree-yun*
Thranlaire	*Thran-lair*		
Verbena	*Ver-be-na*		

Locations

Álnair	*Al-nar*	Luwyneth	*Lew-wen-eth*
Cendillis	*Sen-del-es*	Malpars	*Mal-pars*
Culhos	*Cul-hos*	Mérosorc	*Mare-os-orc*
Dairíon	*Die-re-on*	Oswë-kí-aurfai	*Os-way-kee-or fie*
Haldoron	*Hal-dor-ron*	Shaimar	*Shy-mar*
Idon	*I-duhn*	Torerock	*Tore-rock*
Kinpar	*Kin-par*	Vetus svet	*Ve-tus sve-t*

Charms

Aoratos	*ei-ora-tos*	Ketevos	*Kay-ter-vos*
Astarai	*As-ta-rye*	Mendolenai	*Men-dol-en-aye*
Cosain	*Co-sahn*	Soporus	*So-por-us*
Exoculos	*Ex-oc-u-lus*	Undolthgare	*Un-dol-th-gare*
Foläga	*Foe-lay-gar*	Vaelus Medesta	*Vah-lus Meh-des-ta*
Glaciocaptus	*Gla-si-o-'Kap-tus*	Vinaro	*Vin-ah-ro*

Other Terms

Agnador	*Ag-na-dor*	Neushallough	*New-shal-low*
Aríol	*Ah-ree-ol*	Pelatarrof	*Pel-a-tar-roff*
Bolpode	*Bowl-pod*	Praeterium	*Pray-ter-re-um*
Drakaron	*Dra-ka-ron*	Rafapel	*Raph-ah-pel*

Fatakrít	*Fah-TAH-creet*	Rolvian	*Rol-ve-an*
Foramens	*For-a-mens*	Sanelda	*San-el-dah*
Kámari	*Car-mar-ee*	Transonus	*Tran-so-nus*
Karatos	*Kar-AH-tos*	Trínondras	*Trin-on-dras*
Mórskarin	*More-ska-rin*	Tuagust	*Tu-a-gus*
Myrkroth	*Mere-kroth*		

Phrases

Ai Numen Fai, cenya oron sí nalbë. Tuae El'damo, Kor íquista.	*Aye New-men Fie, sen-ya or-on see nal-bay. Two-ae el-da-mo, cor ih-qwis-ta.*
Arídakor nai arnor.	*Ah-ree-da-cor nai ah-nor.*
Kai sartor, ílamae os.	*Khai sar-tor ih-la-mae os.*
Píaken, atshi nolista kor.	*Pee-AH-ken, at-she no-lis-ta cor.*
Teronwë das kel'numen.	*Ter-on-way das kel-NEW-men.*

PROLOGUE

'Destroy them all!'

Mórfran's harsh order carried over the sounds of crackling fire. The dryads fought valiantly against the rabble who obeyed their leader's command with brutal enjoyment. Then agonised screams rang out as several dryads felt their tree become engulfed by the merciless inferno spreading through the forest, the flames creating a hazy glow in the late afternoon sky.

'So shall perish all who would stand against our master.'

Mórfran cast a last disdainful look at the scene then turned away. The low hood draped over his face concealed the malevolent expression in his eyes, but not the cruel sneer about his mouth, nor the dreadful scar that marred his right cheek.

'Mórfran, they may have been telling the truth,' his companion pointed out. 'Maybe they have no knowledge of where it may be located.'

'Nonsense, Janarius. This is one of the oldest parts of the forest and dryads have very long memories. If they refuse to assist us by revealing what they know then they are of no further use and deserve to die. Also, this will serve as a warning to all others that we will not tolerate any opposition. Our master grows impatient, and another failure such as the one committed by that fool Plancy will be met with the utmost displeasure. I, for one, certainly do not intend to be the recipient of his ire. If these tree spirits cannot help me succeed, then I will annihilate every single one of them.'

As though in defiance of his words, a fierce bellow rang out like a loud battle cry. Whirling about, the two men saw a dryad of immense height shoot out of his ancient oak tree. The tree spirit sped towards the dark heart of the forest, hurling several of the human attackers out of his way as he went.

'Should we follow him?' Janarius asked.

Mórfran shrugged indifferently, already dismissing the incident as unimportant. 'Here or somewhere else, he'll be just as dead once we burn his tree to ashes.'

Chapter 1

THE DRYAD'S WARNING

Rhiannon was *bored*.

There were only so many dress fittings a girl could stand, and she had reached her limit at five. She was now on her eighth!

The grey-haired and plump form of Madame Dubois stuck another pin into the hem of her gown. Rhiannon squirmed as the itch on the back of her neck returned.

'S'op 'oving young 'ady.' Her words almost incomprehensible around the collection of pins she held in her mouth, the talented but eccentric dressmaker shot an exasperated glare at the fidgeting girl.

'I'm sorry, Madame,' Rhiannon apologised, 'but I've spent the last half hour impersonating a dummy. Also, my neck is itchy.'

Madame Dubois spat the pins from her mouth and stood up with a distinct huff of impatience. 'Fine! Scratch your neck! But my masterpiece shall never be finished in time for the ball if I must stop every time you —'

'Jumping toadstools, Rhiannon! Aren't you finished yet?'

Startled by the interruption, both females turned towards the owner of the voice.

There, his golden-haired head poking through the curtains draped across the entrance to Madame Dubois' fitting-room, was –

'Your Royal Highness!'

'David!'

The Prince of Álnair smiled upon hearing the relief in Rhiannon's voice. 'Still sticking pins into you, is she?' he asked lightly.

'Please, Your Royal Highness, you must not see my creation before it is finished,' Madame Dubois cried.

'Never fear, Madame,' David reassured her with a boyish grin, 'when I'm in your presence my eyes can only ever see the beauty of your charming face.'

The blatant flattery instantly softened the old woman's expression.

'You're a terrible flirt,' she declared, though it was apparent she enjoyed the compliment when her mouth curled up into a smile.

'David, did you want me to come with you *right now*?'

Rhiannon's desperate emphasis on her last two words elicited a hastily muffled laugh from David. 'I did, but I can wait until Madame is finished.'

The glare he received from Rhiannon's golden eyes would have made Sir Raeden proud.

'Oh no, no!' Madame Dubois hurried forward and began to loosen the back laces on Rhiannon's gown. 'We will not keep you waiting. The dress is almost finished. I shall complete these last adjustments without Miss Rhiannon, and have it delivered to the palace by tomorrow afternoon.'

'You're very good,' David informed her warmly. 'I'll just be outside, Rhiannon, once you finish getting changed.'

And with that his head withdrew back through the curtains.

'Such a nice boy,' Madame Dubois announced, lifting the delicate silver-blue gown over Rhiannon's head of unruly chestnut ringlets to reveal a chemise of fine white cotton underneath.

'Always so charming! Now, put your own overdress on, dear. Lucinda can help you.'

'Thank you, Madame,' Rhiannon murmured.

Once the friendly assistant Lucinda had tightened the last lace on her dress, Rhiannon hurried out of the room, down the spiral staircase and across the main floor of Amelia's Apparel & Haberdashery Boutique. She shot out the doorway to where David stood waiting with Gareth Harulf, his Robesman for the day, standing a short distance behind him.

'You! I could cheerfully throw something at you!'

To Rhiannon's indignation the heir to the throne of Álnair was unperturbed by this threat of bodily harm. He remained nonchalantly leaning against a lamppost with a smile on his lips.

'Why did you say you'd wait?' Rhiannon demanded. 'What if Madame Dubois hadn't –'

'I knew she wouldn't keep you if I said I'd be waiting,' David interrupted calmly. 'Anyway, I don't know what you've got to complain about. I got you out of there twenty minutes earlier than we originally planned.'

Rhiannon sighed. 'I suppose, but it felt like forever! She doesn't let me move and if she could, I'm sure she'd stop me from breathing!'

'She is brilliant at what she does but she does tend to get a bit carried away,' David admitted. 'In fact, she stuck me with a pin when I was about five after I wouldn't stop turning around to see what she was doing. She swore to my mother it was an accident, but I have my doubts.'

'I just wish this whole thing was over and done with,' Rhiannon moaned. 'She changed her mind *again* about what design will look best, and spent the first ten minutes unpinning what she did yesterday.'

'It's certainly a situation where Wyvern would be useful,' David remarked as he led the way across the busy thoroughfare to the city centre of Cendillis. 'He'd simply tell her he expected it finished within the hour and she'd have it done.'

At the mention of her guardian, the concerned expression, which had been appearing frequently on Rhiannon's face for the past few days, returned. 'I wonder what's taking him so long to get back. It's been almost four weeks since he left after the race.'

'I'm sure he's fine,' David replied. 'He'll be back soon – and after putting up with him for a couple of days you'll start wondering how soon it will be before he leaves again.'

Although David's last comment made a small smile appear on Rhiannon's face, it was clear her worry over Sir Raeden's prolonged absence would not be easily dismissed.

'He'll be all right, Rhiannon,' David assured her, his tone now serious. 'Endrille has often said he's the best fighter she's ever seen, and he's not the sort to take stupid risks. Once he finishes whatever it is he left to do he'll be back.'

'I just can't help thinking about why he would've sent for Endrille rather than come back himself.' Rhiannon gestured helplessly with her hand. 'What if he *is* hurt, and they're not telling us?'

'If he'd been injured my father would've been duty-bound to tell you. It's more likely he found something that Endrille needed to see for herself. They'll both be back in the next few days. When that happens the only thing he'll want to know is how you've done catching up on the lessons you missed.'

'Well, thanks to you, John and Izana I'm getting through them quite quickly.' Rhiannon sighed. 'I would've got more done if I hadn't lost nearly a week having to attend the trial for Crumper.'

David's face darkened at the mention of the rider who almost caused Rhiannon's death during the race.

'I'm sure even Wyvern wouldn't have expected you to get much done during that horrendous ordeal,' he stated grimly. 'At least it's over now with Darvill Crumper imprisoned on Culhos.'

'And Plancy dead.'

David frowned. 'They still haven't discovered how he got hold of the poison before his trial. All the guards have been questioned by the Trínondras and each one has been cleared of any involvement. But it is certain that Plancy took his own life to avoid having to tell the truth about why he wanted the Dragon's Cup, and also so he couldn't give the names of anyone else involved with his scheme.'

'David! Rhiannon!'

At the sound of the familiar voice, they both turned around to see John striding towards them, his curly mop of auburn hair making him easy to spot in the thick crowd. Behind him, and walking at a more sedate pace, was a tall, willowy woman.

'That's Cordelia,' David murmured. 'If she's a bit formal, just ignore it. John says she's been like that ever since she finished her first year at Ryegoth's.'

Intrigued, Rhiannon stared at John's older sister. Unlike her brother, Cordelia had long dark hair that was as straight as a ruler, and a small delicate face dominated by a pair of large blue eyes. She also walked with a smooth grace, the complete opposite of John's firm stride.

'She's quite pretty,' Rhiannon observed.

David shrugged. 'I suppose so,' he remarked without much enthusiasm. 'All I see when I look at her is John's sister who was always telling us to go away and play somewhere else.'

'I'm so glad I saw you two!' John announced with evident relief as he caught up to them. 'Delia's just spent over two hours looking for a book in the library, and she was about to drag me off with her to Moberly's Book Emporium to find another one!'

'John, really! Stop making a spectacle of yourself.' Cordelia turned to David. Her well-modulated voice was pitched low when she said, 'Your Royal Highness, I apologise for my brother's uncouth behaviour.'

'Delia, I've known your family all my life,' David pointed out. 'I gave up being shocked by John's behaviour years ago. Now, let me introduce you. Rhiannon, I'd like you to meet Cordelia Tremaine. Delia, this is Rhiannon McBride, daughter of the line of Mórell.'

Rhiannon felt extremely conscious of her untidy appearance when Cordelia turned to look at her. But, to her credit, John's sister merely smiled and said, 'It is a pleasure to meet the winner of the Dragon's Cup. You did extremely well and you have my congratulations.'

'Thank you.'

'I also understand that the ball being held tomorrow is in honour of your birthday,' Cordelia continued. 'Unfortunately, I shall be unable to attend, but I do wish you the very best. I just hope none of my brothers causes you any embarrassment by pulling a foolish prank.'

John gave an inelegant snort of laughter. 'I doubt the triplets will be able to get their hands on Rhiannon's cake like they did with yours,' he said. At Rhiannon's questioning look he told her, 'They put something into it that turns your teeth purple. Delia refused to speak or smile for a week until it faded.'

His sister, not amused by the memory of the incident, frowned in John's direction.

'We had best be on our way.'

At David's tactful interjection the siblings both turned towards him.

'I'll come with you,' John promptly declared. 'Delia has the carriage to get her home.' He then looked at Gareth who had been maintaining a discreet distance, and said with the authority of Chief Robesman, 'I can take over for you, Gareth.'

The older man looked at David who nodded and waved a casual hand. 'It's all right with me,' he said. 'You can have the rest of the day off if you like.'

'Thanks, David.' Gareth then turned to John. With a complete change of tone, he said, 'I request you ensure My Lord's safety at all times.'

'My life shall I place in his service,' John replied.

His duty done, Gareth smiled at them all, including Rhiannon. Ever since the race, his cool manner towards her had softened to a slightly friendlier one.

'Don't let these two encourage you to do anything dangerous, Miss Rhiannon,' he said. 'They have a habit of getting themselves into trouble.'

'Oh, I won't. I think I've had enough of danger for now.'

'What? You mean you don't want to go cliff-diving?' John asked in exaggerated dismay.

Cordelia, who had accepted her brother's abandonment with sisterly forbearance, admonished him to behave himself. Then she took her leave of David and Rhiannon.

'Would you like me to accompany you, Delia?' Gareth said unexpectedly. 'I came on Orvar and could see you home.'

Cordelia looked at him. 'Only if you swear to behave yourself, Mr Harulf,' she answered. 'I have not forgotten your partiality for fighting. Even on the last day of term you could not resist.'

'I noticed you stayed to watch the duel.'

'Only because I couldn't get through the crowd of both staff and students who'd gathered around me.'

'What's this?' David interjected. 'Gareth, were you fighting at the Academy again?'

Gareth waved dismissively. 'It could barely count as a fight,' he said. 'Harris has no skill with a blade. He challenged me after taking offence at my pointing that fact out to him when he was boasting he would win the Duelling Tournament this year. I simply sparred with him using training swords. I didn't harm him. Much. Just a few bruises that would have disappeared after a few days.'

'Hmph!' Cordelia turned away with a toss of her head and set off down the street.

'I think you offended her,' David observed, a hint of laughter in his voice.

'Rubbish!' John refuted with all the authority of a brother. 'She's inflicted her fair share of bruises on me when we've sparred, and she enjoys fighting. I don't know why she's suddenly trying to pretend she doesn't.' He looked at Gareth. 'If you still want to go with her, feel free. You could always just challenge her to spar with you. She never could resist accepting one.'

'Or you could simply say you're sorry,' Rhiannon suggested. All three males turned to look at her. 'Well, if she's already angry an apology might work better than a challenge.'

Gareth considered this for a moment. 'It might work,' he said, and nodded to Rhiannon. 'Thank you. I'll give it a try.'

Then he set off after Cordelia, his long fair hair glinting in the sunlight.

'Is it just me, or does he seem unusually interested in my sister?'

'It's not just you,' David answered.

'More fool him. She wants to be an apothecary like Mum and she said she's not interested in courting anyone for the next two years. Now, where are we going?'

'Officer Morton has our horses at Camberwell Fountain, we're meeting him there.'

'Excellent, that's not too far from where I left Asaph. And after that?'

'David agreed to take me to see the colony of vasker otters near Haldoron Bridge,' said Rhiannon. 'I've been wanting to go there ever since I read about them.'

'It'll take us at least an hour and a half to get there from here if we use the Narrowgate road,' David said, 'so we'd best hurry up and get the horses.'

'Well, let's not waste any more time talking,' John declared, 'let's go!'

It did not take long for them to retrieve their horses and convince Officer Morton they had no need of an escort. They hurried down the cobblestone roads, through the Narrowgate entrance of the defensive wall, then a labyrinth of alleyways to the outskirts of Cendillis.

A sea of colourful heather shimmered across the expanse of grassy fields. Rhiannon gazed beyond them at the tall trees of Shaimar Forest visible in the distance.

'Why did we come this way?' she asked. 'The main road is back there.'

'It's quicker to cut across the fields,' David explained. He pointed slightly to the southeast. 'Haldoron Bridge is over there. If we followed the main road we'd take twice as long to get there.'

'We'd also have to deal with all the other people using the road,' John added.

'Then over the fields it is,' Rhiannon agreed, urging her mount forward.

'Have a care going over the first rise,' David warned her, 'sometimes the ground's a bit slippery, and Flavian won't like it if you bring Kateri back with a limp.'

Having become familiar with the head groom of the Royal Stables, Rhiannon knew all too well how irate he would be should one of the horses under his charge be returned to him suffering an injury.

'I'll be careful,' she promised, and thankfully, after an enjoyable ride across the fields, all three horses and their riders made it to Haldoron Bridge without incident.

After dismounting, David, Rhiannon and John left the horses to follow along behind as they walked towards the impressive structure. Rhiannon, who had only ever seen the bridge whilst flying on a dragon or from a distance inside the castle walls, stared at it in awe.

Made entirely from stone, and set atop enormous pilings, it spanned the long width of the Deora River from bank to bank. Benevolent-faced angels sculpted from white marble on high pedestals surmounted the fine balustrades guarding each side. And along the length of the bridge, lampposts lined the walkways reserved for those who chose to cross on foot.

'This is incredible!' Rhiannon exclaimed.

She stepped onto the bridge and rushed to lean over the side to stare down at the water.

The Deora River flowed merrily under the bridge, its rippling surface sparkling in the afternoon sunlight. To her delight, Rhiannon caught a glimpse of several little furry creatures playing with each other near its east bank.

'Look! There they are!'

Obediently following the direction of her pointed finger, her two companions gazed down at the water to see three young vasker otters wrestling with each other.

'Can we get closer to them?' Rhiannon asked.

'There's a spot upriver in Shaimar Forest where you can see the rest of the family. You can even get close enough to pat one if they like you,' David answered. 'Most people tend not to go there as the track leading to it is a bit rough. But it's worth the effort when you get to see them.'

'How far is it from here?'

'It's not too far,' John said. He cast a doubtful gaze at Rhiannon's gown. 'But as David mentioned, the path leading there isn't easy.'

Rhiannon lifted up the hem of her gown to show off a sturdy pair of boots. 'Then I guess it's fortunate I'm wearing these.'

'They'll do,' David declared and led the way across the bridge. As they reached the other side, he gestured towards the road continuing northeast. 'That's the main road to the city of Ardara.

It takes about ten days to get there by carriage, since you can only travel over the mountains during the day due to the steep inclines and sharp turns. The southeast road leads to the town of Kelmore and that one there leads to Ryegoth Academy,' he continued, pointing to a narrower road, which branched off towards the north and disappeared into the dense woodland of Shaimar Forest. 'It's pretty much deserted during the holidays.'

And indeed, compared to the other main road, with several carriages and people mounted upon horses travelling along it, on the northward road there was not a single traveller to be seen.

'So where's the path we're taking?' Rhiannon asked.

'Over here.' David turned to the left and walked off into the long grass bordering the road. The gentle summer breeze blew through the lush green growth, the movement transforming the grass into a sea of emerald waves. 'It's close to the riverbank, so be careful you don't slip,' he cautioned.

Rhiannon glanced over her shoulder to check on the horses. She noticed they had only followed them a short distance into the long grass before coming to a halt.

'They'll be fine,' David said when she mentioned it. 'No one would dare try to steal them, and they'll come if we call.'

'Besides, they won't be able to follow us all the way once we pass into Shaimar Forest,' John said. 'The path wasn't designed for horses.'

A little while later as she sidestepped a small burrow and ducked another low-hanging branch in the forest, Rhiannon had to concede the truth of John's words. If the horses tried to walk along the path, one of them was sure to end up with a lame leg.

'We're almost there,' David said from the bottom of a steep slope of naturally formed steps. 'Be careful not to rush when you come down these rocks, there's moss on some of them.'

Rhiannon looked at the ground and gingerly began to walk down the steps.

All was going well until the third one when her foot slipped.

She toppled forward with a startled cry.

A strong arm hooked around her waist and pulled her back. Her body was lifted as easily as though she weighed no more than a feather, while her rescuer declared, 'You should place your steps with more care, small one.'

Rhiannon glanced up at the owner of the fair voice and beheld the graceful, feminine features of a young dryad.

Its eyes stern, the tree spirit gently set Rhiannon down beside a pale-faced David. 'This path can be treacherous, even to those familiar with its dangers,' the dryad said. 'Be vigilant, children.' Then, without another word, it disappeared back inside the trunk of a tall beech tree.

'Are you all right?'

Rhiannon nodded at David's concerned question.

'No harm done, thanks to our friend,' she replied.

'You're lucky the dryad caught you,' John commented. He cautiously descended the last of the steps. 'Otherwise that would've been a really nasty fall.'

'Do you want to go on?' David asked.

'Of course,' Rhiannon replied in some surprise. 'You don't think that was enough to scare me, do you? I faced worse dangers during the race!'

David conceded the truth of this, having been told all about the obstacles she had faced. He turned away and continued onwards, though he was quick to offer his hand to assist Rhiannon when they at last reached the muddy shore near the shallow edge of the river.

Not wanting to risk ending up face first in the mud, Rhiannon gratefully accepted his help in walking through the mire to where several otters could be seen. Some of them were lazily floating on their backs in the river, while others sat up from their position on the shore to stare curiously at their human visitors. There was only one who ignored them and continued juggling three rocks between his paws as he rolled onto his back.

'They're adorable!'

The instant she spoke all the otters turned to look directly at Rhiannon. The ones in the water rolled over and swam to the shore. Then they all tilted their noses into the air to sniff cautiously.

'They're already curious,' David murmured softly. 'Stay still, Rhiannon. If they sense there's no threat about they'll come over to you.'

After a moment it became obvious the small creatures had come to a decision. With a bounce in their steps, they raced across the muddy land and circled around their target with a chorus of delighted squeaks. Several of them began nudging and rubbing against Rhiannon's legs with their heads.

'They want you to pat them,' John told her with a smile. 'I've never seen them take a liking to someone so quickly before.'

Rhiannon eagerly bent down and stroked the head of the two otters closest to her. The others immediately gave a whine of protest.

'I only have two hands!' she laughed.

'Leave off, you little rascal!'

Rhiannon looked over her shoulder to see the smallest otter batting playfully at David's boot. She also noticed that despite his words of rebuke, the Prince of Álnair had a smile on his face as he crouched down to tease the assailant of his footwear with one gentle hand.

She turned her attention to John and grinned when she saw him attempting to extract his cloak from the claws of another otter trying to climb it.

'I really needed an outing like this after the drama of Crumper's trial,' she murmured.

For several minutes the otters gambolled about their visitors, never seeming to tire in their playful antics.

Then a dreadful agonised scream shattered the peaceful atmosphere.

David and John drew their swords.

Rhiannon, having left the castle without her own, pulled the dagger from her boot.

Their survival instincts coming to the fore, the otters all scurried away towards the river.

The three humans turned to face whatever had made the ghastly noise.

David and John stared into the shadowy depths of the forest, moving instinctively in front of Rhiannon. Their taller forms blocked her view completely.

Rhiannon huffed impatiently. She stepped to the side and peered around David's arm.

'What do you think it was?'

'I don't know,' David whispered. 'I've never heard anything scream like that before. What concerns me, however, is the possibility that whatever inflicted the pain may be approaching us.'

At this ominous possibility all three of them shifted into a defensive stance.

David and John tightened their grip on the hilt of their swords.

Rhiannon raised her dagger.

A violent stirring of the forest trees filled the air with the loud rustling of leaves, like the wild turbulence before a storm.

Then, from out of the dark shadows of the woods, a great figure appeared. Its tall, masculine form disfigured and severely burnt, the creature was in immense pain as it stumbled and fell to the ground. Several otters scampered towards it, squeaking in concern. Looking up, the dryad gazed at David with desperate eyes and raised one beseeching hand.

'O Prince! Hear me!' the creature cried in a rasping masculine voice that still retained a faint musical quality.

David sheathed his sword and was moving before John's

horrified exclamation of, 'It's a dryad!' burst from him. He ran forward, his feet slipping and sliding in the mud, and hastened to the dryad's side. He grasped its outstretched hand in his.

'What has happened? Who did this to you?'

The dryad grimaced again as a shudder of pain shook its body.

'My tree is almost gone,' it gasped, 'I am very old, my roots grow deep for miles beneath the forest, but now the cursed fire has reached the last root and I have not the strength to make it to Valieoth Castle. You must tell the king the heart of Black Woods has been destroyed by those seeking the location of the Dragon's Eye. They are led by one called Mórfran. There is an evil presence growing in the north, beyond the dark height of Mount Perdus. It is spreading throughout the land.'

The dryad broke off. A strangled scream sounded in its throat.

'Can't you help him?' Rhiannon asked desperately, crouching down beside David.

'No.' David did not take his eyes off the writhing tree spirit. 'Had the fire only been burning the visible body of the tree, we could have saved him. But a cursed fire that is already burning the last root under the ground? We would never arrive in time to put out the flames. I have met him before while travelling with my parents. He's Phalóran, and he comes from the ancient oak which lies within the heart of the Black Woods. He would have crossed the Wildlands to reach us.'

'Fifteen days and nights have I journeyed,' the dryad whispered. 'I despaired of being able to pass on my warning before I died, but then I heard your voices. O Prince, there is a darkness coming, and its power is increasing. Beware the one called Mórfran. He bears a scar on his right cheek. Protect the Dragon's Eye. Keep it safe from him. Keep it safe.'

Then the tree spirit lifted its eyes towards the sky and cried out. 'My life is extinguished! The flames have consumed my tree completely!' And with a shudder of pain Phalóran vanished.

Horrified, Rhiannon stared at the empty space where he had been. Not a trace of his existence remained. For a long time, no one spoke. Then David stood up. Grief and anger had cast a stern shadow in his eyes. He held a hand out to help Rhiannon to her feet.

'Come on,' he said. 'I need to inform my father of this immediately.'

Neither John nor Rhiannon offered any protest. They followed David in silence until Haldoron Bridge could be seen beyond the edge of the forest's border. Then Rhiannon, with a hesitant glance at David, asked, 'Do you know what he meant about the Dragon's Eye?'

David did not slow his pace as he said, 'I do. It's an object the House of Valieoth is sworn to protect. I'll only find out what it does from Endrille once I become king, but I know its location. What troubles me is that someone else knows it exists. It's imperative I tell my father someone is now searching for it.'

When they exited the forest, David gave a long whistle. The clear, piercing sound carried on the gentle breeze to where the three horses stood grazing near the river. Upon hearing the summons, their heads lifted and as one they turned and galloped towards their riders, their hooves thundering on the ground.

After the horses stopped before them, David hastily assisted Rhiannon to mount Kateri, before swinging himself onto Cineád's back with effortless grace. Once John was astride Asaph, the prince of Álnair did not waste another moment in talking. He urged Cineád into a fast gallop, and led the way back to the castle, a grim expression on his face.

Chapter 2

A GRAND PARTY

It did not take long for David, Rhiannon and John to find King Stephen after they reached Valieoth Castle. They quickly informed him of the dryad's words. However, he did not seem surprised, or even shocked by the news.

'Thank you for telling me so promptly,' was all he said.

It's almost as though he was expecting to hear it, Rhiannon thought later that night in her bedroom as she sat studying at her desk. And what is the Dragon's Eye?

She closed the rather tedious book (*Professor Grimshore's Essay of Dimensional Alteration*), which she had been trying to focus on for the past twenty minutes, and abandoned any further attempt at studying. Instead, she reached for the small book she had been meaning to read for a while. She had discovered it among the piles of textbooks she had bought at Moberly's Book Emporium during the Christmas holidays. With everything that had happened, she had not had a chance to even open the thick leather cover to discover what *The Lost Secrets of Merlin* might contain.

Rhiannon opened the book to a random page, and had her attention instantly captured by the words written upon it.

Of the many secrets none is more intriguing, or more controversial, than the location of Merlin's secret laboratory. Though many have searched for this place, which is reputed to still hold many of the mage's personal records and notes on his experiments, each attempt has met with failure. There are now those who question whether the laboratory even exists, despite the deathbed testimony given by Merlin's assistant, Cornelius Tichley.

Master Tichley said he had been privileged to see inside the laboratory, but had sworn an oath to never divulge its location.

One person who insists it does exist is distinguished Professor of History, Renwolf Tysus. Prior to his retirement, Professor Tysus insisted the laboratory existed, even theorising that its entrance may lie somewhere inside Valieoth Castle.

'Inside Valieoth Castle,' Rhiannon whispered, a spark of excitement flaring to life inside her. 'I wonder if David knows anything about it.' She looked at her watch and groaned. 'It's too late to disturb him now.' She regretfully put the book down, changed into her nightdress, then crawled into bed. She clapped her hands once to dim the lights and snuggled under the warm coverlet. 'I'll ask him about it tomorrow.'

However, in the mad rush of last-minute preparations for the ball, Rhiannon never got a chance to speak to David alone.

Queen Maiwen, thrilled to finally have a young girl she could fuss over and spoil, spent the day ensuring Rhiannon would look her best with the help of multiple beauty treatments. Then, upon the arrival of Rhiannon's gown from Madame Dubois, she insisted they go through an extremely large jewellery collection to find the perfect necklace to match it.

Unsurprisingly, David avoided all these displays of feminine titivating by disappearing immediately after breakfast. He returned to the castle just in time to get changed into his formal high-collared blue tunic, white breeches and black polished boots, and a white cloak trimmed with gold. With a shining coronet adorning his head, he presented himself in the Great Hall for his parents' approval just moments before Rhiannon arrived.

Her golden eyes gleaming, Rhiannon stepped through the grand entrance to the Great Hall, then stopped at the splendid scene in front of her. The brightly lit hall was bedecked in a colourful array of ribbons and garlands of flowers, while the delicate chains of crystals hanging from the mural-covered ceiling cast dancing rainbows on the marble floor. On the raised dais at the top of the Great Hall, King Stephen and Queen Maiwen were standing beside David in front of the long window, the brilliant sunset creating a golden haze about their forms and the two fine thrones behind them.

Rhiannon slowly made her way forward. She could not help but be flattered by the light of admiration in David's eyes when he turned and saw her short, sturdy figure arrayed in Madame Dubois' expensive masterpiece. Her mirror had shown how the gown of shimmering silver-blue chiffon and white satin expertly outlined her now developing figure, but it felt good to have the fact confirmed by David's appreciative smile. Part of her hair formed a coronet around her head, while the rest cascaded down her back in a flow of ringlets. To complete her fine attire, around her neck was Queen Maiwen's necklace of sapphire and pearl set in a delicate floral design.

'Stars above, Rhiannon! You'll outshine every other girl looking like that!' David exclaimed, stepping down from the dais to stand in front of her. 'The embroidery makes it look like you've got crushed jewels scattered on your dress.'

Rhiannon nervously smoothed her hand down the light material of her gown. 'You don't think I look ridiculous?'

'Of course not! You look lovely.'

'Well, I feel like a little girl playing dress-up with her mother's clothes.'

'Take it from me, you don't look like a little girl at all.'

'No indeed, my dear,' Queen Maiwen said in agreement. Clad in a silver gown that twinkled with every step, she approached Rhiannon and embraced her. 'You look very elegant, and I'm sure everyone who sees you tonight will be of the same opinion.'

'I had best order the guards to be extra vigilant in case some young man tries to make off with you.'

Rhiannon flushed scarlet at King Stephen's gently teasing comment.

'He'd soon regret it,' David said. 'Not only would he have my Robesmen and me to deal with, but Rhiannon would soon have him laid out on the ground with her foot on his throat. I've seen her do it to some of the guards.'

Rhiannon shot a glare in David's direction before explaining to his startled parents, 'It was during my lessons with Sir Raeden. He had a few guards attack me, and I was only allowed to use my body to defeat them.'

Their expressions transforming to ones of amusement, King Stephen and Queen Maiwen were sincere in complimenting her on her skill. Then a gracious smile of welcome appeared on their faces as the first group of guests was announced, and they moved away to greet them.

'You just had to make it sound like I'd been randomly attacking the guards, didn't you,' Rhiannon muttered.

'Of course,' David said, chuckling. 'I couldn't resist the opportunity of boasting about your more violent achievements. Plus, I had to remind myself of them after seeing you look so refined and proper in that gown. You look like a fashionable, impeccably-behaved lady.'

'What's wrong with that?'

'Nothing really, but every fashionable and impeccably-behaved lady I've met, apart from my mother and some of her friends, have always been dead bores. I didn't want to tarnish my opinion of you by giving you that appellation.'

Rhiannon smacked him on the arm.

'See! That, right there, helps me remember that you're more interesting than most of the other girls who'll be here,' David said, grinning.

'You're weird.'

The approach of the first group of guests put an end to their conversation.

Rhiannon watched David effortlessly assume his polite public persona. She thought it would be impossible for anyone to guess how much he disliked their obsequious attentions and fulsome compliments. Throughout the next half hour, she noticed the only time he really relaxed was when he greeted Izana, Eamon, Derrick and Gareth. The four Robesmen treated him with respect, but absolutely no formality, and Rhiannon happily realised they were all beginning to treat her the same way.

Izana smiled as he wished her happy birthday, adding he was willing to continue their study and sparring sessions in the new school year if she wanted his help. She did not hesitate to accept.

Eamon beamed at her, cheerfully saying she looked as fine as one of his arrows. She took that as a compliment, knowing how meticulously he fletched his own.

Derrick, looking a little pale from a recent infection but his manner still stoic, told her the colour of her gown was suitable and her appearance was elegant. She took that to be the equivalent of someone else saying 'you look great'.

And Gareth, having dismissed all his initial reservations about her, declared she looked splendid before thanking her for her wise advice the previous day. It turned out Cordelia *had* preferred an apology.

A few minutes after Gareth had stepped away to greet Lord

Sharbel, David and Rhiannon looked up to see John approaching them.

'Looks like this is going to be a rather crowded party,' he said after greeting them both. 'Thankfully, that should make it easier to hide from my little sister.'

David groaned. 'Please don't tell me Alice is going to be here.'

'Special treat since it's Rhiannon's birthday ball.' A mischievous twinkle appeared in John's green eyes. He added slyly to David, 'She's quite determined to ask you to dance with her, on account of you being her future husband.'

'What!' Rhiannon's exclamation of shock rang out loudly.

David shot an exasperated look at John. 'I'm not her future husband. The silly girl decided she wants to marry me when she's older and keeps telling everyone what her dress will be like. It's downright annoying.'

Rhiannon's frown disappeared. She smiled, feeling strangely relieved. 'So you're not betrothed to her.'

'Of course not, child betrothals have never been permitted in Álnair.'

'Then I wouldn't take what she says seriously,' she said dismissively. 'She'll probably declare she's going to marry dozens of boys before she's ten. Quite a few girls do, you know.'

'Did you?' David asked, not quite disguising the note of interest in his voice.

Rhiannon shifted uncomfortably. 'Not really. The boys I knew were either tormenting me or ignoring my existence. Not the kind of behaviour to evoke feelings of a positive kind.' She glanced again at him and added, 'Let Alice have her dreams if they make her happy. Believe me, she'll grow out of her infatuation with you as soon as another boy catches her attention. At the moment she's probably wanting to be a princess. Once that wears off, she may want to be a Defence Instructor. Then she'll start saying she's going to marry Sir Raeden.'

David and John howled with laughter.

'Now that would be amusing,' John chuckled.

'I'd want to see his face the first time she announced it,' David remarked with no small amount of glee, only for his smile to fade into a wry look of resignation when he caught sight of John's parents entering the Great Hall with the marriage-minded menace set between them.

Four-year-old Alice Tremaine looked a picture of innocence in her green dress and bouncing red curls, but upon catching sight of David, she gave a cry of delight and ran towards him, oblivious of her mother's attempts to stop her.

Her baby teeth shone like brilliant little pearls as she beamed at him and babbled, 'Pwinth David! Mama says I'm not to twouble you, but I'm not. You wike to dance wiv me, so may I pwease dance wiv you? I pwactised and pwactised a wong time!'

David sighed ruefully before bestowing a small smile on his pint-sized tormentor. 'Of course I'll dance with you, Alice, but as it's Rhiannon's birthday I'll have to dance with her first. I'll come get you after my dance with her.'

Alice frowned. 'You pwomise?'

'May Endrille sit on me and squash me to jelly if I don't,' David said solemnly.

Alice gave him a beatific smile, then turned to Rhiannon. 'Happy burfday, Wiannon,' she said politely.

Rhiannon thanked her, then bent down to say, 'That's a beautiful dress you're wearing.'

Alice preened. 'Mama buyed it for me,' she said proudly. Then her eyes widened as she looked properly at Rhiannon's gown. 'Thath pwetty! When I mawwy Pwinth David my dweth ith gonna be wike it.'

Rhiannon controlled her laughter at seeing David glare at John, who was snorting with amusement. 'I'm sure you'll look lovely,' she said kindly.

The arrival of Lady Isabella Tremaine mercifully diverted Alice's attention.

While her mother quietly began to scold Alice for running across the room, David, Rhiannon and John made good their escape to an alcove that lay partially concealed behind one of the large pillars lining the hall. They passed through the curtained entrance and sat on the padded stone seats adjoined to the walls.

'They'll start the dancing soon,' David said, 'but before that happens my father will open the ball by presenting you to the guests. Then I'll lead you out onto the floor for the first dance. After that you can dance with whomever you like.'

'It's just a shame I didn't have a say in who was invited,' Rhiannon sighed, looking out at the crowd of people who now filled the Great Hall, and one person in particular. 'Marcus definitely wouldn't have got an invite.'

David grimaced as his gaze found his cousin who was complaining to a sympathetic Felix Costanzo.

'He does have an unpleasant way of ruining any party,' he said.

'Although, I have to say I didn't think it was very nice of your uncle to embarrass him like he did when they arrived,' Rhiannon reflected.

'Marcus got embarrassed?' John's interest was immediately caught. 'How?'

'Uncle Oliver congratulated me on my progress at school, then said Marcus should strive to be more like me.' David's tone conveyed how little he had enjoyed the scene. 'He certainly didn't try to hide his disappointment over the fact Marcus doesn't share his talent in Natural Science. Maybe if he didn't praise my efforts every time he sees me, Marcus might be content to hate me from a distance.' He pointed to where Felix was now muttering something to a glowering Marcus, and added, 'I'm sure it would also decrease Felix's opportunities to encourage his resentment of me.'

'It's never a good feeling to be compared to someone else all the time,' Rhiannon agreed, thinking of when she had stood listening to her foster parents sing Annabelle's praises while dismissing her own efforts on the piano. 'If Marcus has to put up with that, I suppose I can understand why he's so nasty.'

'I wouldn't put all the blame for that on David's uncle,' John said. 'Even when we were younger, Marcus was nothing but a little fiend. He'd do anything to try and get us in trouble, particularly David. And he'd always throw a tantrum if he didn't get his own way. We tried to be nice to him by including him in our adventures, but as soon as it worked to his advantage he'd run and inform our parents so we'd get into trouble. Then while we were being lectured, he'd be watching with a little smirk on his face.'

David suddenly laughed. 'Mind you, there was one time when it didn't play out quite how he expected. Do you remember?'

John frowned in thought, then slapped his knee. 'That's right,' he exclaimed. 'When he told Sir Raeden instead of your father.'

'It's the one time I didn't mind getting a lecture from Wyvern,' David recalled fondly, and told Rhiannon, 'it was the night before my ninth birthday and Marcus and John were staying over in the palace. John and I went out at midnight to find a star crystal.' At Rhiannon's puzzled frown, he explained, 'They're a special sort of jewel found on the ocean floor. They're quite hard to find as you can only see them in the moonlight when they're in the water, but when air touches them, they become permanently visible. Anyway, Marcus had overheard us talking about looking for them before dinner and he was watching from his window when he saw us on the beach. Then he ran and told Wyvern.

'I'll admit I felt absolutely terrified when I first looked up and saw Wyvern glaring at me as he stood on the sand with the moon shining on him. But when he marched John and me back to the palace, and he wiped the smirk off Marcus' face by informing him that he was in just as much trouble for not telling someone what we planned as soon as he heard us talking about it, I didn't care what Wyvern said to me, or what punishment I got. Marcus' outraged screams and tearful sobs when he realised he'd got himself into trouble made it one of our best adventures.'

'I take it he didn't snitch on you again after that?' Rhiannon said.

'Oh, John and I were careful not to give him the opportunity. If we were planning something, most of the faeries would call out a warning if he started to come near us. They don't really like him either.'

A sudden hush descending on the crowd gathered in the Great Hall drew their attention. David looked out, rose to his feet and turned to Rhiannon.

'Father's about to call your name. You don't want to miss your cue,' he said, holding out his hand. 'I suppose it's my cue too,' he added, 'since I'm supposed to escort you to the dais. Come on.'

Rhiannon placed her hand on top of his, and stood up. A tinge of nervousness had her asking, 'Will I have to say anything?'

'Just smile when everyone cheers, then thank them. They won't expect much more than that this time.'

Relieved, Rhiannon allowed him to lead her out of the alcove, John's cheerful promise to find them after the first dance sounding out behind them.

David and Rhiannon slowly walked towards the dais where King Stephen and Queen Maiwen were standing in front of their thrones. King Stephen made an imposing figure as he stepped forward to formally greet his guests, his tall form majestically clad in robes of deep blue linen and his long golden hair gleaming beneath his crown. However, no one could mistake the warm smile on his lips, nor the affable tone of his voice when he spoke.

'Welcome, my dear friends, to this celebration in honour of a special young lady. She has only been in Álnair since Christmas last year, but already it is difficult to imagine life in Valieoth Castle without her. A few weeks ago she became the youngest champion to win the Dragon's Cup, and today is her fourteenth birthday. It is both my pleasure and privilege to present to you Rhiannon McBride.'

The guests broke out into loud applause.

David escorted Rhiannon up onto the dais. Then he stepped back, leaving her to face the crowd alone. She looked out at the sea of faces, smiling tentatively. A flurry of eager movement caught her attention. In an instant, her smile became a real one. She stifled the laugh rising in her throat at the sight of the Tremaine triplets already helping themselves to the selection of light refreshments on the side tables.

'They better leave some for the rest of us.'

David's quiet mutter from behind her informed Rhiannon that he too had seen them, and she could not prevent the small giggle that escaped her lips.

The crowd's applause began to fade.

Rhiannon bowed her head and with a small smile said a simple word of thanks.

At a gesture from King Stephen, the musicians, a small group of faeries, lifted their harps, flutes and fiddles and began to play.

The elegant, lilting melody had the guests retreating to the sides of the Great Hall. Then David led Rhiannon to the middle of the floor to finish the opening of the ball by performing the first dance of the evening with her.

Rhiannon's breath stuttered and caught in her throat when David placed a hand on her waist to draw her into a series of smooth turns. Somehow, it felt different to all those times he, Izana and John had performed the same move during the light-hearted lessons Queen Maiwen had organised for her. He bent his head, his face hovering above hers. His clean, woodsy scent blended with hers of vanilla honey. She could even feel his warm breath against her skin. Rhiannon felt herself blush when she realised she had been silently staring into his eyes all throughout the turns.

'You're doing very well,' David complimented her, tactfully not mentioning her flushed cheeks. 'No one would guess you were still treading on my feet three days ago.'

His last teasing comment drew an answering smile from Rhiannon.

'It's not my fault you have such big feet,' she retorted, moving to circle about under his outstretched arm. Her gaze flickered over the crowd. Then she gave a start of surprise. An extremely tall man with black hair was standing partially concealed in the shadows by the entrance.

'What's wrong?' David queried in concern, gracefully covering her small lapse in concentration with a deft whirl.

'I thought I saw Sir Raeden near the main doors.'

They both used the movement of the dance to glance towards the doorway, only to see it empty of anyone matching Sir Raeden's description.

'I could've sworn he was there,' Rhiannon murmured.

'Perhaps he was, and if he is here you'd better focus on your steps. You don't want to trip and fall to the ground while he's watching.'

'Good point,' Rhiannon agreed, and forced herself to concentrate solely on completing the dance.

When the last note was played, she gave a low curtsy to David's bow, and sighed in relief. 'At least that's over.'

'You needn't make it sound like dancing with me is so terrible,' David complained, his masculine pride wounded.

'Don't be silly,' Rhiannon said with a smile, 'I didn't mean that. I just hate having so many people stare at me like I'm an exhibit on display.'

'Welcome to my life,' David said, and led her from the floor. 'Now, do you want to go and see if it was Wyvern?'

'I do, but you can't come. You promised to dance with Alice,' Rhiannon reminded him.

'And a promise is a promise,' John said as he stepped in front of them. 'Off you go, David. My mum has Alice over there, and she's ready to battle her way over here if you don't hurry.'

David looked in the direction of his next dance partner and manfully resigned himself to his fate.

'We can look for Sir Raeden when you get back.'

David snorted at Rhiannon's words. 'You say that like it will be a lovely treat,' he said, and walked off towards an ecstatic Alice who was literally bouncing in anticipation.

'Is Sir Raeden back?' John asked, looking over the crowd of people standing near them.

'I thought I saw him near the door,' Rhiannon replied, 'but when I looked again he'd disappeared.'

'Hmm.' John gazed about them again and frowned. 'I can't see him, and he's so tall he'd be easy to spot, even in this crowd. Perhaps he –' His voice abruptly broke off.

Rhiannon turned away from the sight of Carina Egelbert staring wistfully around the Great Hall to look at John. She was startled to see his expression had become one of blank astonishment. Following the direction of his gaze through the dancing figures, she saw what had distracted him.

A girl. An exquisitely beautiful girl with long black hair and creamy skin, clad in a gown of rich green velvet and silver satin. She was standing beside a distinguished looking gentleman who was conversing with Lord Sharbel. As Rhiannon watched, the High Chancellor released a booming laugh and shook his head. Then he bestowed a friendly smile on the girl and said something that brought an answering smile to her lips.

Rhiannon glanced back at John and choked back a laugh at the starstruck look in his eyes as he stared unblinkingly at the girl.

'John. John.'

When calling his name drew no response from him, Rhiannon slapped him on the arm. Hard. 'John!'

The Chief Robesman to the Prince Royal looked down and frowned at his assailant. 'Why did you hit me?'

'You were too focused on staring at that girl to answer me when I called your name.'

'Oh.' His clean-shaven cheeks tinged red with embarrassment, John ran a hand through his auburn curls and apologised. 'I've never seen her before and was wondering who she could be.'

Rhiannon rolled her eyes. 'You weren't thinking of her name,' she said bluntly. 'You were too distracted by her appearance to think of anything else but how she looked.'

John's blush deepened. Indeed, he looked so awkward Rhiannon relented, and rather than teasing him, only said, 'She is quite lovely, and I definitely would've remembered if I'd seen her before.'

'They weren't among the guests I met before the ball started,' John revealed. 'They must've arrived late.'

They both looked over again in time to see several boys move towards the girl like moths drawn to a flame, all of them vying for her attention.

'She certainly won't have to worry about not finding a dance partner,' Rhiannon remarked lightly, 'not with the way all those boys are swarming around her.'

At these words, John's sense of loyalty and honour evidently broke through the fog surrounding his mind. 'They should be swarming around you,' he declared, 'after all, it is *your* birthday.'

'Thank you, but I'm not really one to crave that amount of attention.'

'You sound like David. He hates pomp and ceremony and people fawning over him all the time.'

'I can understand why,' Rhiannon commented drily, 'if that is an example of it.' She pointed to where David was trying valiantly to dance with Alice, but was rather hindered by the fact that the red-headed imp wouldn't release his hand when the steps called for it, and by the girls who kept trying to attract his notice as he passed.

John gave a bark of laughter. 'The girls attempting to flirt with him won't get very far,' he said, 'but for all she's a little pain with her obsession about marrying him, he's not really bothered by Alice's behaviour. He told me once that at least she's honest and doesn't have any hidden motives for chasing after him.'

'Because she announces what she wants whenever she sees him?' Rhiannon guessed.

'Exactly.' John looked over at his little sister's merry countenance and smiled. 'She's always been a cheerful girl and to David she's the baby sister he always wanted. I've tried making a present of her to him, but my parents won't let me.'

'How selfish of them.'

Hearing the humour in Rhiannon's voice, John's smile became a cheeky grin. 'It is, isn't it. I thought it was very generous of me to offer David one of my sisters – after all, I've got two of them.'

'And deep down inside you love them both, and would hate it if you lost one,' Rhiannon said warmly.

'This also is very true,' John conceded with a nod.

The music coming to a rousing conclusion drew their gazes back to the dance floor in time to see Alice twirl one final time under David's arm, then go down in a lopsided curtsy with an adorable smile on her face.

'She really is a little darling, isn't she,' John said proudly, and watched as David returned Alice to their mother's side.

After saying a few words to Lady Isabella, David turned and made his way towards John and Rhiannon.

'Do you two mind if I find somewhere to collapse,' he moaned as he reached them. 'John, I don't know where Alice gets all her energy, but if you discover the source you'd make a fortune selling it.'

'To old men like you?' John asked, and offered his arm to David with an exaggerated show of concern.

'If I had my walking stick I'd beat you over the head with it,' declared the Prince of Álnair. He turned to Rhiannon. 'Did you see anything of Wyvern while talking to this clodpole?'

Rhiannon shook her head. Then she twinkled impishly. 'Although, John did fall in love with a girl he saw.'

'Oi, who said anything about falling in love with her?' John demanded indignantly.

'So he's fallen for another one, has he?' David said in exaggerated exasperation. 'He averages one a month.'

Decorum forgotten, John punched him on the arm.

Rhiannon sniggered. 'If you know her, I'm sure he'd love an introduction,' she said to David, and pointed the girl out to him.

Unlike John, he merely looked at the beautiful girl for a moment, then announced, 'That's Branwen Sedgewick. She's not a clever conversationalist by any means, and given a choice I'd prefer talking to her younger sister Cassandra, the girl standing behind her with the dark curls. Cassandra lives here in the palace and gets private lessons. You wouldn't have seen her before as she tends to keep to herself. Their father is the man standing next to her, Lord Lamorak Sedgewick. He lives near Ardara, and Branwen attends a large school in the city. I'm surprised to see them here. They've never visited the castle before, not even to see Cassandra.'

'So why does Cassandra live here?' Rhiannon asked, gazing curiously at the girl who looked to be the same age as her.

'She accepted the position of First Seer and needs access to the Book of Prophecy,' David said. 'She has the gift of neushallough, to quite an extraordinary degree in fact, and whenever she has a vision it needs to be put into the book, which is kept in a secure part of the palace that only she and the current ruler of Álnair can enter. No one knows when a vision will come to her, so it's not unusual for her to walk off in the middle of a conversation and disappear for a while. Because of that, whenever he's here, my father has to check the book each morning to see if anything important has been prophesied.'

David turned back to John and offered, 'If you like, I can introduce you to Branwen. I've met her a few times when I've been to Ardara with my parents on official visits.'

John observed the crowd around Branwen, which had increased significantly from when he first saw her, and shook his head. 'Too many people about,' he said. 'You can always introduce me another time. Let's just go and see if Wyvern has returned.'

Neither David nor Rhiannon offered any objections to this proposal. They followed John, who led the way towards the main doors, only to be stopped several times by people wishing to speak to Rhiannon. Leila Hardinge, Viola Rastell and Innogen Calloway spent ten whole minutes exclaiming over her gown and her achievement in winning the Dragon's Cup.

When they finally slipped out of the Great Hall, the three of them all heaved a sigh of relief.

'I thought we'd never get through,' said David.

'At least when we had to stop it gave us the chance to check if Wyvern might be nearby,' John replied.

'Where should we look first?' Rhiannon asked. 'Would he go straight to his office?'

'No.' David lowered his head in thought. 'He'd have to report to my father, and he usually does that in the king's private office that's located on the floor above the Praeterium. In any event, something must have happened, because I saw Lord Sato speak to my father as we were talking to Mrs Mereweather, then they both left.' At Rhiannon's confused expression, he explained, 'My father never leaves the Great Hall in the middle of a social function unless it's important.'

'Do you think he'll mind if we go to the office to see if Sir Raeden is there?' Rhiannon asked.

'He doesn't have to know we're going to check,' David said, a grin appearing on his face. 'There's a secret passageway that goes from a concealed entrance near the Room of Tranquillity up to the office, a quick and convenient way for the old kings to walk between the office and the Praeterium. We'll be able to hear if they're in there.' He lifted his right hand to display his signet ring. 'This will let us inside the passageway.'

'Then what are we waiting for!' Rhiannon exclaimed, anxious to be off. 'Let's go!' And she set off determinedly towards the Room of Tranquillity with David and John hurrying after her.

Chapter 3

OF TROUBLING REPORTS AND STRANGE BIRTHDAY WISHES

The secret passageway was not quite what Rhiannon had expected. Its narrow entrance, concealed in the tall marble pedestal bearing a gold statue of a griffon, and opened by the touch of David's signet ring into a tiny indent on one of the pillar's floral ornamental carvings, led to a wide spiralling stone staircase that could easily fit across it three large men standing abreast. It was lit by yellow lights held aloft in the sconces lining the walls. The lights had flickered to life the moment they stepped through the door.

'We'll need to be quiet,' David warned as he and John followed her into the passage. 'These stone walls may be thick, but there's a chance someone could hear us if we make too much noise.'

With a tap of his ring against the back of the marble slab, the entrance was resealed, then they made their way up the winding steps in silence. At the top of the stairs was a long walkway leading to a wall with a metal handle attached to the stone.

'Is that the opening to the office?' Rhiannon whispered.

David nodded and crept forward. He gently pushed against one of the stones. A sliver of blue light radiated around it. The hard surface transformed, becoming as translucent as a butterfly wing.

Then they heard two voices. One was King Stephen's. The other was unquestionably Sir Raeden Wyvern's.

A tremendous sensation of relief flooded through Rhiannon at this confirmation of her guardian's safe return. But her joy was short-lived when she focused on his words.

'The evidence I found definitely indicates extensive experiments have been conducted. The talisman found on Plancy was set to transport him to a location point in the Forbidden Mountains. I followed some recent tracks which led to a laboratory within the woodland. The experiments appear to have been going on for some time. It was impossible to ascertain precisely how many dragons and magi were killed during the course of his tests. However, what I found left over from the last experiment would seem to indicate at least a dozen of each had been used for that one alone.'

'Could you identify the purpose behind all the experiments?' King Stephen enquired.

'Not conclusively. Unfortunately, the notes I found were vague, and I believe they were the only records kept. I have brought them back with me, but, from my initial perusal of them, it would appear the main focus of the last experiment was centred on increasing the magical potency of living cells. Reference was made to using the Dragon's Cup as the active stimulant, possibly due to the high levels of powerful energy already contained within it.'

'Which explains why Plancy sought the aid of Darvill Crumper.'

'Precisely. Lady Endrille informed me that during his trial Crumper confirmed he was unaware of the reason why Plancy desired to gain possession of the Dragon's Cup. I also only found traces of three other people inside the laboratory, and none of those traces belonged to Crumper. He was merely a tool Plancy intended to use and discard.'

'He would have killed him?'

'There is no doubt in my mind that was the ultimate fate Plancy had in store for him. The notes make a reference to using the fresh living tissue from a mage, with a later entry referring to the first test sample to be taken from "Rider D.C." Had Darvill Crumper succeeded in beating Rhiannon to the finish and been handed the Cup, he would have vanished without a trace and become an unwilling participant in Plancy's experiments.'

'Then he is lucky Rhiannon did not immediately succumb to the effects of the somlyne.'

'Yes.' Sir Raeden's voice was hard. 'He was lucky, and I was fortunate my ward was not killed through my oversight of not insisting all the riders be searched prior to the race.'

'Raeden, you cannot blame yourself for what happened to her. In fact, if it had not been for your quick identification of the poison and administering the thranlaire, she would not have survived.' When no answer was forthcoming, King Stephen sighed. 'Very well. I can see I will not convince you. But when apportioning blame, do not forget my own.'

'Sire —'

'No.' The word was said very firmly, in the tone of a king making a royal decree. 'We both thought adequate protections had been put into place with hidden guards positioned at each section of the race, and therefore we are both to blame for what happened to Rhiannon.'

A brief silence followed King Stephen's words.

Then, his voice pitched so low as though he did not want to risk anyone overhearing him, Sir Raeden enquired, 'Is she all right?'

'She has suffered no ill-effects from either the somlyne or thranlaire. However, Darvill Crumper's trial did place a significant strain on her. My son and John took it upon themselves to ensure she escaped for a few hours each day, and they have also been assisting her with her studies with some help from Izana. There was an incident yesterday that I believe disturbed her when the three of them encountered a dying dryad.'

'What!'

King Stephen briefly recounted the tale to him.

'This is ill news indeed,' Sir Raeden said gravely after King Stephen had finished. 'But it confirms the rumours I reported of Mórfran seeking the location of the Dragon's Eye. Lady Endrille disclosed to me its purpose and of the few entrusted with that knowledge. For Mórfran to only now be searching for it leads to the logical conclusion that his own knowledge of it is recent. Lady Endrille cannot even be considered as having betrayed its existence, therefore of the four human individuals who could have told him, there are only two feasible suspects.'

'*Four* human individuals? Before these events and your recent awareness, there were only three who knew about it.'

'Five years ago, there was another and her death has never been confirmed.'

King Stephen gave a loud sigh. 'If she has been a captive of that man all this time I dread to think what she has suffered. And I now see your point. Until one is certain, all possibilities must be considered.'

'Precisely. We could rule out one possibility tomorrow using the witness chair in the Praeterium. Has anyone been despatched to investigate the incident in the Black Woods?'

'Arastar left last night.' A small pause descended. Then King Stephen added quietly, 'Raeden, I did not tell them anything about Mórfran.'

'Thank you.'

There was a soft rustle of silk and the firm tread of boots from inside the office and then King Stephen spoke again.

'Now, before all my guests decide to come looking for me I had best return to the festivities below. Will you soon join us?'

'I shall change into more suitable attire, then speak to Lady Endrille and apprise her of what you have told me prior to making an appearance.'

'Rhiannon shall certainly be relieved to see you. I understand from David that she has been quite concerned for your safety.'

In the secret passage, Rhiannon frowned at David. He shrugged and mouthed, 'He asked about you.'

'I would hope she has been equally concerned about catching up on her studies,' came Sir Raeden's reply, his voice sounding farther away from the wall.

'Master Elgalad did mention she has made several visits to the library. And, before you ask, he said the books she took were mostly for study.'

'Just because one borrows a book, does not mean it gets read,' Sir Raeden pointed out.

The sound of a door clicking shut cut off King Stephen's laugh and muted his reply.

David reached out and touched the gossamer stone. Instantly, it hardened to its original state.

'We'd better get back,' he said, 'but we'll go to the North Courtyard and take the stairs outside up to the West Terrace. We can enter the Great Hall from there.'

'Won't we run into your father?' John asked.

David shook his head. 'He'll take the private staircase that leads straight to the antechamber adjoining the Great Hall. Come on.'

Without waiting for a reply, he took off down the long walkway, leaving Rhiannon and John to follow him in silence. After making it outside undetected, they walked through the North Courtyard. The eyes of the stone dragons seemed to follow them when they passed the large fountain, while soft lights turned the spray into twinkling falling stars as it poured forth from the cold marble hands of the two children riding the central dragon.

A warm breeze gently stirred the light chiffon of Rhiannon's gown, while beyond the eastern wall in the orchard, the quiet rustle of a sea of leaves could be heard. In the clear evening sky above, the stars shone brilliantly, and the luminous glow of the full moon bathed the world in a pure white light.

No chatter disturbed the peace of the wide courtyard as they moved along the empty pathways towards the West Courtyard, but in the distance, they heard music and laughter.

'I wonder what Plancy was trying to do with those experiments?' Rhiannon's question broke the cautious silence they had maintained while in the palace.

'It was nothing good, that's for sure,' said David, 'since it involved killing dragons and magi, plus an attempt to kill you for something he needed.'

'Do you think we could get a look at his notes?'

'I doubt it,' was David's reply, while John's voice was stern when he told her, 'Whatever you do, don't sneak into Wyvern's office to try and find them.'

David snorted. 'She doesn't have a death wish. Besides, he wouldn't leave them out in the open for anyone to find.'

'You could ask your father what Sir Raeden found, and then ask if we could see the notes once he tells you about them,' Rhiannon suggested.

'He wouldn't agree to that,' David answered. 'They'll either be destroyed, or sealed away as evidence once Wyvern finishes examining them, and no one will be able to see them unless Endrille approves it. What I really want to know is what woman they were talking about, what my father meant when he said he didn't tell us anything about Mórfran and why Wyvern thanked him for it.'

John's forehead creased in thought. 'I've got no idea about the woman. As for Mórfran, maybe he's a relative of Wyvern and he's ashamed of the connection.'

David shook his head. 'No, it isn't anything as simple as that,' he said slowly, 'if it was, my father wouldn't have sounded so grave. It has to be something much more serious.'

Rhiannon frowned. 'Maybe it's a similar thing to what you told me about Merlin and Fendrel. They could've been friends, and then Mórfran betrayed Sir Raeden.'

'That is a possibility,' David agreed after giving the idea some thought.

'Not that we're likely to ever find out the truth,' John reflected, 'either about Mórfran or what Plancy was doing in his laboratory.'

'Laboratory,' Rhiannon repeated absently. 'You know, I was reading something last night about one that belonged to —'

Rhiannon broke off when a sudden uprush of wind sent a wild assault of dirt and leaves towards her. The sight of the swirling debris evoked a flash of memories: A hot afternoon in Brakenhurst; a dizzying kaleidoscope of colours; her body being transported to a different world.

A feeling of panic flooded through her.

Then two arms were holding her securely. Her face was pressed against a solid chest covered in blue cloth, her protector's head bent over hers to help shield her from the onslaught.

Rhiannon clung to the smooth blue fabric, praying for the wind to die away and hoping she wouldn't find herself transported back to Brakenhurst.

A pause. Then a blinding flash of light.

Rhiannon buried her face in the fine tunic.

Please don't send me back! she pleaded, her thoughts a jumbled mess.

'It's over now.'

That was David's voice!

Rhiannon cautiously lifted her head and looked up.

Golden hair. Fair skin. Deep violet eyes framed by dark lashes staring intently into hers. Definitely David. And behind his head she could see the famous constellation of twelve bright stars that was only visible during the summer months in the land of Álnair – The Ring of Agnador.

'I'm still here,' she whispered.

'A little dishevelled, but still here,' David agreed, gently plucking a leaf out of her hair. 'That was rather close. We're lucky we weren't just a step closer, or I would've been seeing what Vetus svet looks like.'

'Aye, and what a grand adventure that would be,' a deep, cheerful voice declared. 'Me and my kin would have a fine time showin' ye and the pretty lass around the place.'

A wide smile spread across David's face. Rhiannon was surprised when instead of just stepping away from her, he took hold of her hand, turned around and said warmly, 'King Brian, you old rascal! I was hoping you might show up. I've been wanting to introduce you to Rhiannon for months. Rhiannon, I'd like you to meet King Brian of the Leprechauns. King Brian, this is Rhiannon McBride – Dragon Cup Champion, daughter of Mórell's line and birthday girl.'

Rhiannon looked down and beheld a smartly dressed figure standing no more than three feet in height. He wore a rich swallow-tailed coat of red laced with gold and a green vest. His legs were clad in white stockings and black breeches buckled at the knee, and on his feet were shiny black shoes with gold buckles. On his black hair he wore a gleaming crown of gold, and his green eyes sparkled merrily.

'I thought leprechauns wore green coats and top hats,' she blurted without thinking.

'Aye, and so some of me people do,' King Brian said, 'especially when they wish to play tricks on the folk in Vetus svet. But I do prefer the red.'

'It does make you look rather dapper,' John said with a grin.

King Brian saluted him. 'A thousand blessin's on ye, John Tremaine, for those kind words,' he declared. Turning back to Rhiannon, he said, 'It is an honour to meet you, Lady Rhiannon, daughter of the great mage Mórell. My kin will always remember her with great affection, for she once saved the life of me sister's son when he was wounded by an iron spear. Know that if ever ye seek the aid of the leprechauns we shall lay all our talents and skills at your service. Simply call me name, and one of my kin will appear if I'm not here – providin' of course there be no storm a'brewin'. If there be one thing we don't like, it be the sound of the heavens a'rumblin'.'

'Thank you, Your Majesty,' Rhiannon said, overwhelmed.

'Ah, and you have my congratulations on your triumph at the Dragon's Cup,' King Brian went on. 'I was impressed that none of my jewels made their way into your tunic. A young heart that can resist the lure of leprechaun treasure is a wise one. And this night when I'm in me home, in honour of your birthday I shall raise a toast to your coffin. May it be built from the wood of a hundred-year-old oak tree that I shall plant a week from tomorrow.'

Rhiannon blinked at the rather bizarre birthday wish, and darted a quick, uncertain glance at David. Then she looked back at King Brian, only to find he had disappeared.

'He does that,' David informed her, 'never stays around to say goodbye.'

'He seems quite nice,' Rhiannon said blankly, still dazed by the fact she had met a leprechaun, who had also said he was going to drink a toast to her coffin!

'He's a good sort,' John said, then looked at his watch. 'Tare an' ouns! We'd best be getting back. It'll be almost time for supper.'

Rhiannon stepped forward and felt a tug on her hand. She looked down to see it still firmly clasped in David's. She looked up and her gaze met his. A wave of bashful confusion washed over them. Flustered, they both stammered an apology and hastily released each other, a faint blush staining their cheeks.

John watched them in silent amusement but in a display of maturity, refrained from teasing them. 'Come on, you two,' was all he said, and led the way up the wide stone staircase to the West Terrace.

They re-entered the Great Hall unseen by anyone except Professor Egelbert, who merely greeted them with an absent-minded, 'Too many variables in that equation. Do you think I should reduce the amount of myaelan?' and then proceeded to walk outside without waiting for an answer.

The last dance before supper was about to commence. As it was a reel requiring two sets of three people to form each circle of six, David, Rhiannon and John quickly joined the other groups on the floor.

In the merry atmosphere of the dance, the serious conversation they had overheard between King Stephen and Sir Raeden was soon pushed from their minds. Frequent bursts of laughter could be heard coming from their area of the room – especially when Rhiannon forgot to turn left instead of right, and nearly sent herself and John crashing into the group behind them.

Then the musicians were playing the last few bars of music at a frantic pace that had all the dancers breathless. Rhiannon gasped with laughter as David and John spun her around in quick succession. The last note sounded out. In a triumphant flare, the dancers all joined hands and raised them high to enthusiastic applause.

With cheeks flushed from exertion, and eyes brightened by happiness, Rhiannon turned around, a laughing comment to David on her lips. Then she froze.

'John,' she said, a hint of concern in her voice, 'I think Alice is going to be in trouble.'

'What do you mean?'

Rhiannon pointed.

John and David followed the direction of her finger towards the main doors and found themselves staring at the sight of Sir Raeden entering the Great Hall with a tearful Alice in his arms.

'She's done for,' John groaned. 'She only gets that look on her face when she's disobeyed my parents and got found out.'

'And she was caught by Wyvern of all people,' David said sympathetically.

Rhiannon set out across the floor, forgetting all about supper in her eagerness to speak to her guardian. David and John shared a resigned look and went after her.

Before they reached Sir Raeden, John's mother hurried up to him from behind and accepted the return of her daughter with a grateful smile. As they were now only a short distance away, they heard her words clearly.

'O Sir Raeden! I've had half the faeries inside the palace looking for her! I only turned my back for a moment, and then she was gone. Thank you so much for finding her. I'm so sorry for the inconvenience she caused you.'

'It was no bother, Lady Isabella,' he replied briefly. 'I chanced upon her as I was returning through the north gardens.'

'Alice! You've been told not to go out there unless someone goes with you.'

At her mother's scolding words, Alice's bottom lip trembled piteously. 'I wanted Pwinth David,' she cried unhappily. One big fat tear trickled down her cheek. 'I see'd him go out.'

A few people turned their heads to stare at the miserable girl who was now standing dejectedly beside her mother and sniffling loudly.

'Disgraceful behaviour!'

'A child that age doesn't belong at a ball. Her parents should have left her at home.'

'I've never seen such appalling manners.'

Rhiannon heard the acerbic words, and it became obvious to her that so had the three Tremaines, along with David and Sir Raeden.

David stiffened; her guardian sent a blistering glare towards the impertinent speakers, sparking their hasty retreat; Lady Isabella and John turned red in mortification; and Alice burst into noisy tears.

Then David moved forward. Ignoring everyone else, he plucked Alice up from the floor and swung her onto his hip. 'You silly little goose,' he gently teased her. 'Did you think I wouldn't come back to have supper with my favourite little redhead? No, no, don't strangle me. Come, where is that pretty smile of yours?'

A small tremulous smile appeared.

'That's better. We mustn't have tears at Rhiannon's ball. Now, it was very naughty of you to follow me,' David chided softly, 'you know that, don't you?'

Alice hung her head.

'Neither John, Rhiannon nor I saw you,' he went on, 'and we were just lucky Sir Raeden saw you before you fell into one of the fishponds. None of us wants to see you hurt, Alice, so you must never go out there alone again until your parents tell you it's all right. Do you understand?'

Alice meekly nodded her head. ''m sowwy,' she whispered.

David brushed an unruly curl off her brow. 'I know you are and no doubt you're feeling hungry too. Am I right?'

She gave a more energetic nod.

'Then we'll have to find you something to eat.' He looked at one member of his silent audience. 'Lady Isabella, despite her misbehaviour, may I take advantage of my position and insist that Alice remain for supper. I could not enjoy my food if I knew she was going hungry.'

Lady Isabella gave a faint smile. 'As Your Royal Highness wishes,' she said and stepped forward to take Alice from him.

When her head was close to his, she murmured, 'Thank you, David.'

He smiled but did not reply.

'We will still be speaking of this when we get home, young lady,' Lady Isabella told her daughter. Then she turned towards Rhiannon. 'I am so sorry we disturbed your birthday celebrations,' she said sincerely. 'I hope you will forgive us.'

'Oh, it's all right, you don't have to apologise,' Rhiannon reassured her. She smiled at Alice. 'Also, I'll need a lot of help to eat all this food, otherwise I'll have to eat it all myself and get as round and fat as a well-fed pig. Don't you agree, Alice?'

Little Alice nodded so enthusiastically that her red curls bounced.

'And she's not just talking about the desserts,' John said with brotherly candour, reaching out to ruffle her hair. 'Make sure you eat some vegetables, Appletop.'

Alice's face crinkled up in disgust. 'They taste ugly,' she began to protest only to be silenced by her mother's stern glare. Lady Isabella thanked both Sir Raeden and David again, and led her youngest daughter away towards the supper tables set up in the Banquet Hall.

John turned to David. 'I'm grateful too, for what you did,' he said quietly.

David gave a self-deprecating shrug. 'I merely used my position to ensure no one else will criticise any of you for her presence here, or her behaviour. I know she did the wrong thing, but when those sharp-tongued harpies upset her I wanted nothing more than to make her feel better.'

'Well, you certainly did that,' said Rhiannon before turning to her guardian. 'Sir Raeden, you came back for my birthday!'

He looked down at her, his keen blue eyes conducting a swift assessment of her appearance. 'My mission was completed, which enabled me to return. As I am here, pray accept my best wishes for the occasion. You also have my felicitations for your good taste when choosing your gift. Sapphires and pearls are appropriate gemstones for a girl your age.'

Rhiannon laid a questioning hand against the necklace she had thought belonged to David's mother. 'This, Sir? But, I thought Queen Maiwen only lent it to me.'

'I requested she present you with a range of necklaces to permit you to choose one, but not to reveal it was to be your gift. I was certain if you knew the truth you would not select anything.' Sir Raeden's lips gave a faint twitch, although his voice was still cool when he added, 'I have not forgotten your penchant for wanting to earn everything you receive, child. And, no, you may not return it.'

The faint sting of tears burned Rhiannon's eyes. She blinked rapidly to dispel them. 'I will not insult you by refusing to accept it,' she said in a low voice.

Sir Raeden gave a slight smile, recognising his own words from when she had presented him with a gift on his birthday. 'Very wise,' he replied urbanely. 'And, now,' he continued in a sterner tone of voice, 'may I know what caused you to leave the party, which then led to Miss Tremaine's venturing outside?'

Rhiannon hesitated for only a second before deciding a partial truth was better than an actual lie. 'I was worried about you and wanted to see if you had returned. Then King Brian showed up and we spoke to him for a little while.'

Sir Raeden looked at her, his sharp gaze seeming to pierce her mind. 'I am gratified by your concern,' he said at length. 'But that is not the whole truth.'

Rhiannon could not help the guilty flush that swiftly coloured her cheeks. David was no better. Only John maintained an unperturbed countenance, his expression carefully neutral as befitted his position of Chief Robesman, and not in the least like someone who was also guilty of eavesdropping.

Fortunately, or perhaps unfortunately, Sir Raeden put another interpretation on Rhiannon's and David's high colour. He ordered both of them and John to follow him out of the Great Hall to a small, private room, then proceeded to reprimand David.

'Until both parties are sixteen, an official courtship is not permitted. An informal one may be entered into whilst the couple is younger, however, in both situations a certain level of conduct is expected from both the lady and the gentleman. As the Prince of Álnair, a higher standard of behaviour is demanded of you. If you must cater to these youthful inclinations for an informal courtship, at least have the good sense to refrain from committing an act that might be deemed inappropriate. Going outside for a private moment during a formal event like this ball is just such an act. Despite the presence of a Robesman, there are some who would not hesitate to see scandal in the most innocent of scenes. For instance, there may be a perfectly reasonable explanation for the small leaf caught in my ward's hair and the grains of dirt on her dress, but an idle and malicious tongue could use their mere presence to concoct the vilest of slanders about her.'

'They were from the foramen,' Rhiannon interrupted, her face a brilliant shade of red as she hastily patted her hair to find the offending leaf. 'That was how King Brian arrived. David didn't do anything, we just talked.'

Sir Raeden frowned at her. 'If I had even the slightest suspicion that he had not behaved as befits a gentleman towards you, I would not be here *talking* to him. He would be feeling my displeasure with every blow I inflicted out on the training field.'

'I will never insult Rhiannon's honour in a way that would merit such punishment.'

At the calm, commanding tone in his voice, all three of David's listeners turned to look at him. The boyish flush had faded from his cheeks, leaving them pale but resolute. His violet eyes stared unflinchingly at Sir Raeden, and he stood with a dignity that showed a glimpse of the king he would one day become.

'I give you my word on that,' he continued solemnly. 'She's my friend, and I cherish her trust and respect too much to do anything that could make me lose it.'

Rhiannon stared at him in wonder, a warm glow enveloping her heart at his words.

John smiled, and what might have been a hint of satisfaction flashed in Sir Raeden's eyes. However, her guardian only replied with a brusque, 'Be sure that you do not.'

Rhiannon broke the silence that followed by asking her guardian if he had discovered anything to explain Plancy's desire for the Dragon's Cup.

'Perhaps,' was the curt reply, 'but you need not concern yourself with the matter. Suffice it to say that in failing to take possession of the Cup, whatever plan he had for it will not come to pass. Now, I will escort you back to the Great Hall where you will oblige me by not leaving it again for the duration of the ball, unless you are in the company of Queen Maiwen.'

'Yes, Sir,' Rhiannon said obediently, swallowing her disappointment over his less than detailed response to her question. 'And, Sir,' she called as Sir Raeden made for the door, 'I'm glad you made it back safely.'

Her guardian paused and looked back at her. 'As am I,' he replied in grim humour, 'for I am interested to know how you have fared in your studies.'

To David and John's surprise, these words elicited only a gamine smile from Rhiannon as she followed Sir Raeden out the door. They could not know she was simply grateful to finally have a guardian who was concerned over her progress in anything.

Chapter 4

MORE THAN FRIENDSHIP?

A host of curious eyes immediately focused upon David and Rhiannon when they re-entered the Great Hall. When those same eyes beheld the tall form of Sir Raeden walking behind the pair with John beside him, their glances lost their speculative glint. After all, there was nothing scandalous in a girl wanting to speak to her guardian away from a crowd. Only Izana continued to closely study the small group, his sharp mind taking note of Rhiannon's pink cheeks when she looked up to find David's face very close to hers as he removed something from her hair. The Robesman resolved to keep an eye on them during the remainder of the evening.

Supper passed uneventfully for Rhiannon and then it was time for the birthday cake to be brought in from the kitchen. It was magnificent. A masterpiece of white icing and gold roses that glistened in the dancing lights of the candles placed upon it.

Rhiannon clutched at David's hand, staring at the beautiful creation in disbelief. 'That's my cake?' she whispered.

'It's certainly not mine,' he answered, glancing down at her with a smile.

She counted the candles. 'There's fifteen,' she murmured.

'Old Álnairian tradition, remember?' David said.

A memory of him explaining the tradition at his own birthday celebration in January came to her. 'The extra one represents the light of life and the wish the person will live for another year.'

David nodded. 'Don't forget to remove it before you blow out the others, then give it to Hestor,' he said, pointing with his free hand to where the Chief Steward stood.

Unexpectedly, a strange sense of nervousness struck Rhiannon. 'I've never had to do this in front of more than three people before.'

'You'll be fine. And the palace won't fall down if you don't manage to blow out the other candles in one breath.'

He led her closer to the table where the cake had been placed, then slid his hand out of hers.

Rhiannon hesitated briefly, but then her shoulders straightened and she took the last three steps to reach the table. She removed one of the candles and took a deep breath. Determined not to fail, she blew as hard as she could. One by one the flames flickered and died, until only one remained. Her lungs almost empty of air, she pushed out the last little puff. The light danced valiantly, but then went out.

A few hearty cheers sounded from the large crowd of guests, while others politely applauded.

Rhiannon gave the candle in her hand to Hestor, who placed it in the small crystal holder in his hand. Then he took up his position near the connecting doors to the Great Hall in readiness for leading the group to the South Terrace.

Rhiannon picked up the silver knife and began to cut the cake. The blade tip glided through the thick icing as if it was melted butter. She pushed the knife down and had almost sliced halfway through the cake, when someone called out, 'Be careful not to cut the bottom!'

Her hand slipped. The sharp blade hit the crystal platter beneath the cake with a loud *chink!*

She glanced up to see Queen Maiwen and John watching her. Both looked inordinately pleased with themselves.

'Now, that definitely sounded like the bottom got cut,' one of the guests called out.

'David's standing closest to you, Rhiannon,' one of the Tremaine triplets called out helpfully, 'you have to kiss him now.'

Rhiannon remembered the tradition she had mentioned at the prince's birthday party and her gaze flew to where David was standing with a shocked look in his eyes.

'What's going on?' queried a few of the guests.

Their neighbours, who had attended David's party in January, briefly explained. 'It's a tradition from her old home in Vetus svet. If you cut the bottom of the cake, you have to kiss the person of the opposite sex who's closest to you.'

A ripple of mirth spread throughout the crowd.

'Go on then, dear,' one old lady said, entertained by the novelty of the idea, 'and I'll be sure to enforce that tradition on my next birthday!'

Most of the other guests voiced their agreement.

Izana simply stood and watched in silence.

Rhiannon looked helplessly at David.

The Prince of Álnair stared back, then he walked the short distance separating them and offered his cheek to her with calm formality.

Rhiannon's eyes widened, while one thought kept racing through her mind: My first time kissing someone and it's going to be David in front of a room filled with people! She stretched up and hastily brushed her lips against his cheek. The warmth of his skin scorched her flesh.

When she pulled away both their faces were bright red.

David cleared his throat and raised one hand to adjust the high collar of his tunic, the oddly nervous gesture widening the eyes of all his Robesmen.

'Rhiannon, don't worry about cutting the first slice out,' King Stephen said, his voice almost lost in the noise of the guests' laughter and applause. 'Just walk over to Hestor and we'll go out to the South Terrace.'

'Thank you, Father,' David murmured. He gestured for Rhiannon to go ahead of him.

Rhiannon walked towards the connecting doors, grateful to no longer be the focus of everyone's attention. As she passed Sir Raeden she saw his expression was the most inscrutable she had ever seen. She really did not want to know what he thought of the new tradition she had introduced to Álnair!

She followed the Chief Steward through the Great Hall to its main doors, then cast a furtive look at David when he drew level with her outside. His countenance was still red and there seemed to be a new tightness along his jawline. He was obviously still feeling uncomfortable about having her kiss him.

'I'm sorry.'

He turned his head at the sound of her subdued apology.

'For what?' he asked.

'If I had never mentioned that tradition, no one would have known about it and I wouldn't have embarrassed you.'

David was silent for a moment. Then he said in a quiet, earnest voice, 'You didn't embarrass me, Rhiannon.'

'I didn't?'

'No. And I don't really mind that tradition. If it appeared I disliked it that was only because I knew being the centre of that scene was distressing you.' He looked at her as they continued walking down the wide hallway. 'I meant what I said to Wyvern. You're my friend, and your trust and respect are important to me.'

Rhiannon felt again the strange warmth that had surrounded her heart when she had heard him say it the first time.

'I – I've never had anyone call me their friend before,' she said hoarsely. 'You've now done it twice in one evening.'

'I'll say it once more to make it official,' David said, smiling. 'You, Rhiannon McBride, are my friend, and if no one in Vetus svet was able to see how special you are, then you are definitely better off here with us.'

Rhiannon returned his smile. 'I wouldn't disagree with you,' she said. After a small pause, she asked hesitantly, 'Does this mean I can say you're my friend?'

'To be honest I'm slightly hurt you haven't already,' David answered lightly.

'I just wasn't sure whether it was allowed.'

'Allowed?'

'With you being the prince, I thought there might be some rule about me saying in public that you're my friend.'

David frowned. 'If there is such a rule I've never heard of it. Then again, all the people I count as my friends were all chosen for me before I could crawl. It was simply good fortune we all got along so well, especially John and I. But even then they're not really just my friends. They all have positions here at the castle, which means they have a duty to me. You're the first friend I've ever chosen for myself.'

'You mean you don't have any friends outside the castle?' Rhiannon asked in astonishment.

'I do, but again, they're all people I've known since I was born and their parents are known to mine. Whenever I snuck out of the grounds I'd use another name to try and make friends, but Wyvern or one of the guards always found me and ruined everything by using my title. I still slip out now and then, but I've given up trying to make friends. Now, I just go to see how all the people are faring and learn what I can about how they live, what they do. And anyone I meet through school, or in any other place I visit under my own name, never gets past the acquaintance stage. Most of them are either overwhelmed by my rank, or want to use me to further their own ambitions. Before you arrived it had reached the point where I was wondering if people were only being nice to me because of my position.' He grinned at her. 'That's probably why you fascinated me after that evening when we first met. You weren't intimidated by my title and you didn't try and use me to get anything. In fact, you have the distinct honour of being the only person to ever yell at me mere moments after I introduced myself. Not that I blame you for that after the way I spoke to you,' he added. 'I'm only surprised you continued to speak to me.'

'You apologised, and it was the first sincere one I had ever received,' Rhiannon said. Then, a teasing note entering her voice, she added, 'After that you didn't seem like such an arrogant prat.'

David laughed. 'See! You're not in awe of my illustrious title and you don't give toadying compliments. Only a friend would be that brutally honest.'

Their arrival at the large doors leading out to the South Terrace brought their conversation to a close.

Rhiannon stepped through the doorway and onto the terrace. Looking at the long stone balustrade, she saw the line of Hope Lanterns hovering above it. They were identical to the ones she had seen at David's party. The crowd of guests following King Stephen and Queen Maiwen spread out along the wide space of the terrace. Soon a hush descended upon the large gathering.

Hestor the Chief Steward approached the first lantern and spoke. 'May the light of life inside Rhiannon Marie McBride continue to burn for another year.'

Rhiannon leaned against the tall pillar behind her to watch as the first lantern was lit. In the light of the flame its transparent material took on a golden-white glow. She felt a familiar sense of enchantment come over her when the light spread to all the other lanterns and they began to float into the sky, then drift out over the Dairíon Ocean.

The first lantern burst into a dazzling shower of violet and gold lights.

The second disappeared in a radiant scattering of green and red.

As another array of colours lit up the sky, Rhiannon became aware of a slight heat near her arm. She glanced down to see a pale, masculine hand resting near hers on the pillar. The long fingers were a hairsbreadth away from hers.

Rhiannon looked up and found herself staring at David's profile. His head was tilted back and he was slouched against the pillar to bring himself down to her height. He did not say anything, just kept his eyes focused on the disappearing lanterns, but she knew he was aware of the closeness of their hands.

Returning her gaze to the sky, she swallowed nervously. Then she tentatively moved her hand until her little finger brushed against David's. His reaction was immediate. He did not speak, or look at her. He only curled his finger around hers and left it there. She was grateful for the slight shadows of the terrace that concealed her flaming cheeks.

She was practically holding hands with a boy!

Her heart almost stopped in shock. And yet, she felt no fear. No inkling of danger. Only trust and affection. She knew instinctively she was safe with David, and she was certain if she never mentioned this moment after tonight he would not bring it up himself. Why he wanted to hold her hand, or finger in this case, she did not know, but the small gesture brought her a sense of peace and contentment she had never known before.

'I'm glad you came to Álnair.'

David's words were so soft they were almost inaudible. But Rhiannon heard them. Her finger tightened its grip on his.

'Me too,' she whispered.

A burst of pale blue light lit up the terrace as another lantern vanished in a shower of sparks.

David finally lowered his gaze from the sky to look at her. The warmth in his eyes matched the one in his smile as he said, 'Happy Birthday, Rhiannon.'

Then they watched the rest of the Hope Lanterns disappear in companionable silence, their linked fingers never separating until it was time to return to the Great Hall.

They walked inside, unaware of the several pairs of eyes that had been watching them closely.

Rhiannon passed the remainder of the evening in a cheerful humour. After the cake was eaten, the dancing recommenced. She smiled upon seeing an obviously happy Carina Egelbert escorted to the floor by Sir Raeden. Her own partner, she was astonished to discover, was none other than King Stephen!

Then she danced with each of David's Robesmen. After that her partners ranged in age from the bashful ten-year-old son of one of the guests, to a white-haired old man, whose name she missed, and who seemed bent on informing her on the whole history of Valieoth Castle. Her hand for the last dance was claimed by David.

It was while she was standing in the Entrance Hall with him and his parents and saying goodbye to the last of the guests that Rhiannon saw the old man again. She politely said goodbye to him, then waited until he was out of earshot before asking David for his name. The answer completely surprised her.

'Professor Renwolf Tysus!' she repeated.

'You recognise it?'

Rhiannon nodded. 'It was in a book I read last night on M—'

'Goodnight, David.'

The voice of David's maiden aunt made them both turn to look at her.

Lady Phoebe Donahue, a tall, Junoesque woman with fair hair and a proud countenance, gave her nephew a brief nod. 'You conducted yourself quite well tonight, but there is still room for improvement,' she said without preamble. 'You also still show a disturbing lack of decorum in permitting those of lesser rank to address you without any honorific. I trust you will see that this is corrected. It is important that your retainers and subjects learn to see you as their prince and show the proper respect.'

'Yes, Aunt Phoebe,' David replied with the politeness of one long inured to hearing this form of criticism.

She nodded, then focused on her next target. 'Your deportment was quite acceptable, Rhiannon. However, you must work harder to attain the perfect elegance of manner expected in one of your lineage. You must also learn to be more discriminating in your choice of dance partners.'

'My dear Phoebe, the hour is far too late for these strictures,' Queen Maiwen said from behind her sister's back. 'I shall visit you tomorrow and you may tell them to me over some of your cook's famous sweetcakes.'

Lady Phoebe turned and frowned at her shorter, but older sister. 'I know very well you always ignore all the advice I give you,' she said bluntly.

'Not all of it, I always heed your advice when it comes to purchasing a new gown. Now, come, your carriage is waiting, and I am sure all of us wish to seek our beds for what remains of the night.'

Lady Phoebe allowed herself to be led away with only another brisk comment to David and Rhiannon to heed her words, and a brief, 'Those curls need trimming, Mr Tremaine,' to John who had come over to say his goodbyes while his father made his to King Stephen.

'Has she always been like that?' Rhiannon asked faintly.

'Ever since I've known her,' David answered. 'Quite the martinet, isn't she. But, underneath all her fondness for rules and etiquette she can be rather nice. She visited me every day for a month after I developed a high fever when I was five.' He looked at John. 'I forgot to ask Gareth before he left if he's still covering for Derrick. Is he well enough to be back on duty yet?'

'He's over the infection he picked up and I've told him he can resume his duties tomorrow. I'll also be here. Lord Sharbel has asked my father to speak to the new guards, so I'll be accompanying him.'

'You won't get here too early, I hope,' David said, smothering a yawn.

'Never fear, we don't want to deal with a sleep-deprived princeling,' John teased him. 'We'll come at eight after the Morning Office.'

'John, the carriage is here.'

The faint note of pained fatigue in Sir Julian Tremaine's voice had his son quickly saying goodnight, then hurrying across the Entrance Hall to assist his father out to their carriage.

'It's now time for bed, my dears,' Queen Maiwen declared after the great wooden doors had closed. She led the way towards the dais for the transonus system which lay inside a discreetly designed alcove set behind a large pillar. 'I hope you enjoyed the ball, Rhiannon.'

'Oh, I did. It was so kind of you all to organise everything.'

King Stephen immediately disclaimed any hand in it. 'I fear my talents do not extend to planning balls for young ladies,' he said. 'Full credit must go to my wife and her bevy of helpers.'

A discussion of the ball took place, which lasted until they reached the alcove. Then David's parents said their final goodnights, mounted the dais and pressed the rune for the Upper West Wing. They vanished in a flash of white light.

Rhiannon gave a huge yawn and stepped up onto the dais.

'I'll see you to your chamber,' said David, following her.

'You don't have to do that,' she replied tiredly, 'especially since it's so late.'

'It's simple good manners. You're exhausted and could trip in that long gown.'

Rhiannon decided it was pointless to argue with him, and after they arrived on the dais in the Upper South Wing, she didn't bother objecting when he helped her descend from it.

When they reached the arched doorway to her bedchamber they both stopped. David looked at his watch.

'Just a few minutes shy of midnight,' he said. 'It's still technically your birthday.'

'I guess so.' Rhiannon frowned when she saw him reach into his tunic pocket and pull out a small wooden box. 'What's that?'

'It's my present for you. I didn't want it to get lost in the mammoth pile in the Great Hall.' He placed the box into her hand. 'I've never chosen a present for a girl by myself before so I hope it's all right.'

Rhiannon smiled, her tiredness forgotten. 'I'm sure it'll be lovely,' she said and opened the box, half expecting to find a watch inside.

The hallway was suddenly filled with dead silence.

David's eyes widened in dismay as his friend mutely stared at the contents of the box. 'Don't you like it?' he asked anxiously.

Rhiannon immediately looked up and met his disappointed gaze with an incredulous one. 'Of course I like it. How could I not!' she said, then carefully lifted a shiny chain from its bed of white velvet. At its end hung a vibrant blue stone the size of a small thimble set inside a delicate circle of silver vines. The jewel had shimmering white flecks in its depth that twinkled like the light of the stars reflected on the surface of the ocean.

'It's a star crystal,' David said. 'I started to think I wouldn't be able to find a blue one in time for your birthday, but last week when I went out again to look in Luwyneth Cove I found it near the Kinpar Rocks.'

Rhiannon gave him a startled look. 'You found it yourself? But

David, you said earlier you can only see star crystals in moonlight when they're in the water. And isn't Luwyneth Cove supposed to be a few hours' ride from here? Couldn't you just have found one on the beach below the castle?'

'It's not the first time I've gone swimming in the middle of the night,' he answered, 'and Valnas, one of the other battle dragons, flew me there after dinner a few times after I gave up trying to find a blue stone at the beach here. Although, since they are the rarest kind, I wasn't surprised when I didn't see any.'

'I can't believe you went to all that trouble just to get me a present,' Rhiannon said in a small voice. 'No one's ever done that for me before.'

'I thought your gift should be as unique as our friendship,' David explained. 'I knew you didn't have any jewellery so I had the silversmith design the necklace so you'd be able to wear it whenever you liked.' He looked at the sapphires and pearls adorning Rhiannon's neck and sighed. 'I didn't know Wyvern was going to give you that one. Mine must seem quite shoddy to you in comparison.'

'Never,' Rhiannon refuted, thinking of the time and effort he had taken to get the stone for her. 'I shall treasure them both,' she said, giving him a warm smile.

David blinked at her glowing look, then shielded his mouth behind one hand as he feigned a small cough. 'Well, I should let you get off to bed,' he said awkwardly. He went to step back, but then hesitated.

Rhiannon had only a moment to wonder what was wrong when he abruptly stepped forward and bent down to place a gentle kiss on her cheek.

Instantly, her face flamed with colour.

'Goodnight, Rhiannon,' David said softly, then quickly straightened up and walked away, but not before she had seen his own cheeks suffused with a scarlet hue.

She stared at his retreating back, her hand with the necklace dangling between her fingers resting against the place touched by his lips.

'Goodnight,' she finally whispered.

It was not until she was inside her room, and tucked under the coverlet on her bed, that she came out of her distracted state to realise she had completely forgotten to ask him about Professor Tysus and Merlin's laboratory.

'I'll definitely ask about them tomorrow,' she muttered into her pillow, then felt again the warm brush of David's lips on her skin. 'He probably did it to be nice,' she told herself. 'Don't overthink it. Focus on something else. Like the location of Merlin's secret laboratory. If Sir Raeden won't involve me in finding out what Plancy was up to, I'll find that laboratory instead.'

'Aren't you worried that she may decide to look into the matter herself if she isn't told what Raeden discovered? She's the one who almost died due to Plancy's actions.'

King Stephen looked at his wife who was removing her jewellery and frowning at him in her dresser mirror. He gave her a slight smile. 'From what he told me of his private discussion with them, I believe she and our son have happier things on their minds.'

'What!'

'Come, my dear, I know you have been watching their friendship develop these past few months with increasing hope. And did you think I missed your delight in playing matchmaker this evening when the cake was being cut?'

Queen Maiwen released a rueful laugh. 'Very well, My Lord,' she said with playful meekness, 'I will own I have become quite fond of Rhiannon, and given our son's previous habit of having nothing more than the politest of conversations with any female around his own age, I certainly have not missed the interest he has taken in her.'

'Just remember they are still young, Maiwen. You needn't start writing the wedding invitations tomorrow.'

'I was three years younger than Rhiannon is now when I first met you thirty-one years ago,' his wife reminded him. 'I knew then, as I knew eight years later when you first asked to court me, that I would marry you.'

'Yes, you made that quite plain when you declared it in front of the entire court during a visit with your father,' King Stephen remarked drily. 'At fifteen I had thought myself incapable of being embarrassed, only to be proven wrong by a bold little termagant with a loud voice.'

Queen Maiwen smiled mischievously. 'You did turn rather red,' she recalled with satisfaction. 'David looked just the same tonight while he was dancing with Rhiannon, and after she kissed him.'

'Given your inordinate pleasure at the memory of our son's youthful bashfulness, you will be delighted to know he was similarly afflicted during another part of the evening. Raeden informed me he confronted them about their disappearance from the Great Hall, which fortunately no one else appears to have noticed apart from yourself and Alice Tremaine. Apparently, they both flushed rather guiltily when he asked them about it, while John maintained a discreet silence.'

He chuckled in amusement.

'While Raeden was chastising him for his actions, our normally impetuous son told him quite calmly he would never do anything to dishonour Rhiannon. Raeden said it was the first time David has fully mastered his temper when confronting him over an issue and spoken to him in such a composed manner without once averting his eyes. It would appear his fondness for Rhiannon is exercising quite a powerful effect on his behaviour.'

'He's growing up,' Queen Maiwen said, 'and she's good for

him. He's still impulsive at times, but I have noticed he's not as reckless as he was before she arrived. He's also voluntarily doing extra duties. I discovered him in his study last Saturday reading one of Lord Sharbel's reports. Can you guess what he said when I asked him why he was doing it? He said it was because Rhiannon was working hard on completing her homework for Sir Raeden and he'd realised he should be working just as hard to properly prepare himself for when he assumes his full duties as Prince of Álnair.'

'I should take advantage of his new interest and give him some of my own work to do,' King Stephen said lightly.

'Please, my love, we don't want to squash his enthusiasm so soon,' his wife replied with a hint of laughter in her voice. 'Leave it a few months, then give it to him.'

'And then see how long it takes before he's trying to scale down the palace walls again to escape the monotony.'

Queen Maiwen shuddered. 'I've heard he manages to sneak out of the grounds occasionally when he wants to get away. I'll never forget the first night he tried to do it and broke his ankle when he attempted to climb over the outer wall.'

'Dearest, he was seven when he did that. He's a bit more sensible now in choosing his methods of escape. Besides, if Rhiannon has captured his interest, he'll be too focused on spending time with her to get up to anything too dangerous. And she won't have time to dwell on what happened with Plancy, or anything else for that matter.'

Chapter 5

A Lurking Threat

On the dark shadowed cliff overlooking the ocean, an exquisitely dressed figure scowled at his male companion. 'I'm doing the best I can to find a clue as to its whereabouts,' he protested. 'It's not as simple as looking for a lost item in the Unclaimed Property Room, you know.'

His companion waved a dismissive hand. 'Don't kill the messenger, my friend. I'm just telling you what Mórfran told me to say.'

The dark-haired man huffed impatiently. 'It's not my fault his plan with the potion failed. He can blame Plancy for that.'

'He does, and were the fool not dead he would be learning a new definition of pain.'

The man shuddered. 'I've no doubt about that.' He gazed in the direction of the palace behind them and asked, 'Did he say anything about the girl? Have the plans changed?'

'No, they haven't changed. Our master wants the pleasure of experimenting on her himself, so for the moment your only task with regard to her is to observe. I met her this evening and must say I did not think her anything special.'

The man scoffed. 'Nothing special? Certainly her looks aren't anything compared to your daughter's, but the girl survived being hit by the Glaciocaptus Charm and poisoned with a pure dose of somlyne. I'd love the chance to test a few things on her myself.'

'Well, you'll have to forgo that desire, won't you. Or at least until after our master is finished with her.'

'By the time he's done she'll probably be useless.'

'Maybe so, but you don't have a choice. Should anything happen to her our master will not be pleased.'

~*Chapter 6*~

Confessions and Laboratories

Rhiannon left her bedchamber the morning after the ball filled with eager anticipation. She was determined to find out as much as she could about Merlin's secret laboratory, but first she had to attend Morning Prayers then finish any chores Sir Raeden might require her to do now that he had returned.

Unfortunately, the sleep-in she had indulged in meant she arrived after the commencement of Morning Prayer in the palace chapel, so she missed seeing David who was already cloistered inside the Royal Tribune. Afterwards there was no time to linger about in the hope of speaking to him, so she quickly made her way to her guardian's chambers, then knocked on the door to his workroom.

'Enter.'

The laconic command made Rhiannon smile as she opened the door.

Most people would say 'come in', she thought, and stepped into the room.

'Rhiannon, you were not at breakfast,' were her guardian's first words upon seeing her.

'I overslept, but Aleda made sure I got something.' And forestalling his next words, she said, 'I came to do my chores.'

Sir Raeden looked pointedly around at the immaculately clean laboratory. Not one jar of ingredients or one apparatus was out of place.

'I have scarce set foot in here since my return last night. What chores could I have for you to do?'

'I'm not sure, Sir, but I know you would enjoy thinking some up.'

Sir Raeden stiffened, but his lips twitched.

'You appear to have developed an impertinent tongue in my absence,' he said coolly.

Rhiannon, having not missed the flicker of amusement in his face, blithely informed him, 'I had a very good teacher.'

'Whom I do not hesitate to say shall find himself without his own tongue in the near future if he persists in teaching you to speak in such a fashion.' He gestured towards the door. 'You may go. Tomorrow I will look over your homework. You may bring it to me after eleven.'

'And my chores?'

Sir Raeden gave what from anyone else would be called a sigh. 'I shall endeavour to have a whole list of them for next weekend. Will that satisfy you?'

Rhiannon nodded. 'Thank you, Sir.'

'Impossible girl. Now, be off with you.'

Rhiannon obediently turned to leave, then paused. 'Sir?'

Her guardian unhurriedly retrieved a heavy tome from the tall bookshelf behind him, sat down at a workbench and opened the book. 'Yes?'

The brief answer was all the encouragement Rhiannon needed. 'Sir, do you know anything about Merlin's laboratory?'

'You are standing in it.'

Rhiannon gaped at him. 'What?'

A cold glare had her quickly amending her response.

'Sorry, Sir. I meant, do you mean this was actually Merlin's laboratory?'

'Yes.'

'His secret laboratory?'

'No, his official one.'

Rhiannon blinked. 'He had two?'

'Presumably.'

Sir Raeden flicked over a page.

'Sir, why do you have his laboratory?'

'He no longer had need of it.'

Rhiannon almost groaned. For someone so strict, her guardian had the oddest flashes of humour. 'No, I mean, why didn't Master Zhen get it? He's the Natural Science teacher.'

'Francis was offered it, but he refused. He believed he was not worthy to use it. I do not hold with such foolish notions. It is a laboratory, not a shrine or hallowed ground.'

Now *that* sounded more like her guardian! Rhiannon bit her lip to stifle a grin.

'Sir, have you found anything in here that looks like a concealed door? Something that could lead to a secret room?'

'No. And I do not believe Professor Treshart would have assigned you any homework on Merlin's secret laboratory. She considers its existence a myth.'

'It's not for my history homework,' Rhiannon told him. 'I read about it in a book I bought by accident after Christmas.' She cast a curious glance at Sir Raeden. 'Sir, do you think it's a myth?'

'No.'

This captured Rhiannon's attention. 'Have you ever looked for it?' she asked.

'Once.'

As no further information was forthcoming, Rhiannon said, 'Could you tell me anything about what you found out?'

'No.' Sir Raeden turned another page.

'Why not?'

'I have no information to provide that cannot also be found within the pages of any book on the subject. What I know, I have read. You should do the same, then conduct your own search.' He finally lifted his head to give her a stern look. 'However, should I learn you are neglecting your normal studies to do that research, then I shall not hesitate to engage a tutor to watch over you in the evenings until you have completed your assigned work.'

Rhiannon hastily assured him this would never be necessary.

'Good.' Sir Raeden lowered his gaze back to the open book. 'And, Rhiannon, Prince David has an unfortunate predilection for leaving the grounds alone when the mood strikes him. You will oblige me by not following his example. Should your quest lead you outside the castle grounds, you will take an appropriate escort.'

'Yes, Sir.'

'Now, take yourself off, McBride, and leave me in peace.'

At the appearance of his teacher voice, Rhiannon quickly headed towards the door with an obedient, 'Yes, Sir.'

Once outside the room she carefully closed the door behind her, then set off at a run towards her bedchamber to change. Her cleaning outfit, an old brown robe, tunic and breeches, was hardly appropriate for roaming through the castle grounds.

She exited her bedchamber twenty minutes later freshly gowned and wearing a sensible pair of boots. The House Faeries cleaning the ceiling in her chamber had helpfully informed her David was visiting Lord Sharbel in the High Chancellor's Tower with Sir Julian, John and Derrick.

She hurried down the hallway towards the transonus dais in the alcove opposite the staircase. When she reached it, she leapt up onto the dais and pressed the rune on the stone console for the High Chancellor's Tower. There was a flash of white light, and then she was standing on a dais situated near the top of a long flight of stairs in a brightly lit hallway. A perfect line of wide windows ran along three of the walls, giving a wonderful view of Cendillis Harbour, Shaimar Forest and Haldoron Bridge in the distance.

Rhiannon looked to her left to see David coming out of an open doorway. A fiery heat instantly spread across her face. Her cheek tingled where his lips had touched it the night before and her breath caught in her throat. Even though she had gone looking for him, she hadn't thought she would feel this flustered upon seeing him again. Then she noticed four men exiting the room behind him. The butterflies fluttering in her stomach slowly retreated into their cocoons.

'He should not be too much longer,' Lord Sharbel was saying. 'I understand they were going to visit Cassandra before his audience with King Stephen.'

John turned at that moment and saw her.

'Good morning, Rhiannon,' he called.

David swiftly looked in her direction as she voiced her own greeting, then quickened his pace to reach the dais ahead of the others. His smile widened when his gaze landed on the star crystal pendant adorning Rhiannon's neck, although all he said was a warm, 'Good morning. I thought we wouldn't see you until lunchtime.'

'Sir Raeden didn't have any chores for me to do and I wanted to talk to you. And John,' she added hastily, as the Chief Robesman reached them, with Derrick not far behind him.

'No need to spare my feelings,' John assured her. 'Derrick and I will just go off with Lord Sharbel and my father and leave you two alone.'

'If I could I'd take you up on that offer,' said David. He turned back to Rhiannon, a look of regret on his face. 'Unfortunately, we won't have much time to talk. Lord Sedgewick and his neighbour are meeting with my father, and I've been asked to attend. I'm not sure how long we'll be. John also wants to meet Sedgewick's daughter Branwen.'

'Oh.' Rhiannon felt a sharp pang of disappointment which had nothing to do with having to put off asking him about Merlin's laboratory. She forced a smile to her lips. 'That's all right. I'll just go for a walk. I've been wanting to see the woodlands in the Middle Ward.'

'Derrick can go with you,' David said. 'He's quite a good dendrologist and can tell you all about the different trees.'

'There's no need for him to come with me, I'll be fine by myself.'

'It is always best to have someone accompany you into the woods, Miss Rhiannon,' Derrick's prosaic voice informed her. 'It may not be the size of Shaimar Forest; however, people have still sustained injuries whilst walking through it.'

Rhiannon might have ignored the man's comment and insisted on going by herself had it not been for David saying, 'I know you can look after yourself, Rhiannon, but I also know how swiftly accidents can happen. I'd be able to concentrate much better during the meeting if I knew you had someone with you.'

His words had Rhiannon recalling her conversation with Endrille after she had first awoken in Valieoth Castle. Endrille said David had been greatly disturbed when he found her apparently dead body in Shaimar Forest. Her friend's desire to have someone go with her into another woodland now made sense, and her resolve to set out alone faded.

'Very well,' she consented.

Her reply brought an expression of relief to David's face.

'Thank you,' he said, then looked at his Robesman. 'Derrick, until Rhiannon releases you, or I arrive, you're to remain with her.'

'Understood.'

Derrick stepped up onto the dais to join Rhiannon. His detached countenance had not changed at all.

'And don't let her make you smile.'

The only response Derrick made to David's light comment was to slightly quirk one eyebrow.

Then, as Derrick exchanged the Robesmen Pledge with John, Rhiannon looked back at her friend and saw Lord Sharbel quietly speaking to him. A faery with scarlet hair and silver-grey eyes was hovering behind their heads.

Rhiannon had a feeling the time for conversation had just run out.

David gave a small sigh and nodded to the faery who immediately vanished. He glanced back up to find Rhiannon watching him.

'Lord Sedgewick is almost at the meeting room,' he said.

'Then I'd better go. We wouldn't want you getting into trouble for keeping them waiting,' Rhiannon replied. She reached out towards the rune for the gate tower in the second inner wall. 'I'll be out of your way in a flash,' she punned weakly, then pressed the rune. 'See yo—'

A flash of white light cut off her words and left David staring at a vacant dais.

Seeing his downcast expression, John moved aside and gestured for his father and Lord Sharbel to use the transonus system next. 'Try not to terrify the new recruits too much with your stories, Dad,' he said.

Sir Julian laughed and carefully mounted the stone steps. 'And take all the enjoyment out of this visit?' he asked. 'I'm sure they'll love the one about the dreamreapers near Mount Perdus.'

Lord Sharbel followed the retired knight and after reminding David and John not to delay their own departure, pushed the rune to send himself and Sir Julian to the soldiers' quarters in the Lower

Ward. The white light engulfed the two men and they disappeared from sight.

John turned to look at David, who made no move towards the dais.

'Is it strange that only eight months ago I'd run for the stables to avoid walking in the woodlands with any girl, and now I want nothing more than to be able to swap places with Derrick?'

David's question was quiet and John, with no levity in his voice, said, 'It's not strange. Apart from some of the girls in school and Cassandra, all the ones you knew were either focused on flirting with you, or insipidly agreeing with everything you had to say or too intimidated by your rank to say anything. Rhiannon doesn't do any of those things.' He paused, then added with a trace of a smile, 'I also saw the necklace, David. It certainly wasn't bought from any jeweller in Cendillis, or anywhere else in Álnair for that matter. I've seen enough of your sketches over the years to recognise your designs. No doubt you snuck out during the night a few times to find that particular star crystal. That tells me you really like her, so wanting to spend time with her is perfectly understandable.'

A brief silence fell. Then, 'I kissed her,' David confessed.

'You kissed … What!' John forgot all decorum and spun David around to face him. 'When? Are you sure you weren't dreaming?'

'I – I wouldn't dream that!' David protested loudly, his cheeks a shade brighter than John's hair. 'And it happened last night after I gave her the necklace. She smiled at me and I just really wanted to kiss her.' He shook his head. 'I didn't even ask her permission. I gave my word to Wyvern that I'd always treat her with respect, and then I went and acted like that.'

'What did she do?'

'She just stared at me.'

'She didn't respond?'

'Not really.'

John frowned. 'She didn't even say anything?'

'I think I heard her say goodnight as I was walking away.'

'Then she couldn't have been upset,' John concluded with all the wisdom of his seventeen years. 'And she didn't seem angry just now, though she did seem a bit flushed when I first saw her.'

'She turned red when I kissed her,' David said quietly, staring blankly at the dais. He was silent for a moment, then admitted, 'You were right, John. I do like her. I've had feelings for her for a long time, and when I held her last night to protect her from the debris of the foramen I became certain of them. I'm not sure when they started, but I noticed them on the night of my birthday after she first mentioned that tradition from Vetus svet. You pointed out she was the one I'd have to kiss, and I found myself looking forward to hearing the knife hit the crystal platter. I was so disappointed when Alice took her place. Then later, when I saw Rhiannon out on the South Terrace, and she looked so happy watching the Hope Lanterns, I desperately wanted the ability to make her smile like that all the time. Then everything went wrong. She had to train for the Dragon's Cup, and I didn't want to do or say anything to distract her. I was hoping to have an opportunity after the race, but, of course, the situation with Plancy put an end to that, and then with her worrying over Wyvern there was never a moment that felt right.'

'You'll definitely need to discuss what happened,' John told him. 'You can't just kiss a girl, then never talk to her about it.'

'I know, only how do I even start the conversation? I can hardly say, "Excuse me, Rhiannon, I hope you weren't offended when I kissed you on the cheek last night, but I —"'

'Cheek!' John's startled exclamation cut him off. 'Are you telling me you're all tied up in knots over giving her a simple kiss on the cheek?'

David stared at him. 'Did you hit your head when I wasn't looking a second ago? Isn't that what I just told you?'

'No, you said that you kissed her. I thought you meant on the lips.'

David choked and turned a brilliant shade of crimson.

John shook his head. 'David, a kiss on the cheek is usually considered inoffensive, although you should definitely still find out beforehand if a girl is happy for you to do it. I'd suggest you go and talk to Rhiannon after the meeting, and find out what she thinks about your feelings for her. We don't want things to get uncomfortable between the two of you because of a misunderstanding.'

David gave a wry smile. 'Yes, Izana.'

'Hey, I'll have you know I have my moments of insightful wisdom too,' John protested, and led the way onto the dais. He waited until David had followed him, then remarked casually, 'You know, if you two get married, Wyvern would be like your father-in-law.'

The scarlet-haired faery Lystro, returning to advise the prince that his father and the two guests were now waiting to start the meeting, was greeted by the sight of Prince David landing a heavy blow to the shoulder of his chuckling Chief Robesman before they both vanished in a flash of white light.

'I really don't know why they always send me a second time to fetch him,' he told the empty hallway, 'he never fails to set out just as I arrive!'

While David was making his apologies to his father and their guests for keeping them waiting, Rhiannon and Derrick were slowly walking towards the eastern woodland in the Middle Ward. Behind a border of elm trees, the great branches of tall oaks and yews swayed in a warm breeze, the dance transforming their leaves into a whispering green sea in the morning sunlight.

'The western side is being used by the guards today,' Derrick explained as he led the way off the wide stone road dividing the two woodlands. 'You should always ask the sentries at the gate tower if there is any training underway before you enter either forest.'

'As I've no desire to be accidentally attacked again, I'll be sure to do that.'

Rhiannon peered into the depths of the woods and noticed there were several glades illuminated by streams of golden light. In the largest one she could vaguely make out parts of a circular structure made of white and blue stone.

'What's that?' she asked, pointing towards it.

Derrick's gaze followed her finger. 'It's a gazebo,' he said. 'Would you like to go there?'

Rhiannon nodded. 'I'd love to see it, if you don't mind.'

'My wishes are irrelevant. David has placed me at your service which is all that matters. The easiest way to get there is by the stone path which connects to the road. It is an excellent place to go when you desire solitude, and you would be able to go there alone quite safely as the path leads directly to the bridged entrance. There is a small stream which flows underneath it, and a copse of myaelan trees has been planted on its northern side. As we get closer you will see them. The tallest one ever recorded was four feet in height, but most of them only average about three and a half. The red bark is used to create restorative teas for those recovering from debilitating illnesses, while the purple flowers are the base ingredient for the potion to save those who have been attacked by a dreamreaper.'

'What's a dreamreaper?' Rhiannon asked, already sensing she would not like the answer.

'It's an incorporeal being that attacks people in their dreams and destroys their mind from within their subconscious. They are created by the lingering echoes of dark magic and can form centuries after an incident occurs. A group of them was found by Sir Julian and his men fifteen years ago near Mount Perdus, the location of some of Fendrel's darkest experiments. Another cluster was later discovered in the Caves of the Fallen where a large number of young Parvus Dragons had been slain by Fendrel's followers.'

Derrick's voice remained impassive throughout his explanation. Rhiannon could not decide whether that made his words creepier or not.

'What do they look like? I'd like to know so I can make sure to run in the opposite direction if I see one,' she said.

'You cannot see them, they can only be felt in the prickling of the senses. An inexplicable wave of uneasiness followed by an icy sensation around the chest is normally an indication that one is nearby. If you ever go on a journey and feel like that, you should immediately get a beeswax candle and have it lit when you go to bed. The scent and the light will prevent them from approaching you in your sleep.'

Rhiannon frowned. 'But how can you tell if someone is being attacked by one if you can only feel their presence?'

'A dark glow appears over the victim's face. The only way to prevent their mind being completely destroyed is to immediately awaken them once the attack is detected, then orally administer a restorative made from the myaelan flowers.'

'Can they be killed?'

'It takes a very strong and skilled mage to destroy one, as they have no physical body. The mage essentially needs to expel it from existence using a chant that is repeated three times in Drakaron. That may sound easy, however, the essence of a dreamreaper is dark magic, which cannot be defeated by mere words. It is the conviction and pure intent of the mage saying the words that ultimately destroys them.'

'What's the chant?' Rhiannon asked.

Derrick came to a halt near the path leading into the eastern woodland.

'I shall not tell it to you in Drakaron,' he said, 'for you would not understand the words – unless you share David's gift of mastering a language in two months.'

'That's a definite no.'

Derrick nodded. 'Then, in English, the chant is this:

Purest of light, come to my aid.
Grant me the strength to defeat this evil.
Foulest of beings that taint this land,
I expel thee from this world.
All that is evil, I command thee: be gone!
Let no part of thy malice remain in this realm.
Thou art banished, thy power destroyed.
May the Blessed Light dispel thy darkness,
and grant me victory over thee.
O dread reaper of mind and soul, thy time is ended,
thine influence broken.
May the source of all light and life overwhelm thy black shadow,
and drive it hence.
As smoke is driven away,
so shalt thou be driven.
Accurst being of darkness,
Be gone!'

Derrick's voice fell silent.

Rhiannon shivered. 'Is there any chance of one of them getting into the palace?' she finally managed to say.

'No. The palace gardeners have long been cultivating several *Rosa virginis –*'

'The … Virgin's Rose?'

'That is the English name, yes,' Derrick said. 'They're a rare blue rose that can purify any area where they grow of the residual effects of dark magic. It is really quite fascinating. All other flowers and plants will shrivel and die if forbidden sorcery is cast near them, but the *Rosa virginis* remains unchanged and will cleanse the atmosphere of the foul taint. No dreamreaper has ever formed where they grow. There is even an old tradition that says if a bride wears a wreath of *Rosa virginis* at her wedding she will be protected against any ill-will wished upon her.'

'So, the *Rosa virginis* prevents the dreamreapers from entering the palace?'

'They stop them from developing in these grounds. Their ability to protect an area from a formed dreamreaper hasn't yet been studied.'

'Why not?'

'The rose is extremely rare and will only blossom in certain environments. Consequently, experimentation is difficult. Not to mention expensive.'

'You mean there's no guarantee that the roses are able to keep formed dreamreapers from entering the grounds?' Rhiannon asked in alarm.

'You needn't worry about that,' Derrick reassured her. 'Endrille placed an enchantment around all the buildings in the castle grounds that prevents any dreamreaper from entering. Other people may ask her to do the same around their own homes. However, she can only do it on permanent dwellings. The barrier cannot be placed on a carriage or a tent, therefore most travellers will ensure they take a supply of beeswax candles with them in the event they find themselves having to sleep in an unprotected place.'

'I'll be sure to always pack one,' Rhiannon stated emphatically.

'A wise precaution,' said Derrick. He looked over her shoulder in the direction of the western woodland. A quick intake of breath was all the warning Rhiannon received before he bellowed out, 'PROFESSOR TYSUS!'

Rhiannon twisted around to see the white-haired nobleman pause on the southeast border of the other woodland.

'Pardon me, Miss Rhiannon,' Derrick said, 'and please remain here a moment.' Then he hurried towards the retired professor.

Rhiannon obeyed his request for all of two seconds before following him. She did not want to miss the opportunity of asking Professor Tysus about Merlin's laboratory!

'Why, if it isn't Lord Fasani,' Professor Tysus was saying as she hurried to catch up with Derrick's much longer stride. 'And Miss McBride! What brings you both out here today?'

Ignoring his query, and after giving Rhiannon a stern look of reproof for following him, Derrick abruptly told him, 'You cannot go into that woodland, Professor. The castle guards are conducting a training exercise. Surely, you were informed of that by the sentry at the gate tower?'

Professor Tysus frowned. 'Hm, is that what he was talking about? I must own, dear boy, that I was not paying him much heed. I had the most wonderful idea for another book on the life of Helga Stronsky, the woman who created the transonus system, you know. I came to seek an audience with King Stephen to get permission to do some research on the one in the castle. It really is quite marvellous with all those daises connected to it!'

'If you desire to meet with King Stephen you will need to make arrangements with Lord Sharbel,' Derrick said briefly, and began to lead him away from the western woodland.

'Oh, of course! I wouldn't dream of imposing upon the king's time unannounced. Such a busy man. I happened upon Lord Sharbel just now in the Lower Ward when I arrived. He said he will see me in fifteen minutes, although by now I suppose it would be closer to ten, to make an appointment, and kindly gave me permission to visit here in the meantime. It has been quite a number of years since I had the pleasure of walking through these woods. I recall one of my favourite places to go was a particularly fine yew tree, which had three stone benches placed into its hollow trunk.'

Rhiannon, knowing her time with him would be limited to ten minutes, interrupted what appeared to be the start of a long reminiscence of past walks by saying, 'Excuse me, Professor, I'm wondering if you could tell me anything about Merlin's secret laboratory.'

She could not have picked a subject closer to the professor's heart.

'Dear girl, I could tell you a great number of things. Firstly, do you know I firmly believe it is located within Valieoth Castle itself?'

'Yes, sir, I do. But I'm curious as to why you believe that?'

'Logic demands it, child. His official laboratory and living quarters lay within the South Wing of the palace, and his assistant's records say he rarely left these grounds in the forty years he worked here after his friendship with Fendrel fell apart. Then after the battle when Fendrel had been placed in exile, he remained inside the palace until King Brian returned him to Vetus svet. It was during that time he took his assistant, Cornelius Tichley, to the secret laboratory. In his written testimony given on his deathbed, Master Tichley states Merlin took him there to assist with an enchantment. He did not go into detail about it, but did say it was to seal the laboratory, along with all of Merlin's other records. If you're interested, you may read the whole document for yourself in the Hall of Archives. It really is quite fascinating.'

'Do you think the secret laboratory is linked to his official one?' Rhiannon asked.

'At first I did consider the possibility, for it would appear to make the greatest sense, would it not? He could then easily go from one to the other. But then, I reconsidered. Merlin guarded its location, even from his assistant, until he wished to seal it away. He would not have put the entry inside a chamber where someone was often to be found.'

'So, the entrance is most likely to be in one of the less important rooms,' Rhiannon said slowly. 'Somewhere that people seldom visit.'

'Precisely, my dear. Of course, that does not really narrow the possibilities down in a place the size of Valieoth Castle. The main palace alone has over four thousand rooms so it's still like trying to locate one special grain of sand on the beach. I have examined the original plans numerous times. The measurements between all the rooms are accurate, and as Merlin could easily have cast a dimension-altering enchantment, this cannot discount the areas where the space between the rooms is no wider than a particularly narrow wardrobe.'

'Are the plans in the archives as well?'

Professor Tysus nodded. 'They are, along with the ones for all the other buildings located in the grounds and the defensive walls which were built during the war against Fendrel, but you will need special permission from the king to view them, and they are never to be taken outside of the restricted area of the Hall. That certainly made it difficult when I wanted to check the measurements of all the buildings. I had to make detailed notes of the calculations to use, which I was ordered to destroy after I had finished checking them off. In the end it was all for nothing. I could not uncover so much as a single loose stone.'

Rhiannon was disappointed but not discouraged by his words. 'Is there a particular room you think is more likely to contain the entrance?'

The professor waved one wrinkled hand. 'No, no, dear girl. Never limit your search right from the beginning.' He laughed when he saw Rhiannon's surprised expression. 'I'm old, child; not senile. You would not be asking me about the laboratory unless you intended to look for it yourself.'

'Professor Tysus!'

They all turned towards the open doors of the gate tower.

The sentry standing in front of it, upon seeing he had caught their attention, called, 'Lord Sharbel has returned to his office. He has requested you make your way there now.'

Professor Tysus raised his hand to indicate he would be there, then returned his attention to Rhiannon. 'It has been a pleasure talking to you again, Miss McBride, and it is reassuring to know there are still some young minds prepared to believe in the existence of Merlin's secret laboratory. I wish you the best of luck in your search, and sincerely hope you have more success than myself in finding it.'

Rhiannon smiled. 'Thank you, Professor, and good luck with writing your new book.'

'Doing the research is always the hardest,' he observed, 'after that the writing is not so difficult. As for you, Lord Fasani,' he said, turning towards Derrick, 'I believe you will be entering your last year at the Academy next month. I am sure you will excel in your studies, just as you have always done, but good luck to you as well, dear boy.'

He shook Derrick's hand, directed a low, courtly bow towards Rhiannon, then walked away.

Rhiannon looked up at Derrick. 'Is it weird getting called a boy at your age?' she asked.

'What is a boy but a young man,' he said equably. 'To Professor Tysus I will always be a young man. He was the History teacher at the castle school up until five years ago when he retired, so he has known me since I was twelve.'

Unexpectedly, Rhiannon gave a snort of laughter.

Derrick tilted his head and frowned. 'I was not aware I was being humorous.'

'Oh, it wasn't you,' Rhiannon told him. 'I just imagined him calling you a boy when you're the same age he is now and you have a head of white hair instead of brown.'

The stoic Robesman then did something Rhiannon had never

thought to see him do. He smiled. It was only a slight upturn at the corners of his mouth, but it was still a smile.

'Were I to reach the momentous age of ninety-eight I believe I would not mind what anyone called me, least of all a man who had lived for almost two centuries,' he said.

Rhiannon gaped at him. 'Ninety-eight!' she exclaimed. 'I thought he was only about sixty.'

'When he was sixty he was still participating in duelling championships throughout Álnair,' was Derrick's even more astonishing reply. 'He retired from doing that at eighty-five.'

Rhiannon was still trying to come to grips with this revelation when her companion went on to announce, 'David's meeting with his father appears to have concluded.'

The morning suddenly seemed much brighter. Rhiannon looked up, but the sun had not come out from behind a cloud. The brilliant circle of golden light was still alone in the clear blue sky. Lowering her gaze to the gate tower, she saw David and John passing Professor Tysus through the open doors. Both of them appeared surprised to see her and Derrick still on the road.

'Did you decide to walk from the Entrance Hall?' David queried when he reached them. 'I thought you'd be inside the woodland by now.'

'We were going to the gazebo, but then started talking to Professor Tysus,' Rhiannon said. 'How did the meeting go?'

Before answering her, David suggested they continue to their original destination. Then, as they walked along the road, he said, 'My father wanted me to practise my mediation skills. Lord Sedgewick and his neighbour started arguing over who owns the stream that runs between their properties. Each of them was claiming ownership and demanded the other pay them to use it.'

Even Derrick looked curious at this disclosure. 'And King Stephen asked you to resolve the issue?' he said.

'Yes. I'll be sixteen in five months, and then I'll be responsible for dealing with some of the minor disputes that get presented to my father during the holidays.'

'So, what did you do?' Rhiannon asked.

'He basically told them in the most diplomatic way to stop acting like quarrelsome children,' John said when David took too long in answering. 'Then he declared that as the stream comes off the Idon River and ends past both their properties, it belongs to neither of them. They can both use it, but on a ratio system with the other landowners so each can access the amount of water their property needs from what's available.'

Derrick nodded in approval. 'A very good decision,' he said. 'Were they satisfied?'

'Sedgewick wasn't happy about it. He's a nobleman and his neighbour's a farmer. He thought David should have sided with him.' John grimaced before he continued, 'If I hadn't wanted to meet his daughter I cheerfully would've thrown him out of the room.'

'Was she at the meeting?' Rhiannon enquired in surprise. 'Did you get to speak to her?'

'She sat at the back of the room,' John replied, his previous interest in the girl absent from his voice. 'We spoke briefly, but she didn't say a lot, certainly not as much as what Professor Tysus did to you, I'm sure. He loves to talk to people.'

'I'm grateful he does,' Rhiannon declared fervently. 'He was able to tell me more about Merlin's secret laboratory.'

'Merlin's secret laboratory?' David and John said in unison.

'It's what I wanted to talk to you about earlier. I read about it in a book on Friday night. I'm determined to find it.'

'Good luck with that,' John said with a laugh. 'People have been searching for that place ever since Master Tichley revealed its existence.'

David, however, did not laugh. He looked at Rhiannon and asked, 'Why do you want to find it?'

'Curiosity, I suppose. They say a lot of his personal records are there, and I've always been fascinated by the legends about him.' Rhiannon paused, then said, 'I don't suppose you'd want to help, would you?'

David shrugged. 'Why not. I tried to find it a few times myself when I was younger, but never had much success. I take it Professor Tysus told you he believed its entrance is somewhere in the palace?'

Rhiannon nodded. 'He did, and that it was most likely to be in one of the less frequented rooms. He also mentioned some plans that are stored in the Hall of Archives.'

'We'll need my father's permission to view them,' David said, 'but that won't be a problem. He's busy for the next forty minutes and then he was going to be signing a stack of documents for Lord Sharbel. I'm sure he won't mind signing the pass for us to access the restricted area at the same time.'

'So, we could start looking today?' The sparkle in her eyes matched the excited lilt in Rhiannon's voice.

'I don't see why not. You've nearly completed all your homework, so Wyvern can't object to you spending some time on this.'

'I've already mentioned it to him. He said so long as I don't neglect my normal studies he doesn't have a problem with me researching it.' Rhiannon grimaced before adding, 'He also said that should my search lead me outside the castle grounds, then I'm not to follow your example by going by myself.'

'He has a good reason for that,' John interjected and cast a dark look at David. 'I've lost count of the number of times he's snuck out and some disaster's befallen him.'

'I survived each of them, didn't I,' David remarked. Turning to Rhiannon, he said, 'You know I'll come with you if you need to go outside the walls. And if one of these mother hens isn't here, we can take one of the guards, or just go by ourselves.'

By ourselves! He means alone, Rhiannon thought, and felt a burning flush in her cheeks, as memories of what had happened the last time they were alone filled her mind. Before meeting David, she hadn't even received a hug from a boy, let alone a kiss. What was she supposed to do if he did it again?

'I suppose we could,' she said eventually.

Rhiannon's heightened colour and delayed response had not gone unnoticed by her male companions. Derrick gave her a sharp, assessing look; John coughed and nudged David, who hesitated briefly before saying, 'Rhiannon, do you mind if we walk ahead of Derrick and John?'

'No,' she replied, startled. 'Why?'

'I'll tell you once we reach the gazebo.'

Unseen by Rhiannon, John gave David a slight nod before he and Derrick slowed their pace and dropped behind.

By now they were on the woodland path, and Rhiannon could see the structure of white and blue stone behind a wall of trees.

'This used to be one of my favourite places to play,' David said as they walked under a canopy of oak leaves. 'I'd go swimming in the stream, or climb the trees. I certainly got very good at hiding in them – and ruined quite a lot of clothes doing it too.'

He continued talking in a similar vein until they turned a corner. Then he fell silent as Rhiannon stopped to gaze at the scene before them.

Lit by golden sunlight, the open gazebo of blue and white stone in the glade was built over a wide stream. It possessed a domed roof and three marble bench seats, and was accessible only by one entry via a little stone bridge. The myaelan trees Derrick had told her about were in full bloom, the purple flowers filling the air with a delightful scent, like that of lily and jasmine mixed with iris. Several little wrens chirped happily in the surrounding woodland.

David glanced over his shoulder and saw John and Derrick

standing a short distance away. To his surprise, he saw Izana was now with them. The fair-haired Robesman was leading his horse, while staring at him with an inscrutable expression. David raised his hand in greeting before returning his attention to Rhiannon when she spoke.

'It's so peaceful. Do you still come here often?'

'Not as much as I used to, there's a lot more for me to do now than when I was younger.' He began walking again. 'I come here sometimes when I really want to be alone. All my Robesmen know to look here first if I disappear unexpectedly, but if they see me they stay behind the trees and keep watch from a distance – although, sometimes John and Izana will come over and talk to me if they think I need advice.'

'Don't the others do that?'

'No. If they're on duty they'll send for John or Izana to come if they're concerned. It's not that they don't want to do it themselves,' he added upon seeing her frown. 'It's just John and Izana seem able to help me understand things more clearly. In fact, it was John who made me realise this morning that I really needed to speak to you.'

Rhiannon halted midway across the small bridge. 'Speak to me?' she said, bewildered. 'David, you've been speaking to me daily since I first woke up in the palace.'

'No, that's not what I –' David broke off, then ran a hand through his hair. 'I've got no idea how to say this,' he muttered.

'Whatever it is can't be that bad. Just say it.'

He hesitated but then nodded. 'All right,' he said, and straightened his shoulders. 'Rhiannon, I'm sorry I kissed you last night.'

The words of apology stung, rejection of her seeming to lace every word. A sharp pain pierced Rhiannon's heart and a burning sensation filled her eyes. Then her old defences began to swiftly rebuild themselves. Her face turned into an impassive blank slate, and her voice was cold when she said, 'Fine. Is that all?'

Her icy tone was not hard to miss.

David stared at her in dismay. 'What's wrong? Did I not say it properly?'

'Oh, you said it well enough. Now, if you don't have anything else to say, I'll be off.'

She went to turn away, only to find her hand captured by David's.

'I have a lot more to say,' he declared. 'I don't know why you're upset over my apology, but I certainly didn't intend to hurt you.'

A flash of anger broke through Rhiannon's defences.

'You didn't intend to hurt me! You say you regret kissing me and expect me to be what? Happy about it?'

'Regret kissing you?' David said, looking astonished. 'I didn't say that!'

'Yes you did.'

'No, I said I was sorry I kissed you.' David paused, then shook his head with a sigh. 'Clearly, I'm not saying it very well. I'm fluent in seventy-three languages, but I'm yet to attain even a basic understanding of how to talk to females about certain things. Rhiannon, I definitely don't regret kissing you, but I'm sorry I did it without asking your permission.' A fiery blush spread across his cheeks as he continued awkwardly, 'I've never felt like this before, and I'm probably making a mess of everything.'

Rhiannon's anger faded at these words. Her own face now rather flushed, she looked down at their clasped hands. 'How – How do you feel?' she asked nervously.

David cleared his throat and shifted his feet. 'Ever since the night of my birthday party I knew I liked you,' he confessed. 'But it wasn't until last night that I realised how strong my feelings are. I was going to speak to you, to tell you how much I like you. And, if you don't feel the same way, that's all right,' he added hurriedly. 'I won't pester you or anything. I just wanted you to know the truth. When I gave you the necklace I certainly wasn't intending to kiss you without warning. I'm so sorry if it made you feel uncomfortable. If you'd prefer me not to touch you again, I won't.'

He seemed to recall he was still holding her hand and hastily let it go.

Rhiannon stood on the bridge in silence, her emotions thrown into a whirlpool of confusion. She had come to care for David very much; in fact, in some ways he was her best friend. She felt happy when she was with him, and his friendly nature only ever made her feel safe. The kiss had not changed that, although it had distracted her quite a bit. And there had been times when she felt a strong connection with him, like when they were on the South Terrace the previous night. However, she wasn't sure if her feelings were as deep as David's appeared to be, and it wasn't right to let him think they were.

So she told him, explaining her feelings as best she could, which must not have been very eloquently, for David's countenance took on his own polite mask as he listened.

'It's all right, you don't need to say anymore,' he interrupted when Rhiannon began to repeat herself. 'I appreciate your honesty. I won't mention it again.'

'You dummy! I wasn't saying I'd never feel the same way. It's simply, right now, I don't know. This is a first for me too. I've never had a boy interested in me before.'

'Then they all must've been both deaf and blind,' David said promptly, and a smile reappeared on his face. 'A maybe is certainly better than a definite no. I won't rush you, Rhiannon. Take whatever time you need to figure out what you want. Just knowing you may one day feel the same as I do is enough.'

'Do you mean it?'

'Of course. You only just turned fourteen and I'll be sixteen in a few months. There's no hurry. I can wait.'

Rhiannon could only think of one way to show her gratitude,

not only for his patience but for his understanding: She stepped forward and hugged him, whispering a word of thanks into the soft cloth of his tunic.

David closed his eyes, relishing the warmth of her embrace.

Then she was loosening her hold and stepping back. 'And I won't object to an occasional kiss on the cheek.'

Startled, David looked down and saw her gaze was on his face. 'After all, some friends do it all the time,' she continued, 'and … well, um …'

David suppressed a grin when he saw her pale cheeks turning a dusky shade of pink. 'Yes?' he said encouragingly.

Rhiannon swallowed. 'Well, I liked it,' she muttered. 'And asking for my permission each time you want to do it is a bit ridiculous, so I won't expect you to do that.'

'That's kind of you,' David said, and swiftly bent down to kiss her cheek. 'In exchange I promise I won't do it every time I get the inclination,' he murmured as he pulled away.

'He's kissed her on the cheek again!'

The hushed voice came from within the long branches of an ancient elm tree, and one of the two men standing at its base sighed.

'John, would you get out of the tree,' Izana said. 'David and Rhiannon don't need you spying on them at every moment.'

'I'm not spying, I'm watching.'

'You're spying. Let them have some time together without it being turned into a spectator sport.'

There was a short silence, followed by a rustle of leaves. Then John landed on the ground with a soft thud. 'I suppose you're right,' he conceded. 'But I can't help feeling anxious for David's sake. The present he gave her was one that shows she means a great deal to him. Certainly a lot more than what he's probably allowing her to think right now. If it turns out she's only slightly infatuated with him like Alice is then he's going to be devastated.'

'I do not believe you need concern yourself over whether Rhiannon returns his feelings,' Izana said quietly.

John and Derrick looked at him closely.

'Why, do you know something?' John demanded.

'Only what I've observed,' Izana replied. 'She may not have realised it herself as yet, but she is just as taken with him as he is with her. I had numerous opportunities to study them during our sparring sessions and formal classes, and what I saw was a couple firstly becoming very good friends, and then devoted companions. There was also their behaviour last night.'

'If you're talking about them leaving the ball with only me in attendance I can assure you there wasn't any romantic reason for it,' John said. 'Rhiannon thought she saw Wyvern while she was dancing with David, and she wanted to check if he'd returned.'

'Having myself seen Sir Raeden in the doorway, I did not think your absence would be for any other reason, which is why I did not follow you,' Izana elucidated. 'The behaviour to which I refer is their interaction with each other inside the Great Hall and on the South Terrace. And, no, I will not tell you the specifics of what I observed. As you are aware, sometimes it's a Robesman's duty to keep watch silently and never mention what they may see or hear.'

John leant back against the elm tree and crossed his arms. 'Sometimes I really want to hit you,' he declared.

'You could try,' Izana replied, unperturbed by the threat. Then he said in a more solemn voice, 'John, you know my loyalty to David is beyond question. I would never permit anyone to become close to him if I had even the slightest suspicion they were not sincere in their displays of affection. I am convinced Rhiannon's may be trusted, but she needs to identify her feelings at her own pace.'

John studied Izana's serious expression in silence for a moment.

Then he said in the tone of one making an incredible discovery, 'You like her too.'

'As a brother may be fond of his sister,' Izana said briefly, and held up a hand when John went to speak. 'I will not say more on the subject, save only that while my loyalty to David shall always come first, I will not hesitate to protect Rhiannon should the need arise.'

'And for that I thank you, Izana.'

The three Robesmen looked in the direction of the tree line to see David standing there with Rhiannon beside him.

'Thunder an' turf, David! How did you two get so close without us seeing you?' John exclaimed.

'It wasn't hard to sneak up on you when you weren't paying attention,' David answered. He turned to the fair-haired Robesman and said, 'If ever the time comes when my Robesmen must make a choice between protecting me or Rhiannon, I'm relying upon you to choose Rhiannon, Izana.'

Izana bowed. 'I promise I will not fail you.'

Rhiannon stepped forward, a slight frown on her face. 'I think I'd be quite capable of looking after myself,' she declared, then turned quickly to Izana, saying, 'Not that I'm not grateful for what you said, or for how you feel. It's just, I'm not helpless. I can defend myself.'

'As I have reason to know,' Izana said, his slight smile showing he had taken no offence at her words. 'However, there are times when even the most accomplished fighter shall need assistance or protection. It is in those times that I will intervene.'

Rhiannon's frown deepened. Then her stiff posture relaxed, and a rueful smile curled her lips. 'Sir Raeden warned me not to get overly confident about my abilities. I suppose that's what I was just doing, wasn't it.'

'Don't worry, we've all thought we were indestructible only to learn that we aren't,' John said. 'Although, some of us are taking longer to learn that than others.' He sent a very pointed look in David's direction.

The Prince of Álnair looked offended. 'I haven't done anything reckless for a while,' he protested.

'One day is not a while,' John retorted.

'What did he do?' Rhiannon asked.

'While you were with Queen Maiwen yesterday, this idiot was practising switching mounts with both horses running at a full gallop.'

'David!'

Rhiannon's shocked exclamation had her friend rushing to reassure her.

'I've been doing it since I was twelve, and I've done dozens of other tricks since I was three,' he said.

'You'll end up breaking your neck,' John warned him. 'I'll never understand why your father gave Flavian permission to teach you half of those tricks.'

'Because he knew David was determined to learn them,' Derrick said.

Izana nodded. 'And having someone teach him was certainly better than having him go off alone to try and do them.'

'He would hardly have been alone, as I'm sure you would've been with him,' said John. Turning to Rhiannon, he told her, 'Izana's just as mad as His Royal Highness over there. Some of the stunts they've done in the past have been completely insane. Gareth is just as bad.'

'So, you've never tried any of them?'

'He used to do them with us,' David said, 'but after I had a slight accident when I was eight he didn't want to do them anymore.'

'A slight accident! David, you broke your arm and were unconscious for two days!'

The details sounded familiar to Rhiannon. 'Was that when you tried to take a jump while riding two horses at once?' she asked.

'Yes,' David said, astonished. 'How did you know about that?'

'Aleda told me. And I can understand why John wouldn't want to see you doing crazy stunts after he saw something like that.'

'I know what I'm doing,' David announced calmly. 'I'm not an amateur rider who's only sat on a horse a few times. I've been training for years.'

'He is extremely good at it,' Izana confirmed, 'and the tricks certainly give an advantage when we do mounted combat.' He turned to face David. 'I came over today to see if you wanted to get some practice in before the new term starts.'

'Normally I'd jump at the chance, but Rhiannon wants to search for Merlin's secret laboratory. We'll be going to the Hall of Archives once I have the pass from my father to enter the restricted area.'

'If you'd rather go with Izana, I won't mind,' Rhiannon lied convincingly.

'And leave you to find the laboratory alone? Don't be silly,' David said, smiling. 'Besides, Izana is brilliant at reading plans. We could use his help.'

'You shall have it,' Izana promised.

'Excellent,' David declared, 'then let's start heading back. My father should be in his study soon, and it'll only take me a few minutes to get the pass. Then we can begin the search.'

Chapter 7

THE HALL OF ARCHIVES

Just as David predicted, it did not take them long to get the pass from his father. Upon being told the reason behind their desire to see the castle plans, King Stephen simply nodded, told his son to ensure he did not take any plans out of the restricted area and signed the pass without hesitation.

The small group then set out for the Hall of Archives.

Located on the third floor of the Lower East Wing, the hall could only be entered through a pair of heavy wooden doors reinforced with metal bars. These were guarded by two sentries who returned their prince's greeting with friendly politeness, then opened the doors.

The group stepped over the threshold and Rhiannon beheld the splendour of the Hall of Archives for the first time.

Lit only by the pure white light emanating from a collection of silver lamps, the hall glowed with a gentle brilliance. Five tiered balconies lined its long walls, each one connected to the next by a fine staircase of polished marble. Thousands of books and scrolls filled the shelves on every level, while people seated in elegant chairs perused their selections in silence.

Rhiannon's gaze stopped on a curiously shaped device in a

small alcove to her left. Atop a short stone pillar engraved with runes was a wide silver bowl containing a large clear orb.

'What's that?' she asked.

David looked to where she was pointing. 'It's an híosta-kel. A listening stone. There's one on every level. I'll show you how they work when we get to the restricted area.'

Rhiannon cast another look around the hall. 'Where is it?'

'Right up the top. We could take the stairs, or there's the hall's transonus system, which will certainly be quicker.'

Rhiannon did not hesitate in her decision. 'Transonus it is.'

The group made their way to the dais next to the staircase at the far end of the hall. After they all stepped up onto it, David explained the line of runes on the control panel to Rhiannon. 'Unlike the castle's main system, these runes represent the level you want in here. It goes from lowest to highest.'

He pressed the one on the far right. In a flash of light, the group was transported to the dais on the top level. To the left of them was the staircase, and on their right two guards stood on the landing behind a partition gate. Both guards stepped forward when the group approached them, then opened the gate once David showed them the pass.

'There are only two other people inside, Your Royal Highness,' one of them mentioned as the group walked by him. 'We can request they leave if you wish it.'

'Thanks, Captain Whitman, but that won't be necessary,' David replied before leading the way towards the fully stocked shelves halfway down the wide balcony. 'We don't keep just the plans here as you can see,' he informed Rhiannon. 'There's also the original manuscripts of important documents, the most valuable records from our history, and these.'

He went to a shelf and pulled out a blue oblong-shaped crystal. He checked one side, then handed it to Rhiannon.

It was cool and smooth in her hand. One side had a small line of runes along its length. She blinked when a stray shaft of light shone through the blue stone. Something had moved! She held the crystal up for a closer look. Beneath its hard surface a liquid substance shimmered and shifted. 'What is it?'

'It's a sha méel, although most people call them voice crystals these days. They're used to store a spoken message or testimony. You can listen to them with an híosta-kel. All the ones up here are either too important or too dangerous to put in the shelves below. There's some over on the other side that were done by Fendrel. They were discovered in his laboratory underneath Mount Perdus after the war. I've only heard them the once. I never want to do so again.'

Rhiannon pointed to the runes on the crystal. 'What do these mean?'

'It's the name of the person who's speaking and the date they did it. The one you're holding was done by Merlin. I thought you'd like to hear it before we start looking at the plans.'

Rhiannon stared at him. Then at the crystal. Then back at David. 'Do you mean you have a *voice recording* of *Merlin*?'

'Several actually. You won't be able to understand him as he only speaks in either Old Álnairian or Drakaron, but I could translate what he says for you.'

Rhiannon was too stunned to reply. She mutely handed the sha méel back to David. He took it with a smile, then turned to his Robesmen.

'Did you want to come and listen, or stay and start on the plans?'

All three chose to go with them.

'Right then. The híosta-kel is over this way.' David took them to an alcove a bit farther down that was identical to the one Rhiannon had seen on the first level.

All five of them gathered around the stone pillar, which was about four and a half feet high.

David put the crystal back in Rhiannon's hand and showed her an opening in the side of the orb. 'You put the crystal in here,' he instructed. 'It can go either way. The liquid inside it carries the sound and is activated when it's inside the orb. Don't worry when a drape appears over the entrance – it's just to stop the sound from disturbing everyone else in the hall.'

Rhiannon slowly inserted the sha méel into the orb.

A red drape appeared over the entrance to the alcove.

The orb began to glow.

The liquid inside the blue crystal started to swirl.

An array of colours sparked to life inside the orb. They flickered and moved like fireflies trapped in a glass ball.

Then a voice spoke. A deep, pleasant voice, speaking the musical language of Drakaron.

'He's speaking about his stasis enchantment,' said David. 'He put a book in the ground for six months after placing the enchantment on it. He retrieved it and there wasn't any damage. Now, he's going through some calculations for strengthening the enchantment so it will last longer.'

Then he fell silent, allowing Merlin's voice to fill the small space of the alcove.

Rhiannon's gaze was transfixed on the colourful lights of the híosta-kel, while her mind processed the fact that she was hearing the voice of a man who had died centuries ago.

Eventually, Merlin's voice came to an end. David pulled the crystal from the orb and the red drape disappeared.

'That was definitely surreal,' Rhiannon declared as they left the alcove to return the sha méel to the shelf. 'Can anyone make one of those?'

'I suppose,' David replied, 'but only people like Merlin, inventors and professors have done it.'

'How long do the crystals last?'

This time it was Izana who answered. 'Any sha méel created will last indefinitely. The crystals are unbreakable, and the substance inside them is incapable of being damaged.'

'You certainly make things to last here in Álnair. Back in Vetus svet they've got devices people use to record their voice, but they all get damaged sooner or later. These crystals are much better. Are there any done in English?'

'There's quite a few,' David said, opening a large cabinet to pull out a handful of scrolls. He handed them to John, who put them on the nearest table. 'Professors Egelbert and Tysus have created some. Even Wyvern's done several.'

'He has?' Rhiannon said, startled. 'On what?'

'His experiments. He's performed quite a number of them, including the ones which twice got him awarded the Imperial Order of Merit. The first one was for a salve he developed called Rafapel. It regrows severely damaged or burnt skin. The second was for creating Vaelus Medesta.'

'What does it do?'

David's top half disappeared inside the cabinet to reach the last of the scrolls, making his reply muffled.

'It reverses the effects of Exoculos,' Izana said, taking over the explanation. 'A mage named Dathan Scroop designed Exoculos forty years ago to blind a group of his fellow students at the Academy. They had each succeeded in beating him academically, and he was not the sort who could accept being second to anyone. After the truth was discovered he was arrested and imprisoned, but he refused to give any assistance in undoing the damage he'd inflicted. Several professors tried to find a way to help the students, but each attempt ended in failure. For several decades nothing changed until after Sir Raeden did his experiments. When the time came to test the counter charm, he had no lack of volunteers as they all knew of his success with Rafapel. None of them were disappointed. Each person had their sight restored, and Sir Raeden received his second Imperial Order of Merit before he was twenty-two.'

'Twenty-two!'

David grinned at the astonishment in Rhiannon's voice.

'Unnatural, isn't it,' he said lightly. Then gesturing towards the small mountain of scrolls, he announced, 'They're all the original plans and design notes for the palace. The plans are bound with red ribbon and the notes are black. All of them have a preservation charm placed on them, so don't worry about damaging them. Derrick, you can help Izana with the plans. John and I will go over the design notes. Rhiannon, you can choose what you want to do.'

'I'd like to look at the plans, even if they won't make any sense to me.'

'I'll explain as we go,' Izana said.

Their tasks allotted, the group was soon divided between two long tables with their bundle of scrolls. At one table Izana unrolled the first scroll to reveal a floor plan. At least, that was what Rhiannon thought it was. She asked Izana and received a nod of confirmation.

'It's for the first part of the palace they built, the North Wing,' he said. 'Now, what we'll have to do is open all the scrolls and lay them out in a complete representation of the palace. What we want to do is make a list of the possible rooms in order of their distance from Merlin's personal chambers. He would've preferred a room he could access quickly, and the transonus system wasn't made until 980 so it most likely will be somewhere in the South Wing. However, we'll check all areas of the palace just in case. We can't discount any room due to size, or if it's at the top of a tower. Merlin was smart. He could've done a dimension-altering enchantment to create a wide enough space for a spiral staircase down to a lower area, even beneath the palace. This'll take a while so let's get started.'

For the next few hours, Rhiannon's vocabulary was expanded

to include words like cubit, liminal, mullion, stylobate and interstice as Izana scrutinised the plans, then explained them to her while dictating a list of rooms to Derrick.

David and John sat at their table, reading through the design notes and making lists of their own.

The change of the guards went unnoticed, as did the departure of the two other visitors to the restricted area. The group worked diligently until, with a great sense of relief, all quills were lowered when there was not one page of notes or scroll to be checked.

'Just in time for lunch,' David declared, glancing at his watch. 'Well done, everyone. I think we've got all the information we can get from here.' He went over and looked at the list in front of Derrick. 'Izana, you didn't give any calculations.'

'It wasn't necessary. The rooms I gave are the ones which would've been accessible to Merlin in order of their proximity to his quarters, and the frequency with which they would be visited by others.'

'I see.' David eyed the list again. 'There's rather a lot.'

'And all have to be thoroughly searched,' John said. 'I say we stop for lunch, then start looking. With five of us we should get through a few of them.'

His suggestion met with everyone's approval, so they carefully rolled up the scrolls and replaced them in the cabinet. Then they left for a lunch of cold meat, salads and fresh bread in the King's Dining Hall.

Both lunch and dinner had long since been consumed and it was late when David and a disappointed Rhiannon accompanied Izana, John and Derrick to the Imperial Stables. The search of the first ten rooms on Izana's list had not been successful.

The three Robesmen led their horses out to the stable yard,

the lamplight casting their long shadows across the cobblestones beneath their feet.

'We'll be back tomorrow,' John promised. 'We can look for the lab again in the morning.'

Rhiannon shook her head. 'Izana and David gave up practice today to help me. It wouldn't be right if I asked them to do it again.'

Both David and Izana immediately said they wouldn't mind, but she was determined to be fair. 'I'll have plenty of other opportunities to search. Besides, I'd like to see some of your riding tricks.'

David grinned. 'All right. I'll send a message to Gareth. And to Eamon – he'll be offended if we leave him out of a group event. Tomorrow we practise, the next day we search.'

Izana's horse, a beautiful chestnut mare, suddenly snorted and tossed her mane.

Izana lowered the bridle in his hand and gently stroked her neck. 'No, Regina. We're not practising now. Tomorrow.'

Regina snickered, playfully trotting away from him.

'Come on, girl,' Izana coaxed her. 'Don't be stubborn.'

'What's she doing?' Rhiannon asked.

'She does this every time she wants to go to the arena. She loves performing no matter what time it is.' Izana bestowed a look of great affection on his horse. 'Regina, come here.'

Rhiannon could have sworn the mare's eyes were laughing in the bright light of the lamps as she looked at her owner across the yard.

'Izana, I would prefer to leave this evening,' Derrick called from the back of a large grey stallion.

Unfortunately, Regina seemed determined to have her own way. Every time Izana approached her, she danced out of reach.

'She's waiting for him to fetch the bridle we use for practice,' David said. 'I don't think she'll give up anytime soon.'

Rhiannon didn't think so either. She looked at the three Robesmen and could not fail to see John's barely concealed yawn. Coming to a decision, she stepped forward and called, 'Regina!'

The mare stopped. Slowly, her head turned and she looked at Rhiannon.

'I know you want to play, but it's late and Izana is tired. You wouldn't want him to get hurt, would you?'

Regina grew still. Then her head drooped.

'He needs to go home and so do you,' Rhiannon continued. 'You'll both be coming back tomorrow, and I promise you won't have to stay in the stables all day. I'd really like to see what you and Izana can do, but I won't be able to if he hasn't had enough sleep and can't come. So please go to him.'

Silence cloaked the stable yard after Rhiannon finished speaking.

Then Regina plodded towards Izana, her hoofs striking penitently against the cobblestones. Her docile manner had everyone present staring at her in disbelief.

When the mare reached Izana, she nudged his shoulder with her great nostrils.

'Oh, it's all right, Regina. I'm not angry,' Izana reassured her, smoothing his hand down her nose. He placed the bridle on her, then turned to look at Rhiannon who was now the centre of an intrigued audience.

'Somehow I don't think it was just natural friendliness which made the horses respond to you during your riding lessons,' said John. 'You spoke to Regina as though you knew she'd understand every word you said. Come to think of it, those otters seemed to react the same way.'

'You have the ability to converse with animals.'

The quiet observation came from Derrick.

'Well, I can talk to them and they understand me,' Rhiannon said.

'A useful ability,' John remarked. 'I can't believe none of us noticed it sooner.'

'I suppose there weren't many occasions where you could,' Rhiannon pointed out. 'I repeated what you and David said to the horses when I was learning to ride, and I know better than to talk to any of the wolfhounds on guard in the palace. Also, we only did theory in Creatures and Beasts during the week I attended lessons in the school. And since I've done it for so long I guess it never occurred to me to tell any of you about it,' she finished apologetically.

'Don't worry about that,' David said. 'It was more fun finding out like this. I don't think I've ever seen Izana so surprised in my life.'

'I'm gratified I could provide you with some entertainment.'

Izana's wry comment was followed by his swinging himself up into the saddle on Regina's back. He looked down at Rhiannon. 'You have been given a special gift, one which many wish they possessed. But it must be used wisely. An animal hearing you speak will understand every word and will trust you. Because of that they will obey your commands, even if it places them in danger. I do not believe you would ever intentionally ask them to put themselves at risk; however, you might say something in jest within an animal's hearing that they will take as a real command. Therefore, please be careful in what you say around them.'

Rhiannon stared at him in shock, scarce believing he was telling the truth – until she remembered the magpies at Brakenhurst High School, and a particular incident involving her foster sister Annabelle and several irate black swans at the Brakenhurst Town Festival the previous year. Annabelle had come across her feeding the swans by the river, and lost no time in ordering her to carry the pile of things she had bought at the stalls. Annabelle had strolled away to Rhiannon's muttered, 'It'd be funny if you chased her into the river.' A short while later, in front of the stunned populace of Brakenhurst, the swans were going after her foster sister like avenging warriors, their bugle-like calls sounding out like a battle cry as they pursued their fleeing target straight into the water. At the time she had thought Annabelle must have done something to upset them, but now, after Izana's words, she realised the swans had been obeying her muttered comment.

'I'll be careful,' she promised. Her gaze shifted from Izana to Regina. 'If you like, I'll swear to never give her another command again.'

At this, Izana smiled. 'That won't be necessary. I trust you. Besides, when teaching our horses new tricks your ability would be very helpful in getting them to understand what we need them to do.'

David added his support to the idea. 'Sometimes, Cináed, Regina and Orvar get frustrated if we have to correct them several times when they're learning a new trick.'

'In that case, I'd be glad to help. And maybe you could show me how to do some of the simpler tricks.'

David promptly agreed, his voice drowning out John's muttered comment about having to now deal with four reckless idiots.

Upon reaching the North Courtyard, David and Rhiannon said their goodbyes to the others and began to make their way towards the main entrance of the palace. They had not gone far when they heard a familiar voice from an enormous form landing on the ground beside them, its fiery red mane and mahogany and silver scales shining in the soft glow of the lights illuminating the courtyard.

'Greetings children.'

'Endrille!' David and Rhiannon cried happily in unison.

'My dears, it is wonderful to see you. And, Rhiannon, I hope you enjoyed your birthday celebrations.'

'I did, but I would've liked to have seen you.'

'I regret my late return prevented that from happening. Sir Raeden worked tirelessly to complete his investigations so we could return in time, but unfortunately, we did not succeed in arriving during the day as he had hoped.'

Rhiannon thought of her guardian's manner and words of the previous evening. Why hadn't he wanted her to know how hard he had worked to return in time for her birthday?

'Well, I'm just happy you both got back safely,' she said. Then hoping Endrille might be more inclined to answer questions than Sir Raeden, she asked, 'Did you find anything to explain why Plancy wanted the Dragon's Cup?'

'Did Sir Raeden not give you an answer when you undoubtedly made the same enquiry to him?'

'He just said "perhaps", and we shouldn't concern ourselves with the matter,' Rhiannon admitted reluctantly.

'Then I would suggest you obey him.'

'Couldn't you overrule him just a little?' David asked.

'No, I could not. Should the time come when you need to be told what was discovered, I am certain Sir Raeden will inform you himself.'

'I think there's a greater chance of John declaring he loves flying than Wyvern ever doing that.'

'Perhaps. We shall have to wait and see what happens first,' Endrille said placidly. 'Now, I understand from your father that you are searching for Merlin's secret laboratory. Did you have any luck in finding it?'

'We only started looking for it today,' David replied.

'I know.'

'We appreciate your confidence in our sleuthing abilities, but we didn't find anything.'

'Not even a small crevice in a single wall.' Rhiannon looked enquiringly at Endrille. 'You wouldn't happen to know where it is, would you?'

'I know the location of many places. Some are hidden, some are not.'

David groaned. 'Endrille! Every time someone's asked you about it you never give a straight answer. Can't you do it this time? Or at least give us a clue on where the lab could be?'

'Knowledge easily acquired is never valued at its full worth.'

'I believe she just told us no,' Rhiannon said.

'And as usual without actually saying it. All right, Endrille, we'll do it your way.'

Endrille's eyes glinted with amusement. 'There's no need to be disheartened. Be of good cheer, for I did not deny the existence of the laboratory.'

A small laugh escaped David. 'No, you didn't. I guess that's something.'

'Your Royal Highness! Prince David!'

At the sound of the loud call, Rhiannon and Endrille saw David grimace before he turned to greet the owner of the voice who was striding across the courtyard towards them.

'Good evening, Lord Sedgewick. I'm sure you remember Lady Endrille and Rhiannon.'

The nobleman directed a courteous bow to both females, along with a brief salutation, then genuflected towards David. 'Your Royal Highness, I have been attempting to speak with you again since this morning. I do not believe you fully understood the situation between myself and Jeremiah Hoyle.'

'I understood enough, Lord Sedgewick,' David interrupted, 'and my decision still stands.'

Lord Sedgewick gave an overly hearty laugh. 'Come now, My Lord Prince, you've had your fun. We all know how much you enjoy a fine jest, but it is time to consider the issue with proper solemnity.'

'A jest.' David's voice was calm, but, looking at him, Rhiannon saw a white tinge around his mouth and his eyes glittering fiercely.

'You believe I would repay the king's trust in me by making a game of a serious matter?'

Realising his mistake, Lord Sedgewick hastily sought to appease his prince. 'No, of course not, Sire. But, perhaps your youth —'

'Were I three times the age I am now I would still make the same decision,' David cut him off. 'The decree signed by the king was to be delivered to you tomorrow; however, we will go and fetch it this minute so I may personally place it in your hands and put an end to this matter.' He turned towards Rhiannon and Endrille to bid them a warm goodnight, then set off in the direction of the palace, the rigid set of his shoulders proclaiming his displeasure with every step. Lord Sedgewick silently trailed behind him.

Rhiannon stared at their retreating forms and frowned. 'I've seen David angry before, but not like that. I think his voice gave me frostbite.'

'He does not take his father's trust in him lightly,' Endrille explained. 'Lord Sedgewick was extremely foolish to imply he would betray that trust for the sake of amusing himself. David may dislike several aspects of being a prince, but he always performs each task given to him by King Stephen to the best of his ability.'

Having come to know David's honourable streak well, Rhiannon knew Endrille was speaking the truth. He might occasionally moan about his duties, but David certainly never shirked them or treated them in a frivolous manner.

'I've noticed he does take some things very seriously,' she said.

'He has done ever since he was a child,' Endrille replied. 'Especially anything involving the safety of Álnair, the well-being of others and keeping the trust of those whom he loves.' She gave a faint smile tinged with sadness. 'When he was very young he saw the scar under my left wing. His eyes flared with a fire I had never seen in them before. He thought I had been attacked and declared he would punish the ones responsible. I told him the scar was from an injury I received in Vetus svet long before he was born. He would not be satisfied with anything less than the whole story. When I finished telling it to him, he had the most determined look on his face. He stood before me and promised to always help and protect those threatened by evil, whether they were human or of any other race. He has never forgotten that oath.'

The image inside Rhiannon's mind of a much smaller David solemnly staring up at Endrille's towering form to make the vow morphed into the memory of him standing in front of her in the forest, sword in hand and ready to defend her against a possible attack.

'No, he's never forgotten it,' she said quietly. A brief pause fell. Then, her voice hesitant, she asked, 'Could you tell me how you got the scar?'

Endrille's breath came out in a long sigh. 'I will, but it is not a pleasant tale.' She lifted her head to gaze up at the silver moon shining brightly in the clear night sky. A stray breeze blew through the courtyard, the strong scent of saltwater mingling with the delicate fragrance of summer blossoms and fruit trees. 'It was on an evening very much like this one when I was sent to Vetus svet to investigate the disappearance of several dragons near the ruined city of Akkad. While I was there I happened upon a group of Erímos hatchlings. They were all very young, not yet even capable of flying a short distance. I spoke to them and discovered their parents had been missing for two days. After ensuring they were safely settled beside the Purattu River, I set out to locate their mother and father.

'Throughout the night I searched the surrounding area, but it was not until the sun was at her zenith the following day that I found them. They had been slaughtered. There was also a heavy trace of enchantment on their bodies which I recognised as the Glaciocaptus Charm. Fearing the magi who murdered the parents might be seeking their offspring, I quickly returned to the river.

Unfortunately, I did not arrive first. The magi had found the hatchlings and had killed one of them. The remaining three were seeking to escape by climbing up a steep cliff to an old cave. The magi, who did not immediately flee upon my arrival, either turned to fight me or remained focused on their original intent of slaying the hatchlings. My scar is from an attack I intercepted meant for one of them.

'In my pain and desire to protect the orphans behind me, I lost my restraint and released a burst of flame. Six of the magi who stood nearby were severely burned. Their companions were not eager to continue the confrontation after that and dragged them away. When they had gone, I gathered the surviving hatchlings and brought them here to Álnair. Afterwards, I had my wound examined. It could be healed, but too much time had passed for it to be done completely, and the scar will always remain.'

'I'm sorry.'

Endrille looked back at Rhiannon to see her face turned unnaturally pale with shame. 'Dear child, you owe me no apology. You are not to blame for the actions of those who lived before you.'

Rhiannon shook her head. 'David told me what happened during the Time of Persecution, but he never mentioned you had been hurt. How can you bring yourself to still consider us your friends? How do you not hate us for what we did?'

'Though acts of evil were committed against the dragon races, there were also many acts of love. The ones who treated my wound, and the injuries of many other dragons for several years until the pathways were closed, were two young magi from the O'Faenart clan: Conall, who became the first High King of Álnair, and his twin sister Mórell. It is their likeness which is captured in the statues over there in the fountain. The dragon they are riding is Ryegoth, and surrounding them is a depiction of each of the five other dragon races that they helped.

'As for your second question, every sentient being has the gift of free will, and to love or to hate is a choice. In my anger over what had been done against the dragons, I could have chosen to hold rancour for the actions of the people who attacked me against all members of your race, but I did not. I acknowledged the wrong done by them towards me and my kindred, and certainly did what I could to prevent them from committing those acts again, but I chose not to hold hatred of the guilty ones in my heart, or allow thoughts of vengeance to consume my mind.

'The pain over their actions will always remain, but the heart and mind should work as one. Your heart cannot be filled with love if your mind is preoccupied with evil thoughts. Hate is an insidious poison that will slowly run through your veins, infecting all of your body until you are consumed with it. You would nurture hatred in your heart to the exclusion of all else. In your dreams you would kill those whom you hate, then awake to find them alive and healthy. You would not realise the only one you are killing is yourself. This is why we all should be charitable in our words, for we cannot speak poison about someone and then expect to gain the Blessed Light's grace when the venom still coats our tongue. Therefore, we must always remain vigilant against any hint of evil that may creep into our thoughts, for if not checked it will spread to our heart and destroy us completely. Instead of nourishing hatred by plotting revenge and holding onto my anger towards those who wronged me, I chose to forgive. For only through forgiveness can we heal and continue to love.'

Rhiannon entered her bedchamber a short while later with Endrille's words still echoing inside her head. She thought of Plancy and Crumper. The two men had almost killed her. Could she forgive them? Did she want to forgive them? Endrille had admitted to being angry over the acts of betrayal perpetrated against her and the other dragons, and yet she had chosen to forgive the wrongdoers. She did not pretend the attacks and numerous deaths had never occurred. She only chose not to lose herself in her emotions and seek vengeance against the guilty. Punishment was given, but with mercy. Even Fendrel had received exile, not death.

Rhiannon slumped down onto her bed. If Crumper weren't in prison and Plancy not dead, would she be seeking a way to pay them back for what they had done? She honestly didn't think she would. She'd want them caught, but the thought of spending time thinking up ways to get revenge on them held no appeal whatsoever. She would much rather think of something more pleasant.

An image of David smiling at her popped into her head and she instantly felt warm all over, like a comforting blanket had been wrapped around her body. She reached up and clasped the star crystal pendant resting against her breast.

David. Her first friend and defender. Was he thinking of her too?

A soft knock on her chamber door drew her out of her agreeable thoughts and back to the present.

'Come in.'

At Rhiannon's invitation the door slowly opened to reveal David's mother.

She hastily stood up. 'Lady Maiwen!'

'There's no need to get up, my dear. Please, sit back down. I shan't remain above a moment.' Her graceful figure arrayed in a gown of deep mauve, Queen Maiwen approached Rhiannon and held out a silver picture frame. 'I simply wished to give you this. A belated present of sorts.'

'But you've already given me a present. Several, in fact. There wasn't any need to get me anything … else.'

Rhiannon's voice trailed off on the last word. Mesmerised, she looked at the photo in the frame.

It was her! But not in the impersonal setting of a school photo like all the ones taken of her in Vetus svet. No, this one captured her re-entering the Great Hall after the lighting of the Hope Lanterns, accompanied by the people she cared about. David was beside her, his head lowered towards hers with a smile on his face. Close behind them were his parents, his five Robesmen and Sir Raeden. And there, her little face bright with laughter as she tried to evade her brother's hand to reach David, was Alice.

'I arranged for one of the House Faeries to take it,' Queen Maiwen said. 'I hoped you would not have an issue with having one taken of you.'

'No, no issue at all.' Rhiannon traced the photograph with a gentle finger, half expecting the three-dimensional figures to jump away in protest. 'It's lovely.'

'As it should be, given the people in it.'

The Queen's light comment drew a slight grin from Rhiannon. 'I suppose we're all dressed rather splendidly. I know I've never looked better.'

'Or happier.'

The quiet remark had Rhiannon looking up to meet Queen Maiwen's perceptive gaze.

'My dear, the day you were given your lineage report and discovered the truth about your parents, you said a great many things about your life in Vetus svet. Your eyes also revealed a past filled with deep loneliness and sadness. Seeing you in this photograph, I cannot help but notice the change in your expression since that day. Many of the shadows are gone from your eyes, and you certainly smile more frequently. It gladdens my heart to know you have found some measure of joy here in Álnair.'

'With you and all the others caring about me, how could I not,' Rhiannon said. 'And David called me his friend last night. No one's ever done that before! He also k—'

She broke off abruptly, the sudden absence of sound plunging the room into an awkward silence.

Queen Maiwen studied the heightened colour of Rhiannon's cheeks, her own expression remaining carefully neutral. 'It would seem he did something that evoked more than happiness within you,' she observed, moving to sit beside Rhiannon on the bed. 'You need not be embarrassed to tell me what he did.'

'But, you're his mother.'

'So I was informed when they placed him in my arms the first time, but we may disregard that for the moment. Just consider me an old, and hopefully wise, confidante.'

When Rhiannon still hesitated she added, 'I promise I shall not repeat anything you say to another soul.'

The gentle reassurance eased much of the uncertainty in Rhiannon's mind. Besides, she longed to confide in someone. She touched the pendant which lay on her breast, and in a soft voice poured out the entire scene of when David gave it to her. Then she told of his confession that morning, along with her response. Throughout it all, Queen Maiwen listened in attentive silence, with only a flash of amusement showing in her eyes when hearing of her son's flustered apology for the kiss.

'Then he said he'd wait until I was sure,' Rhiannon concluded.

'A most proper answer,' Queen Maiwen said with approval. 'And you chose wisely, my dear. It is always best to be honest in these matters rather than profess to a false depth of feeling. But you do like him?'

'Very much, certainly more than any other boy I've met, either here or in Vetus svet. And I trust him.'

'Then that is all you need to know for the moment. Recognising the true depth of your feelings for someone can happen quickly or gradually.' Queen Maiwen smiled. 'From personal experience I can also add that when the attachment is deep, no lapse of time can alter it. So just take each day as it comes, and let things play out at their own pace.'

'I will. Thank you, Lady Maiwen.'

The Queen waved this gratitude aside, bestowed a swift, maternal kiss on Rhiannon's forehead, then stood up. 'We had best end our conversation there. I must confess to having followed my son's example by sneaking away from my entourage, and they'll be organising a search party very soon if I don't return to finish signing my letters. Goodnight, my dear, and be sure to get plenty of sleep – you'll need it to survive watching that hare-brained son of mine throwing himself around on top of his horse tomorrow.'

Rhiannon looked at her in surprise. 'How did you know about that?'

'Flavian is under strict orders to always notify me whenever David intends to practise. I received a message from him a few minutes before I came to visit you. The only advice I can give for when you're watching them race around the arena, performing all kinds of dangerous tricks, is to keep control of any impulse to panic.'

'I'll certainly do that,' Rhiannon answered, happily unaware of how many times she would experience that impulse the next day.

~Chapter 8~

STUNTS AND STRATAGEMS

'Please don't fall. Please don't fall. Please don't fall.'

Rhiannon's muttered litany went unheard by the focus of her attention: A certain golden-haired rider who apparently had no sense of self-preservation.

The Prince of Álnair had one leg hooked over the saddle on Cináed's back while the rest of him dangled upside down towards the ground. And, if that wasn't bad enough, the black stallion was galloping around the large arena, his dark form glistening in the bright morning sunlight.

A surge of relief went through Rhiannon when David straightened himself back into the saddle, both his legs draped to one side. She watched as he smoothly manoeuvred himself to a standing position. Then she felt her heart stop.

Her friend was now bent over the saddle and using the girth to crawl around Cináed's belly – right in between each pair of the stallion's swiftly moving legs!

'Nicely done.'

Derrick's calm observation from beside her did nothing to restart Rhiannon's heart. She clasped her hands together in front

of her mouth, struggling to hold back the command she longed to
yell for Cináed to halt as David went into a series of double vaults.

'Breathe, Rhiannon.'

John's quiet reminder made her aware of the air caught in her
lungs. She released it in a noisy gasp and quickly inhaled again.

In the arena, Gareth spun in the saddle on Orvar, then went
into a shoulder stand against the gelding's dark neck. Thundering
up behind them came Izana on Regina. The younger Robesman's
lithe form seemed to fly as he swung in and out of the saddle in a
dizzying series of moves, then went around Regina's neck without
a single pause. Back in the saddle, he urged his mount forward to
where David and Gareth were now riding abreast. A long metal
pole, taken up by David, was held firmly along their shoulders
and across the gap between them. Izana guided Regina straight
for the open space.

'What's he doing?'

'You'll see,' was all Eamon said in reply to Rhiannon's question.
And see she did!

When Regina passed between Cináed and Orvar, Izana grasped
the pole and pulled himself off his mount. The chestnut mare took
off swiftly, leaving her rider hanging from the metal rod.

Rhiannon had seen people do all kinds of crazy moves on the
high bars in Brakenhurst's Memorial Park, but Izana proceeded to
outdo them all. With effortless grace, he swung and twisted around
the pole like a monkey, all while Cináed and Orvar continued to
race across the ground. Then, in a precisely timed swing, he let go
of the pole and flew sideways to land behind David's back.

Before the admiring exclamations from the watching grooms
had died away, a flash of glossy chestnut announced the return of
Regina in answer to a short, high-pitched whistle.

David released his hold on the pole. Gareth promptly lifted
it away.

Izana went into a crouch and turned, resting one hand on David's left shoulder. Then Rhiannon watched transfixed as he jumped onto Regina's back with the nimbleness of a pouncing cat. And just like a feline, he landed perfectly.

Their horses now running in unison, the three riders slowly reined them in until they drew up in front of the stand where Rhiannon, John, Eamon and Derrick were waiting. They dismounted and placed a hand on their horses' necks. Cináed, Regina and Orvar lowered their heads and sank into a bow.

Loud applause broke out around the arena. Rhiannon joined in with enthusiasm. Smiling, she watched David, Izana and Gareth give their mounts an affectionate hug and a proud pat.

'Did you enjoy it?' David asked after she descended from the stand and approached him.

'You all nearly frightened me to death dozens of times, and I think I've aged twenty years, but I did enjoy it.' She turned to look at the three horses. 'You were magnificent,' she told them. They repaid the compliment by trotting towards her and gently nudging against her chest and shoulders.

'I hope you're not attempting to entice my Orvar away from me,' Gareth said lightly.

'I wouldn't dare offend Kateri,' Rhiannon laughed. 'She already gets upset if I ride out on another horse. In fact, she probably knew when I had a go on Regina.'

Eamon looked at her in amazement. 'Izana let you ride her? When?'

'He did, before you arrived this morning. He and David thought she'd be the best mount for me to learn some tricks. I finally managed a simple vault standing on her back while Izana led her.'

'She did very well,' David said. 'She only lost her balance and fell off twice.'

At John's concerned expression, Rhiannon rushed to reassure

him. 'I wasn't hurt at all. David was walking beside us and caught me each time.'

'She did almost have us both on the ground with the second one,' David recalled with no sign of irritation. In fact, his smile told his more observant Robesmen he had enjoyed being Rhiannon's catcher.

'Well, my noble steed and I are going to continue practising a while longer,' said Gareth, tactfully changing the subject. He laid his hand on Orvar's mane. 'Any of you want to join us?'

Izana took hold of Regina's bridle. 'We'll stay and do a few more exercises. She still hasn't quite forgiven me for leaving her in the stable for most of yesterday.'

'Cináed and I will stay as well,' said David. He patted the stallion's sleek neck. 'He's a bit too energetic at the moment to go back to the stables, aren't you, boy?'

Cináed pawed the ground in agreement.

John, Eamon and Derrick declared they would fetch their own mounts and then return.

'We could have a mock battle,' Eamon suggested.

The other males promptly agreed and David turned to Rhiannon. 'Did you want to join in? You've done quite well in mounted combat against one opponent and it'd be good practice for you.'

Eamon's eyes brightened. 'She can be the queen leading her army, and the other side have to try and capture her.'

Rhiannon shook her head regretfully. 'If I didn't have to go I'd happily take up the crown, but Sir Raeden wanted to check through my homework at eleven.'

'Then we'll hold off having the battle until you finish,' said David. 'It won't take Wyvern long to read through everything. Besides, all the other horses will have to be warmed up before we start. Just come back when you're done and we'll have Kateri ready for you.'

As David predicted, it did not take long for Sir Raeden to check his ward's homework.

Sitting across from him in his office, Rhiannon watched in silence as her guardian swiftly made his way through the pile of parchment in less than twenty minutes. His sharp gaze did not miss a single error, although these thankfully were few, and Rhiannon felt giddy with pleasure when he informed her, 'Given the events you were called upon to face whilst doing these assignments, you've done well.' She was still smiling when she returned to the arena dressed in the jerkin, tunic and breeches she had worn for the Dragon's Cup.

'You look too happy for someone who's recently been in Wyvern's company,' David commented when he saw her.

'He only had to correct a few things. I still have to finish the rest of the homework, but,' she looked from him to Izana and John, 'thanks to you three I'm now cleared to go up a grade in the new term.'

A chorus of congratulations came from her companions, and Rhiannon could not help but compare their sincere response to the casual indifference her foster parents would have shown to the same news. Then she resolutely pushed all thoughts of the Dashmonts from her mind and said, 'Now, how about this battle. I feel like I could take on an army.'

'Flavian has Kateri ready for you.' David pointed to where the head groom was leading the palomino mare towards them.

Rhiannon cheerfully greeted the old man and got a crotchety reply in return. Smiling ruefully, she turned her attention to Kateri who gently nuzzled her shoulder.

'Some of the guards also want to practise, so there'll be thirty on each side.' David signalled for the mounted guards to come over.

Rhiannon noticed that half of them had a red sash over their leather jerkins while the other half wore green ones.

'Did you still want to participate?' David asked her. 'These mock battles can be intense, and being your first time it could get a bit much for you with so many involved.'

Rhiannon looked at all the mounted guards and thought he made a good point. 'I really want to find out how good my skills actually are,' she said, 'and what it feels like to fight in a mounted battle.'

'All right. However, we'll limit the weapons to just training swords and no charms are to be used. If you get hit on either the back or anywhere in the chest that's to be considered a fatal blow. Now, as to the two sides: Eamon, I believe your idea was to have Rhiannon lead one?'

Eamon nodded. 'We could make it a fight between two forces. You could have Gareth and John, whilst Derrick, Izana and I will go with Rhiannon. Whichever side gets their leader captured first, loses the battle.'

David considered the idea for a moment before voicing his approval.

Once the battlelines were set, and all combatants issued with their sword, they mounted their horses and took their positions at each end of the arena. A small crowd collected in the stands, its members eager to watch the impending fight.

Izana rode up to Rhiannon. The red sash in his hand matched the one now adorning his waist. 'Your colours, Your Majesty.'

Rhiannon grinned. 'What, no crown?'

'I fear the enemy has stolen it.' Then lowering his voice, Izana said, 'The monarch normally leads their army into battle, but certain situations call for different tactics. Since capture of you is the main goal, it would be prudent for you to appoint another to command the attack while you remain defended at the rear.'

Perceiving the sense in his suggestion, Rhiannon agreed.

'Furthermore,' Izana continued, 'during the battle, even if you think you're in no immediate danger, do not have Kateri remain stationary. Keep her in motion. A moving target is harder to capture than a still one. And always be aware of your surroundings. Your eyes should constantly be observing what is going on around you.'

'Understood.'

'You'll also need to appoint a personal guard for yourself. His role will be to remain at your side for the duration of the battle.'

Rhiannon finished tying the sash around her waist and considered the group of riders around her. She recognised a few of them, but for the roles of commander and personal guard she would prefer to select people whose skills she knew well. From their training sessions she was aware that Izana was a great strategist, and she had seen how zealously Eamon fought during Defence class.

'All right. Izana, you're in command. Eamon, you're my personal guard.'

The youngest Robesman grinned and urged his bay mare Charis over towards her.

Rhiannon looked at Derrick. 'I hope you don't mind,' she began, only to have him calmly point out that his feelings in the matter were immaterial.

Izana then drew the group's attention to him and proceeded to give his orders for the battle. It came as no surprise to Rhiannon that he had already considered the different strategies David's side could use and devised numerous ones of his own to counter them. When he asked her if she approved of his plans she could only nod.

'The most important thing to remember is the safety of our queen,' he finished, fixing a stern look at the other guards. 'Be vigilant. Our foe is cunning, and he is resolved to have Her Majesty in his power.'

A loud call from the other end of the arena sounded out. They all turned to see one of David's guards lift a banner.

'That means they're ready,' Izana informed Rhiannon. 'Raise our own, Vladilas. Defenders of the Queen, take your positions. Vanguard, to me.'

As these words were spoken, Rhiannon saw a change come over every single man around her. Their faces became set like flint, their eyes grim with purpose. She began to realise that to them this wasn't just a game to pass the time, or even a serious sparring match. This was preparing for an event that could come to pass in the future. They were treating the mock battle as though it were a real one where a 'death blow' was not shrugged off and ignored but treated like a true fatal injury on the field.

The thought sent an icy shiver down Rhiannon's back. As the horses pawed the ground, and the chink of several bridles assailed her ears, she nervously took in the scene around her.

Izana, mounted on Regina and flanked by eight guards, was positioned at the front of the formation. The other guards and Derrick formed two ranks behind them, with Eamon and her placed in the middle of the second. All of them held their swords firmly, ready to be raised at any moment.

Across the wide length of the arena the sandy ground stirred in the warm breeze. On the opposite side Cináed's dark form stood out like a black beacon at the head of David's group. Strangely, John's distinctive auburn hair was not to be seen anywhere near the prince. Instead, it was at the rear of their right flank. Gareth was the one placed beside her friend, his fair hair waving like a banner as the wind caught at its long strands. She saw David lift his sword. Even at this distance she could see the confidence and authority in that one gesture.

The murmurs of the watching crowd faded.

A horse nickered impatiently.

The mingled scents of horseflesh, saddle soap and leather perfumed the air.

A trickle of sweat ran down Rhiannon's forehead.

There was a tense pause, scarce long enough to allow one to blink. Then a fierce cry erupted from both sides, the deep, male voices ringing out like thunder.

In a burst of action, the horses were off.

The charging forces headed straight for each other, unflinching in their attack.

Rhiannon felt a lump of ice settle in her stomach even as the blood rushed through her veins, the horses' pounding hoofs echoing the thud of her heart.

The gap was closing. She could now see the grim set of David's face.

And then, the clamour of battle exploded with the sharp crack of swords. A pained yell rent the air. One of the guards dropped in his saddle.

The fight was desperate: Sword to sword they fought, fierce and intense. Pandemonium reigned. No single voice could be distinguished among the shouted commands, sharp cries and clash of arms. Defence lines on both sides were breaking.

Rhiannon struck out, landing a hard blow to the waist of a green sashed guard who had slipped pass her defenders. On her left, Eamon dodged and felled his opponent with a sharp strike to the back. She hastily looked around her. No side had the advantage as yet, and David was evading all attempts to capture him. Combining his skill with a sword and his riding tricks, the Prince of Álnair was proving an elusive target, outmanoeuvring at every turn the guards tasked with capturing him.

Gareth and Izana were in the thick of the fight, their own formidable skills on full display.

Derrick was ploughing through the melee on his great red stallion Belarnos.

And John was …

Rhiannon brought Kateri around in a full circle, searching for a sign of the Chief Robesman. Finally, she saw him, but too late to give warning to one of her guards. John's sword slammed against the man's chest, knocking him off balance and out of the battle.

Then John's green eyes were fixed on Eamon.

The youngest Robesman brought Charis about and countered a merciless attack, only to suffer the sting of defeat when he misjudged the direction of the next blow. Now one of the dead, he withdrew from the field.

John grinned as he approached Rhiannon.

She wheeled Kateri about to face him.

A triumphant yell pierced the air.

Rhiannon turned her head. Her eyes widened. Gareth and a handful of green-sashed guards were bearing down on her. They were so close she could see the gleam of victory in their faces. She could not hope to defeat both them and John by herself.

In a moment of panic, acting only on instinct, she cried out, 'David!'

He did not appear. But Derrick did. The eldest Robesman emerged from the skirmish in a burst of violence, ruthlessly intercepting Gareth and his cohorts with fearless daring. And then Izana was beside her. Wielding a sword in each hand, his eyes aflame with a protective light, he blocked John's advance.

However, Rhiannon's respite from danger was short-lived. Gareth and two other guards got past Derrick and once again made for her position.

All her other guards were engaged in a violent struggle or were pursuing David.

Rhiannon lifted her sword. She might be captured but she wouldn't make it easy for them.

'Go! Outrun them!'

Izana's shout was followed by a squealing roar from Kateri. The Robesman had leant over and smacked her hard on the rump. The mare took off like a loosed arrow down the arena, carrying

Rhiannon away and leaving Izana alone to face not only John, but Gareth and the two guards.

A wild gallop could be exhilarating. This one was not. The mock battle felt all too real.

Behind her came the ominous sound of fast-approaching hoofs. She bent lower in the saddle, urging Kateri forward with urgent words of encouragement.

Her pursuer drew closer and closer.

Rhiannon thought she could feel the unknown horse's hot breath on her neck. She dared not look back. The wind tore at her bound hair, pulling several ringlets loose.

Then the horse was alongside her left flank. She could see a familiar black head.

Cináed!

Rhiannon swiftly glanced around to see David staring down at Kateri's side, apparently oblivious to her own guards who were in hot pursuit of him. He was completely focused on closing the gap between Cináed and Kateri. She tried by every means she could to prevent him from doing so, but he drew nearer and nearer until she was sure they would collide. She swapped her sword to her left hand and tried to fend him off. A hard return strike disarmed her. Then David did something that left her stunned beyond words. He tossed away his own sword, then, while travelling at full gallop, he plucked her from her own saddle onto his.

For a moment she felt like she was flying, then she landed against his chest with a thud which almost knocked her unconscious. She felt his left arm wrap around her waist.

David reined in Cináed, turned and started to ride back with Rhiannon held across his saddle. Her head was pressed against his sternum, and she felt the vibration in his chest when he shouted in a loud voice, 'I hold your queen captive. Lay down your arms!'

A boisterous cheer exploded from the stands and from David's group.

'Are you all right?'

Her friend's question had Rhiannon looking up to see David gazing down at her with concern.

'I'm fine,' she answered, her breathing fast. 'Just a little dizzy. I certainly wasn't expecting to go flying today.'

David grinned and gave a long, clear whistle to summon Kateri back. 'I hope I didn't frighten you too much.'

She shook her head. 'I think I was too surprised to be scared. I felt more terrified when I was fighting.'

All signs of levity vanished from David's face. 'That's what I was worried about. I heard you call my name and had to stop myself from coming to help you.'

'I panicked,' Rhiannon confessed in a low voice filled with shame. 'I faced a room full of golems in the race and kept my head the whole time, but when I saw Gareth and those guards coming towards me I felt as helpless as a mouse facing the open jaws of a cat.'

'Don't feel too badly about it,' David consoled her. 'Everyone has moments when they feel like that, and it's better to have it during a mock battle than during a real confrontation. For your first time, you did very well.'

'Thanks to my defenders.'

'They helped protect you, but I saw you take down a few guards by yourself. And, like with anything, the more you do it the better you'll become.'

David's words of encouragement were soon repeated by his Robesmen when they reached them. Eamon was also very apologetic for having failed to protect Rhiannon.

'If I hadn't misjudged John's attack you wouldn't have found yourself without a personal guard.'

'You should practise more,' came Derrick's prosaic observation.

'We all should,' said John, his tone that of the Chief Robesman. 'We can never afford to make a mistake in a real situation.'

'That's true,' Gareth said, rubbing his right upper arm. 'If Master Sato had been wielding a sharp sword I'd have found myself missing a limb. Honestly, Izana, I'm impressed. You've become quite proficient at wielding dual blades. Will you be in the duelling tournament this year?'

Izana, who had taken charge of leading Kateri, nodded. 'Yes. I'll be in the Opens.'

'But you won't be seventeen until November.'

'I know. I just want more of a challenge than what I would get in the fifteen to sixteen years section.'

Gareth smirked. 'I'll be sure to give you one. I'm entering too.'

'That comes as no surprise, you've been in it every year since you were allowed to participate.'

Rhiannon shifted against David to look at the two Robesmen. 'What duelling tournament are you talking about?'

'The one held during the Open Day at the castle in the October term holiday,' said Gareth.

'The castle has an open day?'

'Two, actually,' David answered, 'but the summer one was cancelled this year due to the race. Visitors are allowed into certain areas inside the palace, plus the grounds and outbuildings. There's always crowds of people, and craftsmen from all over Álnair are permitted to erect a stall along the road in the Lower and Middle Wards to market their wares.'

'It's also when David likes to pull one of his vanishing acts,' said John. 'He'll dress in the plainest clothes and lose himself in the crowd. All without us by his side, of course.'

No one could miss the exasperated inflection in his voice, least of all the prince in question who smiled without a hint of remorse.

'It's hard to mingle in a crowd with you five hovering around me,' he said. 'And I only do it for five hours.'

'Why only five?' Rhiannon asked.

'I have to make an appearance with my parents at midday on

the north balcony, and after lunch we come here to the arena to watch the tournament. Once that's done these mother hens won't let me out of their sight for the rest of the day so I don't get a chance to escape back into my disguise.'

'But that doesn't stop him from trying,' said Eamon, brushing a dark curl out of his eyes.

'I can well believe it,' Rhiannon answered with a laugh. She looked up at David, her eyes sparkling with humour. 'Even as a child I bet you were trying to sneak off on your own.'

'He did that quite frequently,' Gareth informed her. 'Usually it was King Stephen or Sir Raeden who got the pleasure of bringing him back.'

'Kicking and screaming?'

Rhiannon felt a shudder go through David's body.

'I had too much sense to do that,' he said. 'I simply surrendered quietly and bided my time until the next opportunity to escape came along.'

A noisy burst of applause as their group reached the arena's grand entrance made any further conversation impossible. Passing underneath the fine stone archway leading to the path for the stables, David accepted the loud calls of congratulation for his triumphant capture of Rhiannon with only a smile and a wave.

When they arrived at the wide yard separating the Imperial and Small Stables, several grooms came forward to take charge of the horses, and David lowered Rhiannon to the ground before dismounting himself. He spoke a few quiet words to Cináed before embracing the stallion around the neck. Behind him, Rhiannon and his Robesmen were doing the same to their equine friends.

After thanking the mounted guards for their participation in the battle, David declared he was famished, invited each of his Robesmen and Rhiannon to join him for an early lunch once they had all freshened up, then led the way towards the palace. His conversation with his Robesmen was dominated by a dissection of the fight, and Rhiannon listened attentively as they each offered their own view on what techniques could be improved and which strategies had worked. It was obvious they all had a wealth of experience in similar assessments, and that each had been taught to critically analyse their actions to pinpoint anything which either helped or hindered their group's performance. She would be willing to bet the instructor who had drilled that particular skill into them was her guardian.

Still discussing the merits of various combat manoeuvres, the small group walked up the wide flight of steps to the North Terrace, then passed through the great wooden doors into the magnificent Entrance Hall of the palace. The quiet chatter of the House Faeries where they hovered in the huge domed ceiling, busily wiping down the mural on its smooth surface, turned into a chorus of happy voices calling out numerous greetings upon their arrival being noticed. They all acknowledged the merry welcome as they made their way towards the alcove containing the transonus dais.

They had not progressed far across the spacious hall when a soft noise drew their attention to the left landing of the grand double staircase. There, with one delicate white hand grasping the banister and her wide eyes staring down at the group, was Cassandra Sedgewick. Clad in a long gown of cherry-red linen and with her ebony curls loose about her shoulders, the young First Seer made a striking picture. Rhiannon instantly felt extremely conscious of her own dishevelled appearance.

'Good afternoon, Cassandra.'

David's polite salutation elicited a stammered one from the girl whose face turned the same shade as her gown.

When the Robesmen all added their own greeting as she descended the stairs, Rhiannon noticed Cassandra's bashfulness increase significantly at the sound of Izana's quiet voice. She suspected it was more than shyness which had the seer ducking her face behind a curtain of hair.

What surprised Rhiannon, however, was Izana's behaviour. The normally reserved Robesman was the first to move forward to speak to Cassandra after she reached the last step, and also the one to introduce her to Rhiannon.

'I hope y…y-you enjoyed your b…b-ball,' Cassandra said politely, her stammer pronounced.

'I did, thank you. Although, I do rather prefer smaller parties, don't you?'

Cassandra nodded, but did not speak.

'Was there any part of the ball you liked?' Rhiannon asked, and smiled so nicely the dark-haired girl visibly relaxed before giving her reply.

'The l…l-lighting of the Hope Lanterns.'

'I think I'd have to say that was my favourite too. You know, I was surprised when David told me you lived here. I'd never seen you in the Dining Hall or anywhere else for that matter.'

'I prefer not to go out m…m-much. People get frustrated l…l-listening to me.'

'I don't see why they should, unless you have a habit of telling them what to do.'

Cassandra's emerald eyes were twin pools of disbelief. She stared at Rhiannon in astonishment. Then a choked gasp of laughter escaped her lips. It was a joyous sound that lightened her features and gave her face an animated prettiness. 'No one would ever b…b-believe I could do that. I'm not very good at giving instructions, not l…l-like Sir Raeden. In fact, I thought y…y-you'd be like him.'

Rhiannon looked down at her rumpled clothes. 'I don't think I could carry off his dignified manner looking like this. I must look like something the cat dragged in after that battle.'

A rosy hue spread across Cassandra's pale cheeks. 'I'm sorry. Y…Y-You probably want to get changed.'

'There's no hurry,' Rhiannon told her.

But Cassandra shook her head. 'Lunch will be served s…s-soon. I don't want to keep you.' She hesitated for a moment, then said diffidently, 'We could meet up some other t…t-time.'

Rhiannon gave her a warm smile. 'I'd like that. And I'm happy to go wherever you'll feel comfortable.'

The look of relief in Cassandra's eyes was evident when she said, 'I l…l-like staying in my chambers. I only came d…d-down to say goodbye to my family.'

'Then just let me know when you're free and I'll come visit you.'

'Thank you. My chambers are in the l…l-lower South-East Tower. You could c…c-come—'

Cassandra's voice abruptly fell silent, the sudden absence of sound bringing a frown to Rhiannon's face. She looked at the girl and noticed a peculiar blankness in her eyes.

'Cassandra?'

Rhiannon reached out to lay her hand on the girl's shoulder. Izana swiftly took hold of her wrist.

'You mustn't touch her,' he said. 'The images she's seeing may cause her to strike out at any physical contact.'

Rhiannon looked again at Cassandra who was standing preternaturally still. 'You mean she's seeing a glimpse of the future right now?'

'Or the past. We'll soon know. If it's a vision of a past event she'll come back to herself shortly with her memory of it intact.'

'And if it's of the future?'

'She'll go put it in the Book of Prophecy and then only remember a collection of fragmented images.'

A brief pause fell. Then, with no change to her expression,

Cassandra slowly turned and walked towards the majestic set of doors in the east wall which led to the Gallery of Tapestries.

'Future it is,' observed Eamon.

Izana looked at David. 'I'll accompany her to the entrance of the passage. Some of the visitors who are still here may try and approach her.'

David nodded. 'She certainly couldn't ask for a more vigilant guard,' he said. 'We'll see you at lunch, and I'll tell the guards here to inform Lord Sedgewick of what happened when he comes down.'

Izana bowed, then hastened after Cassandra, being careful not to get too close to the First Seer. The guards on either side of the Gallery entrance swiftly opened the doors, then waited patiently until Izana and Cassandra stepped over the threshold before closing them again.

'I see he's as protective of her as ever,' said Gareth.

'He exhibited the same behaviour during her appearance at the ball,' Derrick commented with all the emotion of someone reporting on a snail race.

'I'll wager it's because he loves her,' Eamon said. 'It would certainly explain why he goes out of his way to see her every time he comes to the castle.'

'You could be right,' John agreed. 'Then again, he might consider her a sister, like he does with Rhiannon.'

'Well, he probably won't be telling us anything,' said David. 'He can be as talkative as a doorknob when it comes to discussing anything remotely personal.' He started towards the alcove once more, pausing only to pass on the message for Lord Sedgewick to the guards standing sentry at the foot of the staircase.

'Has Cassandra been here long?' Rhiannon asked when he finished.

'Four years. After she turned ten she agreed to become the

First Seer at the palace when the previous one died. Out of all the candidates for the position she was the most gifted.'

'Wasn't she a bit young?'

'Perhaps, but the decision was hers to make. Her father also had to agree, which he did with what my mother called indecent haste. If Lady Sedgewick had still been alive she might have objected.'

'It must've been difficult for her, being in such a large place and surrounded by so many people,' Rhiannon reflected, a look of sympathy on her face.

'She didn't have an easy time,' David confirmed. 'Like all children before they're old enough to attend school she'd been receiving tutoring in basic subjects, but her father had only ever arranged private sessions so she didn't have much experience dealing with people. When she moved into the palace she was included in the morning classes for anyone living on the grounds and the twenty boys chosen as possible Robesmen. Unfortunately, Marcus and Felix were also permitted to attend the lessons whenever their parents came to visit my mother. Izana, Eamon and I were taking the classes when she came, and we tried to look out for her. However, one day we were held up in a training session with Wyvern and arrived at the room after classes were finished. Marcus and a couple of his friends were being their usual disagreeable selves and mocking her stammer. I think it's the only time I've ever seen Izana really lose his temper and he terrified them. He booted them out of the room and threatened to give them a proper thrashing if they were unpleasant to her again. They left her alone after that, but the damage was done. She didn't feel comfortable coming to classes anymore so my parents arranged private lessons for her.'

'She must be very lonely,' Rhiannon said quietly, thinking of her own isolated existence back in Vetus svet.

'We still visit her,' said Eamon, 'especially Izana.'

Judging from Cassandra's reaction to the ash-blond Robesman, Rhiannon was sure his visits were always welcome.

'And now she's asked you to visit her.' David stopped next to the dais and looked down at Rhiannon. 'Not many people receive that invitation. Then again, not many have succeeded in making her laugh within moments of meeting her. If you'd like we could go and see her sometime this afternoon.'

Without hesitation, Rhiannon indicated that she would.

'Then we'll disappear after lunch,' John, Eamon and Gareth all announced. 'We don't want to overcrowd her again.'

Later that afternoon, when the sinking sun was transforming the ocean into a glittering sea of gold, Rhiannon sat in the chamber designated as Cassandra's study, thinking that the three Robesmen had been particularly considerate.

She had arrived at Cassandra's door arrayed in a light woollen gown and accompanied by David, Derrick and Izana. But even four visitors had appeared too much for the First Seer who stammered nervously.

Still, she seems more relaxed than she was in the Entrance Hall, Rhiannon thought. And as the conversation between them progressed, Rhiannon discovered something else.

Cassandra was the nicest girl she had ever met. Not one unkind word passed her lips, and she never asked intrusive questions of any of her guests, or made sly remarks like Annabelle had always done with her friends. And while it became evident that she had feelings for Izana (her eyes betrayed her every time she looked at him), the First Seer did not make him the sole focus of her attention. In her halting speech she included them all in the conversation, and appeared genuinely interested in everyone's opinion.

Izana, for the most part, sat quietly, offering the occasional comment, but mainly keeping silent unless it was to smile and gently encourage Cassandra when she became frustrated in her speech. To Rhiannon, his behaviour and the tone of his voice revealed a deep affection for the girl, and she found herself agreeing with Eamon. Izana loved Cassandra.

'So you didn't have any l…l-luck finding Merlin's lab?'

Cassandra's query recalled Rhiannon's attention to the conversation.

'Not yet, and we still have a mountain of rooms to search.' The seed of an idea sprouted in her mind as she looked at Cassandra's interested expression. With deliberate casualness, she said, 'I'm pretty sure all the chambers in this tower were on the list. If it's all right with you, maybe we could search these ones now and you could help us look.'

Cassandra's eyes brightened. 'Y…Y-You wouldn't mind me helping?'

'Not at all. In fact, you'd be the best person to lead the search as you know these chambers better than anyone.'

Cassandra rose eagerly to her feet, positively glowing with excitement. 'You really think it c…c-could be here?'

'According to the list it's a possibility. Isn't that right, Izana?'

To his credit, the Robesman did not betray by one flicker of an eyelash his surprise at the unexpected addition of several rooms to the list. He merely nodded, saying quietly, 'There's a chance it could be here.'

No other inducement was required to obtain Cassandra's consent. Her words tripping over themselves in her enthusiasm, she began walking about the study and pointing out the most likely places for a secret entrance. Each one was patiently checked, and when all the walls had been thoroughly examined for hidden devices, they all made their way into her bedchamber.

As the others proceeded to search the room, Izana stepped closer to Rhiannon. 'Thank you for including her,' he murmured in a voice no louder than the flutter of a bird's wing.

Rhiannon smiled, and could only hope the next part of her plan worked.

For the next hour the search continued under Cassandra's leadership, but despite her disappointment when each possible place failed to reveal a concealed door, the young seer's enthusiasm did not lessen.

Rhiannon waited patiently until the very last of Cassandra's chambers had been searched, and then said, 'We've got time to check a few more rooms in this tower before dinner. Would you like to join us, Cassandra? We could really use your help. I never would've thought of checking near the hearth.'

Too caught up in solving the mystery of the hidden laboratory, Cassandra did not even hesitate to agree and left her chambers without a second thought. By the time the peal of chimes could be heard announcing dinner was ready in the Dining Hall, she was walking down the hallways of the tower without once ducking her head when someone walked past.

'I'm s...s-sorry we didn't find it,' she said as they left the top level of the tower.

'It's early days yet, and there are so many rooms where it could be,' Rhiannon answered. She paused, then asked, 'When we do another search would you like to come?'

'If I'm free I'd l...l-like to.'

'Great.' Rhiannon turned in the opposite direction to Cassandra's chambers and began walking down the hallway. 'One thing's for sure, all this searching makes me hungry. Come on, let's get to the Dining Hall before all the best dishes disappear. You know, I think there's someone who always takes —' She suddenly halted in dismay. Turning, she looked apologetically at Cassandra. 'I'm sorry, I forgot you prefer to take your meals in your chambers. And I still have a whole lot of questions I'd like to ask you.'

Cassandra looked slightly pale, but a new confidence seemed to shine in her eyes. 'That's all right. P...P-Perhaps I could come this time.'

If she had announced her intention to stand in the middle of

Cendillis and give a public speech she could not have astonished her companions more. Even Derrick regarded her in some surprise.

'I don't think I'll be able to do it all the t…t-time, but I'd like to try coming down for some meals.'

David was the first to recover his voice. With a friendly smile he assured her that her presence would always be welcome. Rhiannon beamed at her, while Izana made no effort to conceal his warm look of pride. Derrick merely regained his normal stoic expression.

'I'll apologise in advance in c…c-case I have a vision during dinner,' Cassandra said.

'Oh, no need to do that,' David told her as they started off down the hallway once more. 'It's not like you can control when they happen.'

'Izana said you only remember fragments of them if they're about future events. Can you make any sense out of them at all?' Rhiannon asked.

Cassandra shook her head. 'Once the prophecy is put into the b…b-book it's like the vision breaks apart inside my mind. Only a few images remain, but I c…c-can't understand what they mean. The one I had before lunch is a perfect example. The only d…d-details I remember are a man in a hood with a scar, a broken sword and several young dragons.'

'That must be frustrating,' Rhiannon commiserated.

The First Seer shrugged. 'I t…t-try not to think about it too much. Besides, if the whole thing stayed inside my head I'd probably go insane. S…S-Sometimes the images are quite horrible and I know something bad happened in the vision. At least this way I don't have to remember it all.'

'But you do remember the ones you have of past events.'

Cassandra nodded. 'The day before you arrived from Vetus svet I had one w…w-where there was a woman who looked like you, only she had red hair. She was s…s-standing near a forest saying goodbye to a group of dragons. Endrille was one of them.

When I described the woman to Endrille, she said she was Mórell. S…S-She gave Endrille something. It was wrapped in a cloth so I c…c-couldn't tell what it was, but it seemed important. I asked Endrille about it, only she said the answer wasn't for me to know.'

'That's Endrille all over,' said David. 'She'll give you some information but only what she feels is necessary.' He had hardly finished speaking when the second peal of bells summoning everyone to the King's Dining Hall rang out. 'Well, if you're joining us, Cassandra, let's get going. I'll make sure we all sit together so you're not surrounded by strangers. If you like you can sit between Rhiannon and Izana.'

Cassandra's flushed cheeks and shy glance in Izana's direction did not go unnoticed by her companions. Clearly, David's suggestion was very much to her liking.

It was late in the evening when Rhiannon once again found herself walking away from the First Seer's Tower with David, Izana and Derrick, but this time without Cassandra's company. Dinner had passed pleasantly and Cassandra, after a moment of anxiety which was soothed by a few quiet words from Izana, had joined in the conversation; tentatively at first, but then with increasing confidence as each of her dining companions listened to her with no sign of exasperated impatience over her stuttering sentences. Afterwards, she had not refused when David suggested they all go for a walk down to the lagoon, and her innocent delight in the ordinary pastime of walking along the sandy beach had made it painfully obvious she was not used to taking time to enjoy herself.

'I don't think I've ever seen her so relaxed,' David commented, breaking the silence which had fallen after they left Cassandra at her chamber door. He smiled at Rhiannon. 'Getting her involved in the search was a brilliant idea. Tonight is the first time she's voluntarily attended a meal in the Dining Hall since she started having private lessons.'

'I must say I didn't plan that,' Rhiannon admitted. 'I just thought if she was distracted enough she might forget to be nervous about going outside her chamber.'

'I believe having a girl her own age treat her as an intelligent human being helped make her feel comfortable about being out in public,' said Izana. 'From what she's revealed to me of her life in Ardara, her father was not very patient with her. There have also been several people who've made her feel that her stammer is a sign of stupidity.'

'Unfortunately, none of us, not even Izana, has been able to fully persuade her they're wrong,' said David. 'She believes we're just being kind.'

'We've got two more weeks before school starts. We'll have to see what else we can do to convince her otherwise while we have plenty of spare time,' Rhiannon declared. 'Is she really good at any particular subject?'

'Natural Science,' Izana answered promptly.

Rhiannon halted mid-step. She stood in silence for a moment, her brow furrowed in thought. 'I've still got those essays to write on the different symptoms of Mëlu and Aconite poisoning. I'll ask her to help me research them in the library.'

David looked at her. 'But we've already helped you do the research.'

'Cassandra doesn't know that. I'll just ask her the same questions I asked you. There's also the extra assignment Master Zhen gave me on basic hydrating serums. If I get her to help me with all of them, hopefully she'll start to feel more confident in herself.'

'It's probably safe to assume she already is,' Derrick observed. 'Otherwise, she would never have willingly come down to the Dining Hall.'

'That's true,' David agreed. 'The credit for that goes to you, Rhiannon.'

'Not all of it,' she replied. 'You three also helped by not hesitating to follow her suggestions during the search. You know, now I'm glad the list of rooms to check is so long. It means we'll have more opportunities to get her out of her chambers. We might even get her to the point where she'll start coming to the school. It'd be nice for her to make a few more friends.' A grim look of resolve hardened her face. 'And if anyone dares to make fun of her they'll soon regret it.'

The silence that greeted this pronouncement had her looking up at her companions. 'What is it?' she demanded upon seeing David's grin, Izana's rare genuine smile and an almost amused expression on Derrick's face.

'Cassandra's certainly got herself another fierce defender in you,' David answered. 'You look like Endrille preparing to protect an orphaned hatchling. For a moment I expected to see flames come pouring out of your mouth.'

'If I ever catch anyone mocking Cassandra I can't promise that there won't be,' Rhiannon said vehemently. 'I can't stand bullies, and I know what it's like to be targeted by them.'

All sign of amusement left her companions' faces at these words.

'I'll do my best to look out for her,' Rhiannon continued, 'and hopefully she'll want to be friends.'

'I'm sure she will,' Izana assured her, 'but don't be discouraged if she occasionally becomes silent and withdrawn. That only happens when a particularly bad vision occurs and the images she recalls disturb her.'

'I'll remember. I guess it's fortunate the vision she had today wasn't about anything too bad, otherwise she might never have agreed to leave her chamber.'

~Chapter 9~

Villainous Deeds

A chorus of frightened wails rent the midday air inside the pinewoods that scaled the steep slopes of the mountain. The high pitch of the cries silenced all other sounds in the woods. At the entrance of a large cave, the green scaled body of a Gora Dragon lay deathly still, bloodstained shards of shattered steel glinting near its head.

'Silence those hatchlings and get them to the laboratory.'

Several members of the group of darkly clad figures obeyed their leader who remained standing at a distance, his face unrecognisable underneath the hood he wore, save for the disfiguring scar on his right cheek. Once the captors had departed with the hatchlings, Mórfran gestured towards the dead dragon.

'Take what we need then destroy the rest,' he ordered. He threw down the broken sword in his hand. 'And next time make sure the damn thing is dead before fetching me.'

'Yes, sir.'

As his cowed subordinates hurried to obey him, Mórfran turned to his nearest companion. 'Janarius, take the heart to Him immediately. Report that the situation with the Dragon's Eye is progressing slowly and our contacts shall need more time.

They may have more success uncovering information as to its whereabouts during the Castle's Open Day.'

Janarius grimaced at the task assigned to him but nodded. 'Where shall we meet up again, Mórfran?'

'At the main laboratory in four weeks. There are several more dragon parts to be harvested and I want to gather a few more hatchlings.'

Janarius hesitated then said, 'Is it necessary to take so many of them?'

A cold, malicious laugh passed Mórfran's lips. 'Do you have an objection to it?'

'N-No,' Janarius replied hastily. 'But surely someone will notice if whole nests of hatchlings and their parents continue to go missing.'

'We can easily dispose of any curious wanderer who decides to investigate. Now, on your way, and have that fool Brandal bring me another sword.'

~*Chapter*~

FUMES OF CONFUSION

Rhiannon awoke with a mingled sense of anticipation and disappointment. The first day of autumn and thus the new school year had arrived, which meant learning more about Álnair and using her mage abilities; but it also meant she would have less time to spend on searching for Merlin's secret laboratory and visiting Cassandra. Although the First Seer had grown more confident in leaving her chambers (she had come down for dinner in the King's Dining Hall six times in the past fortnight), she had not reached the point where she felt comfortable being surrounded by the other students in the school and so would continue to have private lessons.

'I wouldn't give up hope of her coming here at some point in the future,' David told Rhiannon after breakfast as they joined the crowd of chattering students gathered near the school. The last chimes from the belltower had them congregated on the lawn around it. 'After those few stints in the library doing research with you she doesn't look so nervous whenever she offers an opinion anymore, and she doesn't stammer as much when a stranger says hello to her.'

'I know. I just wish she could be here now. She clearly likes

149

Izana and this is his last year here. Once he goes to the Academy he won't be able to visit her as often.'

David chuckled. 'It's not like he'll be far away. Ryegoth Academy's only around forty-five miles from the Main Gate. I'm sure he'll make frequent weekend visits. Besides, there's the months when he'll be on duty and will be staying here.'

'Who'll be staying here?' asked Eamon, turning from a conversation with John and his brothers upon hearing their voices.

'Izana,' David replied, 'when he's on duty during his time at the Academy.'

'If you ask me, I don't think he even needs to go there,' Eamon commented. 'Give him the books to read and he'll pass every subject in six months.'

'By cheating, just like he does here.'

The group turned to see Marcus Donahue's pale face twisted into an unpleasant sneer. Felix Costanzo stood beside him.

'I dare you to say that to his face,' Eamon challenged.

'Izana has no need to cheat,' said John.

'Unlike some people we could name, he actually studies.' David cast a pointed look at his cousin.

Marcus scoffed. 'No one can get the high marks he does just by studying. He's probably found a way to have his stuttering slapog see what's going to be on each test.'

David stiffened at the word used to describe only the most promiscuous of women. 'Watch your mouth, Marcus. Cassandra hasn't done anything to deserve having her reputation soiled by you.'

'I'm sure all those visits by Sato to her tower speak for themselves.'

'They're always chaperoned and I won't warn you again.'

'She's a regular strumpet.'

Fury swept through Rhiannon. Then her fist was connecting with Marcus' face.

'Rhiannon!'

David and Eamon hurriedly pulled her back from Marcus' sprawled form on the ground as Felix took a threatening step towards her.

'Lay one hand on her and I'll break it,' David warned him.

All the other students had fallen silent, their attention caught by the prospect of a fight. The Tremaine triplets were staring at Rhiannon in awed delight.

Marcus scrambled to his feet, a hand pressed to his cheek. 'I'll report you for this,' he snarled, glaring at Rhiannon.

'Be my guest,' she retorted, 'but don't think I won't do it a second time if you *ever* insult Cassandra again.'

'Unless I have the good fortune to reach him first. Should that happen, he will recall I can hit much harder than you, Rhiannon.'

The quiet statement had the blood draining from Marcus' face. He turned his head towards the belltower and flinched upon meeting the hard stare of the bellringer: Izana Sato.

The ash-blond Robesman stepped out of the small doorway of the tower with a grim countenance. When he spoke, his voice was chillingly calm. 'Donahue, your poisonous comments about me are a matter of complete indifference to me. You can hire a town crier and have your opinion declared in the centre of Cendillis for all the populace to hear, and I will do nothing but ignore it. But let me make this plain: Where Cassandra Sedgewick is concerned you will keep that forked tongue of yours silent or I'll silence it for you.'

His face now a sickly grey, Marcus strove to recover his haughty manner. 'You wouldn't dare,' he declared weakly, 'my father –'

'Could not stop me.' Izana slowly walked up to Marcus and looked down at him coldly. 'So you would be wise to cultivate a more civilised tongue. Your spite made you an unpleasant child but in a fourteen-year-old it makes you nothing more than a contemptible worm; and should I hear even a whisper of a rumour against Cassandra's virtue I will crush you under my boot.'

The majority of the student body burst into hearty applause.

His cheeks now scarlet, Marcus gave them a glare of intense dislike then hastily withdrew to the far side of the lawn. Felix and a few other students went after him.

'That was brilliant!' The chorus of three identical voices was followed by Daniel, Edward and Robert Tremaine swiftly approaching Izana and Rhiannon. Their blue eyes were wide in admiration.

'What a punch! Did Sir Raeden teach you that?'

'It was a prime hit. Floored him completely!'

'He turned pale when he heard you, Izana! Is that because you've hit him before?'

'Can we prank him during class?'

'If this is how school always starts I'm going to enjoy coming!'

'Izana, can we be there if you fight him?'

'Next time, Rhiannon, go for his nose.'

'All right, you bloodthirsty monsters, enough.' John stepped in and herded his brothers away. 'Just remember you'll get a good wallop off Dad if you pull any funny business during school.'

With the triplets out of the way, David, Izana and Eamon turned their attention on Rhiannon.

'How's your hand?' David and Izana asked together.

She lifted it up for them to inspect. 'All good. Not even a slight tingle.'

'You certainly made him regret his words about Cassandra,' said Eamon.

'Just like you said you would,' David observed. Unexpectedly, he grinned. 'And I find myself feeling extremely relieved you didn't throw a punch at me after you first woke up here.'

'If I had I would've broken my hand.' Rhiannon turned to

Izana. 'Also, if I'd known you were in the belltower I would've let you have the satisfaction of knocking him down.'

'It was satisfying enough to watch you do it,' Izana replied. He gave Rhiannon a small smile. 'It's good to know Cassandra has such a fierce dragon to look out for her.'

'She was quite scary,' Eamon agreed. 'Although, it looks like most of the females present weren't intimidated at all,' he added, laughing, and pointed to the group of girls approaching them who were led by none other than Leila Hardinge.

The Grade Four student was beaming as she declared, 'I never thought you could top beating Marcus in that race but you have! Seeing him hit the ground was the best start to a school term ever!'

The other girls swarming after her chorused their agreement.

'It'll be a long time before I forget the look on his face.'

'It's a shame we weren't closer to the stables. I'd have liked to see him land right on top of a pile of fresh droppings.'

'Eww, Viola! Then we'd have to put up with the smell all day.'

'It would be worth it.'

'I hope he gets a massive bruise. The nasty little troll deserves it.'

'I met Cassandra once and she's the sweetest girl. If you hadn't hit him, Rhiannon, I would've before tossing him into the bramble bush near the gate.'

'Remind me to never upset Innogen,' Eamon muttered to his fellow Robesmen and David.

'I thought you liked teasing her,' John said, failing to hide his amusement.

'I do, but I also like not having my skin shredded by thorns.'

'I hardly think she'd throw you into the bramble bush.'

'I have four older sisters and I've seen them do some pretty scary things to their beaus when they get upset.'

'Eamon, I don't think you need to worry,' said David. 'Innogen likes you. She doesn't like my cousin. The worst she'd probably do is break your yew bow.'

The young Robesman looked horrified. 'In that case I'd rather she did throw me in the bramble bush.'

'I can do it now!'

Leila's excited exclamation drew David's and his Robesmen's attention back to her animated conversation with Rhiannon, which had clearly undergone a change in topic.

'Ever since I saw you win the Cup I've been practising the drills every day so I'll be good enough to enter the tournament in October.'

'Leila, you'll probably go into a daydream right in the middle of a fight like you always do during class,' Innogen pointed out.

'She's right, Leila. Your mind does tend to wander quite a lot unless you're studying those plants of yours.'

Leila tilted her head proudly. 'I've been sparring with John and he said I'm doing well.'

'John Tremaine?' several girls exclaimed incredulously.

Leila nodded.

'How'd you get him to spar with you?'

'She asked me,' John said mildly. 'Even after several years of our families being neighbours I still haven't managed to say no to one of her requests.'

'You haven't let me ride Asaph.'

John gave Leila a fond smile. 'You know I'd let you but the only other person he's ever permitted on his back is David.'

'Fascinating as all these conversations must be, I must insist on you postponing them until after classes are finished.'

The prim female voice drew all eyes to the doorway of the school. There, her spectacles glinting in the morning light, and her white hair creating a glowing halo around her lined face, was Professor Abigail Treshart.

All the students immediately straightened and bowed their heads in greeting. 'Good morning, Professor,' they chorused.

The stern set of Professor Treshart's mouth softened slightly.

'At least you've remembered your manners,' she said. 'Let us hope you've also remembered how to write, for you'll be taking down a lot of notes this morning on the Battle of Torerock.' She descended the steps and gestured towards the door, the movement made imperious by her long green robe. 'In you go, and you will each find a class schedule on your desk for the term. To our new students I will only say this once: When I am speaking you will listen. If you cannot remember this simple rule then perhaps a visit to the stables will refresh your memory – the grooms are always eager to have extra help cleaning out the stalls.'

An hour and a half later, Rhiannon shook out the cramp in her hand and looked around the classroom to see all the other students doing the same. Professor Treshart had not been joking about the quantity of notes they would be taking down.

The Battle of Torerock in 1095BC, which had seen the defeat of a vast army of Karatos, a form of large, carnivorous sea serpents found in the deepest waters of the Dairíon Ocean, by the combined forces of Ríyun Dragons, Water Faeries and merfolk after a century of war, had lasted over a year. This meant there was a mountain of information for them to learn, including the fact that it was during this battle the great warrior Orthoríon died after hearing of the death of Elvanor, the princess Rhiannon had heard the merfolk singing about the night she first awoke in the palace.

As Professor Treshart left the room, a flash of white light from the dais in the foyer announced the arrival of their next teacher, Master Hubert Gadshill. The language professor stumbled into the classroom, his blue robes worn inside-out and a burst of non-English words passing his lips.

'*Dum spiro spero. Dum spero amo. Dum amo vivo.*'

It would seem Latin was his language of choice for today's lesson.

'Who, apart from Prince David, can tell me what that means?'

Several hands went up, including Rhiannon's.

'Miss McBride.'

Rhiannon stood up beside her desk and said with confidence, 'While I breathe, I hope. While I hope, I love. While I love, I live.'

'Correct. Now, Mr Zemit, change the phrase from first person to second.'

As poor Rolfe rose reluctantly to his feet, Rhiannon sat back down and looked across the aisle at David. Instead of paying attention to the lesson, which was superfluous for him anyway, the Prince of Álnair was staring out the arched window beside him.

Rhiannon peered around his head to see what had caught his attention. Her gaze landed on the shiny grey scales and blue markings of a dragon.

Arastar!

The Parvus Dragon was sitting on the wide road leading from the gate to the palace, speaking with King Stephen and Sir Raeden. A short distance from them stood Izana's father, Lord Daiki Sato, Chief Robesman to the King.

Rhiannon's gaze returned to David. With his head turned away from her she could not see his face, but where his right arm rested on top of his desk she saw his hand clench tightly. Unfortunately, for all his absentmindedness, Master Gadshill was just as strict as Professor Treshart when it came to talking during his lectures, and she had no chance to speak with David until their language lesson ended and they were waiting for the arrival of their next teacher.

'What do you think Arastar found out?' she asked under the chattering voices of the other students.

'Nothing good,' David replied. 'Rather than leave his report with one of the guards, he must've requested one of them to fetch my father. The High Council was in session this morning and they're never interrupted unless it's for something important.' He glanced at the class schedule in his hand. 'We've got Natural Science next, then the rest of the day free. That'll give us a chance to find my father if he doesn't show for lunch and ask him what's happened.'

An abrupt hush descending on the other students in the room announced the arrival of their next teacher.

David and Rhiannon immediately turned to face the front and watched as Master Zhen silently walked to the teacher's desk, placed his books upon it, then slowly examined the array of faces looking up at him. His black hair with its sprinkling of silver gave him a distinguished look, as did his immaculate dark grey robes.

'Those of you in Grades Four and Five who elected not to continue this subject may now go,' he announced in his rich, deep voice. 'Grade One students, you will make your way outside where the Lady Endrille is waiting to speak with you.'

The dismissed students promptly gathered their notes from the previous two lessons and departed in quiet haste.

'Today we will focus on the narapet plant,' Master Zhen announced to the remaining students. 'It is most commonly known for its fruit being used to make a very fine but strong wine. However, it is also used in many potions for the treatment of pain and minor infections. Due to the high potency of the fruit's undiluted natural juices, extreme care is required when handling it, as once the pink skin is cut open, and the purple flesh exposed, the fumes are capable of causing intoxication within minutes. Therefore, a properly secured mask must always be worn whenever you have direct contact with the fruit. Now, those of you who remember the assigned reading for the holidays should be able to tell me the optimal time for harvesting the fruit.'

'In the evening,' most of the students replied.

'Excellent. And once they're harvested how long can they be stored before they begin to spoil?'

'Twenty-four hours.'

'Correct, which is why you should only gather the fruit when you know you will have the opportunity to either juice or preserve it within that timeframe. Last evening I collected enough to supply what we will require for the potion we shall be doing next week. They are currently upstairs in Laboratory One and will need to be cut up and bottled. Some of you will come with me to take care of that task, while the rest of you will remain here under the supervision of John Tremaine and write a short essay on the benefits of narapet as an analgesic. Mr Tremaine, you will find the information to be written up on the board marked in these books. Now, those who will join me upstairs are Eamon Bowler, Innogen Calloway, Rhiannon McBride, His Royal Highness David O'Faenart, Viola Rastell and Izana Sato.'

Master Zhen headed towards the doorway and waited for the six students to precede him, then he followed them out.

A short time later Rhiannon stood patiently inside Laboratory One as David finished tying the strings of her mask, then released her hair. The chestnut ringlets pinned in a high ponytail cascaded down in an unruly cloud. She turned around and picked up the other mask off the workbench beside her.

'Now it's your turn,' she said, then paused and glanced up. Despite having grown taller over the past few months, she saw that David's chin was still several inches above the top of her head. 'You'd better sit.'

David looked at the high stool tucked underneath the table.

'I doubt that would help,' he said, and angling his sword away from the ground, he knelt down. 'That should do it, but you'd best be quick, these stone slabs aren't as comfortable as a kneeler.'

Rhiannon stepped around him and after ensuring the mask lay snuggly against his face, fastened it with a secure knot. The soft, golden strands of his hair gently brushed against her fingers. A strange flutter sprang to life in her heart, along with a sudden urge to run her fingers through the fair tresses covering her friend's neck.

'There, all done,' she said, hastily withdrawing her hands and feeling immensely grateful for the mask concealing her burning cheeks.

David stood up with a quick word of thanks and lifted his hand to let Master Zhen know they were ready. His gesture was soon followed by Eamon's who stood next to Innogen at the workbench across from them. Izana and Viola, having been the first ones ready, were placing silver knives, cutting mats, gloves and glass bottles half filled with cloudy liquid on four of the tables.

Satisfied his students would be protected against the inebriating fumes of the narapet fruit, Master Zhen pointed at the four large pails sat atop the bench lining the back wall. Each one was made of wood with a fitted cover and metal handle.

'The narapet fruit are in those pails. They all need to be destemmed, then quartered,' he instructed. 'The flesh is to be bottled, but do not overfill them. The segments of fruit should be able to float freely in the lemon water. Any juice remaining on the cutting mat is to be tipped into the bucket beneath your bench. Once you have completed cutting up the fruit, please put the lids on the bottles, then inform me. You may begin.'

After David fetched the pail of fruit and placed it on their table, Rhiannon removed the cover and took out the first piece of narapet fruit. The size of an apricot, it looked like a small pink ball with its smooth, shiny skin. There was a rich brown stem at the top and two oval-shaped leaves of mossy green. Through her mask she caught the faintest whiff of an extremely sweet fragrance that tickled her senses and had her smiling in pleasure.

'It's best if you take the stem off first,' said David. He plucked the stem out of the piece he was holding and tossed it in the bucket at his feet. 'Some people make the first cut then remove it, but doing it that way results in too much juice being released.'

He placed the fruit on the cutting mat, and using his silver knife swiftly quartered it.

The sweet aroma assailing Rhiannon's nostrils increased.

David picked up the four segments of fruit in his gloved hand and placed them in the bottle of lemon water. The liquid turned a soft lilac.

Rhiannon's gaze followed David's hand as he reached into the pail for a second time. For some reason she found his movements fascinating.

Her stillness alerted David, who frowned. 'Is something wrong? Rhiannon?'

A nudge to her shoulder broke Rhiannon out of her daze and she shook her head. 'Right, remove the stem first, then cut,' she said, and destemmed the piece of fruit in her hand. She slowly cut it into quarters and placed the portions in the bottle beside her.

David waited until she was reaching into the pail again then turned back to the narapet fruit in his own hand. He efficiently had it destemmed and cut in seconds. He quickly did another ten, and each time he placed the segments in the bottle Rhiannon found it increasingly difficult to focus on their assigned task. Her eyes kept wandering to the golden glint of her friend's hair, the colour enticing her until she reached up and patted the shining strands.

'Rhiannon, what are you doing?'

David's hushed question went unanswered. Instead, Rhiannon grasped a handful of his hair and pulled.

'OW! Rhiannon, stop it!'

A second tug was followed by a delighted, 'Itsh not hard at all.'

'Rhiannon!' David reached up, grasped his friend's hand and pulled it away from his head. 'What's got into you?'

A glazed look in the golden eyes staring up at him was his answer. He saw it and immediately called out, 'Master Zhen, Rhiannon's been affected by the fumes!'

The professor hastily came towards them.

'Didn't you tie her mask properly?' he demanded.

'Of course I did!' David caught Rhiannon as she stumbled against him. His cheeks burned when he felt her snuggling against the soft material of his tunic. 'Rhiannon. Rhiannon! Look at me.'

Rhiannon ignored the request and burrowed her face deeper into the light blue fabric. 'This ish nice.'

'David, see if you can turn her around,' Izana said, coming to stand next to Master Zhen.

'She's got a pretty firm grip on my tunic,' David answered.

His Robesman nodded and stepped forward. Gently, he began to coax Rhiannon's fingers into releasing their tight hold on the captured material.

Rhiannon muttered in protest.

'Now, none of that,' Izana commanded firmly. 'You need to let go, Rhiannon.'

The familiar voice drew her attention and she turned her head. Upon meeting the pair of brown eyes set behind a fringe of ash-blond hair, her own eyes crinkled in a smile. 'Itsh Ishana. You look funny.'

'I'm sure I do.' Izana, seizing the opportunity presented to him, quickly examined Rhiannon's mask and discovered something. 'There's a small tear in her mask.'

'What! Where?' David glanced down at the top of Rhiannon's head. 'I didn't see any when I checked it.'

'It's near her mouth. It was probably too small to be seen before, but when she rubbed her face against you the movement must've made it bigger.'

'So she's been breathing the fumes in since we started.'

'And still is.'

'Your Royal Highness, escort her out of here immediately,' Master Zhen ordered. 'The only remedy is for her to sleep off the effects, so take her back to the palace. I will send a message to her guardian.'

'Yes, sir.' David looked across at Eamon, his assigned Robesman for the month. 'I won't need you to come with me, Eamon. Stay here and finish assisting Master Zhen. You can come and find me once you're done.' Then, with a stern note of authority entering his voice, he instructed, 'Apart from John, I don't want anyone else in the school learning of this. Rhiannon doesn't need certain people mocking her about it.'

'We won't say anything,' Innogen and Viola promised.

Satisfied, David led Rhiannon out of the laboratory. After Izana helped him remove their gloves and masks, he set about the difficult task of getting his friend down the corridor. Moving towards the stairwell, he maintained a secure hold around Rhiannon as she wobbled precariously with each step.

'Where'sh we goin'?'

'You're going back to bed.'

'Sh-Shilly! Itsh not dark yet.'

'No, but you need to lie down for a while.'

Rhiannon peered blearily up at him. 'Can't,' she said. 'A-Annabelle alwaysh makesh me clean.'

David frowned but said mildly, 'She won't if I come with you.'

A film of tears filled Rhiannon's eyes. 'Sh-She will. I-I's her shlave.'

'You're not her slave,' David declared, a fire flaring to life in his eyes. 'You're not anyone's slave.'

A watery smile broke out across Rhiannon's face. 'Davish good. I like Davish.'

'And I like you.'

'Yesh. You-You kissh'd me. But not on-on lipsh. Not a prop-proper kissh.'

'I guess it wasn't,' David conceded, his casual tone belied by the faint blush in his cheeks.

'I's never kissh'd before.' Rhiannon tilted her head back and stared at him earnestly. 'Want Davish to kissh me.' And she used one hand to pull his head down towards her.

His face now burning with a fierce heat, David cleared his throat. He hastily looked away from Rhiannon's inviting mouth, then gently removed her hand from his head.

'If I kissed you right now it wouldn't be right,' he said quietly.

A soft sniffle was swiftly followed by a hurt, 'You don' wanna kissh me.'

David sighed. 'I do, more than anything, but you're not yourself, Rhiannon. I won't spoil the first kiss for us both by taking advantage of your current state. When I kiss you I want you to be fully aware of what you're doing. And be able to remember me doing it.'

A brief pause fell, then Rhiannon lifted her free hand and patted David's cheek. He felt an intense warmth emanating from her skin.

'Davish pretty.'

'I think I prefer handsome. You're the one who's pretty.'

By now they were slowly descending the staircase and David, aware of the other students inside the classroom, kept up a quiet monologue until they reached the bottom and were on the transonus dais. He reached out and pressed the rune for Level Two of the Upper South Wing. They disappeared in a flash of brilliant white light.

The instant they appeared on the other dais, Rhiannon moaned and sank against David. When he tried to urge her forwards, she groaned miserably.

'Come on, Rhiannon. Your chamber's not far.'

'No. Don' wanna move.'

'Look, the doorway's just down there.'

'No.' Rhiannon closed her eyes with a grimace. 'Feel sick.'

'All right, I won't make you walk,' David soothed her, and without another word he scooped her up into his arms.

Rhiannon's pale skin turned a sickly grey. One hand flew up to cover her mouth. Then she buried her face in David's shoulder and took a deep breath. His clean, woodsy scent filled her lungs and slightly eased her upset stomach. Drowsily, she told him not to put her down.

'I won't,' he answered. 'Just concentrate on taking some deep breaths,' he encouraged, smoothly descending the dais steps and setting off down the long hallway.

He easily covered the distance to the arched entrance of Rhiannon's rooms. Having succeeded in opening the door, he passed through the antechamber to the main apartment. By this time Rhiannon's breathing had evened out and her eyes were closed in a deep sleep.

'Aleda!'

A shiny ball of light shimmered in response to David's call. The fragrance of moist earth and fresh grass announced the arrival of the small, green-haired House Faery.

'Yes, Dav— Rhiannon!' Her voice rising in alarm, Aleda flew across the room. 'What's happened?'

David walked towards the four-poster bed. 'We were cutting narapet fruit and she inhaled the fumes,' he explained, carefully lowering Rhiannon onto her bed. He moved a chair closer to it and sat down. 'I need you to stay here with us until she wakes up.'

'Of course I shall stay, but shouldn't Sir Raeden be informed?'

'Master Zhen was sending a message to him. He'll probably come to check on her after he gets it.'

Sir Raeden arrived twenty minutes later accompanied by King Stephen and Queen Maiwen. His expression impassive, the knight rested his hand on Rhiannon's forehead, murmured a flow of words under his breath, then announced, 'Normally it would take a day for her mind and body to be free of their effects, but her ability to self-heal has already begun to neutralise the toxins in her blood. When she awakens she will have nothing more than a bad headache.'

Queen Maiwen made a sound of relief while King Stephen said, 'I'm sorry this happened, Raeden.'

'It was an accident, Sire. No blame can be attached to yourself.'

'It did occur in the castle school and all due to a damaged mask.'

'Master Zhen has assured me he will personally inspect all the other new ones before they are used.' Sir Raeden turned to David. 'He also credits you with identifying that she was affected by the fumes. Rhiannon is fortunate you were perceptive enough to realise it. Had she continued to be exposed to the fumes for the duration of the lesson she would have become violently ill.'

David grimaced at the thought and admitted, 'I didn't really notice something was wrong until after she grabbed my hair.'

'She grabbed your hair?' his mother said in astonishment.

'And pulled it.' David rubbed the offended spot at the memory.

Queen Maiwen made a sympathetic noise but the laughter in her eyes was unmistakable.

A low groan of misery from the prostrate figure on the bed returned their attention to Rhiannon. They all watched as her eyelashes fluttered like captured butterflies before slowly parting to reveal a pair of confused golden eyes.

She winced, then grimaced, her lips curling in distaste. A groan sounded in her throat. She blinked slowly, her bleary gaze focused on the ocean-blue canopy above her bed. A puzzled frown creased her brow. With delicate care, she turned her head and saw David and Sir Raeden standing near her head with King Stephen and Queen Maiwen positioned at the foot of the bed.

'What —'

A moan of pain immediately followed the single word. Her eyes clenched shut. Her hands shot up to grasp her head. When next she spoke, her voice was the merest whisper. 'What am I doing here?'

'You inhaled the fumes of the narapet fruit.' Sir Raeden's voice was pitched low. Rhiannon found the deep timbre in it soothing. 'Drink this.'

A gentle hand raised her head and the cold end of a small glass bottle pressed against her lips. Rhiannon obediently opened her mouth and drank. In less than a moment all signs of pain vanished from her face. A smile lit her expression as her eyes opened. Slowly, she sat up.

'Thank you. I didn't know you had liquid sunshine here,' she quipped. 'It feels like my whole body is flooded with a warm glow. The best thing is the pounding in my head has disappeared, along with the foul taste in my mouth.' She looked at the empty bottle in Sir Raeden's hand. 'What was in that?'

'Sanelda. It is an elixir to relieve pain. The effects will last for three hours which should be sufficient time for your body to fully recover.' Sir Raeden placed the bottle inside the front pocket of his tunic and stepped back. 'I trust that next time you handle the fruit of the narapet plant you will be more vigilant.'

Rhiannon frowned. 'But I was,' she protested. 'I had a mask on and I didn't do anything I wasn't supposed to do. The last thing I remember clearly is David asking me if something was wrong and smelling a really sweet scent.'

'You should not have been able to smell anything at all, apart from the cloth of the mask.'

'Well, nobody told me that!'

'And I shall be having words with Master Zhen about that oversight. It was his responsibility to ensure you were fully instructed, not a fellow student's. Which is why I am not going to reprimand His Royal Highness as your work partner. Now, you are to remain abed for the next two hours. After that you may get up, but you will not leave your chambers until the Sanelda is

out of your system. I will have your lunch sent to you on a tray.'
Sir Raeden turned from Rhiannon and bowed to King Stephen.
'With Your Majesty's permission I shall return to my duties once
I have spoken with Master Zhen.'

King Stephen nodded. 'I won't reconvene the High Council
until you've returned, Raeden.'

With a word of thanks and another bow, Sir Raeden took
his leave and departed, but not before giving Rhiannon a stern
warning to heed his instructions.

'I don't know why I have to stay here,' Rhiannon complained
once he was gone. 'I feel fine.'

'Sanelda can sometimes cause dizziness,' Queen Maiwen
explained.

'We don't want you taking a tumble down the stairs,' said
David. Suddenly, he smiled. 'Don't pout, Rhiannon. It makes you
look like Alice.'

Rhiannon glared at him. 'It's all right for you,' she groused.
'You're not the one confined to your room for the next few hours.'

'I can stay with you, and I've no doubt Izana, Eamon and John
will come up once school is finished. They're bound to be worried
about you.'

Realising why the three Robesmen would be concerned,
Rhiannon moaned in humiliation and covered her face with her
hands. 'I don't remember what I did, but Master Zhen said the
fumes caused intoxication.' Anxiously, she peered through her
fingers at David. 'I didn't make a complete fool of myself, did I?'

'No. You just pulled my hair, told Izana he looked funny and
made a fuss about having to sleep during the day.'

Rhiannon sighed in relief. 'So I didn't become a human water-
ing pot and start rambling about my emotions?'

"I like Davish."

"Want Davish to kissh me."

His friend's uninhibited words echoed in David's ears and he saw again Rhiannon's face tilted invitingly towards his.

'No,' he said. 'You didn't.' Then, deliberately changing the subject, he turned to his father, saying, 'I saw Arastar speaking with you earlier. His news must've been important for the guards to interrupt a meeting of the High Council.'

An odd, pensive look flickered in King Stephen's eyes as he gazed at his son. To David and Rhiannon, he seemed to be debating with himself before he nodded.

'Under normal circumstances I would refrain from troubling you, my son. However, given certain information which has been revealed to me perhaps it is best I share these tidings with you now, rather than have you be caught unawares at a later date. You also, Rhiannon.' King Stephen paused, and when he next spoke his voice was quiet and sombre. 'Arastar has brought news of a growing faction in Graynor who are propagating many of the beliefs held by Fendrel. The leaders have all concealed their identities with the exception of one. Aldric Mórfran. His sentiments have been known for a great many years following an incident in the Black Woods, but unfortunately, he has always evaded capture.

'Several people who were caught conducting forbidden experiments have confessed to aiding in the slaughter of several dragons, and Arastar discovered that the disappearance of dozens of others, including hatchlings, is the work of this faction. Tragically, he heard of another case before returning here. Baegolz had felt the bond with his life-mate Torania being severed, but when he searched the area around their lair he found no trace of her body and their hatchlings had vanished.

'The unrest being created by these events is increasing, and should the members of the faction continue to grow in number and its leaders remain uncaught, Álnair will once again find her land desecrated by war within the next few years.'

A horrified silence greeted this revelation.

Rhiannon's face paled. Aleda shivered. Queen Maiwen clasped her husband's arm. And David sank down onto Rhiannon's bed, his young eyes looking strangely old.

'How many times will Endrille have to suffer from this level of betrayal?'

At the frustrated sadness in her friend's voice, Rhiannon reached out to touch his back, but her consoling gesture went unnoticed.

'How many times will innocent blood be spilt because of some twisted and evil ideology? And how can people even support these atrocities?'

Unable to think of any words with which to comfort him, Rhiannon did not answer. However, King Stephen stepped forward and gently rested his hand on his son's shoulder.

'Sadly, not everyone has your good and faithful heart, my son. They allow their own selfish desires to blind them to what is right and do not hesitate to commit the vilest offences. The most we can do is strive to defend the innocent and protect Álnair each time she is threatened by such malevolence.'

David clenched his jaw. 'It doesn't seem like enough.'

'No, it doesn't,' his father agreed. 'However, it is better than doing nothing at all and allowing evil to go unchecked.'

Acknowledging the truth of this, David said nothing, only nodded.

'Which is also why I will be instructing Sir Raeden to arrange for some guards in civilian clothes to be positioned among the crowd during the Open Day events. Should any person be caught disseminating the materials created by the faction in Graynor, or heard to be speaking in support of them, they will be arrested and put before the Pelatarrof.'

Chapter 11

TREACHERY UNMASKED

'David.'

'Mm.'

'What's today?'

'Wednesday.'

'What's the date?'

'Twenty-six October.'

An expectant silence descended on the prince's study. Rhiannon waited for realisation to strike her friend. Through the tall arched windows of the south wall a faint breeze stirred the long green drapes, bringing with it the scent of the ocean. In the cloudless autumn sky, the radiant glow of the rising sun could be seen.

Another moment passed. The only sounds to break the silence were the delicate rhythmic ticks of a fine pendulum clock and the rolling waves of the sea.

Rhiannon decided to try again.

'David.'

'Yes?'

'Why are you reading that report?'

'Because I need to know what's happening in Álnair.'

Rhiannon reached across the large mahogany desk and placed

her hand on top of the report. 'I mean, why are you reading it now? We've got things to do.'

David looked up at her and frowned. 'I thought we weren't searching for Merlin's lab again until after the holidays. We agreed I'd spend them helping my father.'

His confusion was so evident Rhiannon shook her head in affectionate amusement.

'That was the agreement, but this morning we were going to be two unimportant visitors enjoying the Open Day festivities,' she said, gesturing at her very plain gown, reticule and cloak.

David's eyes widened in consternation. 'O stars above! I'm so sorry, Rhiannon.' He rose from his seat, distractedly running a hand through his hair. 'I came to get the money Lord Grenwa organised for me and found the report.'

'And promptly focused all your attention on it,' Rhiannon concluded.

'It's about Graynor,' he offered by way of explanation.

Rhiannon immediately understood. Ever since his father had told them about the faction there, David had been spending a lot of time checking all the reports put on his desk for a mention of them. 'What does it say?' she asked.

'So far, not much. There was a fire at one of the docks and two ships were badly damaged, but thankfully no one was seriously injured. The Chief Consul for the city says the fire doesn't appear to have been deliberately lit, however, they're not ruling out the possibility entirely.'

'If you want to finish reading it I don't mind waiting a bit longer.'

'And have Izana catch us before we have a chance to leave?' David shook his head. 'We'd never get away from him.' He lifted the leather money pouch off the desk and attached it to his belt. The numerous *chinks* from inside the bag revealed Lord Grenwa had filled it most generously.

He stepped out from behind his desk and Rhiannon saw his normal shiny boots and pristine breeches had been exchanged for more well-worn ones. His tunic was also a plain grey with no embellishment. After he removed his signet ring and tucked it into his breast pocket, the only item on him that looked expensive was his sword.

'Won't that give you away?' she asked, pointing at the fine scabbard which bore the House of Valieoth's family crest.

'My cloak will cover it,' David answered and picked up the simple brown garment. He positioned it around his shoulders before pulling the hood over his head. 'Make sure you put yours up too,' he said, gesturing towards Rhiannon's.

She did so but enquired, 'What about the guards at the Main Gate? Won't they be suspicious if we both appear with our heads covered?'

'Not a chance. In summer it's not unusual for visitors to use their hoods as protection from the sun. And during autumn, with the slight chill in the air, the hoods keep their heads warm. We'll also be arriving at the gate using the transonus system so they'll just think we're two servants from the palace. Now, let's go and get some breakfast.' He escorted her out the door. 'All the stalls will be set up by now, and there's one particular man from Cendillis who always has the nicest kámari.'

'Kámari?'

'It's crab meat mixed with ginger and seaweed wrapped in a ball of batter then cooked on a griddle,' David explained, closing the door to his study. He caught a glimpse of Rhiannon's expression and said, 'Just wait until you've tried one. You won't be pulling that face for long.'

Amidst the bustling crowd already gathered on the wide road, Rhiannon stood in front of the first stall inside the Main Gate and stared at the sizzling rows of delicious smelling kámari with suspicion. From the moment they had left David's study he had been attempting to convince her to try one. So far, he had not succeeded.

'But it's got seaweed in it!'

'Only a little bit. Just try a small piece. Please. If you really don't like it, I'll finish the rest.'

About to categorically refuse for the last time, Rhiannon gazed up and saw David's eyes wide with entreaty and a hopeful look on his face. Then she remembered. This would be his first time attending the stalls with a friend. That day in the arena he had admitted he normally sought to escape his Robesmen for a few hours to mingle in the crowd, which meant he had never before shared his obvious love of these particular kámari with anyone.

'All right, I'll try one,' she said, and was instantly glad upon seeing David's reaction. His beaming smile reflecting the happy light in his eyes, the Prince of Álnair assured her she would not regret it and turned to the elderly kámari merchant who had been watching their interaction with indulgent amusement.

'I'll take a serving of them, please, Mr Funabe,' David ordered.

'Your little lady is in for a treat, Master Alexander,' came the friendly response as the man put several kámari in a small bread boat then drizzled a white sauce over them. 'There we are.' He handed the food to David but waved away the bronze coin offered to him. 'No, no. No charge this time. It's an honour you've brought your lady to my stall for her first taste of kámari.'

David grinned at him. 'I certainly wouldn't take her to Tasroe's. You always make the best.'

Mr Funabe accepted the high praise with a bow, then turned to serve another customer.

'Why did he call you Alexander?' Rhiannon asked in a soft voice.

'That's how I introduced myself when I first met him eight years ago. I wanted to try his kámari and he let me have some for free. After my first piece, I must've returned to his stall a dozen times that day. By the fifth visit he was calling me "Master Alexander" and putting an extra piece on each serve.'

'His stall seems very popular.' Rhiannon looked around at the swarm of people waiting to be served. 'Doesn't he have anyone to help him?'

'No. He doesn't have any family and he isn't prepared to risk someone finding out the special ingredient he uses in his kámari.'

There was a note in his voice that had Rhiannon looking at him intently. 'Do you know it?'

David ducked his head, a faint smile on his lips. 'I do,' he murmured, 'but I promised Mr Funabe never to tell anyone while he lived. So please don't ask me what it is. I really hate saying no to you.'

'Then I won't ask,' Rhiannon promised.

After manoeuvring their way through the crowd pressing in like ravenous seagulls eager for a meal at Mr Funabe's stall, they stopped next to a much quieter booth displaying a colourful array of knitted blankets. The stern matriarch from the cluster of ladies gathered around the counter barely spared them a glance before turning back to her companions.

Rhiannon gave a quiet snort of laughter. 'Do you think her attitude would change if she knew you were the Crown Prince?' she murmured.

'I know it would. She's Claudia Roscalli, the mother of the Chief Consul of Cendillis and the city's worst snob. After she died of shock at seeing me dressed like this, she'd come back to life for the sole purpose of saying a few words to me so she could boast about it to her friends. The two women next to her with the silver-blonde hair are the Chief Consol's wife Honoria and her daughter Romilda. Romilda's the same age as you but goes to school in Cendillis, and Honoria is a close friend of my aunt Lucia.'

'So they must know Marcus quite well.'

'He and Romilda have been close since they chewed on the

same teething toys, and my aunt's always talking about wanting Romilda as a daughter-in-law. It wouldn't surprise me if Marcus ends up obliging her by marrying Romilda. But enough about them, the kámari is getting cold and it tastes better when it's hot.'

David held the bread boat out.

Rhiannon, eager to have the experience over and done, selected the smallest piece of kámari and took a delicate bite.

A plethora of flavour exploded on her tongue: The spice of ginger; the sweetness of crab meat; the cream of egg batter blended with the tangy, savoury sauce; and beneath all of those a hint of salt from the seaweed.

Rhiannon moaned in appreciation.

David's eyes gleamed with mischief. 'Sorry, I didn't quite catch that.'

He was ignored as Rhiannon savoured her first bite, then promptly finished the piece of kámari.

'That's fantastic!' she exclaimed afterwards.

'Despite the seaweed?'

The teasing question drew a laugh from her. 'Yes, despite the seaweed. I can understand why you like them so much.'

'Do you want the rest? I can go back and get another serving for myself.'

Rhiannon looked back at the crowd swarming around Mr Funabe's stall. 'You'll be waiting a long time. We can share these ones.'

And so they did. It was not long before the bread boat was empty of kámari and they devoured it too. Thankfully, there were large wooden water tanks set up at regular points along the road so they were able to wash their hands of the sticky residue left by the sauce.

'Is there any particular sort of thing you'd like to see?' David asked, turning off the faucet and shaking the excess water from his hands.

'Not really. I'm happy to just wander.'

'Then that's what we'll do. Though if you do want to stop at any of the stalls, just let me know.' They joined the sea of people walking towards the palace.

Over an hour later Rhiannon thought it wasn't a question of if she wanted to stop but should she. There was such a variety of stalls, selling everything from jewellery to toys, pottery to potions, and tapestries, weapons and clothing that she knew they couldn't possibly stop at them all – not if David was ever going to make it back in time to change for his balcony appearance with his parents! The crowds were also increasing until it was difficult to move faster than a dawdling cat. Conversations ebbed and flowed around them, while the excited chattering of children was interjected by stern parental warnings.

As they neared the first inner wall, the thick crowd of people finally thinned, allowing Rhiannon and David to approach the gate with ease. It also allowed them to overhear the conversation of the casually dressed Councillor Paul Attwater and his female companion as they exited it.

'Paul, are you sure I won't be late for the tournament?' The tall girl with dark curls looked back anxiously over her shoulder.

'Of course I'm sure. We've got plenty of time before you need to be there.'

'But you said that the time you were leaving to take the Imperial Office Exam and you barely made it through the door before they locked it.'

'The one time I made a mistake and you'll never let me forget it, will you?' Paul gave the end of her pale, freckled nose an affectionate tap. 'Don't worry, Nia. I know exactly how long it takes to get from Mr Funabe's kámari stall to the arena. I won't let you be late. Now come on, if we don't hurry and get Mum's necklace from Mother Tierney's stall all the kámari will be gone!'

The boyish eagerness in his voice was so similar to David's

when he'd spoken of the kámari that Rhiannon had to laugh. Paul's gaze turned towards her and his eyes widened in recognition.

'Miss Rh—'

He frowned and fell silent at her hasty shushing motion before his gaze turned towards David. A grin of comprehension slowly spread across his face. He nodded, then waited until the two couples were an arm's length away from each other before greeting them in a low voice.

'Playing the vagrant, Your Royal Highness?'

'With the utmost pleasure,' David answered, smiling. 'I appreciate your co-operation in keeping my identity a secret. And you too, Nia,' he added, turning to her. 'I almost didn't recognise you as the same shy girl who attended Paul's inauguration ceremony a year ago. Rhiannon, this is Nia Attwater, Paul's younger sister. She's the same age as you but attends school in Cendillis. Nia, this is Rhiannon McBride, daughter of the line of Mórell.'

'You're really her! The youngest Dragon Cup champion!' Nia gazed at Rhiannon, a spark of deep respect in her eyes.

'I usually go by the name Rhiannon,' she chuckled, 'it's much less of a mouthful. I heard you say you'd be in the tournament today.'

Nia nodded. 'In our age section, I'm definitely not good enough for the opens yet. It's my first time entering, but I'm determined to at least pass to the final rounds.'

'With that mindset I'm sure you'll make it,' Rhiannon encouraged her.

'Paul, how're the crowds in the middle ward?' David asked.

'They're not as dense as here. It's much easier to move around.'

'That's a relief, I want to show Rhiannon as many stalls as possible in the time we've got left.'

'Then we'd best not delay you any further.' Paul drew Nia to the side and gave a slight bow. 'You'll pardon my lack of manners in not saluting you, Your Royal Highness, but I wouldn't want to proclaim your presence to everyone here.'

David patted his shoulder. 'You're a wise man, Paul. Thank you. Hope you both enjoy the rest of the day. Good luck in the tournament, Nia.'

Rhiannon added her best wishes to his, saying, 'I'll be cheering you on!' then they entered the gates and passed through the inner wall into the middle ward.

Rhiannon's attention was immediately caught by a large tent bedecked in strings of twinkling star crystals, the flashes of brilliant colour sparkling in the morning sunlight. She seriously considered stopping to have a look at the display, until she saw the person speaking with the stall's owner.

'There's Eamon.'

David hastily looked around. 'Where?'

She pointed at the stall.

'Good grief! He must've been helping his grandfather set up the displays.'

'Is that the old man with him?'

'Yes, that's Nórdan Bowler. He's the best jeweller in Cendillis.'

'The one who sent those crystal flowers to your mother last month for her birthday?'

David nodded. 'And the paperweight carved from a single ruby to my father for his two weeks ago.' He pulled his hood down to cover more of his face, then reached out and adjusted Rhiannon's. 'Come on,' he said, taking her hand and leading her deeper into the crowd. 'If he recognises us, Eamon will stick to us like a burr.'

Extremely conscious of the warmth of David's hand engulfing her own, Rhiannon remained silent as they put some distance between themselves and Eamon. The row of stalls lining the road continued, and all around them the people of Álnair laughed and talked, completely unaware their prince was walking in their midst.

''ere now, lad. 'ow's about a pretty bracelet fer yer lass? Only ten pieces of bronze.'

The speaker stepped right in front of them and held up a chain of shimmering white metal. A roguish twinkle sparkled in the man's right eye, his left covered by a black patch. His tunic and blue cloak were faded but showed all the signs of being carefully looked after.

'Such a bonnie lass deserves a fine gift,' he continued.

To Rhiannon's surprise David let go of her hand and reached into his money pouch.

'Here you go,' he said, and placed the coin he extracted into the seller's hand.

The man's eye widened. 'Eh, lad, it be worth ten bronze, not one gold.'

'Not to me.' David accepted the bracelet with a word of thanks, then he and Rhiannon walked away, leaving the stunned man behind.

'Why'd you do that?' Rhiannon asked.

'I thought you'd like it.'

'Not that. Although you know I could've bought it for myself. Why'd you give him a gold coin?'

David did not immediately answer. He glanced back at the man, an odd mix of respect and regret in his eyes before saying in a quiet voice, 'The reason he has to wear an eyepatch is because he lost the eye saving my life. He was once in the Royal Guard and when I was twelve he accompanied my parents and me when we travelled to Ardara. We had stopped at one of the smaller villages along the road when a group of bandits attacked. Do you remember when I told you after the mock battle how everyone has a moment when they'll panic during a fight?'

'Yes.'

'Well, that's when it happened to me. I turned from defeating one of the bandits to see a large man coming towards me. At least, to me he seemed large. He had a thick black beard, shoulders like an ox and was wielding the biggest sword I had ever seen. I froze. All I could do was watch as the blade came down at me. That's when Captain Lonergan appeared. He leapt in front of me and deflected the blow. He fought the man and during the fight got slashed across the face and badly injured in the arm. They couldn't save his eye and he had to retire from the Royal Guard.' David stopped and looked down at the bracelet in his hand before giving it to Rhiannon. 'He makes these to occupy his time. They're not much more than inexpensive jewellery, but to me their worth comes from the hands that makes them.'

'Now that I know his story, I'd have to agree,' Rhiannon said, slipping the bracelet onto her wrist. 'It is pretty. He must sell a lot of them.'

'His stall usually sells out before the end of the day.' David looked at the next range of wares and grinned. 'Here's another one that does. Do you mind if we stop to have a look?'

Rhiannon glanced at the items on display and immediately understood the reason for his enthusiasm. Clocks and watches of all sizes and designs. The stall and the wagon behind it were covered in them.

'Do they sell out because you buy everything?' she teased lightly.

'Unfortunately not,' he laughed. 'All Gustav's pieces are unique and he only brings his very best ones to the Open Days.'

Rhiannon looked at the row of tall floor clocks on the wagon. Some of them were over six foot high. 'How do people get them home?'

'Gustav arranges delivery for all the clocks.' David picked up a silver pocket watch with the figure of a griffin engraved on the cover. He examined it then nodded. 'Perfect. That's Izana's birthday present taken care of.'

'Is his birthday soon? I don't want to be caught unprepared like I was for Gareth's yesterday.'

'Next month on the twenty-ninth, and I did apologise for that. But Gareth liked the bottle of narapet wine you gave him. I still can't believe Wyvern let you have it.'

'It's not like I was going to be the one drinking it.'

'I meant that he let you have that particular one from his collection. It's one of the most expensive vintages you can buy.'

Rhiannon looked at him in shock. 'It is? He never told me.'

'May I help you, young man?'

The gruff, masculine voice was accompanied by the appearance of its owner at David's side, a grandfatherly figure in fine pearl-grey robes with a long white beard and half-moon spectacles.

'Yes, I'd like this one, thank you, Gustav,' David replied, holding up the pocket watch in his hand. 'Also, do you have one with any tree designs?'

Gustav nodded. 'I have several. The best is this one with a rowan tree.'

David examined it as thoroughly as he had the one for Izana before announcing he would take it as well.

'That will be twenty gold pieces.'

Rhiannon watched as David handed the money over without hesitation.

'I'm amazed you only bought yourself the one,' she remarked when they walked away, the two wrapped watches in David's pocket.

'Then prepare to be astonished because it's not for me,' he said. 'It's for Derrick.'

'Let me guess, his birthday is coming up too.'

'Not until the fourteenth of December but I want to give him this before term starts again. I saw his watch yesterday and he really needs a new one.'

Suddenly, a hard force rammed into Rhiannon, knocking her

sideways into David. His arm curled about her protectively and they both looked down as a penitent cry of, "m sorry, miss!' rang out.

A dishevelled boy of ten or eleven nervously gazed up at them.

'It's all right,' Rhiannon said kindly. 'You didn't hurt me.'

'Did you get separated from your mother and father?' asked David, noticing the absence of any parental figures behind the boy.

'Pa's out at sea and me Ma's at 'ome. I came with ol' Brimsby.'

'Who's Brimsby?'

The boy's thin shoulders lifted in an expressive shrug. 'She be a'stayin' at the inn near me 'ome, and she done give me a gold coin to 'ands out some papers.'

'Papers?'

The boy held out the bundle in his right hand. 'She said to wait till she left afore I 'anded them out, but you can look.'

David took the papers and gazed at the top one. As he read the printed words, his eyes narrowed and his jaw tightened ominously. He returned his attention to the boy.

'Do you know what these say?' he demanded.

'I seen the word dragons and tried readin' 'em but there's lots o' big words. I still ain't too good with me letters,' he added self-consciously, 'an' ol' Brimsby wouldn't tell me.'

The papers crinkled under the hard grip of David's hand. 'Where is this Brimsby?'

''er wagon's over there.' The boy pointed towards a stall selling a variety of lamps and candles. A prosperous looking middle-aged woman with a charming smile was talking to a small group as she polished one of the lamps.

'Is that Brimsby?' David asked.

The boy nodded.

'What's your name?'

'Theo.'

David lifted the papers in his hand. 'If you give these out you'll get into a lot of trouble, Theo, so I'll keep a hold of them. Now, how were you going to get home?'

'I seen Mrs Crickleton's stall over there. She'll let me go with 'er if I helps mind 'er rugs.'

'Then off you go.'

Theo turned to leave then paused. He looked back at David, his expression resignedly woeful. 'Should I give ol' Brimsby back the gold coin?'

'I don't think so. She told you to hand out the papers and you did. You handed them to me.' David reached into his money pouch and withdrew another gold coin. He handed it to Theo with an approving, 'That's for your honesty.'

His eyes as round as saucers, Theo stammered his thanks, gave a clumsy bow and took off.

'What do the papers say?' Rhiannon asked.

In answer, David handed her one.

She cast her eyes over it, then wished she hadn't.

'This is disgusting! Endrille and the other dragons are intelligent creatures, not mindless beasts to be enslaved and slaughtered for body parts!'

'And they certainly never asked to be worshipped by humans,' David declared, taking the paper back. He looked up and surveyed the crowded road, then set off towards two uniformed guards positioned a short distance away.

'What're you going to do?' Rhiannon said, hastening to keep up with his long strides. 'Aren't you going to arrest her?'

'I'd have to announce who I am before I did it, and the Crown Prince arresting someone would have every single person stopping to gawk.'

Rhiannon had to concede the truth of that, although she and David soon discovered that seeing their prince dressed like a humble wayfarer was all it took to make the two guards stare.

Their astonished eyes darting from the crest on the sword's

scabbard David had revealed, to his shadowed face, both guards snapped to attention. 'Your Royal Highness!' they said in unison. 'How may we assist you?'

'What are your names?'

'Zevkar and Poringer, Sire,' the elder of the two replied.

'You both received the orders in regard to apprehending anyone found to be supporters of the faction in Graynor, did you not?'

The two men nodded.

David handed them the bundle of papers. 'The woman named Brimsby at the lamp and candle stall over there paid a young boy one gold coin to hand these out. I'm satisfied the boy was unaware of their content. However, Brimsby will need to be questioned by the Pelatarrof. She's to be put into one of the palace holding cells until tomorrow. And please have word about her sent to my father.'

The guards took a brief look at the papers. Their expressions turned grim. 'Consider it done, Sire,' they announced.

'Is either of you a mage?'

Zevkar nodded.

'Good. Do not give Brimsby a chance to cause a scene.'

The two guards promised the arrest would be done swiftly and with the greatest discretion, then marched off.

Rhiannon, sensing her friend would not want to continue to the palace until he had seen Brimsby taken into custody, was not surprised when David asked if she minded waiting until it was done.

'Of course not,' she replied.

And so they watched and waited.

True to their word the guards' arrest of Brimsby was done quietly and with the least amount of commotion. Zevkar and Poringer waited until there were no customers around the woman's stall before approaching her. The instant she saw them coming, Brimsby went to flee, only to be caught by the deep blue light of *Zevkar's Ketevos Charm*. As the mage led the prisoner towards the closest gate tower, Poringer began to dismantle Brimsby's stall and load it onto her wagon.

Despite the quiet efficiency of the arrest it had, of course, been noticed by some members of the crowd. A murmur that a dangerous criminal had been caught began to spread, the supposition prompting a few curious folk to wonder what Brimsby had done. David and Rhiannon walked away to the sound of a young couple announcing their belief she had been the one to burn Mrs Ralvern's farm, while a strident old lady decreed she was another vile creature like the one who killed King Lúrán and Queen Eleanor.

'She was plotting to murder King Stephen and Queen Maiwen, I have no doubt,' was the last remark they heard her say before the noise of the crowd muffled her voice.

'Who were King Lúrán and Queen Eleanor?' Rhiannon asked.

'My grandparents. They were killed before my father's twenty-first birthday.' David's gaze was fixed firmly ahead as he informed a shocked Rhiannon, 'One of the sailors on board the royal ship *Briella Star* murdered them in their sleep. He took his own life after committing the crime, and it was later discovered when the castle healers examined his body that a sickness lay inside his head. They're not sure why he targeted my grandparents, but if my father had been on the ship with them, everyone believes he would've died too.'

'Why wasn't he with them?'

'He was preparing to take his final exams at the Academy, otherwise he would've been. They loved going sailing together. After he received the news, he left the Academy and didn't return. At least, not as a student.'

'He never did his exams?'

'He did them, but his new duties as king took up a lot of his time so his professors arranged for him to take the exams at the palace after the funeral was over. He told me once that he found focusing on something else helped him deal with the grief of being left an orphan.'

'It's true. It does help,' Rhiannon said with the wisdom of experience. Then she smiled up at David. 'So does having very good friends.'

He returned her smile with a warm one of his own. 'Then I'll strive to be the best friend you'll ever have,' he promised, and wishing to distract her mind from any other melancholy thoughts, he took her hand in his and led her towards the next stall which contained a large display of music boxes.

Feeling the strength of David's fingers around hers once again, Rhiannon had to admit the sensation was not unpleasant. In fact, she realised she quite liked it. And when they reached the gate tower of the second inner wall, she wondered why she felt so happy that David had never once attempted to let go of her hand.

She was still puzzling over it when they used the transonus dais to get from the gate tower to the second level of the Upper South Wing of the palace. The flash of white light heralding their arrival on the dais disappeared, and David and Rhiannon stared in shock at the person seated on one of the fine chairs placed near the staircase across from the alcove.

'Izana! What're you doing here?'

In answer to David's startled query, the Robesman calmly lifted his head from his contemplation of the book in his hand and looked at them.

'You're dressed like you raided the Unclaimed Property Room,' he informed David, then offered placidly, 'I knew you would have to return here eventually to make yourself more presentable for your balcony appearance, though you are cutting it a bit fine. You've only got thirty minutes.'

'That's plenty of time for me,' David declared.

He stepped forward, only to be instantly reminded of

Rhiannon's small, feminine hand clasped in his. Knowing Izana would have seen them, David quietly released it and shot his Robesman a warning look, the severity of it slightly lessened by his own red cheeks.

'Where are the others?' he asked as they descended the dais.

'Waiting outside your chambers.'

'Of course they are,' David sighed. He turned to Rhiannon. 'See you back here in twenty minutes?'

She nodded. 'Although I'll probably be ready in fifteen,' she said, and took off down the hallway.

David watched her go until the soft utterance of his name drew his attention back to Izana. 'What is it?'

'You know I'm loyal to you,' his Robesman stated. 'I'd give my life to protect you. But if you ever hurt her, I'll thump you so hard you'll be seeing stars during the daytime for a week.'

David accepted the threat with perfect equanimity. 'I wouldn't expect anything less of you, Izana,' he said, and set off towards his chambers.

Rhiannon, dressed in an immaculate gown of yellow damask as befitted the ward of Sir Raeden Wyvern, and wearing her star crystal necklace, arrived back at the alcove to find David and his five Robesmen waiting for her.

Her friend was now arrayed in a formal blue tunic, white breeches and polished high boots of black leather. His pristine white cloak, richly embroidered with gold edgings, swept close to the ground and partially concealed his sword. On his head the coronet declaring his royal status shone brilliantly.

'You won't be sneaking off anywhere wearing that,' Rhiannon said, pointing to the crown.

'Don't remind me,' he answered dolefully. 'For the rest of the day I'll be trapped in an endless round of polite platitudes and have people staring at me like I'm some weird creature.'

'But you are a weird creature,' John pointed out.

'Did you enjoy looking at the stalls?' Gareth asked Rhiannon while David dealt his Chief Robesman a hard punch to the shoulder.

'I did, except for the incident with that woman Brimsby.'

'David told us about that,' said Eamon, a dark look appearing on his face. 'I hope they send her to Mérosorc!'

'It is fortunate the boy holding the papers bumped into you before he handed any of them out,' Derrick observed quietly. 'He may have found himself in the middle of a nasty scene if he had given one to an extremely volatile person.'

'Like my father,' said Gareth. 'He would've castigated the boy after reading a few lines before handing him over to a guard.'

Rhiannon, recalling how nervous Theo had been after running into her, knew he would have been terrified to have someone shouting at him – like whoever was now venting their displeasure to the guards at the bottom of the long staircase beside her.

The loud voice drew her and the others closer to the banister and they peered over it. Startled, they all stared at the sight of Oliver Donahue, David's normally polite uncle, curtly ordering the guards to let him pass and mount the staircase.

'As Queen Maiwen's brother I am entitled to full access of the palace wings.' This arrogant claim was immediately followed by, 'I demand you stand aside so I may visit with my nephew. I will have you dismissed from the Royal Guard if you hinder me.'

'With all due respect, Mr Donahue, your kinship to Her Majesty permits you access to the private areas of the palace only on the occasions when it has been approved by one of Their Majesties or His Royal Highness.' The red-cloaked captain spoke calmly, and yet there was a note of unmistakeable steel in his voice.

'Until you provide evidence of their approval for today or I receive a verbal command from them, I cannot allow you to pass.'

The captain's words did not go down well with David's uncle. In an acerbic tone he insulted the captain's parentage and intelligence before declaring the Royal Guard to be nothing but sheep.

'Maybe so, sir. However, we are sheep who know our duty,' came the captain's imperturbable reply. 'Now, move along, there's a good gentleman.'

Apparently realising he was waging an unwinnable battle, Oliver Donahue left, but not without first declaring his anger over certain archaic palace rules which treated family members like suspect criminals.

'What was that about?' Eamon exclaimed once he had gone. 'I've never seen him act like that before.'

'He was exceedingly rude,' Derrick remarked.

'Maybe Marcus is rubbing off on him,' said John.

Izana frowned and looked at David. 'Why would he be trying to visit you when he knows you and your parents will be appearing on the North Balcony in ten minutes?'

David shrugged and walked back towards the alcove. 'He's never tried to visit me in my chambers before, not even when I fought Marcus a few years ago and gave him a black eye.'

'Perhaps he was worried about you,' Rhiannon suggested. 'If he heard about you being involved in Brimsby's arrest he might've wanted to check that you were all right.'

'He could've done that after David finished on the balcony,' Gareth replied. 'It's also strange he'd get so angry over a rule he's known about since Their Majesties got married.'

'That was odd,' David agreed as he stepped up onto the dais. 'I've never heard him sound so unpleasant over such a trivial thing. If I'd wanted him to know I was here, I'd have intervened and asked him for an explanation.'

'You're not going to mention it to your parents then?' John asked.

David shook his head. 'My mother would be mortified if she knew how he spoke to one of the guards. I'll speak to Captain Middon about it later this evening. I'd do it now but I better not keep my parents waiting. Come on, there's room for everyone on here if we squeeze together.'

Rhiannon mounted the steps onto the dais and soon found herself squished between David and Izana, with Gareth close behind her. As they waited for John, Derrick and Eamon to join them, she looked from Izana to Gareth and asked when they would need to get over to the arena for the duelling tournament.

'Not for a while yet,' Gareth replied. 'As we're both in the open section we don't have to confirm our attendance until after the age sections are almost over.' He looked down and gave Rhiannon a teasing smile. 'Will you be cheering for me or Izana?'

A spark of mischief shone in Rhiannon's eyes. Recalling the name Gareth had mentioned that day in Cendillis after her visit to Madame Dubois, she answered blithely, 'I thought I'd cheer for Harris.'

A burst of masculine laughter sounded out around her when Gareth gave an appalled, 'What!' and she saw Izana's mouth twitch into an amused smile. Then David pressed the rune on the control panel and they transported away to the Lower North Wing in a flash of brilliant white light.

If Rhiannon had thought the castle road was packed, it was nothing compared to the crowd gathered in front of the palace for the royal appearance. A sea of people and House Faeries swarmed the grounds of the Upper Ward, and a roar of enthusiasm went up at the first sighting of the three crowned figures on the wide balcony accompanied by their personal aides. She had been informed it was customary in Álnair for all the Robesmen of the King and Crown Prince, along with the Queen's Ladies of the Girdle, to be positioned on the balcony during the royal appearance. Sir Raeden as Commander of the Guard was included and to her great surprise, so was she.

In the shadows of the balcony's arched doorway, she watched and listened as the Álnairians expressed their affection for their royal family in an outpouring of emotional cries and cheers. King Stephen, Queen Maiwen and David stood close to the banister and waved in reply. From her vantage point, Rhiannon observed her friend and saw the genuine warmth he was displaying towards the crowd.

'For all his dislike of feeling like a puppet on show at these events he does love his people,' John murmured beside her.

The feeling was obviously mutual. The crowd continued cheering and then burst into song. Everyone on the balcony around her joined in.

> *Arise! Arise!*
> *O valiant warriors, arise!*
> *Truth and honour are in peril,*
> *and blood now taints the sky.*
>
> *Innocence lies slain,*
> *a victim of evil pride.*
> *Harken to the dragons' call*
> *and hasten to their side.*
>
> *Injustice this day shall cease,*
> *and all fell deeds will end.*
> *Stand up and fight for loyalty's sake,*
> *and let your resolve not break.*
>
> *The foe shall flee before us,*
> *no match for our stalwart hearts.*
> *And evermore will it be said,*
> *'Good is the clan of O'Faenart.'*

'It's The Song of Conall, the first High King of Álnair,' Izana informed Rhiannon when the crowd began cheering again. 'He's said to have spoken those words after one of the bloodiest murders of a group of Parvus hatchlings and their parents. The English translation was put to music over a hundred years ago by Elwyn Nasdale. It's now become a tradition for it to be sung on Open Days and after a coronation.'

'Then I'll definitely have to learn it,' Rhiannon said.

'Polansi could teach it to you.'

'Who's he?'

'One of the palace House Faeries and David's old flute teacher.'

Rhiannon was astonished. 'David plays the flute?'

'Ever since he was five. He's quite good at it but now he mainly only plays when he wants to relax or if he's troubled by something.'

Rhiannon thought of everything that had been happening recently and how much it was disturbing her friend. 'He must be getting in a lot of practice,' she murmured.

'Rhiannon!'

The sound of her name being called drew her attention back to the three O'Faenarts.

King Stephen gestured for her to join them. 'You're the first person of Mórell's line to stand on this balcony. Come. Let the people see you properly.'

Hesitantly, she moved forward. This was nothing like being in front of the multitude at the Dragon's Cup. Then, the crowd's furore had mostly been due to the competitive nature of the race, their support divided between each of the Riders. She had also had other more dire things on her mind every time she stood in front of them. But here, on the balcony, she was not the Dragon Cup Champion. She was merely a girl who was owed no particular loyalty or friendship by any member of the crowd. The closer she got to the banister the more her eyes widened, especially when she saw the throng of people gathered on the terrace and grounds below.

When she reached David's side, he smiled at her and instructed, 'Just wave like you saw us doing.'

Rhiannon swallowed, her throat feeling as if shards of glass were lodged inside it. She slowly raised her hand and gave a small wave. Thunderous applause broke out along with a rousing cheer.

Stunned by the Álnairians' reaction, Rhiannon stared down at them. She felt a warm prickling behind her eyes. Old and young faces alike were smiling up at her, the sincerity of their happy greeting filling her with a reciprocal sense of affection. Her nervous expression eased and she waved again, the beautiful smile on her lips gracing her features with a singular sweetness.

The people and House Faeries gathered in the castle grounds loudly voiced their approval.

'You'll never escape their love now,' David said.

Rhiannon turned to see him gazing at her, his expression hard to decipher but his eyes darkened to a deep violet hue.

'In fact, it's a good thing you're not entering the tournament,' he continued lightly. 'If you were, I don't believe any of the other competitors would have any supporters left to cheer them on.'

Several hours later Rhiannon sat in the stands of the castle's great arena and snorted in amusement when she recalled David's words. The Álnairians may have accepted her but she doubted that would have influenced them to transfer their support of the best duellists to her. The clamorous applause following the announcement of each winner of the age sections was enough to convince her that, when it came to duelling, the Álnairians gave their support to whichever competitor was the most talented.

She was pleased when both Leila Hardinge and Simon Truscott from the castle school won their sections. Leila had worked hard with John to help her perfect her sword technique, and she narrowly defeated Nia Attwater, while Simon wielded his sword with enough vigour and expertise to claim victory in the armed combat section, and then used his mage abilities to great effect against a student from Graynor.

But now the tournament was reaching its climax.

The open sections had seen many fierce confrontations. Now, since Izana had claimed victory in the magi competition by encasing his exhausted rival in a hard sphere of crystallised wind and sand, the two finalists who had defeated all their other opponents in armed combat were to face each other – right after King Stephen and Sir Raeden finished their sparring match.

Rhiannon watched the king and her guardian leave the Royal Podium, then descend into the cleared arena. David chose that moment to inform her of the tradition where the King and the Commander of the Guard sparred before the last duel.

Because they were both awakened magi, the fight between them was a mesmerising combination of magic and armed combat. Their speed was phenomenal, and the stark contrast between King Stephen's gold hair and the raven black of Sir Raeden's was the only discernible difference between the two tall men, for their skills and abilities were perfectly matched.

A blinding clash of emerald-green and scarlet sparks lit up the arena, the resulting yellow flash of the blending colours transforming the pale sand on the ground to a brilliant ocean of gold. Then King Stephen and Sir Raeden both lowered their swords. They made the same sweeping gesture with their left hand over the ground. In front of the admiring eyes of their audience, a pillar of sand formed around them and then burst outwards in a shower of glittering silver-blue lights.

'They're declaring a draw,' David explained as an explosion of cheers and applause sounded out from the audience. 'If they'd kept going, we'd probably be here for another couple of hours.'

'I never knew your father was so good,' Rhiannon said. 'Your mother told me she was once a champion duellist, so your father must have been too.'

David shook his head. 'Not officially. Neither the ruler of Álnair nor his heir are supposed to enter competitive events. If we could I'd have been entering this tournament every year after I turned twelve. As it is, I must be satisfied with sparring and mock battles.'

'Thank goodness for small mercies,' John said under his breath.

A loud trumpet blast sounded, announcing the final duel was about to commence.

'Who do you think will win?' Rhiannon asked as two very familiar figures took their positions in the middle of the arena.

David considered the two finalists. 'It's hard to say,' he pronounced after a moment. 'They're both excellent swordsmen, and while Gareth has the advantage of being slightly taller, Izana is nimbler and lighter on his feet. Until their time runs out, or one of them makes a mistake, I don't think anyone could say for certain which of them will win.'

David's words proved to be prophetic. From the first strike of their swords, the ebb and flow of the duel was never completely in favour of either Izana or Gareth. Neither could gain a significant advantage over the other. Each employed every skilful trick at their command to lure the other into giving them an opening, but time and again they failed.

Thrust and parry.

A feint and dodge.

The dangerous dance continued with both participants never flagging or making one misstep.

The entire audience was captivated.

Finalists were granted a maximum timeframe of twenty minutes for their duel, but even the judges became so caught up in the fierce display of skilled swordsmanship that it took the palace bells chiming the hour of five for them to bring the fight to an abrupt halt – a full fifteen minutes overtime!

The booming voice of the head judge rang throughout the arena. 'A draw, ladies and gentlemen! For the first time in fifty-seven years we have a draw!'

Izana and Gareth stepped away from each other and bowed to deafening applause. The audience's cries of adulation continued as the two Robesmen made their way up to the Royal Podium to stand in front of King Stephen.

The ruler of Álnair rose out of his seat and held up his hands for silence. The noise from the crowd faded almost instantly, the sudden quiet allowing King Stephen's words to easily carry to the farthest point of the arena.

'I believe we will all agree that these two young men have demonstrated an outstanding degree of skill during this tournament. They have proved themselves to be exceptional duellists, but it is their gracious conduct towards each of their defeated opponents which has impressed me the most. I therefore take great pleasure in awarding this year's champion duellist title for armed combat to both Izana Sato and Gareth Harulf.'

Two House Faeries appeared beside King Stephen, each one carrying a laurel wreath on a red velvet cushion. Rhiannon watched as David's father, with great ceremony, first placed a wreath on Izana's head and then on Gareth's. The crowd broke into loud applause once more.

'Congratulations,' she heard King Stephen say quietly. 'And I'm grateful my son will have such talented fighters to assist him should the need ever arise.'

Both Robesmen bowed deeply, their expressions solemn. Then they turned and acknowledged the crowd's chorus of praises with a respectful salute, their right arm placed across their chest as they slowly lowered their head. In the glow of the setting sun, their long fair hair gleamed with the radiance of precious metal freshly burnished.

When the cheering finally began to lessen, King Stephen

addressed the crowd again. 'My good people, sadly, this concludes today's tournament. However, you may continue to enjoy the stalls and explore the open areas of the palace and castle grounds for the next four hours. A reminder that there is a colony of Ríyun Dragons resting in the lagoon, so please refrain from disturbing them; their hatchlings have had a rather tiring day. For those approved to encamp within the lower and middle wards for the night, I ask only that you heed any directions given by the castle guards. Now, I pray you will all be blessed with a safe journey home, and hopefully we shall see you back here for the summer Open Day in July next year.'

A rousing cry of enthusiasm greeted his last words and then the crowd began their mass exodus from the arena.

'Izana! Gareth!'

The two Robesmen looked down towards Rhiannon who was hurrying over to them. Their mouths curved up in answer to the bright smile on her face.

'You look like you enjoyed the fight,' said Gareth.

'I did. You two were amazing! And before you ask, I was cheering for you both!'

'She's telling the truth,' said David, but then added with a laugh, 'although, her cheers did tend to reflect whoever appeared to have the upper hand at each particular moment.'

'Well, I do like both of you,' Rhiannon explained to the highly amused champions. 'It was difficult to choose a favourite.'

'I guess you wouldn't have had that problem if David was allowed in the tournament,' Eamon teased, then winced at the sharp kick John directed at his ankle.

None of those present missed the fiery blush in Rhiannon's cheeks, and Izana took it upon himself to divert everyone's attention by asking if anyone had seen Professor Tysus.

'He's never missed a tournament, and I'm interested to find out what he thinks of the draw,' he said.

'Wasn't he one of the champions the last time it happened?' John asked.

'He was,' Derrick replied, 'and he's over there speaking with Lord Sedgewick.'

Startled, the rest of the group looked to where he was pointing and saw Lord Sedgewick was indeed visiting Cendillis again. He was in the second level of the stands, his younger daughter shifting nervously behind him as he spoke to an animated Professor Tysus.

'I'm amazed Sedgewick managed to get Cassandra in here,' said Eamon. 'She's always avoided coming out of her chambers during Open Day.'

'He didn't have anything to do with her coming today,' David revealed. 'We saw her in the library last week and once she heard Izana was going to be entering the tournament, she said she'd come watch.'

A delicate pink shade appeared in Izana's cheeks. Rhiannon saw him glance at Cassandra, his eyes revealing his deep affection for the girl.

'I'll go and ask if she wants to join us,' she announced, and took off before any of her companions could answer.

Ignoring the aisles, she headed for the solid partition separating the Royal Podium from the rest of the stands.

'She's not intending to go over it, is she?' Gareth asked, astonished.

More familiar with Rhiannon's occasional bursts of unorthodox behaviour, David, Izana, John and Eamon promptly answered with an amused, 'Yes, she is.'

And to Gareth's disbelief that was precisely what she did.

Gathering the hem of her gown to up past her knees, a move which had David and all his Robesmen hastily averting their eyes from the sight of her bare legs, Rhiannon stepped over the stone wall and swiftly placed herself on the other side. Not stopping to look back, she missed seeing David pull at the high collar of his tunic, as though the loose garment was choking him, and the heightened colour in his face as he kept his gaze focused on the opposite side of the arena.

Rhiannon quietly approached Cassandra who was yet to notice her presence. As she drew closer, she heard Lord Sedgewick ask, 'What about the areas not accessible to everyone? Surely the plans for those rooms aren't made available?'

'My dear fellow, of course they are, so long as you have the proper approval,' declared Professor Tysus.

'You've seen them?'

'Several times. His Majesty and his father before him, King Lúrán, have been most supportive of my research.'

'You've seen the plans several times? I suppose you must be able to draw them in your sleep by now?' Lord Sedgewick said with a jovial laugh.

'Quite a few of them at least,' came the old professor's honest reply.

'Including those for the Upper West Wing?'

It was at that inauspicious moment for Rhiannon's curiosity that Cassandra turned and saw her. The First Seer hastily stammered out a short, 'I…I-I'll go now, Father.' Her departure went unacknowledged, Lord Sedgewick being too engrossed in his conversation with Professor Tysus to pay her any heed.

The two girls took the more decorous, and therefore longer way to the Royal Podium where David and his Robesmen were waiting. Rhiannon cast a frowning glance back over her shoulder at Lord Sedgewick. The man had not only ignored his daughter but there was something about his interest in the castle plans, especially his specific mention of the Upper West Wing, that made her uneasy.

That was where the apartments for David's parents were located, she remembered. Why would he be interested in the plans for that area? In fact, why would he be asking about the plans at all?

He didn't seem like the sort to take an academic interest in them. Not like Professor Tysus.

Further questions arose in her mind even as she and Cassandra discussed the tournament, and they continued to form when the young seer warmly congratulated Izana on his two champion titles.

'It does seem out of character,' David said after she quietly mentioned to him the conversation she had overheard. 'He's certainly never expressed an interest in seeing the plans in all the times my father and I have spoken to him in Ardara. Still, he won't be able to see them without permission, and Professor Tysus would never do anything to jeopardise his chances of getting into the Archive's restricted area again by doing something stupid like drawing one of the plans from memory.'

'Are you saying that there's no need to be paranoid about Sedgewick possibly being up to something?'

David shook his head. 'No, I'm not saying that, because sometimes, the intuition of a mage is more reliable than all logic and reason. If you feel uneasy over something, particularly an apparently innocent conversation, there's bound to be a reason for it. I'll let my father know; but, for the moment, I believe the Pelataroff will be more concerned over Brimsby's actions than Sedgewick's sudden interest in the plans of the castle buildings.'

~Chapter 12~

A DISASTROUS OUTING

Brimsby was dead.

The residents of Valieoth Castle awoke to the disturbing news the morning after Open Day. The woman's cold corpse was found in her holding cell with a single stab wound to the heart. There was no weapon with the body and none of the guards reported seeing anything unusual.

A full investigation was carried out by the Pelatarrof and Sir Raeden over the course of several months. Christmas and New Year passed, as did David's sixteenth birthday and Easter, and yet not one clue was discovered to help identify the killer. Security was increased in the castle grounds. Even the House Faeries discreetly kept surveillance on anyone walking through the hallways and corridors of the palace.

Lord Sedgewick, having satisfied the Pelatarrof as to his whereabouts when the murder took place, returned to Ardara and nothing more appeared to come of his interest in the castle plans. David reported his father had received no request from the nobleman for permission to access the restricted area of the Hall of Archives before he departed, and Professor Tysus, during one of his frequent visits to research the castle's transonus system, said the man had not sent so much as a short missive to him after their conversation in the arena.

However, Rhiannon still could not shake the feeling Lord Sedgewick's queries arose from something more than idle curiosity. Not that she had mentioned this to Cassandra. There was no lack of opportunity because the First Seer continued to help in the search for Merlin's laboratory, but Rhiannon was reluctant to say anything which might cause a rift in their friendship.

'He's still her father,' she said to David when they reached the door to her chamber after another unsuccessful search for Merlin's laboratory. 'I'm sure if I told her I suspected he was up to something she'd refuse to speak to me again.'

'Perhaps,' he replied, 'although I doubt it. She certainly appears fonder of you than she does of him, which is hardly surprising. In the space of several months, you've shown more interest in her than he has for the past few years.'

'It helps that I live here,' Rhiannon pointed out fairly.

'So do a lot of other people, but most of them don't go out of their way to visit her. Besides, he barely even writes to her. In all the time she's been here, she's only received *two* letters from him,' David disclosed with a moue of disgust.

'She has mentioned that to me,' Rhiannon said. Unexpectedly, she smiled. 'Along with the stories of how you and the others always make an effort to spoil her on her birthday.'

David pointed down the hall to where his rostered Robesman for March was waiting for him. 'Most of the credit for that belongs to Izana. He's the one who arranges everything. He always seems to know what she'll like.'

'Then he can decide the location for our next day out before school restarts next week. I asked Cassandra if she wanted to come tomorrow but when she heard we're going to Luwyneth Cove she said no.'

David looked surprised. 'I thought she'd enjoy going.'

'So did I, but she said she always feels uneasy whenever she considers going anywhere near it. I thought it might've been because she had an accident there once; however, she said it's just that she gets overwhelmed by a sense of impending disaster whenever she thinks of the place.'

'I didn't know that,' David said, looking slightly ashamed. 'We can go somewhere else.'

'I said that to Cassandra but she didn't want to upset our plans. She insisted we go tomorrow and she'll finish off her homework. I couldn't persuade her otherwise.'

'She can be rather stubborn. Just like another girl I know,' David finished with a teasing smile.

'I have no idea whom you mean,' replied Rhiannon, although the twinkle in her eyes belied her innocent tone. 'And before you start naming names, I'll be off to bed. See you in the morning.'

'Good night. Don't forget to dress warmly tomorrow. These last few days of March always bring a sudden cold wind in from the south.'

Rhiannon shivered, remembering being caught out the previous year during a training session with Sir Raeden outside the school. He had not been happy to discover she had forgotten to bring a cloak and gloves.

'I'll remember,' she promised, and when she entered her bedchamber, she made sure to lay out her thickest woollen cloak and her best riding gloves. They would be going to Luwyneth Cove on horseback and she had no desire to arrive frozen stiff and looking like an ice statue.

She changed into her nightgown and got into bed, pausing only to start the music box which now adorned the right bedside table. Of exquisite craftsmanship, it had been David's main Christmas present to her. Decorated by the figures of four beautiful dryads dancing under the canopy of a tall willow tree, the hauntingly tender melody it played was an old Álnairian lullaby.

Snuggled under the coverlet on the bed, Rhiannon laid her head on the soft pillow and closed her eyes. The enchanted music box continued to play, and as she slipped into peaceful slumber, inside her mind she heard the echo of David's voice from when he had sung the lullaby to her on Christmas morning.

The next day, dawn came in a glorious display of radiant light spread across a clear horizon. Not a cloud could be seen in the azure sky and when a party set forth from Valieoth Castle, the Dairíon Ocean was a glittering reflection of its heavenly neighbour.

Accompanied by Izana, John and, on King Stephen's insistence, a small company of guards, David and Rhiannon crossed Haldoron Bridge, then followed the coastline eastwards, their intent to enjoy a picnic lunch at Luwyneth Cove. There was already a chill wind blowing in from across the sea which stirred the cloaks and hair of the riders, and caused the fields of wild heather to dance in a rippling purple-blue wave. The journey would take a few hours; however, despite the cold wind, the spirits of the group were high, for the last patches of snow were now all melted and Rhiannon's exuberant desire to see more of Álnair had put them all in a cheerful mood.

David glanced again at his friend's laughing expression and hoped she would not be disappointed with their destination.

Magnificently beautiful. That was the only phrase Rhiannon could think of to describe Luwyneth Cove. The serenity of its isolation broken only by the distant cry of a gull and the soft murmur of lazily rolling waves, the oval-shaped inlet was a paradise of gold sand and crystal blue water in the late morning sunshine. Guarded by the sentinel forms of the Kinpar Rocks at its watery entrance and the gentle slope of green scrubland behind, the small cove made for a perfect picnic location.

Captain Morton and his men, having been given charge of the

horses, were nothing more than a faint whisper of voices farther up the beach, considerately maintaining an unobtrusive distance from their prince and his companions.

Now clad only in her riding dress of lilac wool and seated on the warm sand with the remnants of a small feast laid out on the blanket in front of her, Rhiannon inhaled deeply, savouring the stimulating sea breeze as she brushed a strand of hair out of her eyes. On her right, David pointed towards the largest of the Kinpar Rocks.

'I found your star crystal near there,' he said. 'In summer, when the water will be warmer, we could ask Arastar to bring us one evening and I'll take you out to have a look at the others gathered around its base. There are so many different colours it's like looking at a tangle of rainbows.'

'You can leave me behind on that occasion,' John announced with a shudder from his place next to Izana on the other side of the blanket. 'Derrick or Gareth will be on duty and I'm sure they'd enjoy flying about in the dark.'

'Gareth certainly would,' David replied before selecting another pastry and lounging down on his side again. He looked at his other Robesman and asked, 'What about you, Izana?'

'I'll come,' was the prompt reply. 'Once I start at the Academy, I won't have much opportunity to go looking at star crystals for a while.'

A slight shadow crossed David's face. 'No, I suppose you won't, and school won't seem the same without you. Not that I'd want you to stay behind for another year to suit me,' he added hastily. He looked pointedly at John. 'I already have someone doing that, despite my telling him it's not necessary.'

'I consider it to be very necessary,' his Chief Robesman replied. 'If I'm not around, who'll keep you from becoming an insufferable popinjay?'

Laughter broke out around the picnic blanket and David, his

expression amused, picked up an apple and threw it at John. 'You seem to have forgotten Wyvern,' he said.

'Not good enough. You only listen to him when you have to.'

'Rhiannon, then.'

'She's too nice.'

'I've called him a complete blockhead several times,' Rhiannon interjected. 'Does that count?'

Izana gave a choked sound of amusement. 'It does,' he smiled.

'See, no danger of me turning into a full-fledged peacock,' David said to John. 'You should start at the Academy in September with Izana.'

John shook his head. 'You won't get me to change my mind.'

'You really must be a glutton for punishment.'

'Not at all. I simply prefer to be on hand in case your impetuous nature gets the best of you.'

'Are you sure you're not my old nurse Frieda? That sounds like something she used to say,' David remarked drily, before putting aside his joking manner to announce, 'but in all seriousness, John, you're being ridiculous. I know you worry, not only over me but everyone you care about, but you don't have to shoulder the entire responsibility for our safety.'

'You won't convince him, David,' said Izana. 'He's been like that for as long as I've known him. The only way to get him to leave is to order him to go; but even then he'd probably find a way to get the Academy to continue to defer his entry until you're due to attend.'

'Having a relative as the headmaster does have its perks,' John admitted. He saw Rhiannon's look of surprise and explained, 'He's my father's uncle, Amon Tremaine. He was the professor of languages at the Academy before he got the position of headmaster, so he and David always have fun whenever they happen to meet. They'll switch languages halfway through a conversation to try and confuse each other.'

'Has it ever worked?'

At Rhiannon's question, David rolled onto his back to gaze up at her, his head close to her hip. 'On me, not since I was eleven,' he said. 'I've managed to catch him out a few times.'

'That's because you cheat and use a language he doesn't know.'

Izana's dry comment drew a laugh from David.

'It's not cheating when both of us agreed the only rule is that the language has to be one known in Álnair. Can I help it if I happen to know a few more than him?'

His question went unanswered.

'Does he mind when you use a language he doesn't know?' Rhiannon asked.

'No, he finds it amusing. He once told me if I hadn't been born a prince, he would've offered me the position of professor of languages when Professor Valancy moved to Graynor.'

'That was only two years ago,' John revealed.

Rhiannon stared down at David who now had his eyes shut against the glare of the sun. With his face relaxed and unguarded he appeared more like a young boy than someone capable of lecturing a classroom of adults for the past two years.

'If you weren't a prince, would you have accepted his offer?' her curiosity prompted her to ask.

A small frown creased David's brow and he considered the question in silence for a moment. Then he said, 'Probably,' his eyes still closed. 'Once you turn fourteen you're allowed to be employed, and, I suppose, until I discovered if I preferred to do something else, being paid to teach a subject I'm proficient in could only be a proper use of my talent.'

'What about the students? Wouldn't it be odd lecturing people older than you?'

A grin of unholy amusement spread across David's face. 'That would be the fun part,' he declared, and when he reopened his eyes there was a mischievous sparkle in their violet depths. 'Getting to tell a group of adults what to do – what fourteen-year-old wouldn't like to do that? Now, I don't know about the rest of you,' he said, changing the subject, 'but I could really use a walk after that lunch.'

When all three of his companions agreed, he quickly stood up and offered a hand to assist Rhiannon to her feet.

After they had all brushed the sand off their clothing (and in David's case out of his hair), the Prince of Álnair and his two Robesmen picked up their swords from where they lay on the blanket and reattached them to their belts. Rhiannon left hers next to the remnants of their picnic.

'We won't be going far, will we?' she asked.

David shook his head. 'Just to the edge of the cove,' he replied. A sudden gust of wind catching at his white cloak made him enquire if she wanted to fetch hers from Kateri's saddle before they set off.

'I'll be fine,' Rhiannon assured him, and started off towards the surf.

David took a moment to call out their destination to Captain Morton then hurried after her. Izana and John shared a look and deliberately allowed the two in front of them to get a decent head start before following at a slower pace.

Their booted feet leaving two sets of footprints in the wet sand, David and Rhiannon were oblivious to the fact they had practically been left alone. A casual question by Rhiannon launched them into a serious discussion on the latest news from Graynor, and David's attention was so focused on relaying the contents of the Chief Consul's last report on a recently imprisoned criminal named Fotgroy that he failed to notice a strange shift in the air.

'They found the mutated bodies in a cell underneath his house. They're not sure how long Fotgroy had been involved with the faction, but he definitely had been conducting illegal experiments on people for at least five months.'

Rhiannon felt her lunch threatening to make a reappearance. 'And he was murdered in his cell?'

'Yes. His body was discovered with … LOOK OUT!'

Rhiannon lurched sideways as David pulled her towards him with a violent jerk, a strong breath of wind sending an onslaught of sand lashing against their exposed faces with biting harshness.

Then the wind vanished as abruptly as it had appeared.

Behind them, they heard Izana and John shouting their names. Blinded by flecks of grit in their eyes, neither saw the air begin to swirl around them, but they felt the rush of movement when the sand transformed into a gold whirlwind rising up to encircle their bodies.

And that was when Rhiannon grew afraid. She knew that sensation!

'David! It's a foramen! We have to move!'

'I'm trying, but I can't lift my feet off the ground!'

Horrified, Rhiannon realised he was right. She had not tried to move when she had been caught inside the foramen in Vetus svet, but now, when she knew she was straining her muscles to shift her feet even a millimetre off the ground, she discovered she could not.

John and Izana's loud calls increased, the echo of their desperate cries a sound Rhiannon and David would never forget.

David's arms tightened around Rhiannon.

Then, the world tilted and they were twirling upwards.

Rhiannon frantically clutched onto David. She recognised the feeling of being tugged into a vacuum and then spun like the blades of a pinwheel in a gale. The star crystal pendant around her neck repeatedly smacked against her chest.

David strove to quell the fear rising inside of him and simply held his friend, fervently hoping their journey through the foramen would soon end.

Still unable to see, neither saw the dizzying kaleidoscope of images morph into a palette of bleeding colours. Their bodies tumbled over and over at an increasing pace.

A sudden intense flood of heat enveloped them.

Then they were swiftly descending.

Rhiannon's hair became a chestnut curtain across David's face; his cloak, a white stream fanning out above them.

The deceleration when it came was abrupt, the sudden change making them both gasp. And then, with the gentleness of a mother placing her newborn child in their crib, the invisible force lowered them onto solid ground with precision.

A slight pause.

The wind disappeared.

Then a quiet stillness and the scent of fresh grass filled the air.

David and Rhiannon hurriedly worked to get the sand out of their eyes, desperate to see where the foramen had placed them. Wiping away the last piece of grit, they blinked rapidly and then slowly looked up, their expressions a blend of apprehension and dismay as they surveyed their new surroundings.

Chapter 13

FAR FROM HOME

Rhiannon and David looked at the narrow country road in front of them. Thick woodland lay on either side of the curved, muddy dirt track, the thin, moss-spotted birch trees rising like giant bulrushes from the sea of green scrubland and reaching for the ominously overcast sky above. Swirling, black clouds thwarted the sun's attempts to pierce the heavy veil. There was a chill in the air, along with a strong, damp scent which foretold of more rain. All else was still and silent, with not even the occasional birdsong from the dense undergrowth to disturb the quiet atmosphere.

Rhiannon shivered at the dismal scene and shot David a worried look. When she had gone through the foramen to Álnair, she left behind only a lifetime of misery and loneliness. She doubted a single person missed her, unless it was Annabelle regretting the loss of her slave. But David had family and friends whom he loved and who would worry over his disappearance. He was certain to be feeling anxious.

For his part, David was struggling to control the conflicting emotions whirling inside him. Mixed with the natural alarm he felt at being taken away from his family and everything familiar to him was a spark of curiosity to see the world of his ancestors – something he had never thought possible for him. He was also significantly concerned for Rhiannon. He knew she had not been happy in Vetus svet and to abruptly find herself returned to it must surely be unpleasant.

Then, a loud growling broke the silence. Both turned in the direction of the noise. It was coming closer, swiftly approaching the curve just a short distance from where they were currently standing.

Rhiannon's eyes widened in realisation.

'Get off the road! Hurry!'

Not stopping to argue with her, David obeyed Rhiannon's urgent command.

The ominous sound drew nearer.

Their feet slipping in the black mud of the road, they hurried to the grassy mound on the right and ran up its steep slope, the wet earth providing little grip for their booted feet.

Then Rhiannon went down, the long skirt of her riding dress catching underneath her foot.

David heard her cry out but was too late to catch her. He heard a sickening thud as Rhiannon's head connected with a sharp rock on the ground. She became frighteningly still.

'Rhiannon!'

David knelt beside her unconscious form, uncaring of the mud and grassy stains he would get on his white breeches. He carefully turned Rhiannon onto her back and lightly touched the side of her head. A warmth, like the one cast by a cheerful fire in winter, caressed his hand. He had only felt something like it three times before: Once when he had checked to see if Rhiannon was alive after being hit by the Glaciocaptus Charm; then when he had been trying to keep her lucid after being poisoned with somlyne; and lastly after she had inhaled the undiluted fumes of the narapet plant.

The growl became a thunderous roar.

His hand dropping to rest on the hilt of his sword, David looked up and prepared himself to confront whatever beast was about to appear.

Then he saw it.

A horseless carriage, powered by some strange magic and issuing a blistering cacophony of noise, the like of which he had never heard before. Of shining silver, built low to the ground, and the width of the entire road, it shot around the corner, its wheels skidding on the wet, unsealed surface. The carriage hood was down, and he caught a glimpse of a woman in the front seat before it zoomed past, flinging a splatter of sloppy debris towards him and Rhiannon's prone body.

'*Cosain!*'

The gold shield appeared, protecting them from the muddy assault. Then David coughed. A horrible smell was permeating the air. It smelt like Professor Egelbert's laboratory after one of his failed experiments had left behind a pungent smell of rotten eggs.

As the roaring carriage disappeared around the next bend, David looked at the spot where he and Rhiannon had been standing. Their footprints were still visible in the middle of the road, only now they lay between the two deep tracks made by the carriage's wheels. Had they remained on the road they surely would have been hit and killed.

'I hope there aren't too many of those things. It can't be at all safe having them using these roads,' he muttered before returning his attention to Rhiannon.

She still had not stirred. An image flashed through David's mind of the first time he had seen her. She had been lying motionless then too, and on the floor of a forest.

He shook the distressing memory away and focused on the present situation. He could see no sign of blood and her breath was regular. Nevertheless, needing the reassurance that there was no danger of her spirit leaving her body, he placed a hand on her forehead, closed his eyes and murmured a flow of words in Drakaron. A soft purple light, almost the same hue as his eyes, shone around their connected bodies.

'If you're trying to wake me, I'm already awake.'

Startled, and much relieved to hear her voice, David reopened his eyes to stare down into Rhiannon's gold ones and blinked as though blinded by a brilliant radiance.

'*Laus Deo!* I was checking to see if you were all right,' he said as the purple light faded.

'And the shiny glow?'

'It was from a healer's diagnostic technique. I'll teach it to you if you like.' A noise of agreement answered him and David gently smoothed his hand over Rhiannon's head.

Reluctant to say or do anything to bring a halt to the pleasant sensation of his fingers touching her hair, Rhiannon sighed and closed her eyes again.

Unfortunately, this had the opposite effect to what she wanted. David removed his hand from her head to grasp her shoulder.

'Rhiannon!'

The note of concern in his voice had her instantly peering up at his face again.

'I'm fine,' she hastily reassured him, and to lighten the mood, she added, 'I've already been knocked unconscious so I should be right until we go through another foramen.'

'Don't joke about that.' David's voice was sharp. 'Seeing you lying on the ground hurt is not something I ever want to see again.'

Observing the lingering haunted look in his eyes, Rhiannon regretted her attempt at humour.

'Sorry,' she offered sincerely, and wishing to divert his attention from her recent injury, said, 'I take it the car's gone by?'

'Car?' David repeated. 'Is that what the thing's called?'

Rhiannon slowly sat up and nodded.

'Yes, it went past,' David confirmed. 'And I hope it's the only one we'll come across.'

A laugh from his friend drew a frown from the bewildered prince as he helped her to stand. 'What's so funny?'

'There's little chance of it being the only one. Where one car is, you can be certain there'll be hundreds more.'

'Hundreds!' David shuddered in horror. 'The noise and smell from one were bad enough. And if everyone drives like that sapskull I'd feel safer walking into a herd of stampeding horses rather than using the same road as —' He broke off when a cold droplet of water landed on his nose and glanced up to see the storm clouds obliterating every trace of the sun.

'Looks like we're going to get soaked if we don't stop talking and get under shelter,' he said.

The rumble of thunder accompanied by a chill uprush of wind seemed to agree with him.

Rhiannon shivered under the single layer of her riding dress, regretting ever taking off her cloak in Luwyneth Cove.

'Here.'

David placed the blessed warmth of his thick cloak around her shoulders, the long garment spilling past her feet to pool on the damp grass like the white foam on a green sea.

'It should help keep you warm while I get this done.'

'Get what done?' Rhiannon asked, accepting David's proffered hand to reach the top of the mound. 'I thought we were going to look for shelter.'

'We don't have time to look for anything, the rain's about to come.' David paused. After a scan of the dense woodland in front of them, he pointed off to the right. 'That glade over there will do.'

'Do for what?'

'You'll see.'

Without any further explanation, David walked towards the clearing, which was by no means of an impressive size, being scarcely wide enough to stand two horses abreast in it. Rhiannon watched in bewilderment as he halted in the middle of the open space, then knelt on the ground.

The few spots of water began to increase in number until the entire forest was filled with the sound of rain blowing through the swaying treetops, the leaves a rustling chorus to the storm's growling symphony.

His cerulean-blue tunic swiftly becoming drenched, the Prince of Álnair laid both hands upon the damp grass and bowed his head. When he spoke, it was in a clear, unaffected voice. '*Ai Numen Fai, cenya oron sí nalbë. Tuae El'damo, Kor íquista.*'

The short Drakaron phrases made it easier for Rhiannon to use her limited knowledge of the language to translate the words inside her head: *O Blessed Light, raise up a mantle over this place. Grant us Your protection, we beseech You.*

There was a short pause. Then a soft glow, like that which heralds the rising sun, shone inside the clearing, its radiance reflecting off the rain in glistening sparkles of colour. The light illuminated David's body, even as the scattering of fallen leaves stirred about him. Rising into the air, their faded shade of pale yellow returned to a vivid, fresh green. As they rose higher, incandescent beams surrounded the circular border of trees like the winding tendrils of a creeping vine. When the leaves reached slightly above David's height when he stood, they stopped. The shafts of light enveloped them and hardened to form an impenetrable canopy over the glade. Then the luminous aura disappeared.

'*Arídakor nai arnor.*'

The Drakaron phrase of gratitude passed David's lips before he got to his feet and turned to beckon Rhiannon to his side.

She did not waste a single second in reaching him.

As she stepped through the tree line and into the glade, Rhiannon felt a slight breath of heated air pass over her which instantly removed all traces of her brief shower in the wild tempest. Looking back out into the forest, she saw the rain bouncing off an invisible barrier where the beams of light had encircled the clearing. And beneath her feet the ground, like her and David, was now perfectly dry.

'It's a temporary shelter,' explained David, removing his sword and leaning it against a tree trunk. 'A few years ago when my Robesmen and I got caught in a storm near Shaimar Forest, Derrick did something similar – only, of course, on a much larger scale.'

'How long will it last?' Rhiannon asked, settling herself on the thick layer of grass.

'Until there's no one left inside the protected area,' David answered, lowering himself to sit next to her. 'Once the rain eases off and the storm moves on, we can try calling out to King Brian. There's no chance of him or one of his people coming out in this.'

A brilliant flash of lightning and a mighty crash of thunder had Rhiannon offering the sage observation that nor would anyone in their right mind.

'Gareth would disagree with you,' David replied. 'He loves being outside during a storm and he certainly would've enjoyed this one. In fact, if he were here, he'd be standing out there laughing while trying to persuade us to join him.'

Rhiannon looked out to where the trees were groaning against the strong wind and the lashing torrent of rain cascaded down the enchanted barrier. She could imagine Gareth's long, fair hair being whipped about as he stood out there, looking up at the sky, his face alight with the thrill of battling against the elements. The mental image made her smile. But thoughts of Gareth naturally led to her thinking of all the other people she had come to know and like in Álnair, and her lips swiftly lost their amused upward tilt.

'How long do you think we'll be stuck here?' she asked.

David heard the slight despondent note in her voice and did

not hesitate to place his arm around her shoulders in a gesture of comfort. 'It all depends on when the next foramens will occur,' he answered. 'But we will get home. King Brian and his people have never failed to retrieve anyone who got brought here.' Seeing that Rhiannon's downcast expression had not eased completely, he added lightly, 'On second thought, let's stay. After disappearing right in front of them, John and Izana will be the worst mother hens once we go back.'

A snort of weak laughter preceded Rhiannon's next words. 'Maybe Izana will defer going to the Academy as well.'

David gave her a slight shake. 'Don't even joke about it,' he said, half-laughing, half-serious. 'He's the type who would do it if he thought he had to. And just like with John, I'd never be able to convince him otherwise.'

Rhiannon was silent for a moment, then asked, 'Does it really bother you so much that John won't go?'

David looked out at the stormy scene in front of them and sighed. 'I hate feeling like I'm holding him back. If it weren't for me, he'd be attending classes at the Academy and learning far more than he can simply by reading the materials the professors at the school provide to him.'

'He may feel obligated to remain with you, but I don't think he'd ever consider himself to be disadvantaged by staying. From what I've seen, he cares more about looking after the people important to him than how well he does in his studies.' Rhiannon paused, then admitted quietly, 'After living in Álnair, I now understand how he can feel that way.'

David's forehead creased in a deep frown. 'Do you mean there was never anyone who was important to you here? You told me no one had ever called you their friend, but surely there was someone you felt close to; a good neighbour or a teacher?'

'There wasn't anyone. In fact, before your mother hugged me

that first time after the hearing, I can't remember ever receiving a single one.'

Memories of all the embraces his parents, grandparents, aunts and uncles had lavished upon him from his earliest years ran through David's mind. That his friend had been deprived of such a simple gesture of affection horrified and angered him. His arm tightened around her, pressing her deeper into his side, and Rhiannon, her heart filled with a need to be closer to him, made no attempt to move away.

'I was never anything special to my foster parents,' she continued in a low voice. 'Maybe if I had been things would've been different. But I didn't have anything they could show off like they did with Annabelle. I'm not beautiful or a music prodigy.'

'I haven't a clue about your musical skill,' David interjected. 'But I know you're the prettiest girl I've ever met.'

Rhiannon knew enough of her friend to know he wouldn't pay her an empty compliment. She looked up and encountered the sincere admiration reflected in his eyes. A faint blush spread across her cheeks even as she ducked her head, saying, 'I was always told I was too short and stocky.'

'Why should that preclude you from being pretty?' David asked, sounding genuinely puzzled. 'Your height and build are like the outer frame on a painting – they provide a shape for the canvas and can be quite nice, but they have little to do with whether the picture is truly lovely.'

Rhiannon tilted her head back to stare up at him. 'So what does?'

'Kindness and malice both leave an indelible mark on a person's face, so to me it's the spirit infused in the blend of colours and lines which make someone pretty or ugly, regardless of what their features may be.' David lowered his head, his warm gaze holding Rhiannon's. 'And you have the kindest and most generous heart of any girl I know, so don't think I'm only saying you're beautiful because I like you.'

Rhiannon felt the breath catch in her throat at the intense emotion she glimpsed in David's expression. It had been over seven months since the day in the castle woodlands when he had last declared his feelings for her so openly.

'Even if all I felt for you was the same brotherly fondness I have for Alice, I'd still say you were the prettiest girl I've met,' David finished softly.

An overwhelming desire to press her lips to his assailed Rhiannon. The feeling suffused her entire being, and with it came the realisation that the affection she had long felt for David had grown to possess the strength and power of the sun. She shifted her body until their faces were only a few inches apart, striving to find the words to tell him. She could see the individual flecks of colour in the irises of his violet eyes.

David's head dropped even lower, the warmth of his breath causing Rhiannon's lips to tingle in curious anticipation.

He's going to kiss me!

The voice in her mind was equal parts deliciously nervous and girlishly eager.

'Rhiannon, I lo—'

David's quiet voice abruptly fell silent. He swallowed hard, a pained expression crossing his face as he stared down at his friend for a long moment. His eyes closed. To Rhiannon's confused dismay he appeared to struggle with himself before finally lifting his head away from her.

'I'm sorry. I almost broke my promise not to pester you, didn't I?' he said, his voice strangely hoarse.

'Huh?'

Rhiannon's bewilderment lasted only long enough for her to remember the words he had spoken to her that day on the gazebo's bridge. Before she had a chance to inform David of her altered feelings he was saying, 'And I'd hate myself if I took advantage of your upset state and manipulated your emotions for my benefit.'

Rhiannon stared at him in disbelief. 'What?'

'I can only imagine how you hate being back in Vetus svet, and with only me here with you, you might confuse gratitude for something deeper.'

Indignation sent a fiery heat to Rhiannon's cheeks. 'Are you saying I'm incapable of identifying my own emotions?' she demanded, pulling away from him.

'No! Well, that is, not normally.'

David's flustered response did nothing to appease Rhiannon's sudden surge of annoyance. 'Meaning that I am incapable under abnormal conditions,' she bit out crossly.

'That's not … I only meant …' Completely befuddled, David shook his head. 'Why're you so angry? I'm only trying to do the right thing. Master Zhen explained that in a stressful situation people can misidentify their emotions and I don't want to do anything which might confuse you about how you really feel.'

'You don't have a very high opinion of the strength of my mind.'

David's own temper started to flare. 'I'm not saying you're weak-minded!'

'You just did!' Rhiannon's cry almost drowned out the sound of the other storm raging outside the enchanted barrier.

'I meant I don't want to do anything which could influence your emotions while you're stuck here with only me for company.' David stood up and turned away. 'I almost kissed you, Rhiannon. And if I had you might've started to think you like me as much as I like you, but once we return to Álnair you'd remember you weren't sure and possibly even despise me for taking advantage of the situation.' His shoulders slumped as he confessed, 'I couldn't bear it if you did that.'

Rhiannon's anger evaporated at these words, along with her

intention of telling him of her altered feelings. There was no way he would believe her if she told him now.

But once we get back to Álnair I'll tell him, she thought. Aloud she said, 'David, I may sometimes want to throw something heavy at your head or put stink beetles in your boots, but I could never despise you.' Gathering the voluminous folds of his cloak and her riding dress away from her feet, she carefully stood up and reached out to touch her friend's arm. 'You're my best friend and –'

'Conan, ya feckin' eejit! Where'n y' goin' this time?'

The exasperated yell barely finished sounding out when a dark, wet form leapt through the treeline and launched itself at the two magi with a chorus of happy barks. A short distance away amidst the slim birch trees, Rhiannon and David saw a tall, white-haired man with the bearing of a veteran soldier striding towards them whilst ordering the dog to get down.

David swiftly grabbed Rhiannon's hand and moved so they both stepped out of the glade. The enchanted barrier collapsed behind them in a shower of falling leaves, while the heavy downpour of rain immediately drenched the pair from head to toe.

'Glory be, an' if'n it ain't a courtin' couple,' the man exclaimed when he drew closer and observed their clasped hands. 'It be a fierce day to be takin' yer mot out fer a walk, lad,' he remarked to David whilst bestowing a benign smile in Rhiannon's direction. 'Come 'ere, Conan!'

The dog, a peculiar blend of collie and setter, ignored the command and sat upon the ground, his heavy tail thumping excitedly against the wet grass.

'Thick as a plank, he be,' the man groused good-naturedly. 'Still, he won't do ye no harm, which is more'n can be said fer this storm if'n ye stay 'ere much longer. It fair looks to be settlin' in fer a while, an' with there bein' no other house but mine fer miles, ye best come with me.'

Clearly used to being obeyed, the man did not wait for their acceptance. He simply whistled for Conan, then started striding through the forest once again, a seemingly endless monologue on the 'monstrous fierce weather' rattling off his tongue and leaving David and Rhiannon to follow in his wake.

David collected his sword from against the tree and reattached it to his belt. 'He seems harmless enough,' he observed quietly. 'And at least we'll have proper shelter for a while. But stay close to me just in case.'

Rhiannon nodded. 'He sounds Irish,' she said as they hurried to catch up with their Good Samaritan. 'But for all we know we could be in southern France.'

'He's bound to have something in his house that will tell us where we are,' David reflected. 'Once we know that we can try and figure out the best place to go to call King Brian.'

After almost half an hour of walking through the woodland and sodden open fields with the man who never seemed to pause for breath in his monologue, they finally arrived at his house. Although, to call it a house was being generous. At the end of a muddy track lined with green hedges, it was more of a cottage made of grey stone with diamond-paned windows and a steady flow of white smoke rising out of one of its three chimneys.

Now eager to get out of the torrential downpour, Conan dashed towards a wooden shed, while the three humans trudged to the front door of the cottage.

'Get yerselves in there,' the man said, opening the door. He flicked a switch and a warm, yellow glow lit up the room inside.

Not waiting to be invited again, David and Rhiannon hurriedly entered, David having to duck his head to miss the low beam above the door. As their host followed them in, they copied him in taking off their water-logged boots, and Rhiannon hooked David's cloak over one of the coat hooks by the door. Then shivering in the welcoming warmth of the cottage, they quickly took in the room around them: The ceiling lined with thick wooden rafters that were inches from the top of David's head; the room itself Spartan in its simplicity, being furnished with only a single sofa, a wooden desk and chair, two bookshelves and a television; a filled clotheshorse placed before a cheerful fire blazing in the stone hearth behind an iron fireguard; a polished stone floor which was spotless; and along with the front door, five others leading off into other rooms.

'Ye'll both be needin' a warm shower an' a change o' clothes. Can't 'ave ye comin' down with a chill now, can we.' The man hung up his drenched coat and closed the door. ''ere, take these.' He grabbed some garments and towels off the clotheshorse and handed them to David and Rhiannon. 'Lass, th' bathroom be o'er there,' he said, pointing towards a doorway to the left of the fireplace. 'An' lad, ye can use th' shower in th' laundry.' He pointed to the door on the opposite wall.

'What about you, sir?' asked David.

The man waved his concern aside. 'A change o' clothes an' a shot o' whiskey will set me right. Now, off yer go an' I'll see ye both when yer done.' Whistling jauntily, he crossed the room to walk through the doorway leading to a narrow hallway and disappeared.

David waited until he was out of earshot, then turned to Rhiannon.

'Don't join him unless you know I'm there,' he said quietly.

Rhiannon nodded. 'I should only be about fifteen minutes.'

'Do you need help undoing the laces at the back of your dress?' David asked, and was bewildered when Rhiannon gave a squeak before hurriedly assuring him she would be fine and took off towards the bathroom.

David, whose mind had only been focused on the difficulty his friend would have in trying to untie the sodden laces, frowned. Then he blushed when a more intimate connotation for his offer occurred to him. Highly grateful none of his Robesmen were there to overhear him (especially Izana), he swiftly headed for the laundry and determinedly focused his attention on nothing but washing away the chill of the storm.

Rhiannon exited the bathroom twenty minutes later feeling considerably warmer and pat-drying her long hair with a towel. Outside, the rain continued to cascade down the front window and thunder rumbled loudly. Hearing a murmur of voices coming from down the hallway where their host had disappeared, she set off towards it. As she passed the desk, a small stack of pamphlets on top of it caught her attention. Swiftly picking it up, she flicked through them and discovered they were mostly shopping catalogues, except for one. The last was a tourist guide map to the sites used in the film *The Quiet Man*, along with other local attractions in Cong, Ireland. She cast a glance over some of them.

A castle. An abbey where the last High King of Ireland had lived.

David will enjoy seeing that, she thought.

A circle of standing stones.

Rhiannon looked at the photo of Nymphsfield Stone Circle. It was almost identical to the one she had seen when she had first flown on Endrille.

It was the entrance to one of the old pathways, she realised. What else? A wood. A cave where leprechauns were reputed to live! That was useful to know.

Not reading any further, she put the pamphlets back on the desk and set off down the hallway towards the voices issuing forth from the kitchen area up ahead.

'Does it rain a lot in this area?' Rhiannon heard David ask as she approached the doorway.

'Sure lookit. I hope yer mot isn't th' sort to take sick from a proper soakin'.'

'No, she isn't.'

'Tha's a blessin'. Me wife were before she went to meet the

Good Lord. Poor Margot, she come down with a fever after bein' caught out in th' hurricane in '86. She died not a week later.'

'I'm sorry.'

'Lord love ye, lad. Death comes to us all. Now get this into yer.'

There was a pause and reaching the door, Rhiannon looked into the small kitchen to see David seated at a table and sniffing the contents of the mug in his hands. The hilt of his sword glistened where it rested against his chair. Then, 'Lemon, honey, cinnamon, cloves and … nutmeg,' he declared.

'Ye've a sharp nose, lad,' the man said in astonishment. 'I only put a pinch o' th' nutmeg in an' most folk can never tell. Ah, 'ere be yer mot,' he added upon seeing Rhiannon in the doorway. 'Come in, lass, an' drink yer hot toddy.'

At his words, David stood up and turned towards her. A cough violently spluttered from his throat and his gaze hastily shifted away from the expanse of bare leg exposed by the oversized flannel shirt she was wearing.

Oblivious to the shock she had given him, Rhiannon stepped into the kitchen, which smelt of roast dinners and baked bread, and resisted the urge to giggle at David's appearance. Baggy maroon trackpants and a grey woollen polo shirt were certainly not what she was accustomed to seeing him wear. His hair was an untidy mess, as though he had not stopped to run a comb through it, and his feet were bare. In fact, the only thing normal about his appearance was the gold signet ring on his right forefinger. Looking up, she saw his cheeks were flushed and hoped he hadn't caught a cold.

'I'm afraid I didn't know what to do with my clothes, so I hung them over the shower door,' Rhiannon informed their host as she took her seat.

'Never ye fret, lass,' she was reassured. 'I'll go sort 'em out in front o' th' fire. Ye just sit 'ere an' drink this.'

A mug of steaming liquid was placed in front of her and then the man was out the door.

Rhiannon quickly took advantage of his absence to inform David of what she had discovered. To her surprise he already knew about the castle.

'He asked me if we were with something called a film crew who are staying there. I didn't know what else to say so I said we were and that we'd got lost while taking a walk. He told me if the storm passes while there's still daylight he'll take us there, otherwise we can stay here tonight and he'll give us a lift in the morning.'

'From what I could see on the map it's not far from the castle to the woods,' said Rhiannon. 'Do you think we could try calling for King Brian from there?'

David nodded. 'It should be easy to find a secluded spot out of sight and hearing of curious onlookers.'

'Will he come if it's still raining?'

'He should, so long as there's no thunder or lightning. But if he's not in Vetus svet then one of his people will come in his place.'

Rhiannon took a sip of her drink, then grimaced. 'Too many cloves,' she observed.

David agreed, but she noted that his good manners would not let him tip the beverage down the sink. Instead, he politely drank the whole thing then hastily filled the mug with cool water to rinse the taste out of his mouth. Suddenly, he cocked his head to listen. The faint thud of footsteps sounded out in the hallway.

'He's coming back.'

Rhiannon immediately launched into another topic.

'Of course, we still have to see the caves while we're here,' she said, loud enough to be overheard. 'They say leprechauns live there.'

'Aye, so they do,' their host said, reappearing in the kitchen doorway. 'But ye should be careful if'n ye see one, lass. They can be mighty tricksy. Why, only last week, a young lad in town swears he seen one near th' abbey. Says it led 'im into th' woods an' led 'im a merry dance till he were turned on his head.'

'The leprechaun turned him onto his head?' Rhiannon exclaimed in disbelief.

'No, no, lass. He were befuddled. Couldn't tell if he were headin' towards th' path or deeper into th' woods. Now, take this an' put it on.' The man held out a woollen dressing robe. 'I'll be bound it'll drown a small mite like yerself, but it'll keep ye warmer than jus' tha' old shirt o' mine.'

Rhiannon accepted the proffered robe and stood up to slip it on. The long garment was like a tent on her much smaller frame, but she huddled into its warmth with a grateful smile.

'An' now we're all dry an' warm I'm thinkin' introductions are in order. Th' name's O'Rourke. Jarlath O'Rourke.'

'David O'Faenart.'

'Rhiannon McBride.'

'O'Faenart,' the man mused. 'Don't recall ever hearin' tha' clan name before. From th' Isle o' Man be it? I've met some folk from there an' real unusual names they had too. Now, McBride! There be a name I recognise. Me colonel in th' army were a Hugh McBride. Fine man, always lookin' out fer me an' th' other lads. Saved me life a time or two he did, even took a bullet fer me once. We all thought he got himself a real bad hole in th' leg, but blow us down if he weren't runnin' round, shoutin' out orders when th' medics arrived. If it weren't fer th' blood on his uniform ye'd never 'ave guessed he were hit. Believed he were indestructible, we did, till he an' his good wife died in tha' car bombin' in Dublin. Ten April 1990 were definitely a black day fer our regiment. Sheet o' metal sliced right through th' colonel's neck, it did. An' his wife took a piece o' shrapnel straight to th' heart. Their son Patrick come all th' way from Australia fer th' funeral with his wife. Ah now, what were her name? Caroline … Clara … Claire. Tha' be it. Claire. Fair broke our hearts it did to see them poor young 'uns with no other family to support 'em, an' her carryin' a babe inside as well.'

'Excuse me, but your colonel's wife,' Rhiannon interrupted. 'Was her name Kathleen?'

Jarlath gazed at her in amazement. 'It were as sure as th' hills o' Tara are green,' he said. 'Now, how would a lass like yerself be knowin' tha'?'

'My parents, Patrick and Claire McBride, lived in Australia before I was born and my grandparents were Hugh and Kathleen McBride.'

'Ye don't say! Well, don't tha' beat all. But now, seein' yer up close I can see ye 'ave th' colonel's gold eyes an' curls. Mind, his hair were pitch black. I 'ave a photo o'er 'ere ye might ne'er seen before.' He reached up and took a picture frame off the window mantel. 'This were taken th' day he were promoted to colonel.' He handed it to Rhiannon, who looked down and saw an image of her paternal grandparents for the first time.

Standing between a younger version of their host and another soldier was a tall man in a distinguished green uniform, his black hair streaked with white curling beneath his peaked cap, and a pretty woman with titian hair and blue eyes. Even had she not been told they were her grandparents, Rhiannon felt she would have known who they were. The man's gold eyes and the woman's short, sturdy build and small nose could have been her own. And from the kind smiles on their faces she knew, had things turned out differently, she would have been much happier with them than with the Dashmonts.

A single tear escaped her and she gave a watery sniff.

''ere now, lass. What's wrong?'

'I've never seen a photo of them before. They were all lost when I was a child.'

'Ye poor mite. Tell ye what, ye take tha' one an' I'll jus' get me grandson t' print off another.'

Rhiannon stared at him, hardly daring to believe it. 'Really?'

'Aye. Scanned all me photos he has, so ye take tha' one an' ne'er forget wha' a fine officer an' gentleman yer grandfather were.'

Rhiannon's words of gratitude drew a reminiscent smile from Jarlath. 'Ye also 'ave his polite way o' speakin','' he said, 'though yer bound t'ave his temper when yer roused I'm sure.'

'That she does,' David inserted with a smile.

Pleased to have an attentive audience for his stories, Jarlath launched into a lengthy reminiscence on his late respected colonel, his tales ranging from hysterically funny to seriously scary. They saw them through the afternoon and past a delicious supper of hot chowder and fresh bread. And all throughout his entertaining narrations the rain beat a steady constant pattern on the windows, while lightning rumbled and cracked across the ominously dark sky.

'Looks like ye'll both be stayin' th' night,' Jarlath said after a particularly loud crack of thunder rattled the windows in their panes. 'I've a spare bed an' me old campin' cot.' The last was said with a pointed look at David. 'Come along an' we'll get ye both settled fer th' night. Now, jus' in case somethin' happens, like th' old tree out back finally comin' down on th' roof, tha's me room through tha' door.' He pointed at the closed door just before the kitchen, then led them down the rest of the hallway to the main living area. He opened the door to the right of the hearth, saying, 'In 'ere, lass. This be th' spare bed. I'll jus' go fetch th' sheets fer it an' th' cot fer yer young fella out 'ere near th' fire. It won't take me a moment t'ave it all ready fer ye both.'

David stepped forward. 'We can do that, sir.'

'Oh, it's no problem.'

'It's the least we can do to repay you for your kindness.' Unconsciously speaking in the same tone he used when addressing his guards during a mock battle, David ordered, 'If you let us know where to find everything we'll see to making up the beds.'

A bark of laughter escaped Jarlath, who shook his head in defeat. 'Ye'd do well on a parade ground, lad. Ye almost had me salutin' with tha' tone o' voice. All right, ye'll find th' sheets an' spare blankets in th' linen closet in th' laundry. Same with th' cot.'

David and Rhiannon went to fetch everything to the sound of Jarlath's, 'Looks like yer granddaughter's found herself a decent lad, Colonel.'

'I think you impressed him,' Rhiannon said to David half an hour later when they were alone, Jarlath having professed himself tired before retreating to his room. The man had been thrilled to discover his male guest was fluent in Irish when David asked him about one of the books on his shelf, and the two had spent all the time it took to make up the beds conversing in the language which she barely understood beyond a few basic sentences. 'What were you two talking about?'

'Me,' David admitted truthfully. 'I think he was checking to make sure I'm worthy of being associated with his late colonel's granddaughter. I also asked if he could drop us off at the abbey tomorrow. If someone believes they saw a leprechaun there they probably did, and it sounds like it's closer to the woods than the castle. He was also telling me where I could find some beeswax candles after I asked if he had any.'

'Why?'

'I told him because their scent helps us relax, but dark sorcery was performed in Vetus svet before the pathways were closed, possibly even near here, and dreamreapers could have formed over time. Unfortunately, these candles won't be like the enchanted ones in Álnair where we can leave them burning unattended through the night, so we'll have to take it in turns to stay awake and keep watch. You can sleep first,' he said upon seeing Rhiannon stifling a yawn. 'Get into bed and I'll bring your candle in.'

It only took a moment for Rhiannon to rid herself of the dressing robe. She put her necklace next to the photograph of her grandparents on the side table, then crawled beneath the thick layer of blankets on the bed. She snuggled beneath them with a grateful sigh just as David walked into the room. The yellow base candle he held was placed inside a clear glass pillar with a ceramic bottom. He put it on the table beside the bed, then placed his hand over the top.

'*Foläga.*'

At the sound of his quiet word, a soft blue-gold light shone and on the wick of the candle a flame flickered to life. As the sweet scent of honey slowly filled the room, David closed the curtains over the rain-streaked window, saying, 'I'll wake you in five hours.'

'At least this way you'll get to sleep in the bed,' Rhiannon told him. 'That cot doesn't look too comfortable, and your feet would be dangling off it.'

'I'll still have to use it,' David replied on his way to the door. 'If Mr O'Rourke comes out during the night he'll expect to see me out there, not in here. But don't worry, it won't be the worst thing I've ever slept on. That prize goes to a bed at an inn called The Iron Griffin on the road to Ardara. Hard as a rock and I swear there were fleas from the owner's cat inside it.'

David shuddered at the memory, then flicked off the light, leaving the burning flame of the candle to cast its reassuring gentle glow over Rhiannon's face. He was about to leave the room with a final goodnight, when a hesitant calling of his name stopped him.

'What is it?'

'Could you ... I mean, would you mind ...'

David frowned at Rhiannon's unusual reticence. 'Is something wrong?' he asked, concerned.

'No,' he was hurriedly reassured. 'It's just, even though I'm tired my mind won't stop thinking about everyone in Álnair. I was wondering if you sang the lullaby my music box plays it might help me go to sleep. Of course, if you don't want to —'

'Don't be silly,' David cut her off. He walked over to the bed and sat on the end of it. 'Close your eyes – and no giggling if I hit a wrong note.'

'I'll try to control the impulse,' said Rhiannon, and greatly relieved she lay down and closed her eyes as David started singing.

> *Listen, my darling, the dryads are near!*
> *Their sweet voices singing, so merry and clear.*
> *The night is filled with their joyful refrain,*
> *'The stars are shining brightly, let us dance once again!'*
>
> *The sun has gone to her bower to rest,*
> *and each weary bird has sought sleep in their nest.*
> *Still, ever the dryads their sweet voices call,*
> *'Come dance with us, children! Come dance, one and all!'*
>
> *Faeries will join them, their faces alight.*
> *The dragons, too, will be filled with delight.*
> *In the moonlight the dryads will laugh and will sing,*
> *'Come play with us, everyone, whether peasant or king!'*
>
> *The forest will thrill to the glorious sound,*
> *like flowers in Spring when the rains bless the ground.*
> *And ever more joyous the dryads shall cry,*
> *'We have hours to go till the dawn breaks the sky!'*
>
> *So sleep, my darling, there is naught to fear,*
> *'tis only the song of the dryads you hear.*
> *Be at peace as you lie against my breast,*
> *and the Blessed Light shines upon our rest.*

The sweet, haunting melody, accompanied by the lulling sound of the rain, soon had Rhiannon in the deepest of slumbers but David kept singing until he completed the entire song. His gaze lingered on her sleeping face and, for a moment, he permitted his expression to reveal the depth of his feeling for her, his eyes containing the tender light of one contemplating that which they hold the most precious.

Then he stood up and left the room, making sure to leave the door ajar so that he could see the candle from the sofa. He glanced at the clotheshorse with their still dripping clothes on it and murmured, '*Astarai.*' In a stream of dull red light, the sodden fabrics were dry. He performed the drying charm on his cloak and the boots by the front door, then selected a book at random from one of the bookshelves and sat down on the sofa. Opening the large tome, he settled back and delved into the histories of the Roman Empire and its military tactics, the excerpts from ancient manuscripts posing no challenge for his linguistic skills. The next five hours were sure to pass quickly.

~Chapter 14~

CONCERNED MINDS AND ANXIOUS HEARTS

'We're sorry, Your Majesties. Sir Raeden.'

Izana and John bowed low to the three shocked people before them, the Robesmen's grim faces retaining their grieved expressions since their hasty entrance into the antechamber of the Imperial Apartments a short time before.

The spacious and luxurious room was filled with a heavy silence, the only sound the crackle of burning wood in the great hearth.

John resumed his report. 'As soon as they were gone, we called for any dragon nearby to take us to Valieoth Castle. Rumanel heard us and she brought Izana and me straight here. She's now on her way to inform Derrick, Gareth and Eamon of what has occurred. Captain Morton has taken charge of bringing all our mounts back.'

'I have Rhiannon's sword,' Izana announced in a sombre tone. He walked forward to place it into Sir Raeden's hand. 'She removed

235

it while we ate and did not reattach it prior to our setting out on the walk.'

'Does David have his with him?' King Stephen asked, his voice tense with suppressed emotion.

'He does.'

'Then he at least shall be spared a lecture when he returns, whenever that may be, unlike my ward,' said Sir Raeden, the whiteness around his pursed lips matching the shade of his knuckles as his grip tightened on Rhiannon's sword.

John spoke up again. 'Your Majesty, we shall accept any punishment you deem appropriate for our failure to safeguard His Royal Highness Prince David and Rhiannon. Had we been nearer to them when the foramen appeared we may have been able to prevent their being taken.'

Compassion momentarily supplanted the paternal concern in King Stephen's eyes as he looked upon his son's two Robesmen. Their feelings of guilt were written plainly upon their faces. It was clear they would suffer the pangs of remorse every day that David and Rhiannon remained lost in Vetus svet.

'Had you been nearer to them then we may even now be missing both of you as well,' he said. 'Neither of you is responsible for their disappearance, therefore no issuing of punishment is warranted. The foramens appear when and where they will, and no blame can be attached to anyone who witnesses another being taken by them.'

He held up a hand when both Izana and John went to speak. 'I know it is impossible not to be worried about them,' he continued, 'but recall that my son has proven himself a capable swordsman and not unintelligent. I am confident he will ensure no harm comes to himself or Rhiannon.'

It took a moment for the truth of this to ease some of the strain on Izana's face.

'Rhiannon *is* familiar with the customs of Vetus svet,' he

reflected. 'She will know how they should conduct themselves without attracting too much attention.'

Queen Maiwen, who had remained silent from the first mention of the events at Luwyenth Cove, suddenly stood up. Her entire being emanating a sense of pained distress, she fled the room without speaking a single word.

The five men left in the antechamber watched as the door leading out to the hallway clicked shut behind her.

King Stephen sighed. He looked every one of his forty-six years when he turned to face the Commander of the Guard. 'Raeden, would you have a messenger sent to inform Endrille of what has occurred, then have a request issued to King Brian for him to attend upon me should he be in Álnair.'

Sir Raeden bowed. 'I shall do it at once, Sire,' he said, and swiftly departed.

'Daiki.'

Izana's father stepped away from his position near the hearth and inclined his head. 'Yes, Your Majesty?'

'Please inform the other chancellors our meeting is postponed until tomorrow.'

The King's Chief Robesman gave a low bow. 'For the same time?'

'Yes. And, Daiki? May I rely upon you to explain the situation to them?'

At the less formal tone of his king and friend, Lord Sato replied in a similar manner, 'You may trust me to do it, Stephen.' With another bow, he briefly laid a comforting hand on Izana's shoulder, then turned and left the room.

King Stephen focused his attention on Izana and John.

'I shall not order you to return home,' he said without preamble, 'for I am certain you will wish to remain within the palace until David and Rhiannon return. However, I will command you to at least visit your families regularly. While Queen Maiwen and I are deprived of seeing our child for the foreseeable future, there is no reason why your parents should suffer the same grief.'

Izana and John promised to faithfully carry out his order.

'Your Majesty, may we inform Cassandra of what happened?' Izana enquired.

'You may. It would be best if she heard it directly from you.'

Then King Stephen accompanied the two out into the hallway and dismissed them. As they left to seek out Cassandra in her tower, he set off down the corridor in search of his wife.

Queen Maiwen's defences crumbled the instant she entered her son's bedchamber.

Her eyes burned with the first prickling of tears as she drifted around the richly decorated room. The deep, warm tones of the red drapes and rugs failed to soothe her troubled mind each time she paused to run a gentle hand over David's treasured items. There was the odd clock Rhiannon had given him for Christmas and the first star crystal he had found with his father. And there was the beautiful clamshell filled with rare deep-sea pearls, a gift from the king of the merfolk, Lord Leronus, in gratitude for David rescuing his baby daughter from the consequences of her own folly when she teased an old and cranky sea lion.

When she came to his desk, Queen Maiwen stared at the ordered chaos upon it. A pile of books sat in one corner, a stack of parchment in another. A collection of watches in various stages of repair lay strewn across the middle; and there, placed close to the inkwell, was the reed flute she had gifted him for his thirteenth birthday. She closed her eyes to better hear the echoing melody inside her mind of when David first played it, the merry tune at odds with the aching lament in her heart.

At length she reopened her eyes and made her way to the large, canopied bed opposite the wide balcony doors. Slowly, she sat upon the thick mattress and felt the soft down inside the white and carnation-red coverlet sink underneath her weight. Stroking its smooth outer material, she recalled every stitch she had put into its making in the months leading up to David's fourteenth birthday.

A book and picture frame on the bedside table caught her attention. She reached over, picked up the small tome and glanced at the cover.

A splutter of watery laughter escaped her lips when she read the title:

Unlocking the Mysteries of the Female Mind
A Handbook of Survival by a Beleaguered Gentleman in Love

'Oh, David.'

The note of maternal affection in her voice transformed Queen Maiwen's sigh of amusement into a verbal caress. She flipped the book open to the marked page and huffed another laugh at the words her son had carefully underlined:

Her mood can change with the suddenness of a summer storm. This is particularly common should she feel rejected or insulted by a seemingly innocuous remark. Therefore, great tact is required when commenting on her appearance.

Queen Maiwen closed the book and replaced it on the table, a faint smile lingering on her lips. She looked at the framed picture. Her own face, her husband's, David's and Rhiannon's all smiled back at her from amidst a bright array of Christmas decorations. Her hand trembling, she picked up the silver frame and stared at the captured image of her son. At almost sixteen he was nearly as tall as his father, while the top of Rhiannon's head barely reached his shoulder.

How long would it be before she could embrace him again? Before she could hear his animated voice in the hallways as he conversed with Rhiannon and his Robesmen?

Queen Maiwen's fingers tightened their grip on the frame. Tears trickled down her cheeks, the glistening droplets falling like tiny liquid jewels upon the glass pane, their presence blurring David's happy countenance.

She clutched the frame to her breast, a broken sob escaping her mouth.

So great was her distress she did not hear when soft footsteps crossed the room towards her. The first she knew of another presence in the room was when a dearly familiar form sat beside her, and a strong arm wrapped itself around her shoulders.

Instinctively, she turned and laid her head against her husband's chest.

'I knew I would find you here.'

His heart aching at the sight of her grief, King Stephen murmured the words into his wife's hair, his gentle tone mirroring the tenderness of his touch as he stroked the long, dark tresses under his hand.

'Dearest, we must believe he will be all right,' he said quietly, striving to control his own feelings of apprehension in order to comfort the distraught mother in his arms. 'We shall see him again.'

'But when?' The demand was sobbed into the increasingly damp patch on his tunic. 'The last person taken from here was gone for over a year before King Brian brought them back. What if he's missing for longer than that? He can be so reckless! Anything could happen to him! To them!'

'Maiwen, we must believe and pray they will be safe. Unlike Master Aberthor, they're both magi who are also trained in physical defence by the sternest perfectionist I know. It's extremely unlikely they will be assaulted by a band of thugs and rendered unconscious for several months.'

The warm tears soaking his raiment continued to flow and King Stephen realised this would be one occasion when nothing he said could stem their tide. After David's birth and the discovery she would not be able to bear another child, Maiwen had tried not to be overly protective of their adventurous son. She had largely succeeded; however, she had never been able to let a day go by without assuring herself of David's well-being. Until she was able to see for herself that their son had come to no harm, he knew the forthcoming days would be the most difficult she had ever had to endure.

It will be the same for you, his mind's voice stated grimly.

The ruler of Álnair acknowledged the truth of the words, aware the longer his son remained in Vetus svet the more the worry inside his own heart would increase.

'He will return to us, my love,' he finally whispered, lowering his head to rest it against Maiwen's. 'And I am sure with King Brian looking for them, David and Rhiannon will not be gone for long.'

While King Stephen was comforting his wife in David's bedchamber at the south end of the palace, John and Izana were engaged in providing consolation to the castle's First Seer in her tower. Devastated by the news of the disappearance of her two friends, Cassandra's initial shock had given way to an overwhelming sense of guilt.

'I always f…f-felt something terrible would happen there,' she cried. 'They w…w-wouldn't have been taken if I'd stopped them from going.'

'This isn't your fault,' Izana told her with quiet firmness. 'You didn't know the foramen would appear. Even if you had, David and Rhiannon may still have chosen to go there. You aren't responsible for the choices others make.'

'He's right, Cassandra,' said John, his tone abrupt but kind. 'And no one blames you.'

The First Seer still looked unconvinced.

'Do you believe either David or Rhiannon would say it's your fault?' Izana asked bluntly. 'Honestly?'

Cassandra opened her mouth, then closed it. After a brief pause, she shook her head.

'No, they wouldn't,' Izana confirmed. 'And that should be all that matters.'

Upon seeing the lingering agitation in her emerald eyes, and knowing it stemmed primarily from a deep concern for her friend, Izana then did something to make John stare in surprise. The normally undemonstrative Robesman stepped forward and enveloped Cassandra in a comforting embrace.

'She'll be all right,' he said soothingly. 'She survived training with Sir Raeden and the challenges in the Dragon's Cup. Besides, David is with her. You may be sure he'll look after her.'

'S…S-She's more likely to try and l…l-look after him,' Cassandra mumbled into his shoulder.

Her comment brought a moment of much needed levity into the room.

'Well, she does suit the role of mother hen more than us,' John remarked with a wry twist of his lips. 'And unlike our fussing, I don't think David will mind hers very much.'

A soft knock on the antechamber's outer door put an end to their smiles.

John went to greet the unknown visitor while Izana released Cassandra and put a more respectable distance between them.

'Leila!'

John's startled exclamation had the two other occupants in the room looking over in time to see the daughter of the castle's Chief Herbalist cross the threshold.

'I'm sorry for the interruption, Cassandra, but I overheard some of the guards talking to my father and had to know if it was true. Were Rhiannon and Prince David really caught in a foramen?'

Leila's question brought the grim expression back to John's face.

'They were,' he answered. 'How did you know we'd be here?'

Her fleeting glance at the only other girl in the room provided a hint of what her reply would be before Leila revealed, 'I guessed you'd come to tell Cassandra. I've visited her a few times with Rhiannon and I've seen the close friendship they have. It only made sense that she'd be one of the first people you told.' She looked closely at John and hesitated before saying diffidently, 'I was also worried about how you were feeling. I know how important they both are to you, especially Prince David, and I wanted to … that is, I was wondering is there … is there anything I can do to help?'

'Of course there isn't!' His sense of failing his Lord made John's voice harsh, and frustrated at his own inability to assist his missing friends, he demanded, 'Unless you somehow possess the ability to open a pathway between here and Vetus svet, which, with you not being a mage, is extremely unlikely, what could you possibly do to help?'

'John!'

Izana's sharp utterance pierced through the cloud of impotent rage storming inside the Chief Robesman's mind.

John, horrified by his outburst, looked down at the kind girl who had been his neighbour all her life. The shimmering hurt in her wide blue eyes flayed his heart.

'Leila, I … I'm so sorry.' His expression contrite, John reached out towards her head and gently placed his hand on her mousy hair. 'I took my anger at myself out on you and I shouldn't have done that. It was nice of you to offer to help, but there's nothing any of us can do to bring them back – only King Brian and his people can do that.'

Leila gave a loud sniff.

'I should've remembered how hot-tempered you can be when you're upset,' she said by way of forgiving him. 'And I know I'm not any use when it comes to casting enchantments. I meant, isn't there something I can do to make things a bit easier for you, even if it's just getting some of your clothes off your mother and bringing them here, since I know you won't want to leave the castle grounds until they're back safely.'

'Oh.' John flushed until his skin was the same colour as his hair; the thought of Leila handling his clothes made him feel warm all over. 'T-There's no need for you to do that,' he hurriedly assured her. 'I'll be going home shortly to collect a few things.'

Leila's face fell in disappointment. John saw this and overcame his embarrassment to say honestly, 'But I'd appreciate having someone besides Izana to talk to, and I can't think of anyone I'd prefer that to be more than you.'

'Even if I end up prattling on about my plants?'

'I hope you do. If I think of nothing but how David and Rhiannon are stuck in Vetus svet for goodness knows how long, I'll go insane.'

John's words dispersed the last vestiges of unhappiness from Leila's face.

As the four occupants of the room became absorbed in a discussion on how their missing friends were faring, it did not escape Izana's notice that the Chief Herbalist's daughter kept a close watch on her neighbour, evidently ready to change the topic the instant John showed any sign of succumbing to madness.

The sun had set and the radiant silver-white stars lay scattered across the moonless night sky when Sir Raeden entered his office. The glow from the lamps spread throughout the room would have made it easy for an observer to see the effect the day's events had had upon him. A heavy weight seemed to press down on his shoulders until he collapsed like a stringless puppet into his high-backed chair. Leaning his head against the cushioned back, he closed his eyes to listen to the rhythmic sounds of the ocean launching a gentle assault over the shoals guarding the lagoon.

A long moment passed. Then, in a well-practised move, he reached inside his open tunic and slipped a small photograph out of its inner breast pocket. He opened his eyes and stared down at it. An expression of haunted regret passed over his features before he concealed it behind his hand at the knock on his door.

'Raeden?'

The call of his name and the polite knock on his office door brought no change to the knight's pose. The only reaction he gave was to say briefly, 'I am here.'

The door opened slowly, revealing the tall form of King Stephen arrayed in a formal robe of subdued green over a dark tunic and breeches. His high boots were immaculately polished, and on his left hand the gold glint of his wedding band and the signet ring on his right forefinger were his only adornments.

The ruler of Álnair entered the room and closed the door. He walked towards the younger man before him, saw the photograph he held and recognised the delicate feminine writing on the back. A look of concern flickered in his green eyes. The first time he had seen the photograph, a much younger Raeden had been holding it just as he was now, but he had had blood seeping through a bandage on his left shoulder and around his abdomen, along with the bleakest expression on his face.

'The shadows of the past are hardest to endure when there is no light to ease their darkness.'

The quiet words elicited a small huff of acknowledgement, but nothing more.

'Come now, Raeden. Your little lantern and mine are not gone forever. They will be back.'

Sir Raeden's hand dropped from his eyes to reveal a slightly less grim visage, his strong spirit incapable of being in abeyance for long.

'Of course they will,' he said, 'if only so my ward can finish cleaning my storage cupboard. She insisted on starting it last weekend and she loathes leaving a task unfinished.'

The photograph disappeared into the depths of his tunic pocket once more, then Sir Raeden looked across his desk at the man now seated in the chair opposite his own and asked, 'Has King Brian attended upon you?'

'The delegation of Leprechauns I met with informed me he is currently in Vetus svet. It is possible David and Rhiannon have already made contact with him but if not, his nephew Eirehon assures me their people will mention the situation to King Brian as soon as another set of foramen occurs.'

'When do they expect that to be?'

'In six weeks. If David and Rhiannon are now with King Brian they should return at that time. If not, we can only hope it will not take long for King Brian and his people to find them and for the next foramens to appear.' A short silence descended, then King Stephen said in a quiet, sombre tone, 'Who knows, perhaps some good may yet come from this separation.'

'Sire?'

'I have often wondered how my son would cope should he unexpectedly find himself without the presence of either myself or his mother. I know it is not a hardship you or I would wish upon anyone, Raeden. However, it is an inescapable fact that at some point David shall have to assume the position of king, and he will need to face many challenges where the responsibility for making decisions will be his alone. Maybe this experience will help prepare him for such a time.'

'It cannot fail to do so to some degree,' Sir Raeden remarked before adding drily, 'although, with Rhiannon as his companion, I sincerely doubt he will be making all the decisions by himself.'

A small smile broke the serious set of King Stephen's mouth.

'In which case he shall hopefully also learn the importance of choosing his battles wisely.'

'He has already shown a marked improvement in that area,' came Sir Raeden's reply, 'along with an increase in his ability to fight them, both physically and verbally.' His lips curled up in a wry show of amusement. 'Even in his dealings with me. His temper still is not always under good regulation, but his confidence and skill to engage me in a battle of wills has certainly risen. I do not believe you need worry over whether he will be strong enough to bear the burden he will one day have to carry.'

'It relieves my mind to hear you say that, Raeden. Of all men, I trust your judgement in this matter the most. And I do not hesitate to continue to entrust my son to your vigilant care.'

Sir Raeden bowed his head. 'Your Majesty honours me.'

'If speaking the truth confers honour then I will honour you further still by saying you have proven yourself one of the greatest and most loyal of those gifted with a Dragonstar. Do not allow anyone to make you feel your family history negates any good you do.'

His eyes a brilliant shade of blue, Sir Raeden declared, 'Had it not been for the example set by yourself and the Lady Endrille I may have become quite a different kind of man.'

King Stephen shook his head. 'I do not believe so. Even at the young age of seven the integrity you possessed was strong, and not even the tragedy you survived could take it from you. Had you been mentored by Fendrel himself, I doubt you would have turned out any differently. And now,' he said in a very different tone, 'what do you say to a brief stop at the main armoury and then an hour in the Inner Courtyard?'

'I say "Prepare to be defeated, Sire",' said Sir Raeden, accepting without any show of reluctance the king's wish to put an end to their discussion.

Both men rose to their feet and as they made their way to the armoury, the only subject touched upon was whether they should restrict themselves to just swords or utilise their mage abilities. Neither mentioned the ever-present concern lingering inside their minds over David and Rhiannon's absence.

~*Chapter 15*~

DARK DELIGHT

'Did you hear? Prince David and Miss Rhiannon were caught in a foramen!'

The man exiting the Praeterium froze. He looked at the small group down the hallway.

'They were at Luwyneth Cove and got taken right in front of their companions.'

Exclamations of disbelief and horror rang out.

The man ignored them all.

Swiftly, he set off towards the stables. He needed to report the good news to Mórfran immediately. While it was to be hoped the girl wouldn't be gone too long, with Prince David missing the king would no doubt be distracted enough for them to increase their activities without garnering too much attention.

It might also help divert Mórfran's attention from his own continuing failure in discovering anything about the location of the Dragon's Eye!

~Chapter 16~

A Surprising Encounter

David and Rhiannon's second day in Vetus svet dawned wet and windy. The storm had passed, but the rain looked to have settled in for a good long while.

However, despite the weather, Jarlath held true to his word and after a hearty breakfast of eggs, bacon, sausage, black pudding, tomato and fresh bread, he started up his old white sedan and drove them into Cong. Fortunately, the slippery quagmire of a track leading to his cottage soon became a sealed road, and Rhiannon's white-knuckle grip on the door rest in the back seat loosened. For the rest of the journey, she simply enjoyed watching the changes in David's expression as he listened to Jarlath extol the virtues of naturally aspirated engines as opposed to turbocharged ones.

When they arrived in Cong, Jarlath stopped talking like a car salesman and began a running commentary on the history of the buildings they passed.

'Tha' be the Market Cross,' he announced as they came to the end of the main street. He pointed to a limestone cross mounted on a circular stepped plinth placed in the centre of the road. 'It be part o' the High Cross erected to commemorate th' dedication of th' Abbey in th' twelfth century, an' it marks th' spot where a just judge were killed in 1350.'

And then, they were turning right and approaching the site of the abbey ruins. The grey stone building dominated the scenery, looking bleak against the overcast sky, while the adjoining graveyard with its tall headstones was hauntingly eerie in the rain. A few tourists could already be seen walking through it wearing bright rain jackets and carrying umbrellas.

'Yer sure 'bout lookin' around now?' Jarlath asked, pulling over to the curb across the street. 'Ye'll get mighty damp.'

'After surviving the drenching we got yesterday I'm sure we'll be fine,' Rhiannon replied, and thanked him for his hospitality. David added his own words of gratitude.

'Well then, ye both take care o' yerselves an' best o' luck with th' film. An' lad,' he added, halting David's exit from the car with one hand, 'look after th' lass an' be sure t' treat her right.'

'I will. You have my word,' David promised. After a final word of thanks, he joined Rhiannon on the pavement.

The white sedan pulled away with a short beep of the horn, leaving David and Rhiannon in the drizzling rain.

'Let's go,' said David, and started off towards the abbey.

Rhiannon adjusted his cloak around her shoulders and hastily caught up with him.

'You might want to hide your sword,' she cautioned, casting a wary glance around them at the sparsely populated street. 'If Ireland is anything like Australia it'll be illegal to carry a real weapon in public.'

Startled, David halted in his steps. 'Then how are people supposed to defend themselves if they're attacked?'

Rhiannon shrugged. 'I've never been able to figure that one out myself, but we don't want to get in trouble if someone sees it and reports you.'

David shook his head over the illogical rule, placed his hand on the hilt of his sword and muttered, '*Mendolenai.*'

A faint glow of turquoise light enveloped the sword and sheath, then both vanished from sight. The only indication they were still there were the trickles of water running down the invisible smooth length of the scabbard.

'I'll have to reverse the charm before calling for King Brian,' David said as they crossed the road to the abbey and the green woodland beyond it. 'Leprechauns consider it highly offensive to meet with them while hiding a weapon, and I've no inclination to find out what their punishment would be for doing it.'

Their walk through the abbey was accomplished quickly, despite the efforts of several tourists to waylay them to have their picture taken. After complying with the first request from a tiny Polish lady, David simply replied to all the others in Drakaron, leaving the individuals scratching their heads in confusion.

From the abbey grounds they followed the unpaved track beneath the thick canopy of trees and crossed the stone footbridge spanning the river, shivering at the icy chill rising from the flowing water.

Their lips blue with cold and their fingertips turning a bloodless white, they did not pause to wonder at the remains of a stone fishing house built over the water, or the fine archway guarding one end of the footbridge. Instead, doggedly focused on getting into the woods, they only stopped when they reached the sign welcoming them to the Cong Nature Trail.

The increasingly heavy rain turned the dirt track beneath their feet into a squelching, muddy mess, and although the air was filled with a pure, fresh scent, the many fine fir, pine and redwood trees failed to prevent the deluge from continuing to drench them until their hair and clothes were plastered to their bodies. The photograph of Rhiannon's grandparents, protected from the elements by a preservation charm, made a faint outline where it was placed in the inside pocket of David's tunic.

'Should we try now and call him?' Rhiannon asked. 'There's no one about.'

David shook his head. 'Someone could come along while we're speaking to him. We'll go farther into the woods and find a secluded spot off the track.'

Offering her his hand after she slipped and nearly impaled herself on a sharp protruding root, he led her through the tangled underbrush.

Twenty minutes later, bedraggled, wet and miserable, Rhiannon plonked herself down on a fallen log. 'The only living creatures within earshot of us now will be the occasional squirrel, pine marten or wild bird who no doubt are already on friendly terms with the leprechauns,' she declared.

'I suppose you're right,' David conceded. He cast a glance around the area and murmured, '*Undolthgare.*'

His sword instantly became visible.

In a clear voice, David heralded their presence, saying, 'King Brian, Lord of the Leprechauns, we, David O'Faenart and Rhiannon McBride of Álnair, require your aid. Please hear us and answer.'

A long pause fell.

The chilling rain continued to pierce the treetops and smack against the ground, but all else remained quiet. There was not even the hushed whisper of a field mouse scurrying to its burrow to disturb the expectant silence.

Then, just when David and Rhiannon were beginning to think there were no leprechauns currently in Vetus svet, a cheerful voice spoke.

'Well, this be a royal visit and no mistake.'

David and Rhiannon swiftly turned towards a huge redwood. A sigh of relief escaped them upon seeing the short, black-haired and crowned figure of King Brian step out from behind it. Not a single droplet of water was upon his face and his clothes were perfectly dry.

The ruler of the leprechauns surveyed the two drenched forms before him, his green eyes twinkling merrily.

'Best to be gettin' ye both somewhere more comfortable,' he observed. With a wave of his hand, the scenery about them disappeared, replaced by the dry warmth of a cave. 'Welcome to me home away from home.'

David and Rhiannon shivered as a soft heat encased them, drying out their saturated clothes and hair in seconds. They took a moment to appreciate the pleasure of being dry once more, then looked around at their new surroundings.

The room they were in was enormous. Lit by a mysterious light, its high cavernous walls sparkled and shone, while the smooth ground glittered as though strewn with millions of stars. In its centre was a marble dais with a small gold throne set upon it. The gentle cascading sound of a waterfall drew their gaze to where it flowed at one end of the wide space, the fresh water streaming in front of one wall to gather in a clear pool. And near the numerous small doorways leading into the room was a host of chattering leprechauns. Clad in a variety of green and red swallow-tailed coats, black breeches, white stockings and black buckled shoes, the diminutive figures rushed over to greet their king's guests.

David bowed and spoke to them in a language Rhiannon had never heard before, but which instantly drew an excited babble of conversation from King Brian's folk. She looked down at her host. 'Was that your language he just spoke?'

'Aye. Taught him meself I did. Took to it like he were one of us.' Then he shouted, 'Silence, ye bletherskites! I be needin' to talk to me guests alone. Be off with ye. And don't let me be hearin' of any tricks bein' played on these two. Prince David, he be, and Lady Rhiannon be the daughter of Mórell's line.'

The leprechauns obediently withdrew, although their chatter did not diminish in the slightest.

King Brian waited until the noise had faded, then invited David and Rhiannon to sit on the steps of the dais.

'Now, tell me how ye came to find me 'ere,' he ordered, sitting on his throne.

He listened without interrupting as they explained what had happened to them from the moment they came through the foramen.

'We had no monetary way to thank him for his hospitality, so I placed a basic protection enchantment around Mr O'Rourke's cottage,' said David in conclusion. 'It should be enough to safeguard his home from any damage, but I would ask if you and your people could check on him occasionally to ensure he's all right.'

'Aye, we can do that. And tis lucky ye are to still find me here. I were goin' back to Álnair to see me wife but then the storm started a'brewin'.'

Distracted by trying to picture what a female leprechaun would look like, Rhiannon nearly missed King Brian's, 'Now, I'm afeard I've got both good and bad news. The good bein' ye both are welcome to stay here and I'll be more'n happy to take ye wherever ye like. And there be no need to fret o'er dreamreapers in here. Our magic is strong enough to keep any of those foul creatures away. The bad is it'll be six weeks afore the next foramens appear. In fact, 10 May by your people's Gregorian calendar to be precise.'

Rhiannon looked at him in dismay. 'Six weeks,' she repeated. 'But what about school?'

'We'll only miss five weeks of it,' David pointed out. 'Besides, I can teach you the basics of what would be covered in the lessons for your grade plus a few other things, like the healer's diagnostic technique. Languages definitely won't be an issue.'

'There be a fine library in Dublin. Ye'd have some peace and quiet to study there,' King Brian informed them. 'I could take ye to it if it be to yer likin'.'

'Perfect,' said David. 'I'll set you some lessons and then find something to read,' he told Rhiannon. 'We could do a few hours in the morning, then go exploring in the afternoon. After all,' he added with a bright smile, 'not even Wyvern objects to educational outings.'

'Provided they actually are educational, which I doubt these would be,' she remarked drily.

David's grin widened. 'Maybe not all of them.'

'Ye'll also be needin' some more clothes,' King Brian interjected.

He urged them to stand up and for Rhiannon to remove David's cloak.

Without speaking, he walked around them, examining their bodies from head to toe. Returning to the dais, he raised and twirled his right hand. A shiny bubble appeared on his palm. Inside the clear surface were tiny versions of Rhiannon and David. With a flick of his wrist, the bubble disappeared.

'Me tailor will have some things ready shortly, and he'll make sure ye'll not look out of place. Dab hand with a needle, he be. But for now, I wants to take ye to meet a good friend of mine. He'll be thrilled to meet ye both.' Another wave of his hand had filmy silver cloaks appearing, one each around David and Rhiannon's shoulders. 'These'll keep ye dry and warm where we're goin'.'

'But, what about your tailor?' Rhiannon asked. 'Won't he need our measurements?'

'He jus' got them. All he has to do is pop the bubble and he'll have a full-size model of ye both. Now, off we go.'

For the second time that morning David and Rhiannon experienced the scenery about them melting away into nothing, then being replaced with something completely different.

They arrived in their new surroundings and stared about them in wide-eyed wonder.

Under a cloudy blue sky, the high mountains encircling them were glorious in their rugged splendour. Green forests lay spread across their slopes like a royal mantle, with the hem reaching to the wide expanse of rippling water that sparkled in the odd ray of sunlight. The shoreline of the lake was littered with pebbles which shifted and crunched beneath their feet. A short distance away came the soft rustle of leaves caught in a cool breeze. The fine mist of rain touched their hair and faces with the gentle brush of a feather.

Strangely, there was not a single dwelling in sight.

'Where does your friend live?'

In answer to David's question, King Brian pointed towards the lake. 'In there. He'll know we're here and should be here soon. He rarely comes up these days, except when I visit him.'

'Is he shy?'

'No, only wary. Over the years too many humans have attempted to attack him, and all because they chose to believe the malicious lies some spread about him killin' a man.'

'It was a misunderstanding, my friend. There was no deliberate intent to lie.'

The deep, smooth voice spoke quietly. Accompanying it was a scent like that of the sweetest myrtle carried on a fresh sea breeze.

David and Rhiannon turned and looked with astonished eyes in the direction whence it came.

The wide, elongated head with a white mane growing atop it and peering out from behind the large boulder in the lake was unmistakeable.

'A Ríyun,' they breathed, and a smile lit their faces.

The water dragon turned its large obsidian eyes towards them and blinked. 'It has been many centuries since last any of the race of Men could properly identify me,' he said. He still made no move to come out from behind the rock.

'Kelandrus, stop bein' impolite and come and meet me guests. David O'Faenart, Prince of Álnair, and Lady Rhiannon McBride, daughter of Mórell's line. Come through the foramen, they did.'

At these words, Kelandrus raised his head, his long neck extending a great distance above the surface of the water. Then he was exiting the lake with the same grace and speed of a water lizard, the five claws at the ends of each of his four short legs propelling him forward with ease. Droplets of water clung to the white mane that grew down the back of his body from head to tail. His large, serpentine, wingless form with its cyan scales glistened in a stray sunbeam, while the end of his long, thick tail twitched like a cat's. He looked all of sixty feet long.

'I bid you welcome to my home,' he said courteously, lowering his body to the ground.

'*Arídakor nai arnor,*' David answered with a low bow.

Thank you from my heart. It sounds nicer when David says it in Drakaron, Rhiannon thought. Then she noticed the shimmer of tears in the dragon's eyes.

'I never thought I should have the pleasure of hearing a mage speak the language of my race again,' he declared, a distinct tremor in his voice.

A look passed between David and Rhiannon, and then a stream of Drakaron flowed off David's tongue. Soon he and Kelandrus were conversing at such speed Rhiannon had no hope of comprehending a single word. Not that she minded. From grimly sombre to smiling mirth, the changing expressions on David's face held her attention as surely as they had when he was listening to Jarlath O'Rourke talk about cars. And while she did not understand the words coming out of his mouth, his love and respect for dragons was evident in every syllable he spoke.

After a considerable time had passed, Kelandrus glanced at Rhiannon. He said something which drew a brief reply from David. Apology glimmered in the dragon's eyes as he turned to her. 'Forgive me, Lady Rhiannon. I fear in my joy I neglected to observe your exclusion from the discussion. Prince David informs me you have only lived in Álnair a short time and have not yet become fully conversant in Drakaron.'

'It's all right.'

'He also has told me of your triumph in winning the Dragon's Cup. I offer my congratulations on your achievement.'

'*Aridakor.*'

Her thank you, spoken in halting Drakaron, drew a kind smile from the dragon even as he remarked, 'After the pathways closed, I did not expect to ever meet another Dragon's Cup Champion, and now I have met two.'

Startled, David and Rhiannon stared at him. 'Who was the other?' they asked.

'Merlin, though when I met him, many years had passed since he'd won it. After leaving Álnair he and his wife went searching for any dragons who had survived the persecutions. A travelling monk named Colmcille, who was a dear friend of mine, told them where to find me.'

A spark of hope flared to life inside Rhiannon at his revelation. 'Did he ever mention his secret laboratory?'

'Only to say that any being seeking to find it would have to search among the things that are lost,' was the discouraging reply. 'After he told me of the war instigated by Fendrel, he did not speak much of his last years in Álnair. He found the memories too painful. The betrayal of his friend left a wound on his heart more grievous than any physical injury could have done. It was many months before he felt ready to leave the tranquillity of these mountains. Most evenings he would ask me to fly him to one of the peaks to gaze at the stars, and some days he would spend fishing in the lake. His wife was not too happy on those occasions when he came home reeking of fish.'

'Morgana never did like them,' King Brian said in some amusement, as though recalling a particularly fine joke.

'No, she did not; but still she would cook them for him. I believe it was only her love and care of him which enabled Merlin to face the world once more. And after he lost her to death, he returned here to await his own.' Suddenly, Kelandrus fell silent. He lifted his head and looked sharply towards the nearby forest. 'There are people approaching.'

David and Rhiannon listened. In the far distance they could vaguely hear the murmur of voices raised in excited chatter.

'I must not stay.' Kelandrus turned to his visitors and bowed his head. 'It has been an honour and privilege to meet you both, and I pray you will pass my greetings and regards to Queen Endrille upon your return to Álnair. *Teronwë das kel'numen.*'

Farewell and be blessed. Rhiannon heard David repeat the phrase in Drakaron and attempted to do the same. Her effort was rewarded with a warm smile from Kelandrus before he turned and swiftly entered the lake. Within moments no trace of him could be seen.

David frowned in the direction of the voices. 'Are those people really coming to hunt him?'

'Probably not, but there'll be others who will,' King Brian replied. 'He's had a few narrow escapes in the past from those seekin' to make a name for themselves by killin' what they says is the monster of Loch Ness.'

'What!' Rhiannon's exclamation rang out loudly. 'Do you mean Kelandrus is the Loch Ness Monster?'

'Aye, that be the terrible moniker they give him. And all from him tryin' to save a man from drownin'. It were a long time ago by your countin', 565AD to be exact. The man were swimmin' in the lake when somethin' went wrong with his heart. He starts flailin' about like a landed fish and sinks beneath the water, so Kelandrus, who were nearby, goes to help him. He were too late to save him, but pulled the man's body up to the surface. Then some folk in boats arrived. Shoutin' and screamin' at our friend they were, sayin' he were attackin' the man, and when they gets him in a boat they declare he killed him. The travellin' monk, Colmcille, came as they were buryin' him and they tells him Kelandrus attacked the man. He believed them at first, but then a few days later he were crossin' the lake when his boat capsized. Kelandrus saved him, and he learnt the truth. They were good friends after that; however, the other folk had already spread their version of the events, and poor Kelandrus has been havin' to watch out for hunters ever since. I tells him he needs to go live with his kin o'er in the Sea of Japan, but he says this be where his Umelda were slain and he'll not be leavin' her memory to fade into nothin' while he lives.'

'Then he's not the last dragon left in Vetus svet,' said David, his relief palpable.

'There be a number of them, with most bein' Ríyuns, but they've been keepin' out o' sight these many a long year,' King Brian answered. He glanced towards the forest where the voices of the approaching group were becoming clearer. 'They'll be here soon. I could leave if ye wanted to stay a while and have a roam about; or if there be another place ye want to go I can take ye there.'

David looked at Rhiannon. 'What do you want to do?' he asked.

She gazed from him to King Brian, then back again. Her eyes bright with anticipation, she said, 'There is one place I need to visit,' and told them the location. The ruler of the leprechauns nodded, 'Ah, Oswë-kí-aurfai, Land of Golden Light. A beautiful country,' he complimented, and in a blink of an eye the wonder of Loch Ness vanished as he took them to their next destination.

⌒⌒

'It's not here.'

Rhiannon's disbelieving whisper echoed in the empty room. All the furniture was gone, even the pale mustard curtains were missing. Through the exposed window the silvery glow of the moon could be seen in the night sky, and the overwhelming smell of fresh paint assailed her nostrils.

'It can't be gone!'

The desperate cry escaped her lips as she ran from the room.

'Rhiannon, what's wrong?'

David's concerned question went unanswered as Rhiannon raced along the corridor, madly flinging open every door and switching on lights to scan each room. The furnishings were all unchanged, and the bedroom which she had last seen looking like a disaster area was immaculate.

Rhiannon dashed up the stairs to the attic, leaping the last two steps to find … nothing. The space was completely cleared out. No boxes of stored clothes. No wardrobe. Nothing.

She turned and plunged down the stairs, passing a bewildered David who followed her down to the ground level. She tore through the remaining rooms only to be confronted with disappointment in each one.

Finally, disheartened and defeated, she slumped down on the piano stool in the drawing room. She had expected the Dashmonts to have thrown out her clothes, but she never thought they would be so eager to forget her that they would get rid of all reminders of her, including the furniture from her bedroom. A tear forced itself past her defences and trickled down her cheek.

When King Brian had transported them to the carport of 15 Dart Street, she had been so hopeful. The Dashmonts' silver Mercedes was gone, the spare key was still under the second flowerpot in the back garden and the house was quiet and empty.

'Rhiannon?' The comforting warmth of David's arm wrapped around her shoulders as he sat down beside her. 'What is it?'

The tightness in her throat prevented her from answering straightaway. She swallowed before disclosing in a small voice, 'The empty room upstairs was mine. I had … the only picture I had of my parents was in a newspaper clipping hidden beneath my wardrobe. I never thought I'd return here after going to Álnair so I forced myself not to dwell on having lost it. Then this all happened and I let myself hope I'd finally get it back.'

A short laugh, devoid of humour, escaped her. 'I was expecting my clothes to be gone, but I guess the Dashmonts wanted to erase any trace of me when I didn't return and decided to toss the furniture as well.'

David sat in appalled silence, horrified that anyone would accept a person's disappearance with so little concern. Just inside the doorway, King Brian stared darkly at the collection of trophies and photographs decorating the room.

'I'm sure had Annabelle been the one to disappear they'd have turned her room into a shrine.'

The soft observation from Rhiannon was said without bitterness, only weary acceptance, as though she had long become inured to her foster parents' preference for their other ward.

David's heart ached at the realisation. He spoke her name, wanting to offer some words of comfort, when she abruptly stood up, announcing, 'Let's go. I never want to see this place again.'

She walked determinedly towards King Brian, leaving David to follow.

The Prince of Álnair rose to his feet, then paused and examined the large photograph on the wall. The girl in it would have been pretty had it not been for the supercilious smile on her face. He looked at the ones surrounding it and noted the absence of Rhiannon in all of them. A glance at the others in the room revealed not a single one of her. He wondered if there ever had been.

Neither David nor Rhiannon felt like going anywhere else

after the visit to Brakenhurst, so King Brian took them back to the throne room in his cave. However, as leprechauns are quintessentially a light-hearted people, Rhiannon's low mood could not survive being surrounded by their merry singing and dancing. That evening saw her frequently smiling during the feast put on in honour of hers and David's first night as guests of King Brian.

Arrayed in some of the clothes King Brian's tailor had industriously prepared in their absence, she and David enjoyed the cheerful gathering, especially after being shown the area carefully prepared for them in the throne room. Situated near a small, natural alcove where a bathroom had been created were two dressing screens, a wardrobe and two beds, the last assuaging their fear of possibly having to sleep on the hard stone ground. And when, exhausted by hours of revelry, they slipped gratefully beneath the blankets, they fell asleep within moments of their heads touching their pillows.

The cave's labyrinth of passageways was still and quiet. Not a single lilting voice could be heard, the leprechauns all having departed for their night-time escapades of rollicking mischief.

In the dimly lit throne room, the soothing sound of the waterfall created an atmosphere of perfect tranquillity. The source of the light, a glass orb situated between the two occupied beds, glowed softly, shedding its gentle radiance on the sleeping faces of David and Rhiannon.

The peace was absolute, before it was shattered by a piercing scream. Another swiftly followed it.

David awoke with a gasp, his frantic gaze darting across the small space separating his bed from Rhiannon's. What he saw had him throwing aside his blankets and hurrying to her side.

'Rhiannon, wake up!'

Tears coursed down her pale cheeks. Her head tossed violently and a babble of incoherent words escaped her lips.

'Rhiannon!'

David sat on the edge of the bed and touched her shoulder.

The reaction was instantaneous. A shrill cry burst from her and her eyelids flew open. The terror in her eyes was unmistakeable. Then she was launching herself towards him.

Blinded by the horror of the nightmare, Rhiannon flung herself at the comforting presence. She pressed her face into the solid warm chest, and clutched at the person with trembling fingers. A hand came to rest on her head and an arm wrapped around her waist. Yet still she could see nothing but the images from her dream:

A smirking Annabelle slipping her arm through David's and leading him away from where she was tied to a wall, her wrists bound with piano strings, the thin wire cutting into her flesh transforming into dozens of hands dragging her towards a black pit; then an ominous malevolence surrounding her when the pit morphed into a dark shadow, the insidious cloud stretching out over Valieoth Castle as a river of blood flowed from the Upper West Wing of the palace, the red stream transforming the Dairion Ocean into a vivid scarlet sea filled with the bodies of dragons and men.

Rhiannon shuddered, and a sob caught in her throat when the next image replayed: *A body washed ashore at her feet. Her hand reaching out to turn it over. A pair of eyes staring up at her, cold and dead and violet.*

A familiar voice called to her. She titled her head back and looked into the eyes from her dream, only these were blessedly alive.

'You were dead!' The hoarse exclamation was ripped from her. 'Everyone was dead!'

'Rhiannon, it was a dream.' David clasped her hand and held it tightly. 'Feel me, I'm right here with no intention of dying anytime soon.'

Another sob broke from her and she collapsed against him, a description of the nightmare spilling from her lips.

'None of it was real,' David assured her when she finished. 'With everything that's been happening at home, then coming back here where you were so unhappy and hearing of Kelandrus being hunted, it's not surprising you'd have a nightmare like that, but that's all it is. None of those things you saw have happened. And I can promise you there's only a handful of females whom I'll permit to lead me anywhere, and that conceited looking girl who made your life miserable is definitely not one of them.'

Rhiannon felt him stroke her unbound hair. A kiss as delicate as the brush of a butterfly wing touched her forehead. She closed her eyes, taking comfort in his words and the physical proof of life still existing within him.

For a long moment neither spoke until eventually the trembling of Rhiannon's body subsided and she reluctantly drew back.

'I'm sorry I woke you,' she said.

'It's all right,' replied David, and upon observing the haunted expression lingering in her eyes, announced, 'it means I get to tell you this now rather than waiting until the morning. I believe I figured out where the entrance to Merlin's secret laboratory could be.'

To this startling disclosure, which only partially distracted her thoughts from the still vivid memory of her nightmare, Rhiannon could only answer with a stunned, 'You have?'

'I can't say for certain, but I'm sure I'll be right. Just before I fell asleep I was thinking over what Kelandrus told us about Merlin saying anyone seeking to find it would have to search among the things that were lost. For a person to be able to do that, the items would first have to be found. After all, Merlin himself knew where they were and therefore they weren't lost in the strictest sense of the word. An item can be lost and found at the same time.'

Rhiannon puzzled over his words for only a few seconds before realisation dawned. 'Of course! If you lost your ring and I found it, you'd still consider it lost until you got it back.'

'Exactly. And Merlin said to search among "the things", implying they had been gathered into one location. In the palace I can only think of one room where that could be. The Unclaimed Property Room. It makes perfect sense. No one would think twice if they saw someone going in there, particularly a man who was reputed to be quite absentminded on occasion. They'd simply think he'd misplaced one of his belongings again.'

'David, that has to be it.' Excitement lit Rhiannon's face for a brief moment. Then she groaned in frustration. 'And we can't check until we go back and that's six weeks away!'

'I'm sure the time will pass quickly enough,' David soothed her, and observing the faint shadows which still dulled her normally bright eyes, he sought to distract her further. 'There's plenty for us to see here, and you'll have the lessons I'll be giving you. In fact, did you want to get a start on learning the healer's diagnostic technique? It might help if you had something else to focus on for a few minutes.' When Rhiannon agreed, he settled himself into a more comfortable position, ensuring their bodies were not touching, and explained, 'Primarily this technique is used by healers on their patients, or parents on their children, to check if something's wrong. When a mage touches another person and says *kai sartor, ilamae os* —'

'One body, two … souls?'

'Yes. When they say that, they can feel all the sensations in the other person's body and also see if the person's soul is in peril of separating from it. It takes a lot of practice to be able to isolate and identify the different sensations, but I can teach you the basics.

The first thing, though, is to get the pronunciation right. *Kai sartor, ilamae os.*'

'*Kai sartor, illarmae os.*'

'No. It's "ih-la-mae", not "ill-arm-ae". Try it again.'

'*Kai sartor, ilamae os.*'

'Excellent. Now, repeat it ten times, focusing on each syllable and what the words mean.'

Rhiannon obeyed and received a nod of approval when she finished.

'Very good. It's important to always ensure your pronunciation is correct.'

'What'll happen if I ever mispronounce one of the words?'

'Nothing. The technique simply won't work. Another important thing to remember is if the person can tell you where the pain is or you can see a wound, your hand needs to be placed either on it or as near to it as possible. If you're not sure, then hand to hand is best. Now, I'll demonstrate it to you so you can see what's supposed to happen. Are you ready?'

Rhiannon nodded.

'All right.' David reached out and touched her hand. '*Kai sartor, ilamae os.*'

Rhiannon saw the soft purple glow appear around their connected bodies. There was no gradual spread of light and she felt nothing apart from the warmth of David's hand on hers. A moment passed, then the gentle radiance faded.

'Well, the good news is that you're perfectly healthy,' David said, smiling. He moved his hand, placing it under hers. 'Your turn now, and I'll only get you to do it the once tonight. You'll feel disorientated the first couple of times. Being inundated with foreign sensations isn't the easiest experience to handle and it can take a while to become accustomed to it.'

Rhiannon hesitated. 'What happens if I lose my focus?'

'The connection will end by itself after a short period, so there's no danger of being trapped.'

'Do I have to close my eyes?'

'You don't have to, but most people find it easier to start off with them shut.'

Deciding that was good enough for her, Rhiannon took a deep breath and closed her eyes. In a clear voice, she spoke the required words.

As the last one fell from her lips, a ribbon of heat encircled her hand and David's.

A great wave of sensations engulfed her.

Her nerve endings sparked and tingled.

She felt the echo of a second heartbeat inside her chest, a rush of blood through arteries and veins which were not her own.

There was a faint throb in her head and an irritating scratch in her throat.

She opened her eyes.

A brilliant, pure light filled her vision; the luminous glow emanated from inside David's body to radiate outwards in a dazzling white aura. Rhiannon lifted her gaze to his face to see his violet eyes ablaze with an intense brightness.

It's his soul, she realised in awe. She stared enraptured at the beautiful sight until it vanished when the soft purple light faded.

'I saw your soul,' she whispered.

'That is one of the purposes of performing the technique.'

'It was … the light was … it was all around you. Inside you.'

'I'm glad to hear it. If it was rising above me then I'd be concerned.'

'Why?'

The humour left David's face, leaving it deadly serious. 'If the soul starts to rise out of the body, then the person's life is in danger. Once it's fully outside the body they're pretty much at death's door waiting to be let in.'

Rhiannon flinched. 'I hope I never have to see that.'

'Most people share the same hope. Now, apart from being bedazzled by the immortal part of me, how are you feeling? Any dizziness or nausea?'

Rhiannon shook her head. 'There was a lot going on at first and I could feel all sorts of things, but,' she paused, a frown creasing her brow, 'you've got a headache, haven't you?'

David stared at her in surprise. 'Only a minor one.'

'And a sore throat?'

'Nothing a few hours' sleep won't cure.' He shook his head, looking impressed. 'You did very well being able to isolate and identify two issues on your first attempt. It's usually a pretty good indication you'd make an excellent healer. When we get home you should definitely speak with the Chief Healer at the castle about training to be one. He'd be able to tell you more about it than I can.'

'I'll think about it but David, you should've said you weren't feeling well.'

'It's nothing dire,' he answered, waving her concern aside. He cast her a covert glance from under his lashes, and was pleased to see the tension brought on by the nightmare completely gone from her expression. Upon seeing her stifle a yawn, and not wishing to say anything which would remind her of the reason for their both being awake, he rose to his feet and returned to his bed, adding, 'However, I've no doubt you're about to nag at me to go to sleep, so I'll save you the trouble and take myself off.'

He smothered his grin with his pillow when Rhiannon's indignant, 'I don't nag!' rang out.

'All right, badger then,' he amended, and felt something soft thump him on the head. 'Thanks, but I don't need another one,' he said, tossing the pillow back to its owner.

Rhiannon huffed and turned her back to him. 'You're impossible,' she muttered.

'So I've frequently been told.' A brief pause fell. Then, 'Rhiannon?'

An indistinct mumble answered.

'I'm glad you're the one here with me.'

A long silence greeted David's words. Finally, 'I am too,' came Rhiannon's quiet reply.

An amicable peace descended, until, 'Even if you do nag at me.'

There was a gasp of disbelief, followed by a snort and then a gurgle of laughter.

'Shut up, David. And go to sleep.'

'Yes, Rhiannon.'

And in the dimly lit throne room, the two displaced magi closed their eyes and drifted off into a deep sleep, both sharing the conflicted hope that the next six weeks would pass quickly – but not too swiftly.

Chapter 17

FISTS AND FANGS

Rhiannon shifted in her seat beneath the pastel-green dome of the large Reading Room in the National Library of Ireland. She glanced at the upright antique clock on the well-polished wooden balcony. Upon seeing the time, she struggled to quell the desire to tell David to hurry up and decide on the next question for the impromptu quiz he had sprung on her that morning. They had been in Vetus svet for two weeks now and he had announced it was time she took one, although she was more inclined to believe he was doing it to distract himself from what he had learnt the day before. After reading a book about the atrocities perpetrated during the wars and conflicts of the twentieth century, his eagerness to learn more about Vetus svet had died a sudden death. Not even the discovery of another dialect in a language he knew had elicited any more than a disinterested, 'Those who speak it are obsessed with killing innocent people. Why would I want to learn it?'

The sound of a throat pointedly being cleared drew Rhiannon's attention back to the present. She looked at David who quirked an eyebrow at her, evidently waiting for an answer. Of course, he would ask the question when she was lost in thought.

'Sorry, could you repeat that?'

'I asked if you could name some of the medicinal uses of yellow-leaf verbena,' David repeated obligingly.

'Yes, I can.'

When she offered no further information, David's mouth twitched but his voice betrayed no evidence of amusement when he prompted, 'Name some examples, please.'

'Isn't that two questions?'

'Not the way I originally phrased the question. Examples, now.'

'Fine. The root and stem are used to make salves and elixirs to treat serious burns and infections. The flowers can be brewed into a tea to improve mental acuity. And when made into a paste the leaves are used to stop severe haemorrhaging.'

'Very good,' David commended her. 'In its purified form it's used to reverse the effects of mind-control agents such as mandrake juice, aconite and serpent's breath, along with countering the paralysing poison of several sea creatures, including bolpodes, coral snails and rainbow eels. You'll get extra marks on your test if you remember to list those.'

'I've heard about the bite of the rainbow eels, but what do the others do?'

'A bolpode will inject its poison through the tiny stingers covering the length of its five tentacles which it wraps around its prey. They normally go after small merchildren or vasker otters, but sometimes a human gets stung if they get too close to one.

'The coral snail shoots a dart to catch its prey and to defend itself. Their shells are rather lovely, so when they get washed ashore quite a number of children pick them up. Unfortunately, the disagreeable inhabitant of the shell is usually still alive and strikes out at them. If you ever come across a bright green shell with scarlet flecks, just leave it alone.'

'I was never one for picking up seashells anyway,' Rhiannon assured him. She tapped her fingers on top of the wooden desk, looking at the sheaf of paper in front of David where he had been keeping a tally of her marks. 'How'd I do?'

'Quite well, although your geography book could use more study when we return to Álnair. Avalon is the isle where the Ancient Dragons raised their hatchlings for the first few years, whereas Draco Island is simply called that due to its shape, and the Realm of Khoshek is desolate and uninhabitable but it's where we source the raw material needed for voice crystals.

'You also need to be more confident when conversing in another language. Try not to make every sentence sound like a question. Even if you mispronounce a few words or your sentences aren't grammatically perfect, say them as you normally would in English,' David instructed before checking the library clock.

Upon seeing it was approaching midday, he stood up and stretched his stiffened back muscles. 'King Brian should be outside soon so we'll leave it there for today. Besides, I don't know about you, but I'm starving. I hope wherever he's taking us for lunch has large servings.'

As luck would have it, the little restaurant to which King Brian took them in a quiet street in Rome not only had large servings of a delicious chicken cacciatore, but the friendly proprietress was so taken by David's handsome features and fluent Italian she was more than happy to keep his plate replenished until he announced he couldn't possibly eat another bite. Afterwards, when they paid using the money King Brian had again mysteriously procured for them, she offered the services of her youngest son to give them a tour of the ancient city, which, she said, was flooded with pilgrims ahead of the papal conclave.

Luciano, a high-spirited eighteen-year-old, spent the next few hours leading them through a vast number of picturesque streets to see the famous monuments of Rome, from the great Colosseum and Trevi Fountain to the ancient Pantheon and crowded Piazza

Navona. Finally, he took them to the majestic basilica of Saint Peter at the Vatican.

Fortunately, the concealment charm placed upon David's sword enabled them to pass through the security check with ease. Then they were walking through the magnificent rooms, admiring the beautiful paintings and sculptures lovingly created by so many artists.

To Rhiannon's relief, David's eyes slowly regained their twinkle and she knew the hallowed atmosphere of the building had helped ease the grief his reading of the day before had inflicted.

'Thank you for showing us around,' David said to Luciano as they exited the basilica. He looked up at the darkening evening sky. 'We should really let you go home now.'

'No, no,' Luciano refuted energetically. 'We share a meal first as friends. I shall buy. Come, I take you to my favourite place.'

Quite willing to spend some more time in the cheerful Italian's company, they accepted the offer and followed Luciano to their dinner destination.

Tommaso's at seven in the evening was a thriving scene of young socialites. It was hidden behind an unassuming sandwich shop, the dark colours of the popular English-style pub relieved by several soft lights and the colourful attire of its patrons. Seating was sparse, although this did not seem to bother many of those in the crowd.

Unfortunately, the loud music grated on David's ears. His mood was not improved when he noticed the attention he was garnering from several females in the room. He averted his gaze from their scandalously designed dresses and provocative gestures, and hastily retreated to a dark corner with Rhiannon and Luciano. To his dismay, he saw another cluster of girls following them. Not only that, but their words soon made it clear he was their target. As they spoke, their glances swept appraisingly and with uninhibited interest over his gold hair, violet eyes and tall physique.

He had never missed his Robesmen running intervention for him so much in his entire life.

He shot a furtive look at Rhiannon. Her tense shoulders and rigid expression told him she was ready to knock down the giggling females who were staring at her plain tunic and breeches with disdainful condescension.

David reached his limit. He opened his mouth and to his listeners a lilting, yet incomprehensible babble spoken in a coldly polite tone issued forth.

The girls shared a puzzled look. They turned to Luciano who only gave a good-natured shrug. Several of the group gave David a regretful smile and turned away. The two who remained were not to be discouraged so easily. Their voices rose in volume to rival the music, their words spoken slowly in their own language.

'He's not deaf,' Rhiannon finally exploded. 'And can't you see he's already with me?' she demanded.

The girls stared at her in disbelief.

David took the opportunity that had conveniently presented itself and took Rhiannon's hand in his own. A smile curled his lips. This time, the Drakaron heard by his listeners was spoken in a warm, caressing voice.

Then David raised the small hand in his and kissed it.

A disgruntled mumbling came from the girls as they finally retreated, leaving David, Rhiannon and Luciano alone once more.

'You wait here,' Luciano instructed, his tone jovial. 'I'll bring the food back. If you go, too much trouble,' he told David. '*Sei troppo bello!*'

'What did he say?' Rhiannon asked after Luciano had left.

David rubbed his neck. 'He said I'm too handsome.'

'Well, he's not wrong about that,' Rhiannon decreed. 'But those girls should learn some manners. Honestly! Couldn't they see I was with you? What sort of person do they think you are?

Besides, it's not like I would let you go so easily. Did they expect me to?'

That caught David off guard.

'You wouldn't let me go?' he asked.

'Of course not!'

A pleased smile spread across David's face. 'That's good to know,' he murmured.

Luciano returned fifteen minutes later bearing a tray of hamburgers and chips and three fruit cocktails. While they ate their meal, groups around them came and went. In among the Italian being spoken the mixture of other languages increased.

It was after Rhiannon left to wash her hands in the restroom when one noisy horde began making a scene. Luciano suggested it would be best to leave.

'They will make trouble,' he said quietly in Italian. 'It's not safe for the signorina to stay.'

David checked his hand instinctively moving towards the invisible hilt of his sword. He understood the language being spoken and no threats were being made against anyone.

'They're demanding more drinks,' he said.

'Soon they will go after any lady here and it will not matter if she refuses them,' Luciano answered with evident disapproval. 'They come to our city, abuse our hospitality and do not work, then their men dishonour our women, and we are told we are not allowed to fight them. But I did one night.' He pushed up his sleeve to proudly display a nasty scar on his arm. 'They tried to hurt my Rosa, so I hit back.'

David cast a worried glance in the direction Rhiannon had gone several minutes before. She had received extensive defence training but even the most skilled fighter could be taken by surprise.

'I'll wait for Rhiannon outside the restroom,' he said.

He stood up and headed to the outdoor courtyard.

'I told you to let me go! I won't say it again!'

Rhiannon's indignant voice quickened his steps.

David ran through the doorway to see Rhiannon deliver a hard blow to a man's stomach, then follow it up with a sharp kick to his right knee.

The man collapsed to the ground with a bellow of pain.

David was fairly certain the man's kneecap had been shattered.

Several people shuffled by, anxious to get back into the building away from the scene, while a few others David had seen arrive with the noisy horde inside turned with baleful expressions towards Rhiannon. The words they spat at her, which she mercifully would not understand, had his blood burning within his veins.

He wasted no time in placing himself before them as they went to advance on her.

'You would do well to use a more courteous tongue when addressing a lady,' he said coldly in their own language. 'Now apologise.'

The men broke into rowdy laughter, while their two female companions jeered, 'Who's going to make us? A mealymouthed suckling like you?' And turning to the men, they urged with fiendish delight, 'Go teach the insolent brat a lesson.'

One of the men snorted. 'With five of us against a mere stripling we'll drive the lesson home real deep.'

With a vicious snarl, the men rushed at David, displaying all the confidence of a pack of wolves attacking a weakened prey. It was clear they believed he would fall without much of a fight.

They swiftly discovered their error.

His concealed sword remaining sheathed at his side, David wove among them, incapacitating each one with ease. Not even slightly winded by the altercation, his tall, lithe form performed each debilitating kick and punch with minimal effort. Compared to sparring with Sir Raeden, Izana and Gareth, these cowards posed no challenge to him.

Upon witnessing their companions suffer such an ignominious defeat, the two women set their sights on Rhiannon. With a screech of rage, they launched themselves at her in a savage onslaught, their own lack of skill in fighting evident in the wild swings they aimed at her head. Rhiannon swatted them away like she would a bothersome fly.

'Luciano is waiting out the front,' David said when all their opponents lay on the ground, either too hurt or too afraid to get back up. Without another glance at them, he turned and guided Rhiannon out of the pub, through the sandwich shop and across the cobblestone street. Luciano stood waiting at the far end of a wide fountain built into a high wall.

The anxious look on the Italian's face transformed to one of relief when he saw them approaching.

'Signorina is well?' he asked in his heavily accented English.

'*Si*,' Rhiannon replied, using one of the few Italian words she had learnt.

A commotion from inside Tommaso's forestalled any further conversation. Several harsh voices were yelling above the booming music. The shouts were growing louder. Then a large group stampeded out into the street, their faces twisted in rage.

'What is it? What are they saying?'

David looked down at Rhiannon. 'It would appear the cowards in the courtyard took offence to my defending you. They've sought the assistance of their friends to hunt down the "golden-haired devil".' There was another burst of vitriol. David's eyes narrowed and his lips tightened. 'They're not being very complimentary about you, either.'

A great roar went up. They had been spotted.

The self-appointed leader of the rabble stepped forward, his face a grotesque mask of hatred while a string of vile threats poured from his mouth. These increased, and his voice attained the hysterical pitch of a rabid fanatic when David continued to stand unflinchingly against them with an unsettling glint of steel in his eyes.

'I won't let them lay a single finger upon you,' David promised, 'but should any slip by me, use whatever enchantment you need to defend yourself.'

'We could just use the Aoratos Charm and vanish.'

'And Luciano, how would he fare if we disappeared?'

As though to emphasise David's question, someone in the crowd hurled a glass bottle at the Italian. He ducked and it shattered against the lamppost behind him.

'Fair point,' Rhiannon muttered.

She raised her right hand, the words of a charm ready on her lips.

Then a flicker of movement caught her attention.

There, underneath the fountain and less than three feet away from the approaching mob, were dozens upon dozens of tiny pairs of eyes. The unmistakeable silhouette of a large feline peered out to glare at the noisome intruders and bare its fangs in a warning hiss.

An idea sparked in Rhiannon's mind. In a loud voice, she cried, 'My friends, that crowd is threatening me. Chase them far away from here.'

A chorus of fierce yowls answered her and from under the fountain streaked a clowder of growling cats. Their sharp claws extended, they leapt at their targets with merciless precision, each deep scratch and piercing bite eliciting a cry of pain from the panic-stricken thugs.

Then came the snarling bark of dogs.

Rhiannon, David and Luciano turned to see a pack of baying canines race out of a narrow laneway and launch themselves into the fray. Snapping at the heels of the now terrified group, the dogs hounded the screaming throng down the street while above them the birds of Rome joined the chase in a thundering flutter of wings.

'Well done,' David congratulated her once the dissonant mixture of sounds faded into the distance.

Rhiannon accepted his praise with a smile while Luciano stared at them both in disbelief. A burst of Italian flowed from his lips and he gestured wildly with his hands.

David nodded and replied before turning to Rhiannon. 'He's not sure how you did it, but he's extremely grateful to you for calling on the animals to defend us. In fact, he would like you to ask them to chase off any future troublemakers in the same manner.'

'I could, but he'd have to promise to make sure they got fed. Some of them looked half-starved.'

Luciano, his exuberance calming slightly, assured her in English that the animals would get as much food as he could supply. Soon after, the cats and dogs returned looking inordinately pleased with themselves. Rhiannon made them the offer, which they eagerly accepted with a crescendo of rumbling purrs and excited barks.

When informed of their agreement, Luciano said, '*Grazie mille, signorina!*' and repeated it numerous times until he finally left them at the front of a modest hotel with another burst of enthusiastic Italian flowing from his lips.

'We'll have to get King Brian to check on him sometime in the future,' David remarked as they watched the happy young man walk away.

'To make sure everything is all right?'

'That, plus I'd like to know if Luciano was sincere about erecting a statue in honour of the "mystic lady with gold eyes".'

'Is that what he said just now before he left?' Rhiannon exclaimed, startled.

'More or less,' replied David. He kept to himself Luciano's exact words of "the mystic lady with gold eyes and her sweetheart."

Perhaps one day he would tell her, if by some good fortune their relationship came to match Luciano's description of the proposed effigy.

~*Chapter 18*~

A Shot in the Dark

Honestly, David. We've been here six weeks and you've seen plenty of girls wearing skimpier outfits in some of the places we've visited.'

It was their last evening in Vetus svet and a visit to central London had seemed a harmless way to pass the time. At least, it had until they reached this particular storefront.

Rhiannon took her blushing friend's arm and pulled him away from the lingerie boutique's night-time display. Secretly, she thought it adorable that a boy who could hold his own in a fight and perform death-defying tricks on a horse was so embarrassed at seeing a simple chemise and pair of garters on a dummy.

'But, Rhiannon, those were a lady's *undergarments*.' The last was said in a horrified whisper as David permitted himself to be led away. 'How can they display them so openly like that where everyone can see them?'

Rhiannon shrugged. 'Someone probably raised a fuss and got permission to do it a long time ago. There's bound to be several shops around here displaying ones for men as well.'

David shook his head. 'In Álnair no tailor or dressmaker would dare do anything so improper.'

283

'Then it's a good thing we'll be going home soon so you won't have to see them anymore. Now come on,' Rhiannon urged him. 'There's a park up this way and I've had enough of walking around these streets. I just want to sit under a tree for a while where I can breathe something other than car fumes.'

No objection came from David, who was willing to leave the stench and noise of the traffic behind. With every city they visited in Vetus svet he discovered the deafening cacophony increasingly unpleasant. The roar of cars and motorbikes, the screech of trains, the rumble of aeroplanes, all of these were rivalled by the hordes of people yelling abuse at one another, or some obnoxiously loud music pounding inside his head with singers whose voices sounded like a screaming goat's. He much preferred the quiet serenity of the old library in Dublin, or the mountains and forests where there was no chance of having their senses assaulted by the foul odours and noises of the cities.

'Hey there, handsome. She your sister?'

And where he didn't have to worry about scantily-clad females trying to flirt with him every ten minutes. David looked at the three women approaching them from out of the shadows of a tall building and inwardly cringed.

Rhiannon shifted closer to him, her hand tightening its grip on his arm. Her eyes narrowed at the heavily made-up faces of the women.

'How old are ya, darlin'?'

'Is tha' hair colour an' yer doll eyes fer real?'

The three came to a halt a short distance from David and Rhiannon, the cloying scent of their perfume overpowering the stench of rubbish drifting out of a nearby alleyway.

'*Píaken, atshi nolista kor.*'

The three strangers stepped back at David's reply.

''ere, wha' was tha'?'

'What did you say?'

'He said, "Sorry, I don't understand you",' Rhiannon informed them, hoping the women would retreat like most of the other females had done whenever she and David used the ploy. Regrettably, they did not.

'Don' he speak English?' the shortest of them asked.

'It doesn't matter if he can't, the girl knows what we're saying and that's good enough,' the first woman said.

The seductive smile fell from her face.

An ominous click was heard.

The woman lifted her hand to reveal the sharp point of a switchblade. The silver metal of the knife gleamed wickedly in the gentle glow radiating from the nearby lamppost.

Beneath her hand, Rhiannon felt David's arm muscles flex and his body attain the tension of a cat preparing to pounce. She discreetly removed her hand. A glance at their surroundings revealed only a handful of oblivious pedestrians farther up the path.

'You're both going to come quietly with us to that alley.' The knife-wielding mugger tilted her head to indicate the alley entrance behind her. An unpleasant smirk curled her lips. 'Regular toffs you are, judging by your fine clothes and jewellery. That necklace you're wearing should be worth a couple of hundred,' she informed Rhiannon, 'and if you don't want your face messed up, you'll tell your boyfriend to … AH!'

The shrill cry of pain rang out loudly. David, in one fluid spin, kicked the knife out of the mugger's hand and unsheathed his sword with a chilling hiss of steel. His muttered *Undolthgare* to reveal its existence accompanied the knife striking the pavement with a metallic clatter.

The three muggers stared in transfixed terror at their now armed victim who was looking at them with cold eyes, the sword held in his unnervingly steady hand poised at a threatening angle. Immediately, a flood of panicked words fell from their lips.

'We weren't really gonna harm ya.'

'What are you?'

'Ya pulled tha' outta thin air!'

'It were only a joke,' the youngest of them cried. She turned to look pleadingly at Rhiannon. 'Tell him we was jokin'.'

'I do not consider threats of physical violence against my friends to be the least bit humorous,' David bit out, his eyes hard and lit by a dangerous light.

'Y-You do speak English.'

'Fluently. And I'll use my knowledge of it to tell you to drop any other weapons you may have on your persons.'

'The … the knife's all we got.'

David fixed them with a gimlet eye and ordered, 'Then get out of my sight before I give you the thrashing you richly deserve for your arrant piece of knavery.'

The muggers turned and fled into the alley without another word, desperate to escape the fierce glare of their former prey.

'I think you scared them half to death,' Rhiannon commented.

'Hopefully they'll think twice before attempting to rob another person,' David replied.

He sheathed his sword, then walked across the pavement to pick up the knife. He examined it in silence before tossing it into a bin. 'Let's go.'

Rhiannon stepped forward to join him.

'NO!' The feminine screech was followed by the loud crash of falling bins. The sounds of a scuffle came from the dark alleyway. There was the splintering explosion of glass shattering against stone. Then a piercing scream split the air.

'Zain! DON'T!'

The shrill voice was followed by the sharp report of a gunshot.

Something wet splashed on Rhiannon's face.

David stumbled and fell.

Behind his falling body Rhiannon saw a man step out of the

shadows of the alleyway. The lead mugger raced out after him. The man's arm was raised.

'*Cosain!*'

A radiant flash of gold light appeared.

There was another gunshot.

The bullet ricocheted off Rhiannon's magical shield with a harsh *ping*.

Fear had her casting another charm without thinking.

'*KETEVOS!*'

The binding enchantment sped towards the petrified attackers, the deep blue streams of light swiftly immobilising them.

Running footsteps and concerned shouts erupted in the distance.

A gurgling noise sounded at Rhiannon's feet.

She looked down, then dropped to her knees, a cold band crushing her heart. David's face was leached of all colour, leaving it deathly pale. A red liquid trickled from his mouth, running down his cheek towards his ear. A dark stain was forming on the right side of his shirt, while a pool of blood was swiftly spreading out beneath him. There was an audible sucking noise escaping through the hole in his chest with every breath he took. When she looked into his eyes, Rhiannon felt her heart stutter at the dark shadows now shrouding them.

'R … Rhiannon …'

David's choked whisper was drowned out by a chorus of voices telling her to move aside.

Someone touched her arm.

Instinctively, she turned, shouting, '*Soporus!*'

There was an explosion of yellow light.

The people gathering on the pavement collapsed where they stood in a deep enchanted sleep.

Rhiannon gazed back at David to find his eyes closed against the night sky, his long, dark lashes in stark contrast to the whiteness of his cheeks. The shallow rise and fall of his stomach, and the wheezing hiss issuing from his wound, were the only indication that he still lived.

Using the hole in his shirt, Rhiannon tore the material asunder, exposing the bloodstained flesh of David's torso. His hard muscles twitched spasmodically. Sweat glistened amidst the blood on his pale skin. Rhiannon hurriedly placed her hands on his chest over the bloody wound, the words of the diagnostic technique falling from her lips.

'*Kai sartor ilamae os.*'

Her pronunciation was flawless.

A soft purple light shone around their connected bodies.

Rhiannon felt the echoing rush of blood through her body, the frantic beat of a second heart inside her own and a sharp, lancing pain in her chest as though a red-hot poker had pierced right through it.

But, most terrifying of all, was what she saw.

The iridescent glow of David's soul was no longer emanating from inside his body. The white brilliance was hovering outside it with wispy thin tendrils of light clinging desperately to the mortal frame.

'*Once it's fully outside the body they're pretty much at death's door waiting to be let in.*'

David's words replayed inside Rhiannon's mind.

A strong surge of desperation washed over her.

Tears threatened to blur her vision. Fiercely, she blinked them back.

She stared at his face and pressed down on his chest, feeling the hot, sticky blood seep through her fingers.

No! I can't lose him. I can't.

Her mental screams repeated over and over again even as she implored, 'David, please. Don't die! Please don't leave me.'

She closed her eyes and leaned forward.

There was an overwhelming sensation rising inside her very being. It came from the deepest depths of her soul. She could feel that part of herself reaching out towards David, wrapping itself around him like a protective cocoon and enveloping him in a loving embrace. Two entities became entwined, forming a single being. Each inside the other.

Please! Help him, I beg you!

A brilliant aura suffused Rhiannon's body, unseen by any human but witnessed by a curious squirrel and several silent birds.

An intense heat engulfed Rhiannon's heart. The blazing warmth flowed down her arms, through her hands and into David.

Take it. Take all of it! Please. Heal him. Save him.

Rhiannon's petition continued, even as she was swamped in a flood of emotions not her own. Unfamiliar images began to play inside her mind. She saw younger versions of all those she knew in Álnair. She watched as they grew older. The feelings of affection deepened, becoming a tidal wave of protective devotion and admiration. She saw herself, but not as she was when she looked in a mirror. Her features and build remained the same; however, this version of her seemed unusually beautiful.

Time lost all meaning. The slideshow of foreign memories played on. In among the deluge of tender feelings came also sparks of agonised guilt and hurt.

Rhiannon's mystical embrace never eased from around David.

The stream of transcendent warmth from inside her to him did not cease.

Then, *'Rhiannon. You have to stop!'*

David's voice was all around her. Inside her.

'Rhiannon —'

'No!' she cried back. *'I have to save you.'*

'You have. Now, please, stop. You're exhausting yourself.'

'But your wound —'

'Is healed. Look, Rhiannon.'

Rhiannon's eyelids flickered open to reveal her golden eyes burning with luminous light.

She removed her hands and stared down at an unblemished expanse of skin. The wound was completely healed with not even a scar remaining to mar David's flesh.

She sensed the unseen part of her slowly disengage itself from around David and pull back into her body. She laid a hand back on his chest and performed the diagnostic technique once more.

The soft purple light illuminated their bodies. She felt the echo of a steady heartbeat inside her own. The pain was gone from her chest. The gushing flow of blood in arteries and veins had calmed. And most glorious of all, the effulgent glow of David's soul was now back in his body, the pure radiance shining more brilliantly than ever.

Rhiannon tilted her head back to look up at the heavens.

'Thank you,' she whispered. Gazing down once more, she reached out and smoothed David's hair away from his face, uncaring of the streaks of blood she left behind on his brow.

'David, wake up,' she called, aching to see his eyes wide open and aglow with life. Vaguely remembering the explosive power of her Soporus Charm, she whispered, '*Vinaro.*'

The aqua light of the counter-charm flowed from her hand onto David's cheek. His eyelashes fluttered.

But then a great pressure was bearing down upon her, exhaustion overwhelming her senses. She collapsed forward, her body falling on top of David's like a puppet whose strings had been cut. Her face lay against his neck, the coppery smell of blood mingled with the clean, woodsy scent unique to him causing her stomach to roil in protest.

Rhiannon tried to move her arms, to push herself up, all to no avail. She could not even lift her head when a gentle hand came to rest upon it and David's dear voice said quietly, 'I told you you were exhausting yourself. Just rest now, Rhiannon. I'm all right, thanks to you, and I'll take care of everything else.'

Too drained of energy to offer a reply, Rhiannon fought a losing battle to keep her eyes open as David sat up with the same smooth grace he had perfected whilst performing stunts on Cináed. His arms were bands of steel holding Rhiannon against him, and she felt the vibrations in his chest when he called out for King Brian. Then it was as though she were underwater. All sounds became muffled and distorted. A curious weightlessness overtook her body. She felt the touch of a warm pair of lips on her brow, and then everything descended into a vat of blissful oblivion as sleep claimed her.

~*Chapter 19*~

GRIM REVELATIONS

Time went unmarked by Rhiannon. She did not see the waning light of the moon and stars, or the night sky lighten into the golden splendour of dawn. However, coming out of the comforting realm of sleep, she was immediately aware of three things.

One: She was curled up under the blankets on a soft bed.

Two: The distinctive cool, moist scent of King Brian's cave surrounded her.

And three: Someone was lightly tapping her nose.

'Go 'way,' she groused tiredly, snuggling deeper into her pillow.

'You're really not a morning person, are you,' an amused voice said, 'and I would let you sleep, but then we'd miss our way home.'

There was a brief, silent pause as Rhiannon's befuddled mind took a moment to identify the owner of the voice. Then:

'You're alive!'

Her eyes snapped open to gaze up into the violet ones looking down at her. The next instant she leapt out of the bed and hurled herself against David. Burying her face into the smooth material of his Álnairian tunic, she hugged him, her arms tightening their hold as memories of his brush with death assailed her.

'Don't ever scare me like that again,' she sobbed, feeling his chest rise and fall with comforting regularity.

'I shall certainly try not to,' came David's gentle reply.

In a soothing gesture, he stroked the hair streaming down her back and lowered his head to rest it against the top of hers. 'I owe you my life, Rhiannon. And I can't think of anyone to whom I'd prefer to be indebted than you.'

Her grip on his tunic tightened. 'I was terrified.'

'Yet you still managed to save me, and all without any training in advanced healing. Though I wish it hadn't come at the cost of you exhausting yourself. You've been asleep for twelve hours.'

'What!' Rhiannon drew back in surprise. 'I can't have been.'

'Yes, you can.' David's expression was serious. 'It's almost ten o'clock in the morning. You used a lot of energy to heal me. On top of that you put a whole group of people to sleep and magically bound two assailants.'

'Oh, I completely forgot about them. Please don't tell me all those people were left lying in the street for most of the night!'

'Don't worry, after King Brian and I cleaned my blood off you and brought you here, we returned so I could wake them up. I also removed the bindings on that unsavoury pair of reprobates. They both looked ready to pass out when they saw me standing over them in what remained of my shirt. The woman thought I was a ghost and went into hysterics. I doubt she'll be in a rush to attack anyone else in future.'

'What about the man? It's not right he won't be punished for shooting you.'

'Who said he won't be punished? King Brian's already promised to have his people pay him regular visits, and they won't be sociable ones I can assure you.'

'I don't see how him suffering through those will make up for what he did.'

'You would have him punished with an action proportionate to his crime?'

Rhiannon reached out and placed her hand over the spot where the bullet had torn through her friend's chest. The undamaged tunic and her white flesh blurred and she saw the blood-stained ones of the night before.

'I don't know,' she confessed honestly. 'There was so much blood and I saw your soul. It was completely outside your body and struggling to remain connected. You were almost dead and I doubt he would've cared if you'd died.'

'Perhaps not, but were I to take retributive justice, who would save his life after I inflicted the wound on him? And if he died, then would not the punishment have exceeded the crime? In the midst of battle, death is often the judgement passed, even on the ones who might never have killed another. But whereas on a battlefield there is a need for such acts, in situations like these there is not. Mercy may be shown in the administering of justice, so that while hard punishment is given, it is not to the full extent to which it could be done. Therefore, King Brian and his people will ensure the man receives sufficient punishment for what he attempted, only without the shedding of his blood.'

'How will they do that?'

'I've left it up to their imagination and I believe he will soon be wishing he'd been taken before a human court to face trial. Being tormented by leprechauns is bad enough when they like you. I dread to think what they will dream up for someone they're punishing.'

'Nothin' pleasant, me young friend. Nothin' pleasant at all,' came King Brian's grim voice.

David and Rhiannon turned to look where he was now standing a short distance from them. They noticed his eyes were without their normal twinkling smile.

'If it hadn't been for Lady Rhiannon, ye'd be dead. And accordin' to a raven who were perched nearby, if she hadn't got her shield up when she did, she'd have been lyin' on the ground right beside you. Me people were furious when they heard what happened, and they'll make sure the man receives his just punishment.' King Brian then changed the subject by announcing, 'The foramens will be appearin' in ten minutes. I'll be takin' ye both to the one near Himeji Castle and anythin' you want to take back to Álnair can be transported by me people who go through the ones in Warsaw and Prague.'

David indicated towards his bed where several booklets he had picked up lay on the coverlet, along with the journal he had been keeping during their time in Vetus svet.

'Just those for me, thanks. The journal and booklets on the left they can leave at the palace, but could you have them take the other booklets to the Basilica of Saint John?'

King Brian nodded and turned to Rhiannon who could only think of one thing.

'The photo of my grandparents is all I want,' she said.

'It's in my pocket,' David informed her, then both he and King Brian waited as she went and hastily changed into her riding dress, tugged on her boots and ran a quick brush through her hair.

After ensuring the star crystal pendant was fastened around her neck, Rhiannon returned to find the ten minutes had decreased to one, and the items on David's bed were gone.

A crowd of leprechauns had gathered in the throne room to bid them farewell. Their smiling faces were the last thing Rhiannon and David saw before King Brian whisked them away to the expansive grounds of Himeji Castle in Japan.

The peace in the exquisite garden was absolute. No tourists remained to walk amidst the last of the falling cherry blossoms, and a lone bird chirped its evening song across the still waters of the moat. The glow of the setting sun transformed the towering white walls of the castle to a glistening gold, and the clear sky was painted a glorious vision of colour from a celestial palette.

A gardener, busily tending a shrub carelessly stepped on by a passing visitor, murmured a coaxing word of encouragement to the plant, unaware of the trio behind him.

Then the omen, warning of the foramen's imminent arrival, came. The sudden, strong gust of wind sent a sea of blossoms and leaves across the garden.

The gardener ducked his head, shielding his eyes from the onslaught.

David reached out and clasped Rhiannon's hand.

In the brief pause when the wind dropped, the gardener spotted them.

A stern lecture in his native tongue flew from his lips.

David called back an apologetic reply, even as the pink and white petals scattered across the ground swirled up in a dizzying display.

The last David and Rhiannon saw of the gardener was the man's astonished expression as the whirlwind enveloped them, and then he and Vetus svet were gone.

Their eyes shut tightly against the whirling kaleidoscope of colours, David and Rhiannon listened to King Brian's gleeful laughter as they spun and twisted through the foramen. Both their empty stomachs lurched uncomfortably with every tumbling turn they made.

Rhiannon's pendant repeatedly struck against her chest.

They began to descend at a great pace.

David's hand tightened its grip on Rhiannon's.

They were slowing in their downward slide.

Then their feet touched upon the hard and firm surface of cobblestone. The clatter of hoofs and chattering voices surrounded them. A horse whinnied in startled surprise.

They had landed right in the middle of a busy thoroughfare.

David dragged Rhiannon out of the path of the snorting geldings pulling a large carriage. A burst of blistering insults erupted from the driver as he urged his mounts onwards.

'We're in Graynor,' David announced. 'That's the Chief Consul's house.'

He pointed in front of them to the prominent building of grey stone and lattice windows. It had a magnificent flight of steps leading to an imposing entrance fronted by six tall columns. The main door was guarded by two sentries, both of whom were arrayed in matching cloaks and tunics of a rich blue, black breeches and high boots.

'Members of the Visgard,' David said. 'Each Chief Consul has a company of them under his command to assist with maintaining peace and order. They also help investigate situations like that involving Fotgroy.'

Rhiannon saw one of the Visgard look up and spot them.

'Your Royal Highness!' he called out. However, he and the city of Graynor abruptly disappeared when King Brian transported them to the dearly familiar surroundings of the Great Hall at Valieoth Castle.

Their arrival behind one of the large pillars near the main entrance went unnoticed by the crowd assembled at the other end of the resplendently lit room, and by the two crowned monarchs seated on their gold thrones.

David and Rhiannon slowly moved away from the pillar, their hearts rejoicing to hear once more the beloved voice of King Stephen as he addressed Lord Sharbel.

'— and inform Lord Grenwa he is to ensure a fair amount is to be paid to all those injured in the accident. Those members of the crew fit for duty are to be reassigned. Any unable to return to their normal duties are to have alternative employment found for them.'

Lord Sharbel bowed. 'It shall be done, Sire.'

'Now, for the report from Malpars on the missing tuagust.'

King Stephen turned his attention to the group of humanoid figures whose grey flesh was only covered by a diaphanous piece of pale cloth. Their white hair and faded blue eyes completed their ghostlike appearance.

'R'lon, it has now been nigh on twelve months since last anyone saw K'el. Has there been any word of him?'

The tallest among the delegation of tuagust stepped forward and gave a low bow from the waist.

'Your Majesty,' he said in a whispery monotone voice, 'we are continuing our search of the island, but no trace of him has been found.'

'We are sorry to hear it,' King Stephen replied, his manner completely sincere.

'We have begun to believe K'el is not lost on the island, but must have ventured too far in the deep waters and been taken by a karatos. He was ever committing the most foolish of acts at the behest of others, and had often been caught by a passing Ríyun swimming farther out than he should have been. A colony of them are making inquiries of all those who live in the ocean to discover if his fate lies within its depths.'

'One must hope it does not and he will soon return to you and your people alive and unharmed,' King Stephen said. 'Our offer to provide assistance in the search shall always remain open until he is found.'

R'lon gave another deep bow. 'Your Majesty is most kind.'

King Stephen responded to the praise with a friendly inclination of the head, then turned towards the three affluently dressed farmers in the audience.

'My people from the plains near Mount Perdus, the question as to who has the right to graze cattle at the foot of the mountain was decided in March by His Royal Highness, Crown Prince David, and received our full approval. You also indicated your acceptance of the decision. We have read your new petition seeking to restrict your neighbours' access to the area and can find no just cause as to why this should be done. Your accusation against them of cattle theft has been proven groundless by investigations conducted by both the Chief Consul of Ardara and a company of our own Royal Guard, and we can find no evidence confirming their involvement in the murder of your herdsmen. While we may empathise with your situation, we cannot approve any action which would seem to unofficially declare the guilt of your neighbours. Therefore, until the truth of the thefts and murders is revealed, we will not permit any cattle to be mustered within a league of Mount Perdus.'

A gasp to his left made King Stephen pause. He looked to the side in time to see his wife abruptly stand up, her gown rustling with the suddenness of her movement.

'Maiwen?'

Her name had barely passed his lips when she released a tearful laugh and flew down the dais steps with an ecstatic cry of, 'DAVID!'

Several House Faeries hovering nearby took one look at the returned Prince and his companions, then vanished to spread the good news to all within the castle grounds.

King Stephen rose to his feet with a hasty request for his audience's indulgence and understanding, and swiftly followed his queen down the length of the hall, his gaze fixed on the smiling face of his son.

Queen Maiwen ran to her only child, threw her arms around him and clung to him with all the loving fervour her maternal heart possessed. A few steps behind her came King Stephen. The monarch's relief was evident to those who witnessed him drawing his family into the circle of his arms and bestowing a fatherly kiss on David's brow.

A moment passed as all three lost themselves in the joy of their reunion. Queen Maiwen declared she had felt in her heart that some terrible harm had befallen her son the previous night. Her happiness at finding him whole, with no visible sign of injury, was the only thing that prevented her from seeing the fleeting shadow in his eyes. Then Rhiannon was being drawn into the welcoming embrace by King Stephen. Between him and his wife, she blinked back the sting of tears at their sincere pleasure in her return and again when they both kissed her on the cheek.

A distraction came in the form of King Brian when, after being thanked by David's parents for his assistance, he loudly assured them that he had been pleased to have their son and Rhiannon as his guests, and they had both behaved with great propriety. Rhiannon suspected the last was said for the benefit of the other people remaining in the Great Hall who were watching them with keen interest. And then he turned to David, assured him he would let him know how the punishment went for his attacker and disappeared with a cheery wave.

'Attacker?' Queen Maiwen did not waste a second before immediately demanding an explanation. The one she received was highly edited by David and culminated in him announcing that Rhiannon had saved his life.

It was while Rhiannon was recovering her breath after almost being smothered by Queen Maiwen's tight embrace of gratitude that all five of David's Robesmen ran through the doorway. Their haste conveying the depth of their jubilation, they quickly surrounded David and Rhiannon as their prince greeted them in his own inimitable fashion.

'How're all my mother hens? My word, John! You look as though you haven't slept in weeks! And is that grey hair I see? Stop it, Gareth! I'm fine. No broken bones or anything. Never fear, Izana; I promise I behaved myself and don't start apologising. That goes for you too, John! Happy birthday for yesterday, Eamon. We'll have to see about getting us all to Fagin's Flagon for a proper toast, now that we're back. A smile, Derrick? Now I know you missed us. And what are you and Gareth doing here? Shouldn't you be at the Academy preparing for your finals?'

'We've been staying here with the others since the day you went through the foramen,' said Gareth.

'But your classes —'

'Our professors send us the week's lessons in advance,' Derrick explained.

'And we've already received the ones for this week,' Gareth announced, 'so we'll stay until Saturday.'

'You could return now if you wanted to. You just want to hear all their stories about Vetus svet.' Eamon's comment elicited nothing more than a blithe, 'Of course,' from the fair-haired Robesman.

'I'll tell you about it,' promised David, 'but first Rhiannon and I would love some breakfast. We had to miss it this morning and we're famished.'

'I'm sure Wenlon would be happy to make you something,' said his mother. 'He may even have some of your favourite lemon tarts already prepared and in the oven.'

David's eyes lit up with delight. 'I tasted so many different ones in Vetus svet but none were as good as his.'

John grinned. 'I thought you looked a bit plump. Didn't you exercise at all?'

'Only enough to work up an appetite for another tart,' was David's smart rejoinder.

Laughter rippled through the Great Hall and Rhiannon's face was bright with it when she withdrew her arms from around Izana.

Then she looked towards the main entrance and met the stern gaze of her guardian.

Sir Raeden strode forward, his long stride covering the short distance between them in a matter of seconds. He welcomed David back with courteous civility, observing that all Álnair would greet the news with much celebration. Then he returned his attention to Rhiannon.

All sounds faded inside the hall as its occupants watched the taciturn Commander of the Guard in silence, curious to see his reaction to the reappearance of his ward.

Rhiannon suppressed the impulse to try burrowing through the marble floor and stood still, certain the unsmiling expression on Sir Raeden's face heralded a stringent lecture.

Her astonishment was therefore tremendous when her reserved guardian stepped closer and placed his arms about her. One cool, tender hand clasped the back of her head, and the scent of sandalwood enveloped her as her forehead was pressed against his tunic.

'Now I may be at ease.' The quiet words were spoken so softly none save Rhiannon could hear them. 'Dear child, to see you unharmed is the greatest joy, and I praise the Lord for your safe return.'

Her guardian's unusual demonstrative behaviour brought a tremulous smile to Rhiannon's lips. She gave an audible sniff and drew back to look up at his face.

'I'm sorry I worried you,' she said, adding with an irrepressible twinkle, 'but I'm sure you knew I'd be back. I couldn't leave your storage cupboard in a mess now, could I?'

A glint of humour transformed Sir Raeden's eyes to a clear sapphire blue.

'It is for that reason I did not finish cleaning it myself,' he observed wryly.

It was late when David and Rhiannon gratefully set out from the Imperial Stables on Cináed and Kateri, accompanied by all five of the prince's Robesmen. After consuming a tempting array of pastries and fruit to ease their gnawing hunger, and a long visit from a greatly relieved Endrille, they had spent several hours in private conversation with King Stephen, Queen Maiwen and Sir Raeden, the three adults having insisted on hearing the tales of their adventures in Vetus svet away from curious ears. Once again, their account of the incident from the previous night was extremely condensed, with no mention made of how near-death David had come. Still, Rhiannon knew her guardian and King Stephen suspected there was more to the story than what they had been told and they only refrained from voicing their suspicions out of consideration for Queen Maiwen. Certainly, the look Sir Raeden gave his ward had been enough to warn her he would not allow the subject to be put aside and forgotten. She anticipated being on the receiving end of a thorough inquisition once he had the opportunity to speak with her alone.

'There's something you're not telling us about last night.'

An inquisition very much like the one David was now facing.

'You're being meticulously careful in choosing your words,' continued Izana, 'which you only do when there's a detail you wish to leave out.'

The other Robesmen were not reticent in voicing their support of Izana's words.

'All right,' David finally conceded. 'I am leaving something out. I won't tell you everything, only that I did get hurt quite badly and Rhiannon healed me.'

As one all the Robesmen turned to look at her.

'I know what you're going to ask me, but I have no idea how I did it,' she announced, holding up a hand as though to ward off the barrage of questions she felt was imminent.

'We were not going to ask you anything,' Derrick stated. 'It is hardly our place to demand an explanation of you when David has made it clear he does not wish us to know all the details. Instead, we offer you our sincerest gratitude for your actions in saving him.'

A chorus of agreement came from the others.

'You should train to be a healer,' John added.

'See,' David remarked to Rhiannon and informed his curious Robesmen, 'I told her that after she succeeded in identifying my headache and sore throat on her first use of the diagnostic technique.'

'You taught her that?' Eamon exclaimed simultaneously with Derrick's, 'That is remarkable.'

'We didn't spend all our time having fun,' David declared in answer to Eamon's question. 'I taught her as much as I could remember from the Grade Three syllabus, along with a few things from higher grades.'

'Will you consider becoming a trained healer?' Gareth asked.

'I've thought about it,' Rhiannon replied. 'But with the exams next month I don't think I'll have time to do anything except focus on the subjects we couldn't cover in Vetus svet.'

'Like Defence?'

Rhiannon shook her head. 'We still managed to practise every day thanks to King Brian. He got us the weapons we needed and found us the perfect arena where we could train.'

A snort of laughter escaped David. 'It was perfect apart from the one time we arrived a bit too early. We appeared in the middle of a ball game and gave the players a good fright. There was one man running up the field who outdid Alice's shrillest scream when we popped up right in front of him. We quickly apologised and left.'

'What about magical defence?' Izana interjected.

Rhiannon gave a gurgle of amusement. 'We did that too, although King Brian wasn't impressed when we held our first duel in his throne room. He threw us both into the pool when he caught us. After that he took us to a desert island where we could use enchantments on each other to our heart's content.'

'But we didn't get an opportunity to go riding,' David lamented. He stroked Cináed's neck with an affectionate hand. 'I've definitely missed it.'

'So, it's a long ride we'll be taking?' asked John.

David shook his head. 'No. I promised my mother I wouldn't

go outside the castle grounds for a few days. We'll just go to the Main Gate and back. That should be enough to shake the fidgets out of our equestrian friends.'

Throughout the ride to the Main Gate there was scarce one moment of silence. David and Rhiannon's stories of Vetus svet were many and the five Robesmen listened in various stages of astonishment, disbelief and amusement as they were told.

However, when the riders were passing through the gate separating the Lower and Middle Wards and the encounter with Kelandrus at Loch Ness was revealed, all five were truly startled.

'Poor fellow,' murmured Gareth. 'To have spent all those centuries being hunted.'

'Does he ever see his kin?' queried Izana.

David nodded. 'According to King Brian he does visit the Sea of Japan when he suspects a group is going to be doing an extensive search for him.'

'Couldn't he just stay at the bottom of the loch?' asked John.

This time it was Rhiannon who answered. 'He used to do that until they developed a way to scan the depths for him.'

'And he actually met Merlin,' said Eamon.

'Not only that, but he also had a clue on where the secret laboratory could be found.'

'What!'

The chorus of voices in response to David's comment drew a smile from Rhiannon. 'Kelandrus told us Merlin said anyone looking to find the laboratory would have to search among the things that are lost. David believes this means the entrance must be in —'

'The Unclaimed Property Room,' concluded Izana.

Everyone stared at him. Then a rueful laugh escaped David.

'I should've known you'd guess the location as soon as you heard the clue,' he said. 'It took me a while to figure it out.'

John looked from David to Rhiannon, his confusion evident as he asked, 'So why aren't we inside looking for the entrance?'

'I thought we could do it tomorrow when we'd have more time to search,' said David. 'Classes end at lunchtime on Wednesdays, so we'll have all afternoon.'

He gestured around them at the short lamps lining the road through the Middle Ward which were already glowing in the faded twilight. 'In the time it's taken us to get here we wouldn't have progressed beyond moving some of the piles of items away from the walls. Besides, we didn't feel like doing anything too strenuous today.'

'I doubt there would've been much heavy lifting involved,' Izana observed, a hint of laughter in his voice.

'Are we thinking about the same room?' asked Eamon. 'In case you've forgotten, Izana, there's dozens of shelves packed to the brim with an odd assortment of items, some of which aren't particularly featherweight.'

'In the Unclaimed Property Room there are, but not in the Small Music Room of the Lower South Wing.'

'Wait a moment.' The frown on Gareth's brow matched the one appearing on the faces of the other Robesmen, David and Rhiannon. 'You just said the entrance to the laboratory should be in the Unclaimed Property Room.'

'I did, but I didn't mean the current one.' At the uncomprehending looks he received, Izana explained, 'According to the plans in the Hall of Archives, the original room for the storage of lost items was altered and converted to the Small Music Room in 1158. It's on the list we created for that very reason. Had it been a music room in Merlin's time I wouldn't have even considered it as a possible location for the entrance. Too many people would've spent hours in there at a time, and Merlin needed a place that wouldn't be regularly frequented.'

When no one responded, Izana looked around to see his companions staring at him in silence. A puzzled frown appeared on his face. 'What's wrong?'

A loud chuckle escaped David.

'Izana, we'd be lost without you,' he declared. 'We'd have spent hours moving lost items and shelving around in the wrong room if you weren't so adept at reading plans and memorising small details.'

'We each have our own talent,' Izana observed mildly, 'and having an architect for an uncle does have its advantages.'

A new energy flowed through the group as they continued along the road. The sense of anticipation and hope radiating from Rhiannon infected her companions until they too were contemplating the possibility of heading straight for the Small Music Room upon their return to the palace. Unfortunately, the chimes summoning them to dinner rang out as they arrived at the stables and the idea had to be abandoned.

'My parents will be expecting us to be there,' David said when the first chime sounded. 'If we don't show up, they'll have everyone out looking for us.'

In spite of her disappointment, Rhiannon conceded the truth of her friend's words and after changing out of her riding dress into a more appropriate gown of blue-silver silk edged with white lace, she hurried to join the merry gathering in the King's Dining Hall.

The banquet laid out to celebrate David and Rhiannon's return was immense. Side tables groaned under the weight of the array of dishes, while even more sumptuous food was being brought out to be presented to the chattering assembly gathered around the long table.

The inhabitants of the castle swarmed the hall, and among

them was a pale-faced Cassandra who arrived accompanied by Leila Hardinge, John and Izana.

Rhiannon returned the girls' greeting across the table, before taking her place between David and Eamon. She took a serving of the sweetly marinated lamb roast, all the while listening to the answer Eamon gave to David's query about his cousin Marcus.

'He often showed an unholy amount of glee at the prospect you might be gone for several months, so don't be surprised if he seems particularly vitriolic tomorrow.'

'I suppose it was too much to hope he might've grown up a bit while we were missing,' remarked David on a weary sigh. 'Did he at least exercise a modicum of tact and not show his delight around my parents?'

'He was crowing about your disappearance to all of us in the East Garden one evening, not realising Their Majesties were approaching.' Eamon cast a covert glance to where on David's other side King Stephen was talking to Sir Raeden. '*He* wasn't best pleased,' he revealed in a low voice, 'and Queen Maiwen was really upset. Marcus apologised immediately, but he's never dined here again since that day.'

'You mean he's been forbidden to come?' David asked, astounded.

Eamon shook his head. 'Their Majesties never said so. Marcus simply chooses not to attend. Izana believes it's because he doesn't want to risk being reprimanded in public again. Unfortunately, we still have to endure his presence at the school.'

'He was definitely one person I didn't mind not seeing for six weeks,' Rhiannon confessed.

'It was good to be away from him for a while,' David agreed. 'Apart from his normal unpleasant personality, did he or Felix cause any trouble?'

'They tried lording it over some of the other students, but John and Izana soon put a stop to that. Actually,' Eamon paused and lowering his voice even further, murmured, 'the worst trouble almost came from the pamphlets someone placed inside the school.'

Rhiannon and David frowned. 'Pamphlets?' they repeated.

'They were like the ones you took off that boy during the Open Day. No one knows how they got into the school. Whoever did it put them there while we were all at lunch. Thankfully, John saw them first and had Master Zhen confiscate them before they were read by the other students. It hasn't happened again, but a similar incident occurred at one of the schools in Ardara and some of the students did read the pamphlet. According to the report Lord Sharbel received, a few of them were intrigued by what they read.'

'Intrigued by an evil ideology that declares dragons are to be enslaved and innocent lives can be used in immoral experiments?' David's disgusted outrage laced his every word.

Eamon nodded and Rhiannon felt the small amount of dinner she had eaten rebel inside her stomach. The sense of nausea increased when the Robesman revealed the disappearance near Shadow Pass of a young Gora Dragon not three days after the incident with the pamphlets.

'No body was found, and the Chief Consul of Ardara believes whoever was responsible for placing the pamphlets in the school is the same one behind the dragon's disappearance.'

'Undoubtedly,' was David's grim observation. 'Have there been any other attacks?'

Eamon swallowed, then admitted, 'Since you were taken in the foramen we've heard of twenty-seven reported attacks. There could be more, but we're not sure.'

Silence from David had Rhiannon turning to see him with his eyes squeezed shut. His face was creased in a grimace of deep anguish, as though a sharp sword had pierced his heart.

'And they still are no closer to capturing the ones responsible?' he bit out between gritted teeth.

'No, but there can be no doubt they're linked to the faction in Graynor who are recreating the experiments of Fendrel.'

'And seeking the Dragon's Eye,' David muttered, opening his eyes to stare unseeingly at his plate.

'My son, the mention of certain topics is best left for more secluded locations.'

King Stephen's quiet words of caution drew the attention of his son, Rhiannon and Eamon to him.

'One cannot always be sure who may be listening, and a remark spoken in passing may cause unwanted conjecture by others if overheard.'

His expression contrite, David apologised and for the duration of the meal spoke only on the sights he had seen in Vetus svet and enquired about Eamon's birthday celebration. However, it did not escape the sharp gaze of Rhiannon and his father that his smile did not reach his eyes, and there was a hollowness to his laughter which robbed it of its normal charm. It was evident the loss of the missing dragons troubled him deeply, as did the cruel acts of the faction in Graynor. When at length the feast came to an end, and the large gathering departed the Dining Hall, it was with no outward sign of surprise that King Stephen agreed to David's request for a private discussion.

Rhiannon watched as father and son withdrew from the Great Hall. Then she looked at the five Robesmen standing beside her.

'How long do you think they'll be?' she asked.

'That need not concern you,' a firm voice announced from behind her.

Rhiannon turned to see her guardian staring down at her with an inscrutable expression in his cool blue eyes.

'There is a certain matter we need to discuss,' Sir Raeden added, 'and I can think of no better time than the present in which to do so.'

~*Chapter 20*~

SIR RAEDEN THE COUNSELLOR

Rhiannon sat across from Sir Raeden inside his office and glanced away from his unsettling gaze. She had forgotten how piercing his eyes could be when he was determined to extract the truth from someone. Staring into the fierce glare of a man-eating tiger would be preferable to meeting her guardian's eyes of unwavering steel and blue flame.

'I want the whole truth about what happened last night,' prompted his quiet, inflexible voice.

Rhiannon squirmed in her seat. 'David and I told you he got injured and I saved his life. Isn't that enough?'

'After witnessing any event which threatens the life of another, it is important to share those details with someone. The memory of it will retain its full power over you and continue to haunt your mind if you do not.'

'I'm fine. Look at me, not haunted at all.'

The bright smile on Rhiannon's face lingered no more than a few seconds before it faded at Sir Raeden's next words.

'Your eyes tell another story, child.'

Those same eyes darted a glance towards the pair that were now a deep cerulean hue.

'The shadows in them descend after a person has witnessed a scene of particular violence,' Sir Raeden continued, 'and it does not take a great amount of intellect to conclude that in your case the incident last night is to blame. You were remarkably hesitant to provide a full account of what occurred, and while I suspect the main motive for doing so was to protect the sensibilities of Their Majesties, I must insist upon you telling me precisely what took place.'

When it appeared his ward would remain stubbornly silent, he added in a much gentler tone, 'Rhiannon, I am not doing this to be cruel, nor do I feel any pleasure in asking you to do something which will cause you pain. Personal experience has proven to me it is easier to bear the weight of a traumatic memory if one speaks of it to another.' A questioning look from Rhiannon made him admit, 'Yes, I too have done this, and there is no shame in it.'

Still Rhiannon hesitated. 'You won't tell anyone else what I say?'

'You may be assured of my complete discretion.'

'Not even David's parents?'

'I suspect King Stephen will receive a full account from his son while they are sequestered from curious ears; however, on my honour, neither he nor Queen Maiwen shall hear a word of this from my lips.'

Rhiannon sighed. 'Very well.'

She sat in silence for a long moment.

Sir Raeden made no attempt to hurry her, instead allowing her to find the words to begin her tale in her own time.

Finally, at length, she spoke. In a voice strained with suppressed emotion, she described the walk down the London street: The traffic noise, the late hour, the unexpected appearance of the three muggers from the alleyway.

'I thought they'd be like the other girls we'd come across and only be interested in talking to David.' Rhiannon shook her head at her past self's naivety. 'I was wrong. They were interested in nothing more than robbing us. The leader pulled a knife and threatened to mess up my face. David kicked the knife out of her hands and drew his sword. He wore it everywhere we went, but kept it concealed,' she interrupted her story to explain.

Sir Raeden merely gestured for her to continue.

Rhiannon told of what happened next: David's cold words, the muggers' hasty retreat, the disposal of the knife.

Then the hardest part was upon her.

Before her eyes flashed the nightmare scene in all its horrifying colour. Her breath caught on a sob as she described the chilling sound of the gunshot, the enchantments she had not hesitated to use, the sight of David gasping for breath as his blood spread across the pavement in an ever-widening crimson pool.

'The bullet went straight through his chest,' she choked out. 'He-he was dying. There was so much blood and I saw his soul outside his body. I-I couldn't lose him. I couldn't.'

Sir Raeden made no reply to this passionate declaration, nor did he draw attention to the shiny streaks of tears spilling down his ward's face. He continued to sit in patient silence and let Rhiannon talk on.

'I felt something in me reach out. It just wanted to hold onto him; give whatever was needed to heal him. I begged for his life to be spared and suddenly I was seeing images of younger versions of so many people from here. They grew older and I saw myself. Then I heard David speak. I don't even know how it was possible. He was still unconscious, but I heard his voice all around me. Inside me. He told me to stop, that I'd saved him.' A gulped breath and a hard sniff sounded from her. 'When – when I checked, the hole in his chest was gone and his soul was back inside his body. I tried to wake him up but collapsed. I heard David say something and I don't remember anything else until he woke me up and said I'd exhausted myself. But he was alive,' she cried, 'and that's all I cared about.'

In answer to this last statement Sir Raeden observed quietly, 'I am certain Prince David did not share your indifference towards your own well-being.'

'No, he didn't,' she admitted with a watery sniffle. After a fruitless search for her handkerchief, she gratefully accepted the one her guardian extracted from his own pocket and offered to her.

Rhiannon set about cleaning away all evidence of her tears, and when she next spoke her voice was muffled by the fine linen. 'I'd been asleep for twelve hours and David said I'd used a lot of energy to heal him.'

'Which imperilled your own life.'

The handkerchief and Rhiannon's hands fell still. 'Sir?'

'As we discovered when you were struck by the Glaciocaptus Charm, and poisoned with somlyne, your ability to heal yourself is not inexhaustible over an indefinite period. From what you have described, you channelled a great deal of that healing power into Prince David, which placed your body under a tremendous strain. I would say having your soul come into direct contact with his —'

'What!'

At Sir Raeden's stern look, Rhiannon murmured a hasty apology.

'Having your soul come into direct contact with his caused an immense release of power,' her guardian continued, 'the result of which was you gave more than you safely should.'

Rhiannon waited a moment to be sure he had finished speaking, then asked, 'What did you mean about our souls coming into contact with each other?'

'The images you saw would have been the prince's memories. There can be no other explanation. This, therefore, must lead us to the logical conclusion they would only have been visible to you once your soul touched his.'

'And that's how I also heard his voice?'

'In all probability.'

'But, Sir, how could our souls have touched in the first place?'

'Child, I am not omniscient and there are some things which will always be beyond our understanding. Even the transference of your own healing power into Prince David is inexplicable. A mage generally is incapable of sharing their innate gift with another. I could not transfer into you my ability to easily comprehend intricate calculations and the interaction of matter on a molecular level, any more than the prince could share his gift for learning a multitude of different languages with any who would ask it of him.'

Rhiannon frowned. 'Maybe it wasn't my own healing power that was transferred to David. Mage healers use magic to save others all the time.'

'That is entirely different. They need acquired knowledge to utilise the magic made accessible to them through the bestowment of a Dragonstar enabling them to perform the healing, which often involves the use of natural medicinal aids. Sealing a wound like the one you described may not even have been possible for another mage; at least, not in time to prevent the prince's death. And had they, by some miracle, succeeded, he would not have been capable of standing, let alone walking, for at least two weeks. No. The power which enabled Prince David to experience a full and expeditious recovery, with no visible evidence remaining of his injury, was the same that preserved your life from the effects of the Glaciocaptus Charm and the somlyne. We therefore must consider it fortunate you were with him when he was wounded. Death would have come swiftly to him had you not been present, and there is no enchantment capable of healing any creature's body once life has departed from it.'

Rhiannon flinched. The thought of David lying dead, his laughing eyes cold and lifeless, was not one she wished to dwell upon. She rubbed at her chest to ease the aching pain in her heart, and heard Sir Raeden speak. She refocused her attention on him in time to hear, '… and it is not uncommon to relive these events during your sleep. I would urge you, each time this happens, to speak of it to someone. It need not be myself. Aleda, I am certain, would be only too happy to assist you and may be relied upon to be discreet.'

'Yes, Sir.'

'I hope this discussion proved of some assistance to you.'

'It did, Sir.'

And in truth, Rhiannon had to admit she did feel marginally better for having told every nightmarish detail of David's close encounter with death. The band of steel, which had been tightly locked about her chest from the instant he had fallen to the ground, had finally loosened. Still, a longing to find her friend and see his face animated with life lay siege of her. She peeked at her watch only to feel a surge of dismay upon seeing how late it was. Nine thirty-five. And they had classes the next day! There was little chance of her finding him tonight and her guardian made certain of that by decreeing it time for her to be in bed.

'You will need to be well rested for your classes tomorrow,' he said, accompanying her to the door. 'Especially your first lesson.'

'Let me guess, it's Defence.'

'It is.' Sir Raeden opened the door, then looked down at her. 'I would prefer not to see you dozing off at your desk.'

'Yes, Sir.'

Rhiannon went to pass through the doorway, only to pause and offer her guardian the return of his handkerchief.

Sir Raeden regarded the scrunched-up and well-used item in her hand and without hesitation, declined it. 'I fear its current usefulness to me ended some minutes ago,' he remarked with singular politeness. 'Just have it laundered and returned to me later.' He waited until she had stepped outside his office, then said in a carefully neutral voice, 'And, Rhiannon, the palace has been much too quiet these past few weeks. I trust I may rely upon you to restore a touch of life to it?'

The hidden meaning in his words soon dawned on Rhiannon. Her lips curled upwards in gratified happiness. 'I'll do my best,' she promised, 'and thank you, Sir; I missed you too.' Then she set off for her bedchamber, leaving her guardian to watch her retreating back with an impassive expression on his face but a faint smile lurking in his eyes.

~*Chapter 21*~

A PLEDGE OF HEARTS

'Xenophile. Xenolith. Xylophone. Yard. Yacht. Yodel. Zest. Zebra. Zoologist.' Rhiannon huffed in frustration. 'Whose idea was it to have only twenty-six letters in the English alphabet? At this rate I need at least another hundred!'

Her latest attempt to distract her thoughts a failure, she rolled onto her back with a groan and stared blankly at the blue canopy above her. Through the open balcony door the cool ocean breeze stirred the drapes, the movement causing the soft light of the moon to cast ghostly dancing shadows into her bedchamber. For what seemed like half the night she had tried every relaxation trick she knew and still the blessed oblivion of sleep eluded her. Even listening to her music box hadn't worked. She had left Sir Raeden's office with no other intent than to go to bed, and yet a sudden bout of restlessness had seen her tossing and turning from the moment she crawled underneath the coverlet.

She gave a single clap of her hands and light flooded her chamber in an instant. Rhiannon blinked to dispel the dark patches obscuring her vision and sat up. She glanced at her watch and gave an exclamation of annoyance. She had only been abed for an hour!

'It's too quiet,' she informed the photograph of her grand-

318

parents, conscientiously returned to her by David before dinner. Their smiles seemed to change to ones of amusement, as though she had said something exceedingly droll. 'I know,' she declared impatiently, 'how can it be quiet with the sound of the waves coming through the door, but it is. I can't hear him shifting around to find a more comfortable position, or his breathing.' A small pause. Then, 'All right, fine. We spent six weeks sleeping near each other and I miss having him close by. But I doubt his parents or Sir Raeden would approve if I snuck into his room and set up camp near his bed.'

Rhiannon tossed back the coverlet and got up. 'I'm going for a walk,' she announced firmly, as though expecting an argument.

The still image of her grandparents merely smiled their silent encouragement.

Her nightgown having been swiftly exchanged for a simple dress of pale mauve cloth and her feet clad in a pair of walking boots, Rhiannon left her chambers and set off down the dimly lit hallway. Her destination already chosen, she did not waste any time in pressing the rune for the second inner gate once she reached the transonus dais.

If the six guards stationed at the gate were surprised to see her out so late and alone, they gave no sign of it. They returned her greeting with cordial politeness, cautioned her against straying from any of the lit pathways and advised her to cast a flare of red sparks if she got into trouble. Then they kept watch as she walked down the road towards the eastern woodland of the forest in the Middle Ward.

Rhiannon approached the pathway to the gazebo and gazed at it in delight. Small lights were set inside the stone pavers, transforming them into a twinkling trail to rival those of the constellations in the night sky. Around her, the thick clusters of trees whispered secrets to each other in the gentle breeze that stirred their leaves and caught at the long strands of her unbound hair.

There was the faint sound of fair but strange laughter coming from the deepest depths of the woodland. Rhiannon caught a glimpse of tall, ethereal figures emerging from their trees to hasten towards the merry gathering.

She breathed in deeply, savouring the clean, fresh scent of the forest which bespoke of recent rainfalls and the sweet fragrance of the myaelan trees.

A few birds sang their lilting praise to the moon as he shone in all his radiant splendour, while the soft trickle of water came from the stream flowing beneath the white and blue stones of the gazebo. A soft, pale light illuminated the structure, making it appear like a floating oasis in the shadowy glade.

The peace of the sight beckoned Rhiannon and she soon crossed the bridge to seat herself on one of the low benches under the domed roof.

Serenity surrounded her and she felt her mind slowly begin to relax.

The passing of time was counted only by the slow dance of the moon across the sky and the shifting shadows across the pale stones beneath her feet.

Eventually, Rhiannon's eyes closed, her senses lulled by the nocturnal lullaby of Álnair's nature.

Yet there was still a part of her that would not rest. A small section of her mind which reminded her of Sir Raeden's warning to never completely lower your guard when in an isolated place by herself. It was that part which nudged her to full awareness when her ears detected the first faint tread of footsteps.

She stood up and peered out cautiously from the shelter of a pillar.

A tall figure was approaching the bridge. The silhouette

outlined by the lights of the path moved with an athlete's grace that was instantly recognisable.

'David!'

The Prince of Álnair showed no surprise at the sound of her exclamation. He called back his own greeting in a strangely subdued voice, then waited until he reached the bridge before saying, 'The guards at the gate said you went for a walk and I thought you might've come here. I saw you when I turned the corner and wondered how long it'd take you to hear me.'

'How did I do?'

'Not too badly, although you must've been miles away in your thoughts to have missed the clucking from the brood of hens behind me.' He gestured with his head towards the area of the path behind the line of trees. 'There's five of them back there, and they all insisted on accompanying me after we finished going through the stack of reports on my desk. To hear them talk, anyone would think I was a helpless child who can't walk three feet by himself.' He stepped off the bridge and gestured for her to sit down again.

'You can't blame them,' Rhiannon said, retaking her seat on the bench. 'They have spent six weeks worrying about your safety.'

'And yours,' he reminded her.

'I doubt it'd be to the same extent,' she remarked without any sign of rancour. 'I'm not their prince.'

'True, but they do like you.' A rueful note appeared in his voice. 'And part of their concern would spring from their fear of my dragging you into some demented escapade. Not that I would do it intentionally,' he immediately disclaimed.

'I know you wouldn't.'

Rhiannon looked up to where he remained standing, wondering if it would be a good time to confess her feelings for him. She had been so careful all the time they were in Vetus svet and now the revealing words were burning to be spilt from her lips. Then she noticed the distracted expression on his face as he stared out at the woodland. Hardly an auspicious opening. It looked as though her feelings would have to remain undeclared for the time being.

'David? What's wrong?' she asked.

At her concerned tone, he expelled a weary breath and lowered himself to sit beside her on the bench with all the energy of a tired old man. When he spoke, his first words seemed apropos of nothing.

'The world seems so peaceful right now, doesn't it? In such tranquil surroundings it should be easy to forget that somewhere out there a group of people are committing the most heinous of atrocities. It's why I came here after all. To forget. At least for a moment. But it's not working.' The hand resting on his knee clenched into a fist. 'The words my father spoke and the ones on those reports continue to burn inside my mind.'

'What did they say?'

David shook his head. 'You don't want to know.'

'Perhaps not, but if talking about it will help you then I'll bear it.' When he still hesitated, she reached out and grasped his hand. 'Come on, David. Tell me.'

A long silence passed until, at length, David gave in and answered.

'Three weeks ago, an underground laboratory was discovered in the fields bordering the Black Woods,' he began quietly. 'A travelling merchant found it by accident when he chased his prize pig through the enchanted entrance concealed in a small mound. Apparently, the fact he was not searching for the entrance was what enabled him to find it. He followed the pig inside and was confronted with the remains of —' He broke off and closed his eyes, his expression one of horrified anguish. 'There were creatures in a line of cells. Chimeras. Most of them were part human, part animal. Many were completely feral, but some had retained enough of their human mind to realise what had been done to them. They begged the merchant to kill them. Not knowing what else he could do to help them, he did, along with all the others. He then discovered several of them were magi when their Dragonstars appeared after they died. He used one to mark the entrance and got word to the Chief Consul who sent a group of the visgard to investigate.'

David paused.

Rhiannon looked at his face to see unmitigated grief allied with a quiet rage in his eyes which had darkened to a deep, unearthly shade of violet.

'They found something else, didn't they?' she asked, and had not believed it possible for a person to inject so much bile into a single word when David bit out, 'Yes.'

Abruptly, he stood up, his hand sliding out of Rhiannon's grip. His next words came out clipped and sharp.

'There was a deeper section beneath the first laboratory. The visgard came across a list of experiments carried out on the unborn children of the women held captive there. In their desire to achieve immortality, the vermin behind the experiments had treated the most innocent and defenceless of beings with the same disregard one shows to the dirt beneath their feet. And the mothers were unable to do anything to stop them. By the time they were found, only two still bore a live child inside their body. All the others had died or been killed so their remains could be studied.'

David lashed out, slamming his hand against the stone pillar closest to him. His entire body crackled with frustrated protective fury.

'They murdered those children as mercilessly and cruelly as they did the dragons whose body parts were used to create the serums. How could anyone choose to be so evil as to even devise such an experiment, let alone carry it out?'

The fierce utterance drew Rhiannon to her feet, the words Endrille had spoken to her the year before resounding in her mind.

'He stood before me and promised to always help and protect those threatened by evil, whether they were human or any other race.'

She felt sickened by what he had disclosed, but could only imagine the helpless anguish he must have suffered upon first learning of the experiments.

'When people focus only on their own ambitions and desires, I suppose it's easy for them to choose evil,' she said, moving to stand beside him.

They both stared down at the waters of the stream, the gentle, hypnotic movement of the stars reflected on its shifting surface at odds with the tumultuous storm raging inside their hearts.

'Did they catch any of the ones responsible for the experiments?' Rhiannon asked.

'No. There must've been a warning system in place as no one ever returned, and none of the survivors was able to provide any information on the men and women who entered their cells. However, they did know the name of the man who regularly came to see what progress was being made.'

'Who was it?'

'Mórfran. They said he never even attempted to conceal his identity. It would appear he does not believe himself at risk of ever being caught.' David shook his head at the man's supreme arrogance. 'No matter how long it takes, I swear he will be punished for what he's done. Once before, someone terrorised all of Álnair with the same crimes and he was defeated. This *spurínus orcfa* will meet the same fate.'

'*Spurínus ... orcfa?*'

Rhiannon repeated the unfamiliar words and unknowingly succeeded in diverting David's mind from the nightmare images inside it. His anger took a sudden dip and he made a dismayed sound in his throat.

'Please forget you heard me say that,' he begged. 'My parents, not to mention Wyvern, would skin me alive if they found out I said it in front of you.'

'Why? What's it mean?'

'Something incredibly impolite.'

'I guessed that. Come on, David. Tell me,' she coaxed. 'If you don't, I'll ask one of our five friends back there to explain it to me.'

'You wouldn't!'

'I would.'

And she made to move past him, only to have him step in her way.

'All right. I'll tell you. Just, please don't ever say it aloud.' He shifted awkwardly, cast a wary glance to where his Robesmen stood concealed behind the line of trees, then bent down and murmured the meaning into Rhiannon's ear.

Her eyes widened.

'David! Language!' But she revealed her true sentiments by adding, 'Although it would make a fitting epitaph for him.'

'He and all his cohorts,' were the prince's words of endorsement. His wrath over the cruel experimentation on the captives and the innocents slaughtered inside the sanctuary of their mother's womb, while still very much alive, was now bridled. Like steam escaping a pressure valve, his outburst had released the heavy build-up of roiling emotions until equilibrium was restored.

'Do you think Merlin may have left anything in his lab that could be used to help track them down?' Rhiannon enquired after a moment's thought.

'It's possible. There's an enchantment magi can use when they get lost, which creates a small guiding light to the destination they want. In one of his journals, Cornelius Tichley said Merlin had been attempting to develop an enchantment using a similar principle that would enable a mage to locate another person, but then the final battle against Fendrel happened and all the records of his work on the enchantment disappeared. He might've destroyed them, or put them in his secret lab.'

'Why would he do that?'

'The potential for such an enchantment to be misused is considerable. He only commenced working on it in an effort to find Fendrel and bring an end to the war. I guess when Fendrel was defeated, and there was no longer any need for it, he thought it best to discontinue his research. If the records are in the lab, it may be possible for someone to finish it off, providing my father agrees of course.'

David turned and leaned against the pillar. The gentle light emanating from the gazebo bestowed on his fair skin the glowing luminance of polished marble.

'There aren't many he would trust with a task like that, and even fewer who would be talented enough to succeed in making any progress. In fact, the only two he would probably consider are Professor Egelbert and Wyvern. Speaking of Wyvern,' he looked down at Rhiannon, concern flashing in his eyes, 'Eamon said he was in a rather dour mood after dinner when he ordered you to go with him. He didn't say anything to upset you, did he?'

'No.' Rhiannon hesitated, then admitted, 'He just wanted to know the whole story about last night.'

'I take it you told him?' When she nodded, David confessed, 'I told my father too, although I couldn't give him all the details of what you did after I was injured, or even explain how you saved me. All I know is that I heard you calling my name and felt an intense heat surrounding me before a flood of images filled my mind. I recognised your old foster family in several of them, then I saw things which could only have been from your life here in Álnair.'

Startled and anxious over what he might have seen, Rhiannon fidgeted awkwardly. 'Sir Raeden said from what I described that I transferred some of my healing ability into you, which should've been impossible.' She swallowed nervously. 'He also said the way

I was able to hear your voice was through our souls touching. It's also how I saw your memories. You … you apparently were able to do the same with mine.'

'I see. Then what I saw weren't illusions conjured up by my mind.' David smiled, recalling a particularly pleasant memory he had seen. But then, unexpectedly, he flushed and pushed away from the pillar. He stared at Rhiannon in burgeoning dismay. 'I'm sorry,' he said hurriedly.

Nonplussed, she stared back at him. 'For what?'

'I'm such an insensitive prat,' he declared, raking a hand through his hair. 'You're uncomfortable, and it's not hard to guess which memory of mine caused you to feel that way. I know you only see me as a friend and that's why I never said anything about you trying to kiss me.'

'I'm not uncomfortable about that,' Rhiannon denied vehemently. 'And I've been wanting to tell you … Wait. What?' She stared at him, gobsmacked. 'When did I try to kiss you?'

A pause. 'You mean you didn't see that?'

'No!'

'Oh.' David turned his gaze towards the woodland where little glimmers of light were floating among the trees. Absently, he muttered about having to warn the guards there were pixies visiting so they didn't inadvertently get trapped inside a magic circle for a few hours. 'Well,' he continued in a louder voice, 'it was when you were affected by the fumes from the narapet fruit.'

Rhiannon clapped a hand over her eyes, her humiliation obvious. 'I didn't. Does anyone else know I did that?' she asked, her voice strained.

'Not a soul. There was no one with us and I never told anyone about it.'

Rhiannon peeked through her fingers at him. 'Why?'

David frowned. 'Why what?'

'Why didn't you tell anyone?'

'It's hardly their business, is it? Besides, it wouldn't have been right to spread tales about you, and after our first conversation in here I knew you'd be mortified if I told you about it.'

'That's an understatement. Even now, when things have changed, it's embarrassing.' Rhiannon lowered her hand away from her eyes, but averted her gaze to stare at the glistening ripples in the stream. Her mouth was achingly dry and her throat parched, as though she had been standing out in the midday sun on a blistering summer day. Even the palms of her hands felt damp. She had been waiting to tell David the truth for six weeks and now, when an opportunity presented itself, her body was treating the moment like the prelude to a bloody battle.

'Rhiannon, you don't have to worry,' David said earnestly. 'You didn't do anything wrong, and nothing's changed as far as I'm concerned. So —'

'David —'

'Just forget about the incident with the narapet fruit —'

'David —'

'And we can go on as we have been, as friends —'

'I LOVE YOU!'

Dead silence descended.

The breeze paused, casting a heavy stillness in the surrounding woodland. There was not even the faint cry of a night owl or the call of a cricket to be heard following Rhiannon's shouted declaration.

Unseen by the couple in the gazebo, David's five Robesmen shared a look of high amusement while shaking their heads over their prince managing to exhaust Rhiannon's patience when she was confessing to him.

As for David himself, he stood frozen in place, gaping in shock. His eyes stared unblinkingly at the girl in front of him. Finally, he managed to utter a stunned, 'What?'

Her declaration having expelled some of her nervousness, Rhiannon took a deep breath and continued in a more subdued manner, 'I've been waiting the past six weeks to tell you, although I certainly didn't intend to blurt it out like I just did.'

'You love me,' David said, his voice oddly devoid of all emotion.

'Yes.'

'In what way?'

Rhiannon's whole face screwed up in confusion. An inarticulate noise of bewilderment escaped her.

'I mean, how do you love me? As a friend? A brother?'

Rhiannon's face flamed with colour.

'As a … as a girl loves a boy she likes, of course,' she announced. 'I realised it the day we arrived in Vetus svet and I became certain of it last night.' Her gaze drifted to the place on David's chest where the bullet had torn through it. In an instant, all her youthful awkwardness disappeared. She remembered the horror and desperation she had felt upon seeing David's blood spreading across the pavement in an ever-widening pool. The heat of tears burned her eyes. 'You were bleeding out, and … and I knew I'd give every last bit of energy I possessed to save you if I had to, even if it cost me my life.'

The immobility that had taken hold of David broke. He slowly reached out as though fearing she might be an illusion and lightly touched her shoulder. 'You really mean it, don't you,' he whispered, his eyes filled with a soft wonder.

Rhiannon gave a small nod. 'You can be so pig-headed and reckless, and when you lose your temper you'd win the award for least affable personality of the year. But if I had to name the person dearest to me it would be you. If it had been anyone else with me in Vetus svet I know I wouldn't have felt as happy as I did.'

'Even when we went to that clock museum in Germany and I spent hours studying the exhibits?' David teased.

'Even then.' A sparkle of warm humour lit Rhiannon's eyes.

'You got so excited, it was funny watching all the staff trying to keep up with your questions.'

They both grinned at the memory.

A gentle breeze blew through the gazebo, stirring the long cloth of David's cloak and Rhiannon's gown. A single chestnut ringlet brushed against Rhiannon's cheek in a light caress.

'Thank you.' David spoke the heartfelt words with simplistic sincerity. 'Until I met you, I thought I would never be able to believe a girl could accept my feelings for her without my title and position influencing her decision.' He took a step closer to her. 'I'm not … that is … there is so much in my heart that I want to say, but I've no idea how to do that without sounding like some pompous official giving his inauguration speech.'

Rhiannon smiled. 'If you were too confident, I'd begin to wonder if you had several girls hidden away,' she teased. 'But seriously, the words aren't important. It's the feeling behind them that matters.' When he still appeared to flounder for a way to begin, she gently prompted him with, 'Just be honest, David. I don't mind how you say it, just so long as you tell me the truth. You once said you like me —'

'I love you.' The declaration came without hesitation. 'I have for a long time.'

The two short utterances opened the floodgates of David's heart and a deluge poured out.

'From the way you smile at the antics of a small otter or a little imp like Alice to the way you have to straighten all the books on a shelf when they're only slightly askew. I love your goodness, your kindness. The strength in those small hands of yours that strike out to defend those you care about. I love you not only for what you are, but for what I am when I'm with you. You make me want to be the best I can be so I need not be ashamed in your presence. To be strong enough to always uphold what is right and do my duty. I promise I will always try to be worthy of your trust and love, to do all within my power to protect you.' He lifted one hand and held it out towards her. 'Please say you'll be willing for me to court you,' he said, a faint hint of scarlet spreading across his face. 'Officially it could only be an informal courtship until next year when you turn sixteen, but I would consider myself pledged to you in truth should you take my hand and ask it of me.'

Rhiannon's breath caught in her throat. 'Is – is this the Álnairian equivalent to a boy in Vetus svet promising a girl he'll always be hers?'

'It is. And I swear I will always remain true to my promise.'

'I don't doubt it, knowing you,' Rhiannon murmured, a pink flush of pleasure staining her cheeks. She beamed happily and placed her hand into his. 'I'm not sure if there's something in particular I'm meant to say, but I'm pretty sure a simple "I'm all for it, Prince David" will suffice.' A hint of mischief twinkled in her eyes. 'Or should I say, "I'm humbled by your condescension, Your Royal Highness, and obsequiously consent to you courting me"?'

The corner of David's mouth twitched, although his voice was carefully neutral when he responded with a casual, 'You can go with the last one if you don't want to be kissed.'

Rhiannon's eyes widened. A gasp of surprise escaped her. Then her mouth curled in a delighted smile.

'In that case,' she said with eager shyness, 'I'm all for it, Prince David.'

David's free hand rose to cup her cheek.

He slowly bent his head towards hers.

'It's just David,' he reminded her lightly and with awkward tenderness pressed a gentle kiss to her lips.

Both their eyes instinctively closed. Neither could afterwards say with any certainty how long the kiss continued. To them time ceased to exist.

In the surrounding woodland, however, several curious pairs of eyes stared at the young couple for a long moment before averting their gaze. When next they looked, David and Rhiannon were seated close to each other on the low bench. The prince's arm was around Rhiannon's shoulders, while her head rested against him. What was being spoken between them in quiet murmurs went unheard by their watchers and so would forever remain a secret to all but the couple involved.

However, it did not escape the notice of those sharp eyes watching them that a new openness now lay upon David's face as he looked at Rhiannon. His smile unreservedly revealed the depth of his affection for her.

'I'd say he's been successfully distracted from thinking about those reports,' the voice belonging to John observed from behind a wide oak tree.

'So long as he doesn't stay distracted during class tomorrow,' came Izana's prosaic reply. 'Sir Raeden is never pleased when he has to repeat himself.'

~Chapter 22~

A TROVE OF SECRETS

It was not *David's* distraction which displeased Sir Raeden the next morning in the schoolroom. Drowsy from her late night and lost in a pleasant daydream, Rhiannon was blissfully oblivious to her guardian's lecture on the disadvantages of using animated anthropomorphic beings as a means of defence. Her body swayed in time to the music playing inside her head. She felt David's arms about her as they danced in a crowded ballroom decorated with oak wreaths entwined with white ribbons and garlands of orange blossoms, myrtle, roses and ivy.

BANG!

Rhiannon's eyes flew open to meet her guardian's icy gaze as he lifted his hand from her desk.

'I'm sorry, Sir.'

The immediate apology did nothing to remove Sir Raeden's look of disapproval.

'It would seem you need to refresh your knowledge of class etiquette,' he said. 'You will return here after lunch and write a detailed essay on the rules, especially the importance of paying attention when a teacher is speaking.'

Rhiannon gave a miserable nod. 'Yes, Sir.'

'Don't worry,' David told her after the lesson had finished and Sir Raeden was gone. 'We can still search for Merlin's lab after you finish.'

'If you start the essay during lunch you could have a good part of it already done before coming back here,' Eamon suggested from behind them.

Rhiannon's expression brightened.

'That's true,' she agreed, and when she later returned to the school after lunch she soon completed three pages of the essay. It did not take long to complete the remaining five, and she handed the finished essay to Sir Raeden and escaped right on two o'clock. Now the search for the entrance to Merlin's secret laboratory in the old Unclaimed Property Room could finally begin.

The search group, comprising Rhiannon, David, his five Robesmen and Cassandra made their way to the Small Music Room in the Lower South Wing. They began to look over every inch of the room for any clue as to the location of the hidden entrance: Running their hands over the walls to feel for any slight indentation, gently nudging against them with their shoulders, even getting down on their hands and knees to have a good look at the high skirting boards.

Unfortunately, it soon became clear the entrance would not be found swiftly.

Although it was called the Small Music Room, with its brightly coloured high ceiling and smooth walls decorated with gold filigree and embossed paintings, and its parquet wooden floor gleaming under the light of four chandeliers, the music room was immense.

It could, David informed Rhiannon, comfortably seat over eighty people in front of the long dais upon which was placed a music stand of singular beauty, a tall harp and cushioned stool, all exquisitely crafted in a stunning combination of dark wood and gold leafing.

Sumptuous curtains in rich shades of green with yellow trim hung over the five arched windows lining the south wall, while on the ornate tables placed intermittently around the room a collection of fine crystal vases cast flickering rainbows that danced to faded melodies across the polished surface beneath them.

'The Grand Music Room is three times the size of this one,' said David. 'This is mainly used for private recitals and rehearsals.'

A wry grin curled Rhiannon's lips. 'I'm suddenly very grateful that the old Unclaimed Property Room was here in this "small" room and not the "grand" one,' she declared with such fervour David had to laugh before they resumed their search along the north wall.

The group spent a long time examining every feasible inch of the main room. Then they were inside the small adjoining chamber on the far west side where several wind and string instruments were stored. The windowless room was dominated by a magnificent open cabinet of solid oak filled with books which took up most of the outer wall.

'It's got to be in here,' declared Rhiannon.

However, even after thoroughly going over the entire space, the entrance to the laboratory continued to elude them.

'Maybe we missed something,' Eamon said.

Rhiannon slumped against the doorframe with a dejected sigh. 'How could we?' she answered. 'We've gone over every surface of the room that would've been within Merlin's reach and we still ...' Her voice drifted off, her eyes catching a glimpse of something unusual.

There, in the small space between the large bookcase and the side wall. From her position, she could see a faint shadow *behind* the bookcase.

'What is it?' David asked.

'It isn't built into the wall.' Rhiannon straightened up and walked towards the old bookcase. 'It looked like it was but it's an illusion. At the right angle you can see the shadow behind it.' She turned to look at Izana. 'Did the plans mention when this was put here?'

'When this section of the palace was first built,' he replied. 'There were several others added later, however, they were all removed when this became part of the music room.'

'So, it was here during Merlin's time.'

Rhiannon felt a renewed surge of excitement rise inside her. Returning her attention to the bookcase, she contemplated it for a moment, then nodded. 'It could be behind here,' she mused.

Her companions did not need any further prompting. They each took a section of the long bookcase and began examining the shelves and framework. Rhiannon and Gareth, being the ones at either end, also reached behind the oaken back to run their hand over both it and the wall.

No one spoke. For several lengthy minutes the silence in the small chamber was only disturbed by the tapping of fingers against wood, or the whispering hush of books being shifted on a shelf.

Rhiannon, deaf to everything except the solid *thunk* which greeted her taps to the side of the bookcase, doggedly continued downwards until she was crouched upon the floor. Her fingers moved along the top of the unseen skirting board. The smooth surface was without flaw. No bumps or depressions could be felt along it.

Wait! What was that?

Rhiannon paused and slid her forefinger back over the tiny indentation in the marble. There was something odd about it. She applied a gentle amount of pressure and felt a slight shift. Almost delirious with anticipation, she took a deep breath, then pushed down hard.

The small section of marble clicked into place and then …

nothing. No grating noise as the wall shuddered and moved. No sudden breeze as an opening was revealed. Nothing.

Rhiannon's head fell forward, her eyes closing against the bitter disappointment of defeat. She had felt so sure she had found it. Wearily, she withdrew her arm and stood up. Perhaps the others would have better luck.

She went to turn away.

Then it happened.

With a *crack*, like that of a jammed window being forcibly opened, the middle of the bookcase slid forward and swung out, narrowly missing Cassandra who leapt out of its way with a startled yelp. Izana steadied her, then everyone in the room moved to peer into the dimly lit opening that had appeared in the wall.

The same height as the bookcase and wide enough to fit three grown men abreast, the entrance was several feet deep before it curved downwards into a circular stairway. The steps were lit by rows of silver lamps lining the wall that flared to life the instant Rhiannon's head passed the opening's threshold.

The astounded silence was broken by Derrick. 'How did it open?'

'I pressed a small button in the skirting board,' Rhiannon answered.

'You found it.' David's awed whisper filled the empty space which had lain undisturbed for nigh on fifteen centuries. 'You really found the entrance to Merlin's secret laboratory.'

In a blur of movement, he lifted Rhiannon up and swung her around in celebration.

'Well done, Rhiannon!' the others chorused in one ebullient voice as, breathless and flushed, she pulled back from David to see the same elation she felt shining in his eyes.

'I wouldn't have found it without your help,' she told him, then glanced around at their companions. 'Or without yours.'

'But you're the one who spearheaded the whole thing,' said John. 'We wouldn't have been looking if not for you.'

'Do you think we can go down now?' interjected Eamon, his eagerness reminiscent of an excitable puppy. 'I'd love to see the lab.'

'It depends on whether the air is dead or not,' replied Gareth, dousing some of Eamon's enthusiasm.

'If it is we can purify it,' said Izana. He stepped past David and Rhiannon through the opening and walked to the top of the stairs. He paused and inhaled slowly.

'Along with the dimension-altering enchantment, Merlin must've placed a preservation charm in here,' he announced. 'The air isn't stale, but it's not particularly fresh either.'

He raised his right hand and a soft murmur of words left his lips. Before the last syllable had faded, a thin, translucent mist swirled to life around him. A wind blew his hair about his head like ash-blond banners caught in a storm. His amber cloak flapped erratically. He stretched out his hand over the stairs. The mist rose in a great pillar, then shot off down the steps in a twirling dance.

From her place just inside the entrance, Rhiannon immediately noticed the change in the air. It had gone from mildly stuffy to the crisp freshness of a fine spring morning in the space of a few seconds.

'That's better,' said John. He looked at David. 'Are we all going down, or did you want some of us to wait up here?'

'I don't see why we can't all go.' David pointed at a small metal lever placed next to the first silver lamp on the wall. 'Unless I'm very much mistaken, that works on the same principle as the ones used to open and close the castle gates.'

Derrick nodded. 'Merlin would've needed a way to control the entrance from both sides. We should be able to reopen it from inside the passage.'

'Let's go then,' Gareth urged from the back and gestured for Cassandra to precede him through the entrance.

The First Seer hesitated, a glimmer of fear in her eyes. 'Are you s…s-sure we'll be able to get back out if this closes?'

Gareth simply walked away from the opening and indicated for her to join him. 'Use the lever to close it,' he said.

After the other three Robesmen had manoeuvred their way into the small area beside him, David reached up and pulled the lever down.

There was no noise this time. The bookcase soundlessly moved back into position. Those inside the passage watched as the missing part of the wall slid up from inside the ground to reseal the entrance. To their relief the silver lamps remained alight, illuminating the space around them with a comforting glow.

'I think we can safely say it works,' said David, and pushed the lever up.

The wall and bookcase shifted like a well-oiled machine, sliding open with quiet stealth to reveal a reassured Cassandra.

Rhiannon beckoned her forward with a cheerful, 'No chance of getting trapped in here. Come on. You won't want to miss this!'

They descended the long circular stairwell in pairs. David and Rhiannon naturally took the lead with Izana and Cassandra following closely behind. Next came John and Eamon, and bringing up the rear were Derrick and Gareth. Not many words were spoken as their footsteps echoed hollowly against the stone walls about them, their minds dwelling on the knowledge that Merlin had been the last person to press his hand against the grey stone, and his feet the last to pass over the steps beneath their own.

After several minutes the stairs curved around and ended at the gaping mouth of a long, narrow tunnel. Hewn out of hard rock and lit by a row of luminous yellow lanterns on each side, its ceiling was several feet above the top of David's head. They proceeded through it, but after taking only a dozen steps the tunnel's entrance had disappeared and they were all standing at the other end in front of a smoothed-out portion of large stone, heavily decorated with intricate engravings.

'It must be an enchantment,' said John, looking back through the tunnel, 'but certainly not like one I've ever read about.'

'Nor I,' announced Derrick. 'It would appear that for each step we took we travelled a considerable distance.'

Eamon nodded in agreement. 'The rock in these walls isn't the same as that at the other end.'

Izana ran his hand over one of the protruding stones. When he lifted his hand away a fine layer of glittering dust coated his palm. 'It's fatakrít. We're somewhere underneath the Del Enger Mountains.'

'How do you know that?' asked Rhiannon.

'It's the only p…p-place where fatakrít may be found in Álnair,' said Cassandra.

David shook his head. 'Merlin, you brilliant, sneaky man.' He turned and explained to Rhiannon, 'Fatakrít is a hard rock capable of withstanding a tremendous amount of heat. With his experiments he would've needed that in case something went wrong. He also probably used natural fissures in the rock to vent the fumes.' He tilted his head back and looked as though he were peering through the layers of dirt and rock above them. 'No one would ever think to look for his secret lab so far from the castle grounds.'

'But,' Rhiannon gazed around her in disbelief, 'how could he have done this all by himself? The tunnel would have to be over fifty miles at the very least!'

'He would've enlisted the assistance of the only ones with the ability to cut through the hardness of fatakrít: King Nuallán and the other faeries who live in the mountains. They have an entire city built deep within this area and the design on that door is identical to the one they use themselves.' David pointed to the engravings of tendrils of grape vines intermingled with images of small birds and flowers. 'They're very fond of wine, and they have a close affinity with nature, especially wrens and finches.' He walked over to the door, placed his hand on the smooth area where a handle would normally be and blew gently against it. 'And they like incorporating that love into their work.'

A ripple of magic flowed over the surface of the door. The engravings came alive with colour and the birds fluttered out of the stone to chirp a happy greeting to their visitors. Then they turned and flew through the entrance.

'Now, it's our turn,' said David, and he took Rhiannon's hand and led her straight for the door.

For Rhiannon, passing through the enchanted door was unlike her encounter with the charmed wall during the Dragon's Cup. It felt like a gossamer wing of the softest, warmest feathers brushing against her skin, and a scent of the sweetest spring flowers surrounded her. Then she and David were standing inside a large, cavernous chamber of ivory stone. The ground had been levelled and glistened with the sheen of a luminous pearl, while on the wall slender veins of silver-white ran through the neatly carved-out rock. There was no other door visible in the circular room, apart from the one through which they had just entered. In the ceiling were half a dozen jagged cracks.

'Is this it?' Rhiannon exclaimed in disappointed disbelief as the others began to arrive behind them. 'Is this his laboratory?'

'It must be, there's no other door,' David answered.

'But it's empty!'

They stared in disillusioned surprise at the bare chamber. There was not a stick of furniture to be seen, nor a single book or sheet of parchment.

But then something caught their attention.

Lit by the orbs of light lining the walls with part of its steel blade embedded in the stone floor was, 'Merlin's sword. It has to be!'

Like a starter's whistle, Gareth's awestruck words sent the entire group hurrying towards the centre of the room to examine the weapon.

None daring to touch it at first, they came to a halt at the outline of a circle cut in a three-foot radius around the sword and gazed at it in wonder.

'Look at the gold on the guard,' Eamon enthused. 'It's not tarnished at all!'

And indeed, the gold figure of a dragon shone resplendently with not a single blemish to mar its beauty. It crouched protectively above a shallow, oval-shaped indentation in the silver-grey metal shaped like a shadow of its outstretched wings.

'There's s…s-something written on the blade,' said Cassandra.

Izana knelt to read the fine script. 'It's in Drakaron. It says, "I am Oraun, forged in ancient dragon fire to sunder dark from light."'

'"Ancient dragon fire"?' repeated Rhiannon. 'That would mean fire from Endrille, wouldn't it?'

David nodded. 'She must've lit the forge of the smith who helped Merlin create it.'

'It looks like it was designed to hold something in the guard,' Derrick observed, and took a step forward to have a closer look.

The instant the tip of his boot passed over the outline of the circle in the ground there was a loud rumble beneath the floor.

The group backed away hurriedly to a safe distance, unsure what the sound might herald.

There was a harsh grating noise followed by the crack of splintering rock. The section of stone inside the circle began to rise. It crept higher until the sword was now stuck inside a plinth set one foot above the rest of the ground. Then it stopped. To the right of it, and closer to the wall, a tall slab of crystallised blue stone materialised. From where they stood, the group could see writing engraved upon its smooth surface. Cautiously, they made their way across the room to read it.

'What does it say?' Rhiannon asked.

David, after only a glance at the Drakaron text, read it aloud.

'"An ephemeral veil lies upon this chamber and under its mantle shall all other enchantments die. To see what cannot be seen, you first must prove your worth. As Oraun was made pure in the flames, so must the soul be of the one who would seek to remove it from the stone. But beware! For just as dross is burned in the furnace, so shall the corrupted vessel be devoured by the fire."' David grimaced as he said the last words. 'That's cheerful. And he simply signed his name to it.'

'So basically, there's a charm on the room which has hidden everything inside it and made using any form of magic in here impossible until the sword's pulled from its stone sheath,' said Eamon.

'Not only that, but some form of fire is going to engulf the soul of anyone who attempts to do it,' remarked John.

'Then the soul will be consumed by the flames if found to be unworthy,' concluded Gareth.

An icy chill raced down Rhiannon's spine. She turned and looked at the sword, recalling David's words to her the night before. In all possibility, within the hidden contents of Merlin's laboratory, there might be something that could be used to locate the ones responsible for the atrocities being committed in Álnair. But could she risk the life of one of the others attempting to get it?

She shook her head. It had been all her own idea to look for the place, so it fell to her to see it through to the end. She began to carefully move away from the others, not wanting to give them a chance to stop her.

'W…W-What do you suppose would make someone unworthy?' Cassandra asked.

There was a pause. Then, his voice sombre, Izana said, 'Merlin's life was one of service. Everything he did was in the interests of aiding others. He sought no glory for himself in his research, and didn't boast of his intelligence or success. Therefore, the ones he would consider unworthy of his knowledge would be those steeped in their own hubris who'd seek to use his work to further their own selfish ambitions.

'The problem I have is believing Merlin capable of placing an enchantment that would kill someone,' Izana continued. 'And the wording on this stone is ambiguous at best. He doesn't say destroyed by fire, merely devoured. Something that is swallowed may be spat back out. It could be that in attempting to pull out the sword, an unworthy person will suffer for as long as they continue to hold onto it. They will experience the pain of the fire, but I do not believe Merlin ever intended to have his protection charm kill … RHIANNON!'

The bellowing of her name was enough for Rhiannon to know she had been caught.

Ignoring the scurry of movement behind her, she began to run. She had to reach the sword before any of the others! Even if Izana was right, she couldn't ask one of them to undertake a trial of pain without first enduring it herself.

She took the step up onto the plinth and reached for the black grip of the sword's hilt, unaware of the figure sprinting up behind her.

David, his white cloak streaming out behind him, saw Rhiannon stretch out her arm and leapt the remaining distance to her side.

His heart pounded in his chest.

There was an odd vacuum of noise in his ears.

He flung out his hand, praying he would be in time.

His momentum carried him forward into Rhiannon's back.

One arm curled around her waist, his other hand desperately straining to grasp the hilt of the sword before hers did.

Their fingers clashed and meshed, then tightened around the hard grip in the same instant.

A blast of energy exploded from the sword, sweeping outwards in a powerful, surging force.

A bright flare of light flashed in violet and gold eyes, transforming them to brilliant orbs of pure white.

Then, a fierce, scorching pain, like that inflicted by a blazing fire, engulfed David and Rhiannon, eliciting from them cries of anguish that would haunt the dreams of their companions for many years to come. The pain, excruciating and unrelenting, increased each time they pulled on the sword, blinding them to everything around them. Yet they refused to yield, unwilling to abandon the other and leave them to endure the torment alone.

Agonised eyes watched their terrible struggle, the image of their suffering imprinting itself deeply in the memories of the five Robesmen and Cassandra. Helpless, they stood on the other side of an invisible barrier which surrounded the couple on the plinth, forcing upon them the repugnant role of idle spectators.

Rhiannon gasped, her face twisted in agony.

David's arm tightened around her, pressing her against his body until they were as one being.

The tremors shaking Rhiannon's limbs were echoed in David's.

Then, O glorious mercy! The sword shifted. A small, miniscule movement which was barely discernible and yet, to David and Rhiannon, it was enough. With increased fervour they pulled again and again, never surrendering to the urge to let go of the sword and bring an end to their suffering.

An eon passed for them as the long blade was released at a torturous pace.

Sweat beaded their furrowed brows and trickled down their strained faces.

The blue veins under their fair skin and the white of their knuckles stood out starkly against the dark grip of the sword.

No respite was given from the pain. It continued to rack their bodies.

Tears mingled with sweat.

The torment seemed endless.

A sharp tug. A startled cry. The singing of steel against stone.

The sword came free.

The mind-numbing pain vanished, a soothing coolness taking its place. Blessed relief washed over David and Rhiannon. They collapsed to the ground, clutching Oraun as the invisible barrier about them fell, and with it, Merlin's veiling enchantment.

However, none of the room's occupants took any notice of Merlin's rematerialised belongings. David and Rhiannon lay sprawled against each other, their eyes closed against the sight, while the other six were completely focused on their exhausted companions.

'David! Rhiannon!'

The concerned cries, followed by firm hands grasping their shoulders, roused one of the two on the stone plinth to a kind of drowsy giddiness, but the other to a state of admiration mixed with a heavy dose of anger.

'I ought to box your ears,' David announced tersely, his pale countenance at odds with the flash and sparks in his eyes as he fixed the top of Rhiannon's head with a stern look. 'What were you thinking, going off to do it by yourself? And before we knew exactly what would happen! If Izana's hypothesis had been wrong, you could've been killed!'

'Like you wouldn't have tried to do the same thing,' Rhiannon remarked shrewdly. She tried to move forward, only to fall back against his chest with a huff of tired laughter. 'Anyway, it all worked out, didn't it? We got the sword out.'

When no answer came from the tense figure behind her,

Rhiannon sighed and moved her free hand to cover the one resting against her stomach. 'I'm sorry I worried you, David, but the whole idea to go looking for the lab was mine from the beginning. I had to be the one to make the first attempt to get the sword. I wasn't going to stand back and let one of you take the risk before I tried myself.' She tilted her head to the side to look up at him. 'You understand, don't you?'

There was a long pause. No one spoke as they watched David's expression. His anger, born from his concern over the danger in which Rhiannon had placed herself, was still smouldering, but a glimmer of empathy now flickered there as well. At length he dropped his head and gently bumped it against Rhiannon's.

'Yes, I understand,' he said quietly. 'You're too much like me for your own good, and I've just realised what I've been putting these five through each time I've insisted on being the first to do something reckless.' He looked around at his Robesmen and gave them a small smile of apology. 'Every time I threw myself headfirst into a madcap escapade, if you only felt half the terror I did upon seeing Rhiannon reach for the sword then I now know why you always tried to dissuade me from behaving with all the care of a gambolling goat.'

'So can we hope to see you being less impetuous in future?' asked John, his tone implying he held no great hope of receiving an affirmative reply, and nor did he get one.

'I can't make any promises,' was all David said, and gratefully accepted the distraction offered by Gareth when he mentioned the immaculate appearance of the sword.

'The blade looks remarkably sharp for having been buried nearly fifteen hundred years.' The Robesman reached out and ran a finger along the smooth metal. 'There's not even a scratch from where it was inside the stone.'

Barely able to conceal his eagerness, he asked if he could hold it.

Rhiannon and David shared a look, then offered him the hilt. His hazel eyes brimming with wonder, Gareth reverently took up the sword and closely examined it.

'It's perfect,' he declared. 'The balance, weight, grip. Even the extra length of the blade isn't an issue. It still feels comfortable to wield.'

'Easy for you to say,' said Eamon. 'You're a beanstalk. I'd probably fall over the first time I tried to swing it.'

Gareth handed Oraun to him. 'Try it,' he urged.

The shorter Robesman hesitantly lifted the long sword and everyone around him saw his expression change to one of surprise.

'It doesn't feel awkward at all!' he exclaimed, and enthusiastically stepped back and swung the sword in a precise downward attack. 'That's brilliant!'

His own desire to try out the sword had David squeezing Rhiannon's hand, then carefully rising to his feet. He stumbled slightly and was steadied by John and Izana.

'I'm all right,' he assured them. 'My legs are just a bit shaky. They'll be fine in a minute or two.'

And to everyone's relief, he was right. He accepted Oraun from Derrick, and proceeded to wield it with all his usual poise.

It was not long before everyone had held the sword and tested it out for themselves. To her astonishment, Rhiannon found she too could lift the impressively sized weapon with ease.

'Merlin must have placed some form of enchantment so it adjusts to suit whoever is holding it,' said Izana, sounding deeply impressed. He turned to look around the room. 'He might even have left a record in here somewhere on how he did it.'

Their attention now returned to their surroundings, the group stared about them, silently taking in every detail of the laboratory.

A complicated apparatus was set in the centre of each of the five work benches positioned throughout the room, while numerous shelves containing a collection of various shaped glass bottles filled with different coloured liquids and powders lined the curved wall. Near the blue stone bearing Merlin's message was a large iron cauldron sitting atop an ancient fire pit with a small bronze bucket placed a short distance away. On the left side of the plinth was a sturdy wooden chair behind an enormous desk which featured only an abacus, a used quill and an inkwell in one corner, and two huge tomes bound in leather in another. A fine bookcase filled with an assortment of scrolls, ancient books and voice crystals covered a substantial part of the wall near the desk, and a high screen of ornately cut stone surmounted by a sculpture of a fish provided a secluded area for a single bench toilet and washbasin.

'Can you imagine how much knowledge is in that collection?' Izana's eyes were transfixed on the bookcase. 'It'll take months to go through those records.'

'Where would you even start?' said Eamon.

Everyone's attention focused on the two tomes on the desk.

'There,' they announced in unison, and led by David they crossed the floor to take their first look at the information Merlin had felt he needed to seal away.

David carefully turned the thick leather cover of the first book to reveal a page filled with lines of flowing script in Old Álnairian.

Rhiannon groaned.

'I completely forgot he'd be writing in a language I wouldn't be able to understand,' she muttered.

'It's a record of his last experiments,' said David.

He closed the book, then opened the next one.

'This one's his personal journal.' He frowned after reading a bit further. 'Actually, no. It's an account of his history with Fendrel. He wrote it after the final battle.'

He turned the page, his eyes skimming the text with practised speed. When he next spoke, no one missed the grim change in his voice.

'He says when they were in Vetus svet, he and Fendrel were sold as slaves to a silk merchant when they were seven. Their village had been attacked by raiders and their parents killed in front of them. The next couple of paragraphs describe their lives with the merchant. They weren't pleasant. One example he gives of their treatment is of their master frequently whipping them for the smallest infraction or mistake. He also notes Fendrel's health was deteriorating with each punishment meted out. He mentions that had they not been caught in a foramen when they were eleven, Fendrel likely would have died before his next birthday.'

Eamon looked at the open book like it was a swarm of wasps. 'I never thought the day would come when I'd think of Fendrel as an innocent victim.'

'One has to wonder why, after experiencing such evil, he would choose to follow that path himself,' said John, a deep frown on his face.

'People react to personal suffering in different ways,' Derrick observed quietly. 'There are those who become embittered until over time they are consumed with hate, while ones like Merlin will become dedicated to doing all they can to help others.'

'Still, whichever we become, we each must be held accountable for our own actions,' said Izana. He looked directly at Eamon. 'Both Fendrel and Merlin were innocent victims of a barbaric practice for several years, however, they each made the choices which gradually determined the type of person they would become. Fendrel's transformation into a callous monster did not happen quickly. He stripped away his own innocence piece by piece with each deliberate act of cruelty he committed.'

'We are what we make ourselves to be,' Gareth pronounced with firm conviction, 'for no one but we can decide how we will respond to the challenges and sorrows we encounter during our life.'

'It appears Fendrel's response was to always look out for

himself,' said David, having read a few more pages. 'All throughout their schooling in Cendillis and at the Academy, even during their partnership before its breakdown over his obsession with immortality, Merlin realised in hindsight there were numerous warning signs of his childhood friend's increasingly narcissistic tendencies.' He flicked through the book until he came to the last entry by Merlin and began to read it. An exclamation of surprise escaped him.

'What is it?' asked Rhiannon.

'The Dragon's Eye,' he murmured. 'Merlin's written about it.' He continued reading, then abruptly closed the book. 'I'll need my father's permission to reveal anything more,' he said, and turning to the two eldest of his Robesmen, he sent them off to fetch the king.

When Derrick and Gareth returned sometime later, they brought with them not only an astounded King Stephen, but also his Chief Robesman Lord Daiki Sato, and Sir Raeden. The latter was not pleased upon discovering the risk his ward had taken in removing Merlin's sword from the plinth. Rhiannon was only spared the full brunt of a stern lecture by David opening the tome on Fendrel and drawing his father's attention to the last few paragraphs.

'I haven't shared any of this information with the others,' he assured his parent once the monarch had finished reading the page.

'I did not believe for a moment you would have,' was King Stephen's mild reply. 'But you undoubtedly wish to do so.'

'They already know of its existence. Rhiannon and John were there when Phalóran spoke of it, and the others have all heard the whispers of it being sought by Mórfran. I think they need to know why he's searching for it.'

King Stephen gazed around at the people gathered in the laboratory. Finally, he nodded. 'Very well, David. Unfortunately, it is evident Mórfran already knows its purpose, or else he would not be seeking it. Therefore, you may tell them what you have read.'

With scant reference to Merlin's notes, David spoke.

'The last entry was done the night before Merlin left for Vetus svet. He wrote that after the battle and the trial of Fendrel and the Myrkroth, or at least those who were captured, Merlin and Endrille realised there was no prison that would safely contain them. They therefore decided to create a place of inescapable exile. They chose the northernmost part of Álnair and used their combined powers to place an enchanted barrier around its borders. Anyone sent there would be marked by Endrille so they could never pass through the barrier.

'They also created an object to maintain the power of the enchantment. Merlin named it the Dragon's Eye and placed it into the care of my ancestor King Fíachra the First and all his heirs. He and the king hid it, and to ensure its safety placed a protection on it which would prevent anyone from revealing its whereabouts, either orally or in writing. The only way to learn of its location is to be shown it by someone who already knows. It must also remain unbroken and untainted or the enchantment will fail.'

David closed the book. 'He finishes by saying he regrets his old friend caused so much suffering, and can only apologise for not having realised Fendrel's evil machinations for what they were until it was too late.'

For a long moment no one spoke.

Finally, Lord Sato asked, 'Without wishing to seem inquisitive, does he mention who apart from Fíachra and his heirs knew about the Dragon's Eye? I do not believe for a moment either His Majesty or you, Your Royal Highness, would have revealed its existence imprudently.'

David shook his head. 'He doesn't mention it at all.' He looked at his father. 'I take it there was someone else who knew about it along with Endrille?'

King Stephen nodded. 'There were two. One has been questioned and cleared. The other we have not been able to locate.'

'Then he must be the one who told Mórfran,' declared Gareth. He stood up, his face like flint. 'Such a traitor deserves to be flogged. Name him, Your Majesty, and we shall find him.'

King Stephen looked at the outraged Robesman, an expression of deep sadness in his eyes. 'We cannot know if the information was disclosed voluntarily or not,' he said. 'As for their identity, this shall have to remain known only to myself and three others for the moment.' He looked around the laboratory. 'In the meantime, the contents of this room need to be thoroughly checked. Raeden, if I might impose upon you to take charge of that.'

'Could Professor Tysus help him?' asked Rhiannon. 'He's spent so much time trying to find this place I'm sure he'd appreciate being able to assist in going through what's here.'

King Stephen considered the suggestion, then agreed. 'Provided you arrange appropriate security measures for all his time in here, Raeden,' he said, 'and it is made clear to him that he is not to mention the laboratory being found to anyone at this stage.' He cast a look at those around him. 'That goes for all of you.'

'Yes, Sire,' they chorused.

David picked up one of the heavy tomes from the desk. 'This is a record of Merlin's last experiments. You might want to deal with it first.'

He handed it to his father, who passed it on to Sir Raeden.

'See what you can make of them. If there are any which may be of use, let me know,' King Stephen instructed.

Sir Raeden inclined his head.

'As for the other book,' the king continued, 'I believe it may be best to place it with the Dragon's Eye for the foreseeable future.'

He took up the book, then glanced at Merlin's sword.

'I would suggest the sword be left here for the moment. I dare not approve any magic being used to conceal it and there would be too many questions raised should one of the staff catch a glimpse of it in the palace.'

Reluctantly, David and Rhiannon had to concede the wisdom in his words. After a brief search revealed its sheath tucked away near the bookshelf, David placed the sword inside a narrow crevice in the wall.

Then King Stephen declared it time for them all to be returning to the palace.

'For the hour grows late, and it would not do for all of us to be missing when the dinner chimes ring,' he said.

The group left the laboratory, and it was as he and his father were bringing up the rear that David quietly asked for permission to show Rhiannon the Dragon's Eye.

'We never would've found the lab without her,' he said earnestly. 'Also, she proved herself worthy of Merlin's sword. Surely that should tell you she can be trusted.'

'David, I was already aware of her trustworthiness,' was his father's calm response. 'She may come now while I place the journal in its new location. No doubt you would like to accompany us, so I shall meet you both at the entrance. I am sure you can think up some way to leave the vigilant watch of your Robesmen.' There was a definite twinkle in King Stephen's eyes as he suggested with deceptive casualness, 'You could always say you want to spend some time alone with Rhiannon.'

'They'd probably say I didn't have any trouble when they followed us last night. I mean, that is, we didn't deliberately ...' David stopped in an embarrassed muddle, a surge of heat flooding his face.

A chuckle of unrestrained mirth left King Stephen. 'My son, calm yourself. I had a rather interesting conversation with one of the woodland dryads this morning and therefore am aware of your accidental meeting.' He smiled indulgently. 'You will no doubt have many more of them, plus some non-accidental ones. I merely suggest you ensure Sir Raeden is never given any cause to take umbrage over your behaviour towards her.'

'I'll be careful,' David promised. 'And I'll think up some way we can escape my mother hens.'

David's method of escape was to jump onto a transonus dais with Rhiannon and hit the first rune he could reach on the console before his Robesmen joined them.

The flash of light heralding their arrival at the Upper West Wing had barely dissipated when a push of another rune had them vanishing again. Their appearance on the dais near the Praeterium went unmarked by anyone, save a few House Faeries who called a happy greeting then continued on their way.

'Where do we go from here?' asked Rhiannon.

David pointed up the empty hallway towards a familiar gold statue of a griffin. 'The Room of Tranquillity,' he replied.

A serene atmosphere greeted them when they entered the room. Overhead, the faint glow of the setting sun painted a stunning array of colours across the enchanted ceiling, while a light breeze stirred the multitude of flowers covering the ground and the leaves on the great elm tree.

'This way,' said David. He led Rhiannon behind the tree to where his father stood waiting on the other side of a circular fountain.

King Stephen greeted them both, then allowed David to reveal the key to opening the entrance.

'The easiest way to remember is Dragon. D.R.A.G.O.N.' David pointed to the numerous decorative figures carved into the basin's outer wall. 'Watch which ones I touch, and the order in which I do it.'

He walked to and fro, briefly touching six figures from among the many marked into the hard stone. A dog. A rabbit. An acorn. A griffin. An otter and a …

'A bird?' Rhiannon queried with a frown.

'It's a nightingale,' said David.

'All right, now your mnemonic makes sense, or was it Merlin's?'

David shook his head. 'In his day they didn't have the same names for some of the animals. It was pure chance the ones he selected and the order he put them in spelt out dragon in English.' He approached one last figure. 'This one you'll have to remember some other way. Maybe since Merlin did the enchantment, just think of how much Kelandrus said he liked fish.'

He laid his palm over the image of the aquatic animal for three seconds.

There was a slight shift of movement in the ground.

A quiet *whoosh*.

A section of grass tilted upwards creating a small square opening.

Rhiannon peered down into it.

A row of lanterns flickered to life. The soft light illuminated a narrow flight of steps carved out of the white limestone flecked with gold streaks leading down to a wider passageway.

Led by King Stephen, the three descended the stairs.

The opening closed behind them, effectively sealing them beneath the ground.

Rhiannon's breath hitched slightly. The lower ceiling and narrower space seemed more frightening than the underground passage to Merlin's laboratory.

'I take it there's a way to open it from inside here,' she said with the faintest tremor in her voice.

David reached back and found her hand. Holding it firmly in his, he told her, 'We don't get out this way, so no there isn't. I guess Merlin thought it too dangerous to have the exit the same as the entrance.'

They arrived at the bottom of the steps. Rather than releasing Rhiannon, David shifted his grip as he moved to walk beside her in the slightly wider passageway.

The comforting warmth of his hand helped ease Rhiannon's lingering uneasiness over the low ceiling. Both David and his father had to bend to avoid their heads colliding with the glittering stalactites protruding from it, and for perhaps the first time ever Rhiannon was grateful for her short height.

'It's doesn't go down too much farther,' said David. He pointed to where the sloped path curved to the right about a hundred feet away. 'It flattens out after that, and thankfully the ceiling increases to a decent height.'

They continued walking until at length the path ended and they arrived at a cavern, its hollowness filled with a peculiar silver-blue glow. The light originated from the item protected by a circular wall of translucent stone in the middle of the open space.

'The Dragon's Eye.'

Rhiannon's awed whisper carried to every crevice in the wall. Mesmerised, she stared at the large orb floating several feet above the ground.

At two feet in diameter with the luminous beauty of a pearl and bearing a swirling pattern of tawny streaks and specks around a dark centre like an iris, the globe looked like the enlarged eye of a dragon.

'This is what keeps the barrier up around Mérosorc.' Rhiannon's words were a statement, not a question.

Still, King Stephen nodded, saying, 'It is, and the House of Valieoth is sworn to protect it. You will soon be fifteen, Rhiannon, the age when each of the first-born sons of Fíachra's bloodline are shown its location. As the direct descendant of Mórell it is only right you should share in its care and defence.' He put Merlin's journal down, placed a protective barrier around it, then laid his hand against the translucent stone shielding the orb. His flesh moved through the stone with the same ease it would pass through water. 'Each year the enchantment is strengthened when someone of the House of Valieoth touches the Eye.' A fleeting touch of his hand discharged a wave of energy from the orb.

Rhiannon felt the magic wash over her like the surge of heated air when a door opens on a hot summer's day. It warmed her skin, and the hairs on the back of her neck stood on end.

'What would happen if someone else touched it?' she asked.

'That would depend on their intent.' King Stephen drew back his hand, then turned to face her. 'If someone were to lay a hand on the Eye with the intent to destroy it, then it is possible they would succeed in tainting it. This is why only the king, his heir and one other has ever been shown its location.'

'Who's the other one?'

'A person entrusted with the knowledge in the event both the king and his immediate heir should die. Endrille shall inform David of their identity after my death, for after they die it will be his responsibility to show their successor.'

'In that case I'm in no hurry to find out who they are,' David announced, 'I'd rather have you around for ten more decades.'

'I shall certainly strive to oblige you, my son,' King Stephen promised with a faint smile. Then he turned and walked straight through the far wall of solid rock.

'Where did he go?'

'You'll see,' replied David, and went to follow his father.

A slight tug on her arm reminded Rhiannon of their linked hands. Her cheeks burned when she realised King Stephen could hardly have missed the affectionate gesture.

'Don't worry, he already knows about us,' David assured her when she mentioned it. 'And he won't mind us occasionally doing this,' he lifted their clasped hands, 'or this,' he swiftly pressed his lips to hers, 'provided we don't make a vulgar display of it.'

Her breath stolen by his kiss, Rhiannon silently stepped with him through the wall and into a small niche in the cliff face. Out its opening she could see the banister of the staircase that led down from the castle to the lagoon, and beyond it the light of the sinking sun transforming the ocean into liquid gold.

'Wouldn't there be questions asked if someone was in this cave when you came through the wall?' she asked, having recovered her breath. 'Some people like to explore any small crevice they see in a cliff. I can't imagine John's brothers going down to the lagoon and not wanting to discover if this hole led to somewhere more exciting.'

David shook his head. 'There's an illusion cast over the opening to make it look like solid rock, and if you press against it from the outside, you won't be able to get through. We just have to make sure no one is passing this particular spot before we exit.'

'Couldn't someone see us come out from above?'

'No. The area outside is shielded by overhanging ivy.'

They both fell silent at a signal from King Stephen when he reached the opening.

There was the sound of firm footsteps descending the stairs.

A man was speaking.

'... and then he tries to sneak past.' The gravelly voice was contemptuous in its disbelief. '"Sir," I says, "I can see your feet under the cart." I arrested him on the spot. Lucky I did! We discovered a stack of those pamphlets on him. But just like all the others when we went to question him, he were dead.'

The speaker, who wore the uniform of a castle guard, walked by the opening accompanied by four other guards. They were heading down towards the lagoon.

One of the other guards spoke up. 'Do you really think his killer came down this way?' he said, sounding sceptical. 'I mean, how would they get through the shoals without being seen by the guards in the watchtowers, or by the merfolk out in the deeper waters?'

'Sir Raeden ordered all parts of the grounds to be checked. I don't know about you, but I've got more sense than to disobey one of his commands!'

'I just don't see how whoever is committing the murders is getting into the grounds,' a third guard said quietly. 'You don't think it's someone already here, do you? One of us in the guards, or someone working in the palace?'

'Who knows. Plancy was on the High Council and look what he tried to do to Miss Rhiannon.'

'Aye, and her bein' not more than an innocent child. It ain't any wonder His Royal Highness looks out for her as he does.'

There was a bark of laughter.

The voices grew fainter.

'O'Malley, she isn't little Alice Tremaine. I think the prince has a far more personal reason for safeguarding her ...'

The voices faded into indistinct murmurs.

King Stephen listened for a moment, then gave the all-clear.

They swiftly left the small niche, stepping onto the flight of steps connected to the landing that marked the halfway point of the cliff face. Behind them, the opening became lost in the hard stone and shrubbery.

'Father, what man were they talking about?'

'The one who attempted to sneak through the Main Gate this afternoon while you were busy exploring,' King Stephen answered. He added grimly, 'His death is a new development.' Looking down at his son and Rhiannon, he ordered, 'You are both to stay in the palace this evening and remain in the company of your Robesmen, David. And there are to be no more late-night walks in the grounds until they've been thoroughly checked, is that understood?'

David and Rhiannon nodded.

'Good.' King Stephen went to ascend the stairs towards the landing, then paused. He turned back and with a glimmer of a smile said in a completely different tone of voice, 'I could not be more pleased over the change in your relationship, however, do make sure you apprise Sir Raeden of it soon, David. I dread to think what his reaction would be to seeing you holding Rhiannon's hand in public with no declaration of intent made in his presence.'

361

Chapter 23

CRUEL MOTIVATION

Mórfran glared at the man partially obscured by the deep shadows of the cave.

'You have had almost a year and yet you've not uncovered a single clue as to its location.'

The man cringed. 'I know, b-but, Mórfran, you don't understand! I have to be careful. If I was discovered searching for it, they'd —'

'I am not interested in excuses,' Mórfran cut him off. With a curt wave of his hand, he had the man screeching in pain. 'I only want results.'

Blood dripped from the man's nose and trickled out of his mouth.

'M-Mórfran, please. Give me more time. I will find something, I swear it.'

Mórfran's expression became a hideous caricature of pleasantness. 'Of course you'll find something, and to ensure you do I will send someone to serve as motivation. I believe you're already acquainted with him from when we sent him to get rid of Brimsby and those other fools. Should you exhaust my patience completely I will not hesitate to instruct him to deal with you in a like manner.'

The man shivered.

'Can we not interrogate the woman again?' he said desperately. 'Surely she can tell us something that will help.'

'What do you think our associate in Ardara has been doing these past few months? Should he succeed in obtaining further information from her, you will be informed of it.'

Mórfran's sneering smile fell. His cruel eyes gleaming with cold purpose, he warned, 'However, our master has no use for followers who prove themselves ineffectual. You are close to proving yourself one of them. Should you fail to provide anything useful before the first day of autumn, then you will join the leaves in their fall.'

~Chapter 24~

SHADOWS IN THE WATER

The last few weeks of school flew by for Rhiannon and David. Sir Raeden had not objected to the informal courtship between them, although he did promise the most dire of punishments should they behave with anything other than the utmost circumspection. So in among studying for their exams, they spent most of their free time together in the presence of David's Robesmen and some of the girls from the castle school. They went for rides into Cendillis or visited Cassandra in her chambers, and after the grounds were declared safe to walk through again there were many evenings spent conversing in low voices in the secluded gazebo and down at the lagoon.

Then the summer holidays were upon them.

Unlike the previous year, when the Dragon's Cup had loomed before Rhiannon, they found the first couple of weeks passing in a happy blur. There were visits to Merlin's Laboratory to discuss any interesting discoveries with Professor Tysus, along with numerous night flights to Luwyneth Cove with Eamon, Izana and Gareth. After her first time seeing the shimmering array of colourful star crystals beneath the clear water, Rhiannon had been determined to find several blue ones. She wanted a matching bracelet for her

364

necklace, but when the Castle's Summer Open Day arrived, she had only managed to find two of the rare crystals.

The Open Day was mercifully free of any unpleasant incidents, making it more enjoyable than the previous one in October. There was a greater number of stalls lining the road this time and the bustling crowds were thicker. David and Rhiannon spent several hours roaming the stalls, their hands firmly clasped, savouring each moment they shared as just an ordinary couple lost in the sea of people around them. When they arrived, flushed and out of breath, for the balcony appearance only seconds before the stroke of midday, both King Stephen and Queen Maiwen greeted them with kind smiles and an amused twinkle in their eyes.

Three weeks later, the same smiles were shared by most of those present in the Great Hall after David contrived to be the closest male to Rhiannon when she cut her birthday cake and was rewarded with a teasing peck on the cheek. It was not until they were out on the South Terrace to watch the lighting of the Hope Lanterns that David, shielded from inquisitive eyes by the dark shadow of a pillar and his five Robesmen, received a proper kiss from Rhiannon for his efforts.

However, despite their happiness, the ever-present threat of the faction in Graynor lingered.

Rhiannon soon became an expert at recognising whenever a new report had been received of another tragedy. David's eyes would turn the dark violet of a turbulent sky after a violent storm and his natural exuberance would become tightly restrained. When this happened, she and his Robesmen would do everything in their power to divert his mind from it for a while.

Just as they were currently doing with a turtle race in the lagoon.

'Yes! Come on, David! Just a little farther!' Rhiannon's gleeful cry rang out across the sunlit water.

'Adjust your balance, Eamon! You're going to fall!' Izana

shouted, only to be almost drowned out by John's roar of, 'Hurry up, Gareth! It's a race, not a Sunday stroll!'

'Markers, take your positions,' Derrick ordered.

Clad only in loose shirts and breeches with a dagger strapped to their thighs, Rhiannon, Izana and John stepped into the shallow water. David, Eamon and Gareth drew closer to the shoreline. David held the lead, but not by much.

Rhiannon bounced in place, the waves laving her legs as her feet sank into the sand. 'Come on, come on,' she urged.

David drew closer, his mount slicing through the water with ease. A sudden dip left his saturated shirt clinging to his flesh. Just a few feet more.

Then Rhiannon cried, 'Aground!'

David leapt off the sea turtle's giant shell to land with a victorious splash in the shallows. The spray of water sent Rhiannon scuttling back with a shriek of laughter, which quickly turned to gales of mirth when David slipped and toppled backwards into the waves.

His Robesmen were not slow in showing their amusement as well.

'I didn't quite get that last victory move,' grinned John. 'Could you demonstrate it again?'

With a wave of his hand, David sent a large surge of water towards him.

A tad too late with his protective shield, John was drenched.

As David turned towards the others, Eamon hurriedly asked, 'Anyone up for a rematch?'

'I'd prefer going out past the shoals myself,' said Gareth. 'It's the perfect weather for seeing the reefs.'

A vote being taken, and Gareth's idea receiving most of the support, Rhiannon enquired of the turtles if they would be happy to take them out. All three nodded.

Eamon looked at the turtles then at the six people around him. 'One of them is going to be a bit overcrowded,' he pointed out.

'Nonsense,' said David. 'Izana's the slimmest out of all of us, so he and Rhiannon won't take up too much space and I'll share with them. Derrick can go with you.'

'We won't be too heavy for them, will we?' Rhiannon asked, as she climbed onto the turtle's enormous shell behind Izana.

'Not at all,' replied David. He clambered up behind her and clasped her waist. 'They can carry up to twice their own weight. You and Izana combined wouldn't even be a quarter of that.'

The turtle might be able to bear their combined weight; however, Rhiannon noticed it was now deeper in the water than when she had ridden it in the race. Her entire bottom half, from the waist down, was immersed in the water.

'He's fine,' David assured her. 'They just prefer swimming under the surface, rather than above it.'

The group glided through the water on their aquatic mounts, passing between the two protruding cliffs and their watchtowers and over the submerged shoals. High tide was approaching, and the sandbars were pale shadows beneath the sea.

The water grew warmer the farther out they went, while the sun's light pierced the rippling sheen of the surface to reveal the beautiful reef below it.

Rhiannon stared at it in wonder.

Schools of colourful fish swam by, sometimes coming so close she could feel their delicate tails tickling her feet. She could even see several merfolk swimming among the coral and peering up at them in curiosity. She gave them a friendly wave. To her delight, they smiled and returned her gesture of greeting.

'If they invite you to swim, just politely refuse,' Izana murmured in a low voice.

Rhiannon looked at him in surprise. 'Why? I'm quite a good

swimmer, and I know the enchantment for encasing myself in an air bubble.'

'The younger ones can get carried away in their games. They'll pull you down too far and the enchantment will collapse. It draws oxygen from the water to sustain the bubble, but the deeper you go, the less oxygen there is.'

A plume of water shot skywards as a body launched out of the sea. Her torso covered in scales of shimmering cerulean to match her fine fishtail, the fair-haired mermaid arched over their heads and dived gracefully back into the water.

'Here come her friends,' David announced.

Rhiannon looked down to see several merfolk swimming up towards them. Even under the water their fair humanoid features were stunningly beautiful and their hair, like the first, was long but in various shades of colour. The males among them wore theirs tied back with a string of seaweed. However, unlike the younger ones among the coral, none of them were smiling.

The merfolk smoothly broke the surface of the water, then issued an urgent greeting to David in a language as fluid as a flowing stream.

David replied in the same tongue before saying in English, 'One of their infants went missing this morning. They believe he could be near here and have asked if we could help look for him.'

A chorus of agreement rang out and a merman with hair the colour of ripened pomegranates bowed his head in gratitude. 'We have not yet searched those rocks,' he said, pointing at the jagged coastline to the east of the castle. 'Or the reef closest to the lagoon.'

'We'll check among the rocks,' David decided. 'If he's injured, it'll be easier for us to climb through them than it would be for you.'

'The stars bless you for your kindness, O Prince,' the merfolk cried, then hastened in the direction of the lagoon.

The turtles, swiftly given their new target by Rhiannon, set out at their fastest pace towards the rocks.

'The tide isn't as high as it was this morning,' said David. 'He may be trapped in one of the small pools created at low tide. They said his hair is still the silver-grey of a newborn, so he'll be harder to spot.'

'Not necessarily,' interjected Derrick. He pointed to where a flock of seagulls sat atop some of the rocks. 'Miss Rhiannon, I believe they would easily spot him if he is to be found on land.'

Rhiannon immediately grasped his meaning. She called out to the birds, asking for their assistance.

In a cawing chorus, the flock took flight over the coastline.

'And everyone remember, if you see him, don't use any enchantment on or near the child.'

Rhiannon frowned at David's warning. 'Why can't we?'

'When they're less than a year old our magic is like a poison to merfolk. It weakens them until they dissolve into seafoam.'

Aghast, Rhiannon turned her head to look at him. 'It kills them?'

'Yes. So if he's hurt or trapped, don't use any form of enchantment to help him.'

The sun slowly began to sink in the west as the search continued. They had found no sign of the merchild and yet no one was prepared to give up looking for him. The three turtles had spread out along the coastline with their human riders, while some of the merfolk were swimming alongside them. Overhead the sky was filled with birds circling the ocean.

Rhiannon rubbed her eyes. The glare of the sun and closely scrutinising their surroundings had left them strained and tired.

'He's definitely not among the rocks,' she said. 'Should

we check some of those coves over there? Wouldn't they go underwater when there's a high tide?'

'They would,' David agreed. 'Well spotted. I'll tell the others.'

He shifted to look over to where Eamon and Derrick were a short distance behind them.

'Bolpodes!' John's shout pierced the air from in front. 'A squad of them have him. There!'

Dark shadows rippled under the water. A long black tentacle briefly surfaced then disappeared.

A shrill battle cry of fury came from the merfolk. They snarled, their incisors extending and growing pointed like a shark's. Their graceful hands and fingers morphed into razor-sharp claws. A frill of mottled green scales erupted out of their necks. Small, semi-translucent fins rose up behind their ears. Like enraged predators they launched forward, seeking to rip and tear apart the creatures who had dared to harm one of their young.

Meanwhile, John and Gareth had drawn their daggers and dived into the water.

'Go over there!' Rhiannon instructed urgently.

The turtle obeyed, his flippers moving them towards the fight at a tremendous speed.

The sea was turning a murky grey with streaks of red and black blood.

Gareth reappeared in a violent spray of water and an explosive gasp for breath. In one arm he held a frighteningly still merchild. He passed the infant to Izana.

'One of them paralysed him,' he breathed out harshly. 'We stabbed its eyes and cut off its tentacles.'

'Where's John?' David demanded, already preparing to enter the water.

'He was protecting our retreat from below. He should've been right behind me.'

Gareth took a deep breath and ducked back under. David swiftly followed him.

A moment passed. None of them resurfaced.

Izana twisted around to give the merchild to Rhiannon. 'Stay here with him,' he ordered.

The small, mildly warm body was placed in her arms, then Izana dived into the water to join the others.

Rhiannon clutched the merchild to her breast, his damp form soaking the top of her shirt in seconds. The flesh of his tiny arms and hands was smooth, and yet his torso and tail were leathery like a lizard's, the scales a light cerulean blue. His amber eyes were frozen open, and the terror in them wrenched at her heart.

'Everything will be all right,' she crooned softly, and running a soothing hand down his head, she stared down into the darkened sea.

A body bobbed to the surface.

Rhiannon swallowed the bile rising in her throat. The bolpode was missing all three yellow eyes from around its domed head. A cloud of black blood surrounded its corpse, no doubt escaping from where its tentacles looked to have been shredded by ruthless claws.

'Where are they?' she whispered.

The other turtle arrived carrying Derrick and Eamon. The two Robesmen spared her only the briefest of glances before diving into the sea after their prince.

There was not a wave or a splash to betray the turmoil taking place within the watery depths. What was happening? Why weren't they coming back up? Was one of them hurt?

More bolpodes floated to the surface, their bodies nearly torn to shreds. Not a single one was alive.

There was a shift, like that of something exploding deep within the sea.

A long pause fell.

No one appeared.

Where were they?

A violent swirl almost threw Rhiannon off the turtle. She struggled to retain her balance, hampered by the tiny infant in her arms.

In a showering spray, five merfolk broke the surface of the water.

A female with hair the colour of marigolds and eyes of clear green gave a great cry upon seeing Rhiannon holding the merchild. With frantic haste, she battered away the bodies of the bolpodes and reached up to take him. A jumbled torrent of Mórskarin passed her lips before she kissed his forehead.

'He was stung,' Rhiannon told her. 'If you don't have any yellow-leaf verbena I'm sure we can get you some.'

The mermaid cuddled the infant in her arms, giving no indication of having heard Rhiannon as she ducked beneath the water. It was left to one of the others to say, 'She thanked you, Lady Rhiannon, and we add our gratitude for your kind offer, but we have our own way to counter the poison of these foul creatures. Your companion, however, shall be in need of what you have offered. After he placed an air bubble enchantment upon himself, he was stung several times, and one of the bolpodes tried to crush him with its tentacles.'

All colour drained from Rhiannon's face. 'Which companion?' she choked out.

'Master John. The Prince and his aides left to retrieve him. They should not be far behind us.'

Rhiannon watched the sea like a hawk, her emotions in turmoil. David was unharmed, but John was hurt. She could not even begin to imagine how David and the other Robesmen must be feeling.

An eon seemed to pass.

Then, just when Rhiannon felt she must surely scream, David

and his five Robesmen appeared. The shiny transparent substance of an air bubble outlined each of their bodies. John was held between David and Gareth, his head lolling to the side. At a gesture from Eamon all the air bubbles popped and David called out in Mórskarin.

The merfolk reacted immediately. They circled Derrick and Izana who were moving their hands through the water and murmuring a flow of Drakaron under their breath. A ripple of light encircled the two magi, fashioning a small craft of crystallised water about them. They reached down and carefully lifted John into the boat.

'Are you not coming?' Derrick asked when David made no move to follow them.

'You two know more of healing than I do and four of us would be too heavy for the merfolk to pull.' David's eyes flickered towards John's ashen face. 'Get him to Apollinaris,' he commanded. 'And be careful of his chest. Several of his ribs are fractured.'

'We'll look after him,' Izana promised.

The four merfolk took hold of the boat and then they were off, their fishtails swiftly propelling them and the boat through the sea towards the palace.

David and his two remaining Robesmen wasted no time in remounting the patiently waiting turtles. Eamon and Gareth each took a separate one, while David sat behind Rhiannon on the third.

Their return to the palace was accomplished in a silence fraught with tension.

Rhiannon tightened her hold on David's arm which was curled around her waist. She could feel the anxiety pouring off him and wished there was something she could say to ease his mind. Without the knowledge of a fully trained healer, she had no way of knowing how the paralysing toxin would impact John's damaged ribs. Would it do nothing or would it complicate their healing?

If I were a qualified healer I would know, Rhiannon thought, and determined then and there to enquire of the Chief Healer what subjects she would need to study to become one.

For I never want to feel this useless again!

'Is he all right?'

The distraught voice of Leila Hardinge preceded her entry into the antechamber of John's rooms in the palace.

From their various positions around the chamber, David, his parents, his Robesmen, Rhiannon, Cassandra, Sir Julian Tremaine and his daughter Cordelia all turned to see the mousy-haired girl dash through the doorway. A streak of mud marred her left cheek and a small seedling lay crushed in her hand.

'Is he awake? May I see him?' Leila pleaded.

'We're still waiting to be allowed in ourselves,' said Eamon. 'Lady Isabella stuck her head out briefly over an hour ago to say the yellow-leaf verbena had started to take effect.'

'The main concern is that one of his ribs is very close to piercing his lung.'

Leila's face whitened even further at Derrick's words.

'B…B-But Apollinaris is an excellent healer,' Cassandra rushed to reassure her. 'I'm sure John w…w-will be fine.'

'Of course he will,' Cordelia declared, surreptitiously dabbing at her eyes with a delicate handkerchief. 'That brother of mine won't let a *bolpode* get the best of him. He'll be walking about and tormenting us again in no time.'

They all fell silent at the opening of the door to John's bedchamber.

Chief Healer Apollinaris Orlone stepped with quiet dignity across the threshold, the expression on his aged face one of imperturbable tranquillity. He closed the door, then looked up to see twelve pairs of eyes fixed upon him.

'How is he?' David asked, his countenance pale.

A small smile curved the lips beneath the healer's neatly trimmed white beard. 'The danger is past,' he answered warmly in his deep voice.

A collective sigh of relief sounded around the room.

'I have knitted the ribs back together,' Apollinaris continued, 'however, young Master Tremaine will need to take things very easy for the next two weeks. He will still experience significant pain when moving and he is not, under any circumstances, to lift anything heavier than a piece of cutlery or a small cup for at least three days.'

'May we see him?'

The eager chorus from the younger members of the group drew a nod from Apollinaris. 'But you are to keep your voices lowered and not remain any longer than a few minutes,' he instructed. 'He is extremely tired and needs his rest.'

Their promise to abide by his order having been given, the group silently slipped into the bedchamber.

The muted tones of lemon and green in the room created a soothing atmosphere around John's reclining form. His mother stood by his bed with an empty potion bottle in her hand.

Upon looking up to see his twelve visitors approaching his bed, a weak smile spread across John's wan face.

'So many people coming to see me,' he whispered, his voice breathless and strained. 'And it's not even my birthday. What's the occasion?'

A choked sound of amused exasperation escaped David. 'I might've known you'd make light of this as well,' he muttered. He reached out and lightly touched his Chief Robesman's arm. 'You had us all worried, John.'

'You certainly did, little brother.' Cordelia stepped forward and smacked his foot with sisterly affection. 'I'm the only one allowed to lay you out, remember?'

John gave a wry grin. 'I remember, Delia; but please, no demonstrations right now. I couldn't fight off a kitten at the moment. Those bolpodes are a friendly lot, but their hugs are a tad too tight.' He paused to press a hand against his chest, a grimace of pain twisting his face. 'Did … did the child survive?'

'He did.' The answer came from King Stephen. 'Lord Leronus sent a message thanking me for the assistance you all gave in rescuing a child of his realm. He particularly mentioned the bravery of you and Gareth in confronting the bolpodes armed only with your daggers.'

'That's my valiant lad,' Sir Julian proclaimed, running a proud hand over his son's curly hair. 'But don't you ever give us a scare like this again, my boy.'

'I'll try not to, Dad. Will you and Mum be staying the night?'

Sir Julian looked at King Stephen. 'If His Majesty permits it.'

To Rhiannon's surprise, David's father gave a rather inelegant snort.

'Jules, don't be such a nodcock,' the king said with a complete lack of formality. 'Of course you may stay and I'll send a carriage for your other four children. There are rooms enough here and I have no doubt they'll be wanting to see their older brother.' A muffled yelp from John when he yawned had him adding, 'Once he's had a chance to rest.'

'Which he will start doing right now,' Lady Isabella declared firmly. She pressed a small bottle into her son's hand. 'You may all come back in four hours once he's had some sleep.'

John offered a token protest, saying he didn't mind if they all stayed. However, his exhaustion was evident in the shadows below his eyes, and the white stain around his mouth betrayed the pain his injuries were causing him.

'Don't be such a clodpole,' David told him roundly, 'if we stayed you'd never go to sleep. We'll come back and see you later.'

He briefly clasped John's shoulder in a gentle grip. 'Remind me to thump you when you're fully healed for scaring us so badly.'

A glint of humour sparked in John's eyes. 'If you forget, I won't be reminding you. I'm not that eager for another bruise!'

'If David doesn't remember, we will,' announced Gareth.

All the other Robesmen voiced their agreement. 'And you'll get a thump from each of us,' they promised on their way out the door.

Rhiannon shook her head over the strangeness of the male species, said her own goodbye to John, then headed for the antechamber. Stepping out of the bedchamber, she realised Leila was not following her. She turned to see the older girl gingerly sit on the edge of John's bed and take his hand in hers. The only other person in the room was Lady Isabella who tactfully had her back turned to rearrange the potion bottles spread out on the desk.

Hearing a muffled sob, Rhiannon looked back at the bed to see John slowly raise his other hand and place it against Leila's muddy cheek. She could not hear what he said, but she saw the fond smile he only ever gave Leila appear on his face. It would seem waiting to see if Leila was all right was superfluous. A kiss between the two on the bed reinforced that thought.

I'm sure she'll be fine, Rhiannon decided, and beat a hasty retreat for the outer door. She entered the hallway of the First Level of the Upper East Wing and found only David, his four other Robesmen, Cassandra and Cordelia waiting beside the nearby transonus dais.

'Where's Leila?'

At Eamon's question a slight blush spread across Rhiannon's face. 'She's saying goodbye to John,' she answered.

Cordelia and Izana cast her fiery cheeks a sharp, considering look.

Izana, mercifully, did not say anything. Cordelia, however, enquired, with no sign of compunction, 'Have those two finally confessed to each other? We've been waiting for John to pull his head out of the sand these past two years.'

'Um, I don't … I saw, I mean, I didn't, I didn't hear anything,' Rhiannon stammered, her blush deepening.

'But you saw something,' said Cordelia, proving she had caught Rhiannon's slip. A glint of sisterly curiosity lit up her blue eyes. 'I wonder what. Oh, don't worry,' she assured Rhiannon. 'I won't ask you to tell me. An action can have any number of meanings attached to it. Besides, it'll be more fun getting the truth out of my brother myself.'

Rhiannon blinked, trying to see the formal lady she had first met the year before in the impish female with the gamine smile now standing in front of her. She could only assume John's close brush with death had stripped away Cordelia's society mask, revealing her true personality.

'David!'

The relieved cry pulled Rhiannon out of her thoughts. She and the group turned as one to see Oliver Donahue hurrying towards them from the staircase down the passageway.

'O my dear nephew, I just heard. To know how close you came to being injured, I had to see for myself you were unharmed. But poor John! Will he be all right?'

'Apollinaris was able to mend his ribs,' David replied while returning his uncle's embrace, 'but he'll need to be careful for the next two weeks.'

'That is wonderful news indeed,' exclaimed Oliver. 'Here was I expecting to hear the direst of fates had befallen him.'

'We certainly feared the same at first,' David admitted.

Oliver looked at the group, his expression one of deep compassion. 'It must've been a horrendous ordeal for you all.'

'It was,' Derrick stated briefly.

'I had something similar happen when I was at the Academy,' Oliver revealed. 'My brother's father-in-law was trampled by a horse and had nearly all his ribs broken. I don't believe any of us slept that night for worrying over him. I suppose it's times like this we all wish we had your self-healing ability, Miss Rhiannon. Still, at least now it's over you may rest easy, although you must ensure John gets enough rest. Don't let him roam the palace too much. In fact, he'd be best off keeping to his rooms so he doesn't exhaust himself.'

'I think that might be asking the impossible, Uncle.'

Cordelia swiftly added her agreement to David's reply. 'My brother has an extreme aversion to being kept in isolation,' she explained.

Oliver laughed. 'Ah, well. I've given my advice. Just think it over and put it to Master John. I'm sure if you tell him that it will help speed up his recovery so he can swiftly return to his duties, he'll consider it.'

~Chapter 25~

MALEVOLENT CONSPIRACY

He was running out of time. The first day of autumn was less than a week away!

The man looked at the creature lurking in the shadows of the cove, seeing no emotion in its faded blue eyes. Instead, the two orbs peered out at him from the gloom with a chillingly vacant stare. They were the eyes of a being stripped of its own will and devoid of all conscience. Precisely what he needed for the plan he had in mind.

'You're here to serve Mórfran, aren't you?' he demanded.

'Yes,' came the whispery, monotone reply.

'And what does he want me to find?'

'The Dragon's Eye.'

'Then by helping me find it you'd still be serving Mórfran. Correct?'

'Yes.'

The man smirked triumphantly. Instead of taking his life, tomorrow this lackey of Mórfran's would help him keep it! He was through being cautious in this search. He'd risk the creature's capture and utilise its abilities in a more effective manner.

There was one family in all of Álnair who had to know the

location of the Dragon's Eye and one of them would betray its whereabouts without even realising it.

The man extracted a small box from inside his robes.

With the creature's talent and the aid of an arachnescope his plan simply could not fail.

~Chapter 26~

A Grievous Betrayal

David stood in the antechamber to his apartments staring at the report in his hand. He looked at his father. 'You want me to what?'

'David, you are fluent in their language and you would be gone only a few days.'

David shook his head. 'I'm not worried about having to go away. Father, the Rolvian clan have isolated themselves completely from the other peoples of Álnair, but they're not savages. Do you really believe this ludicrous claim that they are responsible for the raid on the hamlets along the Ardara road?'

'No, I don't, however, I cannot leave them unquestioned. A king's main duty is to serve and protect all his people. If I allowed my personal sentiments to dissuade me from fulfilling my obligations then I would be a poor leader. All possibilities, no matter how absurd, must be investigated.'

David grimaced. 'Chieftain Ivor Thorson won't take kindly to having his clan's honour doubted.'

'I am sure I may rely upon you to exert the utmost tact when questioning him. Also, I shall have Sir Raeden accompany you.'

David groaned. 'Must you? Couldn't I just take one of my Robesmen?'

'I do wish you did not dislike him so much,' King Stephen lamented. 'He is strict but not cruel, and perhaps one of the most selfless people I've met.'

'He lives to torment me,' David remonstrated. 'If I commit the same infraction as several other students, he always gives me a more severe punishment.'

'I know, and you accept it without once asking me to intervene,' came his father's quiet response. 'But have you ever wondered why he should be so much harder on you than your classmates?'

'He thinks I'm a spoiled princeling in need of regular correcting?'

'Perhaps sometimes,' King Stephen conceded with a laugh. Then his mirth faded, leaving his countenance set in solemn lines. 'David, one day you will be king, and those in position of authority are expected to lead by example. Therefore, greater expectations are held regarding your behaviour than that of say Master Truscott or the future Lord Sato. Underneath your sometimes impulsive nature and fiery temper Sir Raeden sees the same good qualities in you that I do. In singling you out for harsher punishment, he seeks to dissuade you from repeating the misconduct that would only lead to the ruination of your character. That is one of the reasons why I gave him authority over you, as I knew he would not abuse that power.

'One of the other reasons was that I knew if there was one man capable of testing your mastery over your emotions, it would be him. As king, you will face many trials to test your patience. In order to deal with them you need to be able to keep your emotions subjugated to your will. I would suggest looking upon this journey to the underground city of the Rolvian clan as an opportunity to judge how well you can maintain that control.'

'Yes, Father.'

A small smile appeared on King Stephen's face at David's subdued response. He reached out and gave the gold forelock on David's head a gentle tug of affection.

'I know you would much prefer to remain here with Rhiannon, so I will not make you miss any more of her company,' he said. 'You have until four o'clock. Then Sir Raeden will be waiting with Arastar and Níping in the Lower Ward.'

David's countenance lit up in delight. He threw his arms around his parent. 'You're absolutely the best of fathers! I promise I shan't be late.'

Highly amused, King Stephen returned the embrace. 'Such gratitude for so small an indulgence,' he teased.

'It's not small to me.' David pulled back, a resolute expression on his face. 'I love Rhiannon, and we fully intend to marry in a few years.'

A twinkle of loving warmth lit up King Stephen's eyes.

'You are most definitely your mother's son,' he remarked, placing his hand briefly against David's cheek. 'Steadfast and constant once you've made your choice. And it will be a pleasure to call Rhiannon my daughter. Now, be off with you. If you hurry, you should be able to catch up with her before she reaches John's chambers.'

David walked towards the door, then stopped. 'Mother!' he exclaimed. 'After my disappearing to Vetus svet and the incident with the bolpodes, will she be all right if I'm gone for a few days?'

'Knowing you're still in Álnair and with Sir Raeden will help ease her concern. However, I will also have her meet you in the Lower Ward. I am sure she will wish to see you off herself.'

'Will you be there?'

'Unfortunately not. I shall still be in conference with the delegation from Ardara.'

'Oh. Then I'll say goodbye now.' David clasped his father's right arm with his and they shared a warm embrace. 'Love you.'

King Stephen echoed his son's words. Then they both froze. The sonorous, deep tone of a gong was reverberating throughout the walls of the palace. Strong vibrations rippled along the floor beneath their feet.

'The Bell of Elaros.'

'Why has it been rung?'

Their eyes widening in apprehension, father and son ran for the door.

Rhiannon gave a small skip on her way to John's chambers. Today, they would be taking the Chief Robesman outside the palace for the first time since his injury. David had suggested the North Gardens and said he would meet them there after he finished speaking with his father. She had left him and King Stephen outside the door of his apartments to discuss a new report from Ardara.

'And tell Derrick I'm quite capable of walking out there alone,' he had declared before bestowing a light kiss on her forehead.

Rhiannon had not missed the king's indulgent smile when he looked upon them. Her affection for the kind man only continued to grow with each encounter she had with him.

She continued down the hallway of the Upper South Wing, passing the transonus dais without a second glance. Sometimes, it was simply nicer to walk rather than taking the easier route. She descended the staircase and cheerfully greeted the guards at the bottom.

She had only taken a few steps forwards when she paused. The air around her was pulsating, an aftershock no doubt of the deep, resonating gong echoing down every passageway.

The toll came again.

The guards leapt into action as a third peal rang out.

'Get back upstairs, Miss Rhiannon,' they ordered, their

weapons drawn and at the ready. The two wolfhounds beside them tensed, a warning growl rumbling in their throats.

'What is it?' Rhiannon asked, swiftly moving to obey.

'That was the Bell of Elaros. It is rung three times when the castle or its people are in danger. You should return to your chambers. Remain there until you hear it chime once more.'

Rhiannon did not even consider going back to her rooms. Upon reaching the landing, she took off towards David's apartments.

She ran past door after door.

Then a man exited one of them in front of her.

Lord Daiki Sato!

Rhiannon was going too fast to avoid him. With a squeaking yelp, she collided with his side.

His athletic build barely shifting an inch from the impact, the Chief Robesman to the king steadied her while demanding, 'Where are you going?'

'David's … a-apartments,' she gasped. 'He's there with his father.'

'Come along.'

Lord Sato grasped her hand firmly and dashed down the hallway.

Rhiannon, her breaths coming in ragged pants, struggled to keep up with him.

A twist in the passage and then David and his father were almost on top of them.

'Daiki, what has happened?'

'I don't know. But —'

'O Your Majesty!' The high-pitched cry of a House Faery heralded his swift approach from the direction of David's apartments. 'King Stephen!'

'What is it, Lystro?'

'Some evil has befallen the Royal Guard in their quarters. They're all fighting each other. One has already been killed!

Sir Raeden asked me to inform you he and a company will secure the building and restrain the afflicted guards.'

King Stephen's face became set like flint.

'Lystro, should any guards inside the palace show similar acts of aggression, you and your people are to do all things necessary to subdue them,' he commanded. 'Daiki, go to the South-West Tower and secure the transonus dais. I shall be there shortly. David and Rhiannon, come with me.'

Lystro and Lord Sato each gave a quick bow and swiftly departed.

King Stephen led David and Rhiannon to his son's apartments. The instant they entered the antechamber, he hastened through the door leading into David's study. To Rhiannon's astonishment, he went to the magnificent mural of a woodland scene beside the great hearth in the far-right corner of the room. The painting spanned almost the entire wall. He raised his hand and touched his signet ring to the sun's reflection in the painted stream.

Like ripples spreading outward in real water, the stillness of the image shifted from the epicentre of the ring's touch.

'Get in,' King Stephen ordered. 'And you're to remain in there and not come out for any reason until you know it's safe.'

'Father, I can help,' David protested as Rhiannon looked on in bewilderment. 'If need be, I can use the Aoratos Charm to avoid detection in the fight.'

The king shook his head. 'You could still be struck unintentionally. Please, David. I need to know you will both be out of danger should the situation escalate. Promise me you will do as I bid.'

There was a brief pause before David reluctantly agreed to his father's entreaty.

'Good man,' King Stephen praised, laying a hand on his son's head. He briefly touched Rhiannon's with his other. 'Be safe and take care of each other. Now, make haste.'

'Be careful, Father,' David adjured him. Then he took Rhiannon by the hand and stepped into the mural.

Rhiannon gasped as a warm flow of air washed over her.

The scent of evergreens and moist earth filled her nostrils.

The heat of the sun shone upon her head.

In the shadows of the woodlands there came the rustle of unseen animals in the undergrowth. There were quiet scufflings, a few curious chatterings and a soft *plop* from the stream revealed several fish below its surface.

A flicker of movement drew Rhiannon's gaze to the narrow path between the trees. She caught a glimpse of two tiny red squirrels whisking off the path and scurrying up a tall tree trunk.

David touched his signet ring to the ground then quickly drew Rhiannon into the shadows of the trees.

Rhiannon looked back over her shoulder to see King Stephen standing in the study behind a ghostly barrier of silver-grey miasma. Interspersed across the swirling mist were tiny flecks of light, glittering like dust particles caught in a sunbeam.

'Where are we?' she asked.

'A side dimension. Only Endrille and my family know of its existence. The Valieoth signet rings alone are capable of opening and sealing the doorways hidden in several murals spread through-out the palace. We can't be touched while we're in here, but we are visible from the other side, so we need to hide.'

'Can they hear us?'

'No. But we'll hear whatever happens out there.'

'David, go deeper into the shadows,' King Stephen ordered, unintentionally demonstrating this fact. 'You're still too visible.'

David and Rhiannon hurried to obey, particularly when they heard sharp footsteps striking against the marble floor of the antechamber.

'Your Majesty! Prince David! Are you still here?'

Rhiannon relaxed slightly at the familiar voice. 'It's Sir Raeden,' she said in relief.

David did not pause. He continued until they reached the darker shadows among the trees. They stopped and turned to see King Stephen's back facing them, his long hair a golden sunbeam over the green field of his robe.

'Your Majesty?'

'I'm in here, Raeden.'

The footsteps sped up and then Sir Raeden was dashing through the doorway. His cloak a swirl of black cloth edged with gold, he took in King Stephen's solitary presence in the room at a glance. 'I was told Prince David would be with you,' he said without preamble. 'Where is he?'

'Somewhere safe.' King Stephen walked through the gap between the desk and a long sofa. 'Has the situation in the guards' quarters been contained?'

'No, nor will it be for some time. I believe it to be a ruse.'

'A ruse for what purpose?'

'To find the Dragon's Eye. Those seeking it must suspect you and Prince David know its whereabouts. I believe someone is coming for one or both of you right now.'

'Their suspicions will avail them little, as you know, Raeden. Neither David nor I would reveal its location, no matter who demanded it of us.'

'True.' Sir Raeden stood aside to allow King Stephen to pass him. There was a glint of metal. A flash of a blade. He stabbed swiftly at the king's exposed back. 'But we're sure you would accompany each other to its location and for that we only need one of you alive. The other must disappear.'

King Stephen fell, a choked-off inhalation of breath the last sound to escape his lips.

'NO!'

David's anguished scream echoed that in Rhiannon's heart.

Horrified, she clung to his arm and stared at the chillingly emotionless face of her guardian.

Then her blood ran cold.

Sir Raeden's face and form were changing.

Blue eyes became green.

Black hair turned to gold.

Cloak and tunic transformed to robes.

The intimidating height shortened by two inches.

Even the sword and scabbard altered in their design and colour.

Where Sir Raeden had stood was now a perfect copy of King Stephen.

'Now to find the prince.' The imposter paused and tilted his head, as though listening to a voice only he could hear. 'Yes, dispose of him.' He dragged King Stephen's body behind the large desk and dropped his corpse. Then he stepped towards the fireguard in front of the great hearth.

David's frozen state was shattered.

'*Spurinus orcfa!*'

The furious cry accompanied the sharp hiss of steel. His sword in hand, David's wrath was a palpable force as he tore away from Rhiannon and ran towards the barrier.

'Wait! David!'

'Your Majesty.'

The stern voice from the doorway of the study accomplished what Rhiannon's desperate utterance had not: It stopped David in his tracks.

In synchronised surprise, three pairs of eyes turned to watch the grim, dishevelled figure of Sir Raeden cross the threshold of the room. The knight's gaze was fixed upon the man partially concealed behind the large desk.

'Sire, were I to ask the location of your lantern what would be your answer?'

Sheer, unadulterated bewilderment greeted Sir Raeden's seemingly senseless question. His three listeners all frowned in confusion.

Then the false King Stephen raised his right hand and waved dismissively. 'This is no time for riddles. I need to find my son, and you should be out containing the situation with the guards.'

'Perhaps. But I believe I am needed here.' A streak of deep blue light abruptly shot out of Sir Raeden's upflung hand.

The imposter ducked behind the desk, narrowly avoiding the binding enchantment. 'Are you mad?' he yelled.

'Furious,' was the curt reply. 'Who are you? And where is the king and Prince David?'

'Fool! I'm your king.'

'You have taken the guise of the king, but you are not he. My king would recognise the appellation he used for his own son. He would also not be missing the signet ring from his right fore-finger. A ring that no magic can replicate.'

Sir Raeden drew his sword and stepped farther into the room.

'You wear his face and raiment as easily as you wore mine to order the sentries on the stairs to reveal the last known whereabouts of the king and his son,' he continued, his voice rigid with lethal control. 'Whose did you use to contaminate the food in the guards' quarters? And what sorcery enables you to so alter your appearance? If, indeed, sorcery it is. I begin to suspect otherwise.'

With a slash of his hand, Sir Raeden sent the desk hurtling sideward.

The imposter scrambled after its protective cover.

And so was the fallen body of King Stephen revealed to his trusted Commander and friend.

For a fleeting moment David and Rhiannon saw the starkness of his grief laid bare in Sir Raeden's face. Then it was overwhelmed with cold and deadly resolve.

The imposter cowered behind the desk when the knight's

voice, like the fierce growl of a tiger, curdled the air with its threatening resonance.

'Treasonous wretch! You have spilt the blood of a good and just man, for which vile offence I would see you sent immediately for final judgement before God if our laws permitted your execution. As they do not, you shall suffer the sting of our harshest punishment once you have confessed all your dark secrets.'

The desk flew backwards, trapping the imposter against the wall.

'But first you will tell me what you have done with the prince.'

What happened next occurred at such speed David and Rhiannon were not sure if they imagined it.

A tuagust, short and slim with blood staining his mouth and stripped of King Stephen's appearance, leapt up from the space between the wall and the desk and crashed through the large window. Sir Raeden's binding enchantment streaked after him, its bright light reflecting off the shattered glass, transforming the shards to glittering blue crystals.

Sir Raeden ran and leapt up onto the desk. He looked out of the broken window to the area below, then called for Lystro.

The House Faery arrived and instantly launched into an update on the situation with the Royal Guard, declaring it fully contained with no further casualties. But then he saw the state of the room and King Stephen motionless on the floor. His speech faltered, shock rendering his voice silent.

'His murderer lies bound on the roof of the Middle South Wing,' Sir Raeden said brusquely. 'A tuagust, but he's injured so he cannot change his appearance. Please have four of your people retrieve him. I also want a full search conducted of the palace and the castle grounds for Prince David.'

'There is no need for that, Sir. I'm here.'

Sir Raeden swiftly turned in the direction of the subdued voice. Rhiannon did not miss the surprise in his eyes when he saw her follow David through the ghostly barrier and out of the mural. However, demonstrating a rigid control of his emotions, her guardian satisfied himself with a brief nod, then instructed Lystro to also fetch Queen Maiwen and a priest from the palace chapel.

'Escort the queen to the antechamber, but do not bring her into this room. I shall first need to prepare her for what she shall find when she enters.'

Lystro departed without another word.

Sir Raeden descended from the desk and joined David and Rhiannon beside King Stephen's body.

The ruler of Álnair lay in a small pool of his own blood, the deep crimson liquid coating the radiance of his hair, the long strands falling about his still form like the last golden rays in a red sunset. His Dragonstar of silver metal and ruby-coloured stone lay visible around his neck.

Sir Raeden crouched down to examine the open wound in his back.

Rhiannon tightened her grip on David's hand as he stood gazing at his father in heavy silence. The pain and grief in his face tore at her heart, but she knew there was nothing she could say in this moment that would bring him any comfort.

The grim silence was broken by Sir Raeden quietly stating, 'The blade pierced his heart.' He looked up at David, his expression carefully controlled. 'He would have died instantly.'

A muscle ticked in David's jaw and a watery sheen glistened in his eyes. He gave a small nod of acknowledgement, but offered no verbal reply.

'So I – so I wouldn't have been able to save him like I did with David?'

Her guardian shook his head at Rhiannon's hesitant question.

'There was nothing anyone could have done,' he answered. He gently turned King Stephen's body so his back was to the floor, and closed the eyelids over the lifeless green eyes. He bowed his head in mute prayer, blessed himself, then slowly rose to his feet. 'There shall be many who will deeply mourn your passing, great king,' he murmured, 'including myself,' and turning to David he offered a sincere word of condolence which was accepted with another silent nod.

'For the tuagust's trial, I shall need an account of what happened when you feel ready to tell me,' Sir Raeden added.

Rhiannon, seeking to spare David the pain of having to speak of his father's death, began a concise recounting of the events from the moment the Bell of Elaros had rung.

She reached the moment when the tuagust appeared.

To her bewilderment, David broke in, saying, 'He came in the guise of one of the guards.'

As he briefly narrated the slaying of his father in a voice tight with suppressed emotion, Rhiannon wondered why he had not disclosed the precise identity used by the tuagust. She had her answer after she asked about it when Sir Raeden stepped out into the antechamber to meet Queen Maiwen.

'I saw his grief,' David replied in a ragged whisper. 'How could I add to it by revealing that the creature wore his face to kill my father?'

'Oh, David.' Rhiannon wrapped him in a tight embrace. 'I'm so sorry. And now, every time you see him, you'll see that nightmarish scene again.'

David bowed his head and closed his eyes. 'No. I shall not allow a false image to torment me,' he swore. 'What I'll see is him vehemently declaring my father's murderer a treasonous wretch and praying beside my father's body.' His voice broke on the last word. He buried his face in Rhiannon's hair, a muffled sob shaking his frame.

Rhiannon could feel his sorrow as though it were her own, the sting of it lancing her soul. The hot prickle of tears burned her eyes, but she fought them back.

In silence they stood alone in the study, their arms locked about each other. One of the gold clasps securing David's cloak to his tunic dug into Rhiannon's cheek. The discomfort barely impinged upon her mind. Despite the strength in his arms, at this moment, David was in need of her support.

The tread of approaching footsteps eventually brought Rhiannon and David's hold on each other to an end. Reluctantly, they drew apart. David apologetically smoothed the red mark on Rhiannon's cheek before straightening his shoulders. They both turned to see his mother slowly enter the room.

Rhiannon had never seen anyone look so devastated.

Her body held rigidly upright, eyes bereft of tears, her countenance deathly pale and devoid of all animation, Queen Maiwen spoke not a word as she first hugged David, then knelt beside her husband's body. With one hand she traced King Stephen's face, her fingers tenderly caressing every line and groove. A kiss, gently pressed to his still lips, had her hair falling about the two of them in a black shroud. And then his head was held against her breast as her arms enfolded him; the golden glint of his hair mingled with the shadowy darkness of hers, like sunbeams caught in a raincloud.

Rhiannon remained silent as David stepped forward and approached his mother. His own sadness now lay hidden behind a mask of calm composure. He crouched down to wrap his arms around his grieving parent.

A hushed rustle of fabric drew Rhiannon's attention to the door. There she saw Lord Sato sinking to his knees, his anguished gaze fixed upon the royal family. Behind him stood Sir Raeden, Lady Agnes and David's Robesmen.

Inexplicably, Rhiannon's control over her tears crumbled. They poured down her cheeks, though not a sound passed her lips. Her vision blurred, blinding her to everything. Warm arms wrapped around her, the distinct scent of sandalwood revealing the identity of the person without her needing to hear his voice.

Rhiannon buried her face in her guardian's tunic, mourning the loss of a man who had only ever treated her with kindness, and aching for the desolation his death was causing all those who loved him.

~Chapter 27~

OF SALT AND ARACHNESCOPES

News of King Stephen's death spread quickly. All throughout the palace shocked voices denied its truth until they saw stern-faced guards affix a wreath of lilies, purple asters and white and red roses in every room and passage. Then their lamentations joined those of the House Faeries, whose sad, sweet songs could be heard in every wing. Many wept openly, others hid themselves away to give in to their grief, only to have their reddened eyes and tearstained cheeks betray the extent of their mourning.

The king's body was removed from David's study. He now lay in state inside the Great Hall on a bier, bathed in the glow of the afternoon sunlight streaming through the tall windows. A look of peace was on his face, and were it not for the absolute stillness of his body, it would have been easy to believe him simply caught in the realm of sleep. He was arrayed in burial robes of gold cloth with a gold-embroidered mitre on his head and his Dragonstar about his neck. The richly ornamented and enamelled crucifix upon which he had made his coronation vows lay on his chest

397

beneath his folded hands. Four members of the Royal Guard stood sentry around him.

'David, Sir Raeden's here. He needs to speak with you.'

The soft whisper from Gareth drew Rhiannon's gaze away from the still serenity of King Stephen's face to where David stood beside his mother. Both were dressed entirely in white, save for a purple mantle secured about their shoulders and the single purple stripe around the tops of David's white boots.

David acknowledged Gareth's words with a nod. He glanced towards the main entrance doors, murmured a quiet explanation to Queen Maiwen, deflected the almost fanatically concerned queries of his Uncle Oliver, then slowly made his way down the long length of the hall. His five Robesmen and Rhiannon followed a discreet distance behind him.

When they reached Sir Raeden, he spoke his greeting in a low voice and gestured to the door. 'It would be best to speak of this outside,' he advised.

'What is it?' David asked once they were standing in the hallway.

'Firstly, I shall need all your Robesmen, Rhiannon and you to hold out your hands.'

Obviously in no mood to waste time arguing, David held out his left hand. Rhiannon and the others followed.

Sir Raeden reached out and sprinkled grains of white salt on them.

Rhiannon wondered if the grief of losing his friend and king had driven him mad.

Strangely, David and the others merely wiped it off their palms with David observing, 'We're all who we're supposed to be. Now, what is it?'

'It concerns the tuagust.'

At these words, David's expression tightened. 'What of him?'

'He did not survive the fall. Apollinaris examined the body

and discovered a build-up of toxins inside his brain. The amount indicates he was regularly dosed with a powerful blend of aconite and serpent's breath. There were also significant signs of trauma in his brain around this.' Sir Raeden opened his left hand to reveal a small black object on his palm. No larger than a pea, it looked like a curled-up dead spider.

'The controller fully terminated the link while it was still embedded beneath the *pia mater*,' Sir Raeden continued. At Rhiannon's blank look, he explained briefly, 'It's the innermost layer of delicate connective tissue that protects the central nervous system. I believe that would explain the creature's desperate leap out the window.'

David's expression darkened. 'So, the tuagust was not only acting under compulsion, but someone, who would have to possess knowledge of the layout of the palace, was instructing him the whole time he was here using a forbidden arachnescope.'

'Making it almost impossible to trace who is behind this attack,' said Eamon.

'Not quite,' interjected Izana. 'The tuagust knew the location of David's apartments. Only someone who has been in the topmost level of the palace would know where it is. They would also need to be familiar with the serving of food to the Royal Guard inside their own quarters and not in any of the palace dining halls.'

'Which all reduces the number of suspects considerably,' observed Derrick.

'Not necessarily,' Sir Raeden swiftly corrected him. 'This tuagust bears the name mark of K'el on his left hand.'

'The one who's been missing since last year?' asked David.

'Yes. I suspect we may have found who has been killing the prisoners with a connection to the faction in Graynor.'

'But if that's so, he's had access to the palace for months!' exclaimed Gareth. 'The controller could've had him appearing as anyone.'

Izana shook his head. 'It wouldn't be just anyone. The tuagust would need to appear as someone authorised to enter the highest levels, and the controller would need some basic knowledge about the person to avoid raising suspicions. For example, he couldn't risk having a random guard attempting to enter restricted areas, or one of the chancellors forgetting the names of their colleagues.'

'So, the controller has to be someone with knowledge of those employed by the palace and their positions,' Eamon summarised.

'Yes.' John's reply was strained. 'And they might have more mind-controlled tuagusts roaming among us.'

A wave of uneasiness went through Rhiannon at the possibility.

David turned to Sir Raeden. 'Sir, is that possible?'

'Perhaps. There has been no mention of any other tuagust going missing. However, R'lon should confirm the truth for us once he arrives to collect K'el's body. In the meantime, with your approval, I shall implement a complete check of every human within the castle walls and those seeking to enter. Should there be any others, they will be found.'

David did not hesitate to give his consent. 'However, ensure the application of rock salt on their skin is only used to reveal their true form, rather than cutting them. If any are found, secure them and remove any arachnescope planted in them.'

The reason behind Sir Raeden sprinkling salt on their hands now made sense, but Rhiannon continued to be confused. She looked from David to her guardian. 'I still don't understand. What's an arachnescope?'

'It's a communication device crafted by the blackest sorcery,' Sir Raeden informed her. 'Fendrel made them for use on those he captured and wished to turn into mindless slaves. He stripped them of their memories and placed one inside their brains. Each one has a glass sphere linked to it which is used by the controller, who can see and hear everything the victim does once the arachnescope has embedded itself. The controller gives their instructions directly into the slave's mind. They were all supposed to be destroyed centuries ago, however, over time it has become clear some followers of Fendrel who were never identified or caught have several in their possession. Occasionally another will resurface, as it has in this instance.'

Rhiannon felt the burning sensation of bile rise in her throat. 'How … how can they get that inside someone's head?'

'It's animated to crawl inside the nasal cavity. Once it's attached to the brain, it will remain active until the controller recalls it or severs the link by breaking the glass sphere. The severing of the link will inflict major damage to the brain tissue when the dark power animating the arachnescope dissipates, which is why it's imperative to remove it before that happens.'

The roiling in Rhiannon's stomach increased. She thought of K'el. For the first time, she felt pity for him. He had been nothing but a tool for those behind the search for the Dragon's Eye and his life had been discarded with callous indifference. The cruelty of the controller's character was chilling.

'If you find a tuagust with one of these arachnescopes, would they be able to tell you anything once it's removed?' she asked.

'Unlike those under the influence of mind-controlling agents like aconite or serpent's breath, they would have no recollection of anything other than what they had been instructed to do. They would be incapable of sharing the most basic information about themselves, such as their family, friends and experiences they have lived, as the arachnescope can only be used on victims who no longer possess any personal memories.' Sir Raeden returned his attention to David. 'Until it is certain the palace and castle grounds are secure, it would be prudent for you to remain in the company of your Robesmen.'

'Don't worry, Sir,' all five of them chimed, 'we won't let him out of our sight.'

Satisfied, Sir Raeden nodded. 'I shall report back once the

search is complete. Rhiannon, stay with them and do not wander off by yourself.'

After assuring him she would remain with David and the others, Rhiannon watched her guardian walk away with a great sense of unease filling her heart.

'What if he gets hurt by another tuagust before they're revealed?' She looked up at David. 'If I hadn't seen K'el transform I would've believed he really was Sir Raeden and your father.'

'Don't worry,' came Izana's quiet voice from beside her. 'Now that he knows there could be controlled tuagusts roaming through the palace, Sir Raeden will be suspicious of everyone until they've been tested. No one will catch him off his guard. Not even little Alice Tremaine.'

Chapter 28

WEB OF TRAITORS

The king is dead?'

'Yes.' Janarius hesitated, then added, 'As is the tuagust.'

Mórfran's glacial eyes darkened ominously. 'What of the Dragon's Eye? Has the inept bungler found any useful information to justify the loss of our most efficient executioner?'

'He says he now has confirmation that Prince David knows the location of it.'

Mórfran snarled. 'Of what use is that information when the brat will be so heavily protected no one will get within ten feet of him without raising suspicions!'

'I believe the prince is not the only option we have left,' a new voice interposed.

Mórfran turned towards the small entrance hewn into the side of the mountain's cave.

A distinguished figure stepped out of the passage leading to the underground laboratories, a triumphant expression on his face.

'Explain, Lamorak,' Mórfran barked.

'The prisoner finally slipped up. She declared she will never *show* us the location of the Dragon's Eye and nor will any other who takes her place.'

'And that means what precisely?' Janarius demanded.

'It means that with the aid of some mandrake juice, the one who took over her position at the palace should be able to access the Dragon's Eye and destroy it for us.'

Janarius frowned. 'Why not just get her to do it?'

'Imbecile! She's been missing for six years. If she were to suddenly reappear at the palace she would be instantly put in the care of healers, who would not fail to detect traces of the mind control agent we gave her.'

The contemplative gleam in Mórfran's eyes deepened. 'How do you propose we administer the mandrake juice to her replacement?'

'I shall need to attend the king's funeral. Whilst I'm there it would not be unusual for me to pay him a few visits. It will be simple enough to order him to destroy the Dragon's Eye during one of them.' Lamorak smirked. 'With the whole palace preoccupied with the funeral, I doubt anyone would notice if he disappears for however long it takes him to do it.'

Mórfran nodded his approval. 'Excellent. And you may inform your incompetent friend he has gained a small reprieve for inadvertently creating such favourable conditions for this venture. If it's successful he may live. However, if it fails, I will take the greatest pleasure in inflicting the worst torments imaginable on his flesh and blood.'

~Chapter 29~

STRENGTH IN ADVERSITY

Three days had passed since King Stephen's death. The castle school remained closed and a long line of mourners continued to walk up the road from the main gate to the palace. The people and the non-human inhabitants of Álnair longed for a last glimpse of their beloved king before his interment. Day and night they came, young and old alike, their voices singing countless litanies as their solemn procession passed by his body in the Great Hall. Many who came had cheered King Stephen's birth and watched his coronation with affection and pride. Now, they wept bitterly upon witnessing his body laid out for burial.

A great number of dragons were congregating near the castle walls, all of them waiting to farewell their friend when his funeral procession left for the basilica in a few more days. Foremost among them was Endrille. The ancient dragon's grief was evident in the bent of her head, her shadowed eyes and the listless twitch of her tail. All who saw her felt she embodied the sadness engulfing the land of Álnair.

Overall, the atmosphere inside the castle walls was one of quiet sorrow.

Except inside the cavernous space of the Praeterium.

'All I'm saying is that His Royal Highness may not be ready to take up the responsibilities and duties of king.'

'Then what do you suggest be done?'

From her position between Izana and Gareth on one of the long benches, Rhiannon stared in disbelief at the arguing chancellors and councillors. She had thought nothing would be more important to them than comforting David and his mother after it was confirmed no other tuagusts were inside the castle walls.

How wrong she had been.

A handful of members from the High Council and Pelatarrof were wasting no time in voicing their doubts about David's ability to govern, especially given the activities of the faction in Graynor. And leading them was David's own uncle, Oliver Donahue.

'A regent should be appointed until Prince David at least finishes his last year at the castle school.' Oliver raised his hands to silence the barrage of incredulous exclamations. 'I am not impugning my nephew's right to be king in accordance with the Lady Endrille's appointment of his family as rulers of Álnair,' he assured the assembly. 'I am merely seeking to ensure he is not overly burdened with heavy responsibility so soon after losing his father and while completing his education.'

'How would the regent be chosen?' queried several members with suspicion.

'Whoever is given the position would need to be of good family, preferably of a close kinship to His Royal Highness. They would also need to be familiar with the inner workings of both the High Council and the Pelataroff.'

'So, in essence, someone like you,' scoffed Chancellor Borelli.

Oliver gave him a benign smile. 'Or yourself, Augustine. Are you not first cousins with me and therefore with Her Majesty, my sister?'

Rhiannon glanced to where David sat in rigid silence between

Lord Anton and Caiden Alcober on the raised dais. He had not spoken a single word since the arguments had broken out, but she could see his clenched jaw, a sure sign his emotions were being restrained by the merest thread of control.

'We need to clarify what powers the regent would possess,' another chancellor suggested. 'And for how long they would hold their position. If Prince David decides to do further studies –'

'I will not be attending the Academy.'

The curt declaration drew everyone's gaze to the dais.

David rose to his feet, a look of resolve on his face.

'I shall also not be returning to the castle school,' he announced. 'The question of appointing a regent is therefore redundant.'

Oliver stepped forward. 'My dear nephew, forgive my bluntness, but with the troubling news coming in about the faction in Graynor, and the distressing events occurring across the land, Álnair needs someone with more experience making the important decisions while you complete your schooling. A regent must be appointed for you.'

'As His Royal Highness is of age and of sound mind, no regent may lawfully be appointed against his will.'

The cold, acerbic pronouncement from Sir Raeden dared anyone to contradict him. His eyes glinting pools of blue ice, the Commander of the Guard stepped away from the statue of Fjenador to spear the crowd gathered in the Praeterium with a glacial glare of reproof.

'You all should be ashamed,' he rebuked. 'You trouble Prince David with your quarrelling when King Stephen is not yet laid to rest, and some of you add to your offence by openly questioning his capabilities. He lacks neither skill nor intelligence for the position he must assume and none here shall prevent him from ascending to it.'

'But, his education,' one elderly councillor spoke up. 'Surely it can only be to his benefit, and that of all Álnair, if he completes it.'

'Should he consider it necessary, any gaps in his learning may be filled by private tuition,' Sir Raeden declared.

'I shall certainly not lack for tutors,' David remarked. He bestowed a grateful nod in Sir Raeden's direction. 'I appreciate your words of support, Sir Raeden. And now that the matter of appointing a regent has been addressed, would you please open the doors. I declare this emergency meeting at an end.'

'David, do but stop and reconsider,' Oliver protested. 'You're grieving. Your judgement is bound to be impaired.'

David paused. 'By that same logic you, yourself, Uncle, and everyone in this room would be ineligible to make any important decisions. Unless you're saying you are not grieving?'

Seemingly deprived of all words, Oliver could only watch in silence as David left the dais to join Rhiannon and his Robesmen.

'Let's get out of here,' David muttered, grasping Rhiannon's hand. Without another glance at anyone else, he strode down the aisle and through the doors. He did not stop walking until they were outside, the towering height of the palace behind them and his feet a short distance from the edge of the cliff overlooking the Dairíon Ocean. A host of merfolk led by their king were singing a haunting lament, while the mournful cry of a gull carried across the overcast midday sky.

Rhiannon looked up at David to see him staring out at the wide expanse of water, his expression now stripped of all its defences. In the Praeterium he had shown no weakness, confronting the members of the Pelatarrof and High Council with unshakeable resolve. Now his mask was gone, exposing a great inner turmoil within.

'My father loved coming here,' he revealed quietly. 'He always said the view helped calm his mind whenever he was troubled over something. I often thought he must've come here a few times in the days after my grandparents were killed. Now I know better.

If he felt half as lost and inadequate as I do, he would've come at least a dozen times a day for several months.'

'His visits were quite frequent,' a familiar gentle voice said from above. There was a soft thud as Endrille landed on the ground. 'However, they lessened when he realised he did not have to be perfect to be a good king and that many believed in him. I trust you shall not forget that, David.'

'We shan't let him forget,' swore his Robesmen. 'And we'll remain in the palace for as long as he needs us.'

'I'll be here too,' promised Rhiannon. 'You couldn't keep me away.'

David's grip tightened on her hand. He swallowed convulsively. 'I see now what my father meant when he once told me love is the greatest source of strength, that it can make even the faintest of hearts indomitable,' he confessed in a husky voice. 'Some evil is threatening Álnair and it has already taken the lives of so many, including my father's. But with all of you by my side, I know we shall conquer it.'

A light rain began to fall, the tiny droplets of water reflected in the sunlight piercing through the grey clouds.

Rhiannon slid her hand out of David's and wrapped her arm around his waist. He pressed her against his side while the soft drizzling dampness caressed her skin.

As rain renews and brings forth new life, so Rhiannon felt hope spring to life inside her heart. King Stephen's death had cloaked Álnair in a dark shroud and so many were apprehensive of what other tragedies might come.

However, as she looked out over the ocean with David's arm about her, and his Robesmen and Endrille standing guard beside them, she knew, just as the light of day follows the darkness of night, that evil would be defeated and peace would return to Álnair once more.

DEAR READER

Thank you for continuing Rhiannon's journey with me in *Rhiannon McBride and the Dragon's Eye*. It took a bit longer than I expected, but I finally managed to get it published. I do hope you enjoyed reading it.

I appreciate all the messages you have sent me about my first book, *Rhiannon McBride and the Dragon's Cup*. I loved reading all your comments and knowing how much you liked it – with some of you already having read it multiple times! As an author, simply knowing my writing has touched a reader's heart is the greatest gift. So, thank you again for sharing your thoughts and reactions with me.

Rhiannon McBride and the Dragon Slayer, the final instalment of this fantasy trilogy, will be packed full of adventure, danger and magic. And let's not forget the sweet young love of Rhiannon and David. All going well, book three will be ready for publication in 2025.

If you liked *Rhiannon McBride and the Dragon's Eye,* I would love to hear from you. I can be contacted at:

sarahmmturner.com
facebook.com/SarahMMTurner
instagram.com/sarah.m.m.turner

Want to be among the first to know the release date for the next book? Please join my Reader's List here:

sarahmmturner.com/contact-me

Thank you for choosing to share this journey to the magical land of Álnair with me by reading *Rhiannon McBride and the Dragon's Eye!*

My sincerest regards,

ACKNOWLEDGEMENTS

To Almighty God, thank you for blessing me with a creative imagination and a love of writing.

To all my family and friends, thank you for your continuing support and encouragement. I really could not have come this far without you.

To all those who helped bring this book to publication, thank you for making the journey a joyful experience.

And to all my readers, thank you for your interest in Rhiannon's adventures.